ACCLAIM FOR RUTH REID

"The second book in the Amish Mercies series is just as compelling as the first, if not more so. Once again, Reid weaves together a unique plot with hints of the supernatural (the redheaded man is back!), as well as unexpected twists, heartbreaking turns, and resilient hope."

—*RT BOOK REVIEWS*, 4 STARS, FOR *ARMS OF MERCY*

"Reid is in a class by herself with this tender love story with an unusual twist. Fans of Amish fiction and readers seeking a satisfying and heartwarming inspirational novel with a touch of romance will savor this series launch."

—*LIBRARY JOURNAL*, STARRED REVIEW, FOR *ABIDING MERCY*

"Unique and compelling, [*Abiding Mercy*] blends elements of romance, suspense, and a hint of the supernatural in a coming-of-age story that's difficult to put down . . . A delightfully different sort of Amish romance that even non-Amish-fiction fans should try!"

—*RT BOOK REVIEWS*, 4 STARS

"A heartfelt novel."

—*RT BOOK REVIEWS*, 4 STARS FOR *A DREAM OF MIRACLES*

"Reid's second series installment (after *A Miracle of Hope*) works well as a tender romance with a bit of suspense. A solid pick for fans of Beverly Lewis and Melody Carlson."

—*LIBRARY JOURNAL*, FOR *A WOODLAND MIRACLE*

"Ruth Reid is skillful in portraying the Amish way of life as well as weaving together miracles with the everyday. In this book, she writes a beautiful tale of romance, redemption, and faith."

—BETH WISEMAN, BESTSELLING AUTHOR OF THE DAUGHTERS OF THE PROMISE SERIES, FOR *A MIRACLE OF HOPE*

"Ruth Reid pens a touching story of grace, love, and God's mercy in the midst of uncertainty. A must-read for Amish fiction fans!"

—KATHLEEN FULLER, BESTSELLING AUTHOR OF THE HEARTS OF MIDDLEFIELD SERIES, FOR *A MIRACLE OF HOPE*

"Reid gives readers the hope to believe that there are angels with every one of us, both good and evil, and that the good angels will always win."

—*RT BOOK REVIEWS*, FOR *AN ANGEL BY HER SIDE*

"*An Angel by Her Side* brings together not only a protagonist's inner struggle, but the effect on the character from outside forces. In short, the reader rises, falls, grows, and learns alongside the story's champion."

—*AMISH COUNTRY NEWS REVIEW*

"Reid has written a fine novel that provides, as its series title claims, a bit of 'heaven on earth.'"

—*PUBLISHERS WEEKLY*, FOR *THE PROMISE OF AN ANGEL*

"If *The Promise of an Angel* is anything to judge by, it looks like she's going to become a favorite amongst Amish fans."

—*THE CHRISTIAN MANIFESTO*

"Ruth Reid captivates with a powerful new voice and vision."

—KELLY LONG, BESTSELLING AUTHOR OF *SARAH'S GARDEN* AND *LILLY'S WEDDING QUILT*

"Ruth Reid's *The Promise of an Angel* is a beautiful story of faith, hope, and second chances. It will captivate fans of Amish fiction and readers who love an endearing romance."

—AMY CLIPSTON, BESTSELLING AUTHOR OF THE HEARTS OF THE LANCASTER GRAND HOTEL AND THE KAUFFMAN AMISH BAKERY SERIES

STEADFAST MERCY

OTHER BOOKS BY RUTH REID

THE AMISH MERCIES NOVELS

Abiding Mercy
Arms of Mercy
Steadfast Mercy

THE AMISH WONDERS NOVELS

A Miracle of Hope
A Woodland Miracle
A Dream of Miracles

THE HEAVEN ON EARTH NOVELS

The Promise of an Angel
Brush of Angel's Wings
An Angel by Her Side

NOVELLAS

Her Christmas Pen Pal in *An Amish Second Christmas*
Always His Providence in *An Amish Miracle*
An Unexpected Joy in *An Amish Christmas Gift*
A Flicker of Hope in *An Amish Home*
Home for Christmas in *An Amish Christmas*

STEADFAST MERCY

AN AMISH MERCIES NOVEL

RUTH REID

THOMAS NELSON

Since 1798

Steadfast Mercy

© 2020 Ruth Reid

Published in Nashville, Tennessee, by Thomas Nelson. Thomas Nelson is a registered trademark of HarperCollins Christian Publishing, Inc.

Thomas Nelson titles may be purchased in bulk for educational, business, fund-raising, or sales promotional use. For information, please email SpecialMarkets@ThomasNelson.com.

Publisher's Note: This novel is a work of fiction. Names, characters, places, and incidents are either products of the author's imagination or used fictitiously. All characters are fictional, and any similarity to people living or dead is purely coincidental.

ISBN 978-0-7180-8250-5 (e-book)

Library of Congress Cataloging-in-Publication Data

Names: Reid, Ruth, 1963- author.
Title: Steadfast mercy : an Amish mercies novel / Ruth Reid.
Description: Nashville : Zondervan, 2020. | Series: An Amish mercies novel
 | Summary: "She's returning to her old Amish community with something to hide. Something big. He's just trying to make it through his first winter as a farmer. Together they will learn the meaning of steadfast mercy in this sweet Amish romance"-- Provided by publisher.
Identifiers: LCCN 2020005706 (print) | LCCN 2020005707 (ebook) | ISBN 9780718082499 (trade paperback) | ISBN 9780718082505 (epub)
Subjects: GSAFD: Love stories. | Christian fiction.
Classification: LCC PS3618.E5475 S74 2020 (print) | LCC PS3618.E5475 (ebook) | DDC 813/.6--dc23
LC record available at https://lccn.loc.gov/2020005706
LC ebook record available at https://lccn.loc.gov/2020005707

Printed in the United States of America

20 21 22 23 24 LSC 5 4 3 2 1

I want to dedicate this book to my dad, Paul Droste. You are a man I greatly admire for your steadfast faith. Despite numerous trials and tribulations throughout your life, you have remained a faithful servant of the Lord. I will forever be thankful that God gave me a father of prayer. I love you, Dad!

"And after you have suffered a little while, the God of all grace, who has called you to his eternal glory in Christ, will himself restore, confirm, strengthen, and establish you."

1 PETER 5:10 (ESV)

Glossary

ach: oh
aenti: aunt
allrecht: all right
appeditlich: delicious
Ausbund: Amish hymnal used in worship services
bang: afraid
boppli: baby
bruder: brother
bruderskind: nephew or niece
bu/buwe: boy/boys
Budget, The: Amish newspaper
daadi: grandfather
daed: dad or father
danki: thank you
Das Loblied: Amish praise hymn
daudi haus: house for grandparents
doktah: doctor
dochder: daughter
dorstig: thirsty
engel: angel
Englisch/Englischer: anyone who is not Amish

faul: lazy

fraa: wife

geh: go

guder mariye: good morning

gut: good

gut nacht: good night

haus: house

hiya: a greeting like hello

hund: dog

hungahrich: hungry

Ich: I

jah: yes

kaffi: coffee

kalt: cold

kapp: a prayer covering or cap worn by Amish women

kichlin: cookies

kind/kinner: child/children

kumm: come

maedel: unmarried woman

mamm: mother or mom

mammi: grandmother

mei: my

meiya: tomorrow

nacht: night

narrish: crazy

nau: now

nay: no

nett: not

onkel: uncle

Ordnung: the written and unwritten rules of the Amish; the understood behavior by which the Amish are expected to live, passed down from generation to generation. Most Amish know the rules by heart.

reddy-up: clean up

rumspringa: running-around period when a teenager turns sixteen years old

schlofkopp: sleepyhead

schweschder: sister

schul: school

sohn: son

wasser: water

welkum: welcome

wunderbaar: wonderful

yummasetti: a traditional Amish dish made with noodles, hamburger, and cheese

Chapter 1

J onica Muller gazed out the window of the bus as it continued south on US-23 along Lake Huron's majestic coastline. As white-capped waves raced powerfully toward shore, washing the beach with foam before receding back into churning water, Jonica couldn't help but compare her life—her unrestful state—to that of the tossing waves. Since that fateful day last month, things had been a blur, and though she tried to stay strong for her son, losing her parents had left her numb and feeling abandoned by God.

She shifted her attention to the tree-lined road, uncertainty of the future weighing heavily on her mind. Bright red, yellow, and orange leaves shaded the highway. A typical October day. Only nothing was typical about returning to her childhood settlement. Posen, Michigan, was a place of her past. A place she'd told herself she would never return. But that was before the accident—before life changed course.

Jonica closed her eyes. *Lord, did I think this decision through thoroughly—pray enough?*

Unease tightened her throat muscles. She reached for her travel bag on the floor to retrieve a bottle of water and inadvertently awakened her five-year-old son slouched against her side.

Stephen yawned and pushed off her arm, shucking her wool cloak he'd been using as a blanket. "Are we there yet?"

"Almost."

Curiosity sparked his eyes as he stretched his small frame to peer out the window.

Jonica pointed to the water. "That's Lake Huron." She kissed the top of his head. "Your eyes are as blue as the mighty great lake."

He glanced back at her and smiled. "They are?"

"They are indeed." She placed her wool cloak over his shoulders. "The bus is drafty," she said when he started to squirm. "I don't want you sick when we arrive in Posen."

"I'm *nett* a *boppli*." His bottom lip protruded into an irresistible pout.

"Leave it on. Big boys get sick too." Even wearing his coat, he'd been shivering since they pulled out of the station six hours ago.

The temperature was bound to be warmer in the Lower Peninsula, but she hadn't noticed any temperature difference inside the bus after they crossed Mackinac Bridge. Maybe October wasn't the right time to make the trip. Maybe she should have waited until spring to close out her father's affairs.

Within a few miles Stephen lost interest in the scenery and curled back against her arm, then closed his eyes. She combed her fingers through his curly locks, gently massaging his scalp. The rays of afternoon sun highlighted his hair with a slight golden appearance, reminding her of brown sugar. God had certainly blessed her with a sweet *mamm*'s *bu,* someone to pour her heart and soul into training up in the way he should go.

With her parents gone, they were alone. If it wasn't for her faith in God, she might not have gotten through the past month. First, the accident claimed her mother, then days later, her father succumbed to his internal injuries. Shrouded in unanswered prayers and her faith shaken, she had to constantly remind herself that God had spared her son in the accident. She would have fallen apart completely had she lost Stephen too. He'd been walking between her parents when the car came fishtailing around the bend and hit them. How the car happened to miss her son had mystified the police and ambulance crew, and many of the members in her district had called it a miracle.

Jonica pulled in a sharp breath. She'd come so close to losing her only child.

Stephen was her only priority. And despite what some of the district members had been whispering, she could raise him alone. Just because her parents had gone to be with the Lord didn't mean she *had* to get married, as widower Ephraim King had indicated when he delivered his matter-of-fact proposal.

The scene at her father's wake played across her mind, how Ephraim stood in her kitchen, feet shifting, forehead beading with sweat and looking pale, very pale. "I have four youngsters and *nay fraa*." He averted his gaze and gulped. "And you have no one *nau*," he said, his words running together.

She straightened her posture. "I have Stephen."

"*Jah*, but without your *daed*'s support—"

"Ephraim. This isn't the time nor the place for such talk. The sun hasn't even gone down on *mei daed*'s grave."

Another member of the district entered the kitchen with a casserole dish, and thankfully Ephraim used the opportunity to rejoin the men in the sitting room. Meanwhile, his words rang in her ears. "*Without your* daed*'s support . . .*"

Ephraim was a hardworking man and his children were well behaved. He would be a good provider. She wouldn't have to worry about the price of grain or if she and Stephen would have enough wood to heat the house all winter. Her father had liked Ephraim.

So why was she fleeing Cedar Ridge and going back to Posen—where her heartache started?

*

Caleb Schulmann buckled the loin strap under his mare's girth, his mind racing with all the chores he was leaving unfinished to run an errand for his elderly neighbor. With Edna's mind failing, he wasn't even sure there was a package to pick up in Rogers City, but she had insisted and even showed him on the wall calendar where she'd marked *Arrival* on October first.

He didn't mind doing Edna's errands, as she had no family in the district. Besides, after he dissolved his construction company, she had kindly offered her acreage to farm, even refused money for the use of her land. He enjoyed working the fields. Sowing and harvesting kept his hands occupied and, more importantly, gave him alone time—a place to hide.

Caleb climbed onto the buggy bench and waved good-bye to Edna looking out the kitchen window. He pulled onto the main road, the sunny sky grating on his nerves. He should be in the field. The first week in October marked the deadline to plant winter wheat. Between the torrential rainy summer, inexperience, and various other unexpected interruptions, such as running Edna's errands, he hadn't gotten the seed in the ground. Any more delays risked losing the crop to frost. In addition to planting the wheat, he had forty acres to clear before snowfall if he was going to use the land for spring planting. Hopefully Edna's package had arrived and the trip wouldn't be in vain.

He checked the post office in Posen first without success, heading next to Rogers City. It would have helped if Edna had remembered *what* was arriving. Today she'd appeared more confused than ever, rambling about her parents as though they were alive, while standing on a kitchen chair dusting the crown molding. Somehow Caleb managed to persuade her to get down from the chair by convincing her there weren't any cobwebs. Her penchant to climb things when she had a history of balance issues concerned him since she lived alone.

Caleb pulled into the parking lot in back of The UPS Store, got out, and tied Nutmeg to a tree branch. This was as good a place to check for the package as any. It hadn't been that long ago that she'd sent him to the store to send a box to her brother in Cedar Ridge. Perhaps she was expecting something in return.

The store clerk talking with an *Englisch* customer acknowledged Caleb with a nod. "Be with you in a sec." She placed a parcel on the scale and announced its weight.

Caleb roamed the store, scanning the shelves stuffed with different packing materials. Rolls of bubble wrap, large and small envelopes, labels, folded boxes, everything someone would need to ship a package.

A few minutes later, the clerk came up beside him. "May I help you find something?"

"I'm here to check on a package. Did something *kumm* for Edna Muller?"

The worker's face contorted. "We don't receive customer packages. We ship them. If she's expecting a shipment from UPS, it'll be delivered to her house by truck."

"I see." He'd never used the service himself. Even when he was in construction, he'd picked up supplies from the local lumberyard or hardware store himself. "Thank you for your time."

As Caleb turned toward the door, he glimpsed an Amish woman outside the storefront window, seated on the bus bench and shivering. He went out the front door. Two twine-tied boxes sat on the ground beside the bench. As he headed in her direction, a clean scent of tea tree oil carried in the breeze. "Excuse me. Do you need assistance taking your boxes into the store?"

The woman jolted, then slid a sideways glance at him. "*Nay*, I'm fine. *Danki*." Upon meeting his gaze, the lines between her brows disappeared only to return seconds later. She tugged on the brim of her oversize bonnet, covering most of her face.

The woman wasn't from their side of the district. Otherwise she would have called him by name. "I'm Caleb Schulmann," he volunteered, in hopes of setting her mind at ease.

"*Jah*, I know who you are." She shifted her attention to the wool cloak lying on the bench next to her.

"You've sparked *mei* curiosity *nau*." He moved in front of the bench. "You know me, but I don't recall your name. What side of the district are you from?"

"I'm *nett* from this area anymore." After a moment, she lifted her gaze to meet his. "I'm here to visit with *mei aenti* Edna."

Caleb managed to hide his surprise. "Then you must be the package I was sent to pick up."

Chapter 2

J onica followed Caleb's gaze to her wool cloak on the bench beside her. His furrowed brows revealed that he wanted to say
something about her not wearing the winter garment, but the moment their gazes reconnected, he restated his earlier comment. "I
was sent to pick up a package. Apparently, that's you."

She rested her hand protectively on the cloak. "I'm a package,
you say?"

"So to speak." Caleb shrugged.

"That makes *nay* sense." *Aenti* had said in her letter that she
would be here to meet them when their bus arrived.

"*Mei* buggy is parked around back." He motioned to the alley
between two buildings.

"*Danki*, but . . ." No, she couldn't accept a ride from him. She
needed to stay far away from Caleb Schulmann.

He dragged his hand over his face and let out what sounded
like an impatient sigh. He stared down at the sidewalk, his strong
jaw twitching. He hadn't changed much in five years. As the construction foreman for many of the district's barn raisings, he'd
always been broad shouldered from lifting lumber and carrying
roofing material up ladders. Back then, many of the girls her age

7

had a hopeful eye on him, but him being six years older, he'd been indifferent to them all.

A gust of wind sent a shiver down her spine. She rubbed her arms, wishing more every minute that she had waited until spring to make the trip.

Caleb shucked his coat. "Here." He extended the canvas outerwear to her. "Put this on."

"*Nay*, I couldn't." She looked down and studied a crack in the sidewalk. His gesture wasn't more than a simple act of kindness, but even so, she wouldn't accept.

"Jonica, take the coat. You're *kalt*."

She lifted her head. "You recognize me *nau*?"

"*Jah*, I figured out who you are," he said dryly.

She wasn't sure how to interpret his aloofness—or why it mattered. Ignoring his outstretched hand, she lowered her head and stared at the cement once more.

"What do you say we get going? We can finish this talk on the way home."

Home? Posen hadn't been her home in over five years. Not that Caleb had any reason to remember when or why her family had left. The thought of sharing a buggy bench with a Schulmann unsettled her nerves, but with the wind picking up and the temperature dropping, she didn't want to risk Stephen falling ill. Especially since he hadn't completely recovered from the accident. Though he hadn't suffered broken bones, losing his grandparents had impacted him both emotionally and physically. Besides, it'd been a long journey for both of them. The sooner they reached *Aenti* Edna's place the better.

Jonica lifted a corner of the cloak. "Sweetie, it's time to wake up. We have to *geh nau*."

Stephen blinked a few times, then pushed the covering away as he sat up and stretched.

"You have a *kind*?" Caleb rasped.

"Is that a problem?" Jonica was too busy adjusting her cloak around Stephen to worry about the tone in Caleb's voice. "He can sit on *mei* lap if you don't have enough room."

"*Nay*, there's plenty of room. It's just—" He thrust his coat toward her once again. "Put it on. Your lips are pasty and you're trembling like a wet *hund* in winter."

Jonica scowled as an image of a snow-covered dog with big, sad eyes came to mind. Caleb must have taken her hesitation as stubbornness because he shifted his stance.

"Please, I insist. Edna will have *mei* hide if you get sick on *mei* account."

Jonica hesitated, then finally accepted his offering. "*Danki.*"

"How long have you been waiting?"

"*Nett* long." She pushed her arms into Caleb's warm coat, the woodsy aroma engulfing her senses.

He grabbed the boxes with their belongings. "Like I said, the buggy is parked in the back of the building."

Jonica gathered Stephen into her arms and hurried to catch up with Caleb. "Did *mei aenti* actually send you to pick us up, or did you happen to be in town for something else?"

"She sent me."

When they reached the buggy, he set the boxes on the ground long enough to unlatch the back door, then placed their belongings inside. He glanced up at the sky. "I should be planting winter wheat right *nau*."

"Isn't it too late for winter wheat? Crops went in over a month ago up north."

"I still have today. Hopefully." He slid the passenger side door open with more force than necessary and it shuttered back a few inches.

Jonica took that as a sign to drop the subject. Not that she wanted to encourage conversation in the first place. *Aenti* Edna's farm was only ten miles away. She could keep quiet that long. After positioning Stephen on the bench between them, she once again covered him with her cloak.

Caleb reached behind the bench and retrieved a quilt. "This should help keep you and the *kind* warm."

His attempt to make her comfortable in an unnerving situation was considerate. She wouldn't push his patience and decline the thoughtful gesture. "*Danki.*" She spread the large green-and-black quilt over Stephen, who had nestled under her arm. "Would you like part of the blanket, Caleb?"

"*Nay*, I'm fine." He tapped the reins and the buggy lurched forward. A few minutes later, they merged onto US-23 and headed south.

Jonica gazed out the passenger window. It seemed a lifetime ago since she'd left the small Amish district where she'd grown up. The rural farmland surrounding the small town hadn't changed much over the last five years—yet everything was different.

"Is the *bu* sick or something?"

"*Nay.* It's been a long trip." She drew her son closer to her side, his body heat radiating under the weight of the blanket and wool cloak. Stephen wasn't normally shy or this quiet and shouldn't still be this drained when he'd slept most of the trip. Her thoughts flitted to everything she'd packed in the boxes. A thermometer was one thing she'd forgotten. Hopefully *Aenti* would have one. If need be, she would pick one up at Yoder's Market. Assuming the country store was still open.

"He doesn't talk much, does he?"

"He will once he gets to know you—I mean, *nett* you— anyone. It takes him a while to warm up to people."

"His *mamm* too," Caleb muttered.

"You talk under your breath a lot."

A grin stretched across his clean-shaven face. "You have keen hearing. I'll have to remember that."

I read lips too. A trait she'd developed after becoming the talk of the district.

Caleb clicked his tongue and the horse responded by increasing its pace. It wasn't until he'd turned down the gravel road leading to her aunt's house that he broke the silence between them. "I'm *nett* always as thoughtful as I should be." He cleared his throat. "I read in *The Budget* about your parents going home to be with the Lord. You must really miss them."

A lump formed in her throat. "*Jah*, we do." Jonica removed a handkerchief tucked inside her dress sleeve and used it to soak up the tears before they fell. She'd managed to remain strong through her mother's funeral, and while her father was in the hospital and during both their wakes, so why couldn't she contain her emotions now?

She wrung her hands. Would *Aenti* be welcoming? Her letter was somewhat vague. Over the years she had stayed in contact with Jonica's parents but had never written directly to Jonica. Did her aunt still blame her for her parents' decision to move?

Lord, I don't know if I can sign over the haus *where I grew up— where* mei daed *grew up.* She wept uncontrollably as if she were inside a pressure cooker and everything bottled up inside had exploded. Thankfully, Stephen didn't wake up.

"I didn't mean to upset you. I'm sorry."

Caleb's tenderhearted tone made her cry even harder.

He pulled back on the reins and stopped the buggy on the shoulder of the road. "Is there anything I can do?"

Jonica shook her head. A few deep breaths later, she steeled her thoughts. "I don't normally cry so easily." She blotted her face. "I don't know what came over me."

"It's understandable. You recently lost your parents. I'm sure coming back to Posen, seeing old friends and family—well, I'm sure it will stir up memories *gut* and bad."

Jonica squeezed her son tighter. *More than you know, Caleb.*

❧

Caleb wasn't sure how much silence Jonica needed to compose herself. Her unbridled sobs hit a raw nerve. It didn't make sense why she and the boy were traveling alone. Where was her husband? *Leave it alone. It's* nett *your concern.*

He cleared his throat. "Edna will be happy to see you."

She sniffled. "I'm looking forward to spending time with her as well."

Hearing the quiver in Jonica's voice, he wished he hadn't mentioned her parents. He'd merely wanted to extend his sympathies, not trigger a meltdown. It wasn't his place to comfort another man's wife.

A car zipped past, generating a gust of wind that rocked the buggy. The reins slipped through Caleb's hand as Nutmeg unexpectedly lurched forward. "Whoa, girl." He gripped the leather straps and pulled back, stopping the mare. He set the brake. "She still gets nervous on the main road."

The boy pushed the blanket away from his face and sat up taller, stretching his neck. "Where are we?"

"We're almost to your *aenti* Edna's," Caleb said.

"What's your name?"

Jonica pressed the child to her side. "Leave him be and let him drive."

"But all I wanted to know was—"

She leaned down so her mouth was close to the child's ear. "What have I told you about talking to strangers?"

The boy murmured something undecipherable to his mother, then with his head still bowed, he lifted his gaze to meet Caleb's.

"You can give the signal to your horse *nau* to continue the journey."

Puzzled by her urgency, Caleb continued to hold back the mare. True, he'd never met the boy before today, but he and Jonica weren't exactly strangers.

She leveled Caleb with a stare that seemed to go much deeper than surface annoyance, but he could sit here all day and not be able to figure her out. Lately it seemed all the women he knew, including Darleen, his longtime *maedel,* and his mother, had emotional swings that left him not knowing when to duck and run.

Caleb sighed. He did have winter wheat to plant. Still, he didn't want her in tears when they arrived at Edna's. "You sure? I don't want to rush you."

"I'm sure." She tucked the child under the blanket, then shifted on the bench to look out the side window.

Caleb clicked his tongue and Nutmeg lunged forward. "How long do you plan on staying in Posen?"

"Long enough to get the paperwork for the farm transferred from *mei daed*'s name." Her voice strained. "In order for the county records office to make the necessary changes, I have to provide a copy of his death certificate."

Puffiness surrounded her downcast eyes and from his side view, the corners of her lips seemed to be trembling. He shouldn't press her for information now, but he had questions about the property that directly affected him. "At the risk of sounding insensitive . . . what are you going to do with the property? I ask because I've been farming the land, and if you and your husband plan to move here—"

"I'm *nett* moving back," she said with more force behind her words than he'd heard since picking the two of them up.

If she wasn't moving back to Posen . . . "So, you're selling the farm?"

"I'm *nett*, but *Aenti* is. According to the letter I received."

"Selling to whom?"

Jonica shrugged.

"How long has it been since you've seen Edna? I only ask because you might *nett* be aware that her mind is . . . slipping. I think senility is setting in."

Jonica's brows narrowed. "She sounded perfectly sane in the letter I received."

"Edna didn't remember you were arriving today. I was sent to Rogers City for a *package*. She couldn't remember any of the details. Only that she'd marked *Arrival* on the calendar."

Jonica pulled the cover higher up on the boy's neck. "A little forgetfulness is understandable for someone in her eighties."

"Edna's more than a little forgetful." He nodded, though she didn't appear persuaded. "I guess you'll see for yourself soon enough."

"*Jah*, I suppose I will."

A few minutes later he turned into Edna's driveway and stopped Nutmeg near the back door.

Jonica gathered the sleeping child into her arms. "We're here, Stephen."

"Hold on and I'll get the door for you." Caleb jumped out, hurried around the buggy, and opened the passenger door. Bundled in Jonica's wool coat, the rosy-cheeked boy wasn't much larger than a sack of grain, while at the same time he appeared cumbersome for her to hold. "Would you like me to carry him?"

"*Nay, danki*. I can manage." She proceeded up the porch steps.

Edna opened the door. "You made it."

"It's *gut* to see you, *Aenti* Edna." Jonica gave her aunt a one-arm hug.

Caleb grabbed the two boxes from the back of the buggy. For someone not planning to stay long, she packed heavy. He hiked up the porch steps, then paused as the two women continued their greetings in front of the door.

"It's so nice of you to *kumm* for a visit." Edna lifted the cloak away from Stephen's face. "*Nau* who is this?"

The child lifted his head off his mother's shoulder, eyed Edna, then flicked his gaze over to Caleb with weary blue eyes that matched Jonica's. His lips puckered like he might cry, but then he shoved his thumb in his mouth and laid his head back on his mother's shoulder.

"This is *mei sohn*, Stephen." Jonica pivoted slightly to give Edna a better view of the boy. "He's shy."

Edna leaned forward and pushed a stray lock of hair away from Stephen's forehead. "He's a fine-looking *kind*." She stared blankly a long moment, then stepped back. "He's much too old to be still sucking his thumb. A mixture of ginger and clove will cure that problem."

Edna was known in the district for giving new mothers advice, even though she had never had children of her own. The older woman's unsought opinions didn't seem to sit well with Jonica. Her jaw appeared set and her lips formed a thin, straight line. She needed saving before Edna lectured more on the subject.

"Ahem." Caleb looked down at the boxes, then back up at them and grinned.

"*Ach*," Edna rasped. "What are we still doing on the porch? Let's *geh* in the *haus*." She opened the door and waved them into the two-story house.

Jonica took a few steps inside and lowered Stephen to the floor. Her gaze danced around the room as if taking in every nook and cranny. Within seconds, her eyes dulled with haunting sadness. Distracted by seemingly painful family memories, she didn't appear to notice that Stephen had removed her wool cloak and left it in a heap on the floor.

Caleb leaned toward Jonica and whispered, "You okay?"

"*Jah*, why?"

Because you're about to cry again. He'd seen that same lamenting expression on his mother's face when she thought no one was watching. "Where would you like me to put your belongings?"

"Anywhere is fine," Jonica said without looking his direction. Jonica pointed to the floor. "Is that where the cloak belongs?"

"*Nay*." Stephen hung his head. "Sorry."

"Pick it up, sweetie."

Stephen grabbed the cloak and handed it to his mother, who hung it on the wall hook.

"*Kumm* with me, young man," Edna said. "We'll see if there are any treats in the *kichlin* jar." She ambled toward the kitchen.

Stephen took hold of Jonica's hand and tugged.

They started to follow Edna, but Jonica stopped when she reached the archway between the sitting room and kitchen. She glanced over her shoulder. "*Danki* for the ride, Caleb."

"Anytime." He wasn't sure if it was her somber expression or her piercing blue eyes that twisted his insides. Motherhood had changed her. She wasn't the same giggly *maedel* he remembered.

Edna doubled back into the room, scratching her head as though perplexed.

"Is something wrong, *Aenti*?"

"I don't . . . think so." Edna stared blankly a moment, then shrugged. "I guess *nett*." Her attention shifted to Caleb still standing at the front door. "Would you like to stay for *kaffi*, Caleb?"

"Ah . . ." His gaze moved beyond Edna to the sleepy-eyed boy holding Jonica's hand. "*Nay*." Caleb pushed his hat lower on his head. "I have fields to tend." He went outside and was halfway to the barn when the screen door creaked open.

"Caleb." Jonica hurried down the porch steps, his coat in hand. "You'll need this." She held out the garment. "*Danki* for letting me wear it."

"*Jah*, *nay* problem."

The screen door snapped and Stephen came running toward them. "Don't leave me!"

Jonica scooped Stephen into her arms. "I'm *nett* going to leave you, sweetie." She hugged him close and whispered, "I promise."

He rubbed his eyes. "*Nay kichlin* in the jar."

"I'll make cookies later if *Aenti* has all the ingredients."

Stephen wrapped his arms around her neck in a hug, then peered over at Caleb. "Are you a stranger?"

Caleb glanced at Jonica. No daggers pierced him from her eyes. He smiled at the boy. "I hope *nett* for long. *Mei* name is Caleb Schulmann, and let me guess what your name is." He touched his index finger to his forehead, pretending to think about the answer. "Is your name Matthew?"

The child grinned and shook his head.

"Mark?"

Another head shake.

"Luke? John?"

He laughed. "*Nay*, I'm Stephen Muller."

"*Ach*, silly me. Stephen is a fine name." The boy had his mother's family name, which meant she either married one of her cousins with the same last name or . . . Caleb gulped.

"I know how to spell *mei* name: S-t-e—" His letters ran together and he stopped long enough to take another gaspy breath before he spelled his last name. The child lifted his gaze to his mother. "I did it. Right, *Mamm*?"

Color drained from Jonica's complexion. "You don't have a coat on, Stephen. We need to get you back inside." She hurried back to the house, holding Stephen in her arms. At the top of the porch steps, Stephen shot Caleb a quick wave over her shoulder.

Caleb lifted his hand in return, but they had already disappeared inside. He stared at the house. The way her face blanched, she must think Caleb stood, shovel in hand, ready to dig up old skeletons. But that wasn't his nature. Old bones should stay buried.

He donned the coat, breathing in a pungent aroma of tea tree oil that would probably stay with him all day. Caleb tromped toward the field. Good thing he hadn't planned to visit Darleen. She had a jealous streak a mile wide and would sniff out another woman's scent on him in an instant.

Chapter 3

J onica's stomach roiled. She'd spent numerous hours working
with Stephen so when school started next fall, he would be able
to spell his full name, and until today, he hadn't given her any indication that he'd retained anything from her teaching.

She squeezed her eyes closed in an attempt to blot Caleb's
thunderstruck image from her mind, but to no avail. Her secret was
out. Her beloved child hadn't been given his father's surname—
he'd been conceived out of wedlock, born to a wayward teenager.

"I know how to spell *mei* whole name *nau, Mamm.*" Stephen
pulled her back to the only thing that mattered—her son.

Inwardly, she beamed with pride while outwardly, she practiced meekness and gave him a soft kiss on his cheek. "That's *wunderbaar*, sweetie."

"I *geh* tell *Aenti* Edna." Stephen squirmed, then once she put
him down, he ran full speed into the kitchen bursting with excitement. "*Aenti*, I can spell *mei* name!"

Jonica leaned against the front door and took a few cleansing
breaths as she listened to Stephen spell his name for *Aenti* Edna in
the kitchen. Guilt leached from Jonica's conscience. While she had
spent numerous hours fretting over her son's lack of progress, God
had Stephen in His hand the entire time.

"Lord, forgive me. I haven't prayed much since my parents' deaths. *Nett* like I should. But this prayer is for Stephen. *Nau* that he's excited about spelling his full name, I'm worried what others in the district will say. What price will Stephen have to pay for *mei* time of rebellion? For his *daed*'s lack of interest. He's an innocent boy, Lord. Will You please make a way for me to quickly do what needs to be done with the paperwork, so we can leave?"

Tarnished with shame, she stressed over what Caleb Schulmann thought about her past, even though she didn't need his or anyone else's forgiveness. She'd humbled herself before God in repentance long ago, and according to His word, she'd been forgiven.

Jonica stood still with her eyes closed, soaking in the quiet moment. A verse in 1 John, reminding her of God's grace, came to mind. *"If we confess our sins, he is faithful and just and will forgive us our sins and purify us from all unrighteousness."*

Years ago, her mother had been the one to point out the scripture to Jonica and encourage her to put to memory what God had promised. *"Take Him at His word,"* Mamm told her. *"God is faithful. He will forgive, and He alone purifies."*

Tension eased from her body—until Edna's sharp tone came from the kitchen and Jonica opened her eyes.

"You there," Edna repeated. *"Kind,* are you listening?"

Jonica pushed off the door and rushed into the kitchen, where she found Stephen standing on a kitchen chair looking out the window and Edna scowling a few feet away with her hands on her hips.

"What's wrong, *Aenti*?"

Edna paced to the far end of the kitchen and hovered in the corner. "He's going to get hurt. Please, get him down."

Taken aback by the tremble in her aunt's voice, Jonica wanted to reassure her that Stephen had been climbing and standing on chairs since he was old enough to walk, but instead, she plucked Stephen off the chair and placed him on the floor. "*Aenti* isn't used to having a *kind* in the *haus*. I need you to remember your manners."

"*Danki*." *Aenti* exhaled, holding her hand to her chest. "I was worried he might fall."

Jonica wrapped her arm around Edna's shoulder. "Do you remember when I used to stand on the chair at the sink and help you and *Mamm* rinse vegetables from the garden?"

Edna smiled. "I don't always remember everything, but I do seem to recall how determined you were as a child to help your *mamm* and me in the kitchen." She patted Jonica's back. "It's so nice to have you home again. It hasn't been the same around here since . . ."

Jonica couldn't decipher her aunt's sudden loss for words or the older woman's blank expression. Had *Aenti*'s thoughts drifted back to when her parents announced their decision to move up north? Edna had voiced her disapproval at the time, her words harsh and shrouding Jonica with shame. She had already lathered herself in guilt. As the only child—a late-in-life miracle child—her parents had been determined to shelter her reputation the only way they knew how—start fresh somewhere new.

Stephen pushed the curtains to the side and continued to stare out the window. "He's *nett* a stranger, is he?"

Her son was right. Caleb Schulmann was no stranger—he was the boy's *onkel*. But that didn't mean the man could be Stephen's newfound friend. Jonica came up behind Stephen and placed her hand on his shoulder. She spied Caleb out the window, working the field with his coat high on his neck and his hat pulled down low. Hopefully he wouldn't be around the farm after the first frost.

21

Stephen peered up at her. "Can I *geh* outside?"

"Maybe later." If Stephen went outside now, he would go straight to the field and pester Caleb. She took a deep breath and let out a slow exhale, wishing she could release some of the tension knotting her muscles. Jonica gave Stephen's shoulder a nudge, then she turned him away from the window. "Why don't you and *Aenti* visit in the sitting room while I search for something to make for lunch?"

Stephen protruded his bottom lip, testing her resolve. But before she had a chance to scold his defiant behavior, he whirled around with a sudden burst of energy and ran into the sitting room.

"Oh dear." *Aenti* shuffled toward the kitchen entrance. "I better make sure he doesn't jump on the couch cushions. That young man has a lot of energy."

Jonica cringed. "Sorry."

Aenti chuckled. "These old walls haven't echoed with the sound of youngsters in a long time."

"Hold that thought." *Please.* Jonica prayed the moment her aunt left the room. "Lord, Your Word says to be anxious about nothing, but we've only been here a couple of hours and I'm worried Stephen's overzealousness will, all too soon, get under Edna's skin. I want this time together to be moments for us to treasure." *Aenti* Edna was the only family she and Stephen had.

Edna returned carrying an empty coffee mug. "Who are you talking to, Mary Anna?"

"I'm *nett* Mary Anna, *Aenti.* I'm Jonica. Your niece."

"Who?" Edna stared at her vacantly.

"Jonica. Your *bruder* William's *dochder.*" Mary Anna was *Aenti*'s older *schweschder.* Though Jonica didn't see the resemblance, she'd been told by other relatives that she took after Mary Anna.

Aenti's face relaxed. "I know who you are. Did you make more *kaffi*?" She held up the mug.

"I'll put the kettle on the stove. It won't take long." Jonica filled the kettle with tap water, then placed it on the burner. "What would you like for lunch?"

"I ate a few minutes ago."

"You did?"

"We were at the same table. And don't try to get out of doing the dishes." Edna wagged a finger at her. "It's your turn. Or I'll tell *Mamm*," she announced with a smug face, then promptly left the room.

The sink was empty. *Aenti*'s memory wasn't just *slipping* as Caleb had described. She was visiting somewhere in the past. Jonica hunted through the sparsely stocked cupboards and removed a canning jar labeled chicken noodle soup with last year's date. The loaf of sourdough bread she found in the bread box was hard crusted and most likely stale, but it didn't have mold growing on it yet. Maybe once they had eaten lunch, she would have time to inventory the cabinets and compile a shopping list.

After heating the soup, Jonica called Stephen and Edna to the table.

Stephen climbed up on the chair, took one look inside the bowl, then pushed it away, sloshing soup over the side. "*Ich nett hungahrich.*"

Please don't test mei patience today. Nett in front of Aenti Edna. Jonica eased the bowl back in front of him. "Bow your head for the blessing."

Stephen frowned but did as instructed.

Jonica glanced at Edna seated across the table for direction. It had always been her father who initiated the mealtime prayer, and since his death, Jonica had assumed the role. But they were guests in *Aenti*'s house, so she should be the one to decide.

Edna closed her eyes. After several minutes of silence, Jonica peeked at Edna, not sure if she had fallen asleep. *Daed* had always cleared his throat to signal the end of the blessing. Jonica coughed lightly.

Edna opened her eyes. "You must have a lot to talk over with God. I thought I was going to fall asleep waiting for you to finish."

Jonica smiled. Next time she would assume the duty to avoid confusion. She tasted the soup. "The chicken flavor is *appeditlich*. Did you make the soup, *Aenti*?"

"Ida Hosteller made it. She's *gut* about sharing stuff from her garden and whatever canning she does during the year. I am blessed to have so many friends who look out for me."

Jonica sensed her aunt's loneliness but found herself at a loss for words. If she hadn't gone astray during *rumspringa*, they wouldn't have moved away, *Aenti* wouldn't have spent the last five years alone, and her parents would be alive. This was all Peter's fault. Why did he have to be so engrained with that spirit of discontent, and more importantly, why had she thought he would change?

Jonica glanced at her son. "Eat your soup, Stephen."

He slid the bowl away and laid his head on the table.

"I'll put you in bed if you don't eat," Jonica said.

"*Ich nett hungahrich.*"

Jonica gave him a few minutes to change his mind and start eating, but when he didn't budge, she rose from her chair. "Let's *geh* to your room."

Without protest he pushed away from the table and followed her out of the kitchen.

She took him up the staircase and into the first bedroom on the left, Jonica's room growing up in the house. The plain white walls had yellowed some, and it would take a full day to air out the closed-up mustiness, but standing in the room, surrounded by childhood memories, was a balm for her broken heart—if she could forgive herself for allowing what sent her family away.

Stephen climbed up on the twin bed and laid his head on the pillow.

She pulled the covers up. "You can get up if you're ready to eat."

"Okay." He snuggled deeper into the blankets.

Jonica returned to the kitchen and retook her seat. "Sorry about the interruption." She took a sip of the soup. The noodles tasted like her mother's recipe.

"He doesn't like soup?" Edna slurped a spoonful of the chicken broth.

"Stephen isn't normally a picky eater . . . unless he's sick." Jonica put her spoon down as she recalled her son's recent behavior. She'd attributed his flushed cheeks to his running around the house, but with his lack of an appetite, perhaps he had picked up a bug on their long bus ride. "Excuse me, *Aenti* Edna, I think I should check on him. Do you have a thermometer?"

Chapter 4

Jonica sat on the edge of the bed, holding the thermometer under Stephen's tongue. The little spurt of energy he had running around the house had worn him out. He'd refused his lunch, and he didn't put up a fuss when she laid him down for a nap. All signs of his coming down with something.

The bedroom door opened, and *Aenti* Edna poked her head inside the room. "How is Mannie doing? Is there anything I can do?"

"We're okay." Jonica smiled. *Aenti* had already forgotten Stephen's name. An understandable mistake considering she had only met him for the first time a few hours ago. But *Aenti* had also mixed up Jonica's name a few times too since their arrival.

"I can send for the midwife."

"*Nay*, that isn't necess—" The bedroom door closed.

Jonica glanced over her shoulder to discover Edna had left. She checked the thermometer and let out a sigh. Though one hundred degrees was slightly elevated, he'd spiked higher temperatures in the past that hadn't alarmed his doctor in Cedar Ridge. Stephen should feel much better once he'd napped.

After straightening the quilt around her son, she kissed his forehead. "I'll check on you in a little while."

"*Mamm*," Stephen said, "are there *kinner* here for me to play with?"

Meeting her son's innocent gaze, she swallowed hard. "Let's talk about that tomorrow when you're feeling better."

Stephen smiled. "Okay."

Jonica slipped out of the room. She had no plans to mingle with members of the old community, but she had failed to consider Stephen. Of course he would want to play with other children while he was here. But that could open the floodgates of gossip she wasn't ready to face.

Jonica chewed the inside of her cheek. She would have to come up with other things to occupy Stephen's time, keep him distracted. Then, once her father's affairs were in order, they would go back to Cedar Ridge. Indecision about Ephraim's proposal, and Stephen's and her future in Cedar Ridge, made her jaw tighten. A marriage of convenience wasn't wrong per se, but she didn't *want* to choose financial support over love. If her parents hadn't died, hadn't left her and Stephen alone . . .

Tears clouded her vision as she made her way down the stairs. She paused at the bottom of the steps to clear her throat, then proceeded into the sitting room. "*Aenti?*"

Not finding her aunt in her rocking chair, she checked the kitchen, but Edna was nowhere to be found. Jonica removed a cup from the cabinet next to the sink. As she filled it with tap water, she gazed out the window. Edna and Caleb were in the field, and by the way Caleb was nodding, Edna was doing most of the talking. It wasn't until Caleb looked toward the house, then began unhitching the horse from the plow that it dawned on Jonica what Edna must have asked him to do. He was going after the midwife.

Jonica set the mug on the counter and rushed outside, not bothering to grab her cloak on the way out the door. She hurried across the lawn and ducked under the wire fence separating the field from the horse corral.

"There's *mei* niece *nau*." *Aenti* waved her over to them. "I've asked Caleb to fetch Sadie."

"*Aenti*, you left before I had the chance to reply to your question." She came up behind Caleb, who was disassembling the equipment. "You can stop unhitching the horse. You don't need to *geh* after Sadie."

"I don't mind going if the *kind* is sick." He released the horse from the plow.

"He's *nett* sick." Jonica glanced sideways to reinforce her words to Edna, but her aunt was hightailing it back to the house. She turned her attention to Caleb. "Stephen tires very easily and tends to be a child who requires extra sleep."

"Edna said he didn't eat any of his lunch and you were taking his temperature. Sounds like he's sick to me." He dusted dirt off his knees. "I already have the horse unhitched. I might as well *geh* see if Sadie can *kumm* to the *haus* and check him over."

"Please, you're *nett* listening. He doesn't need a midwife." And she didn't need the entire district knowing she was back in Posen—with a fatherless child. Jonica crossed her arms. "How many *kinner* do you have, Caleb?"

He shook his head. "None."

Having given birth as a teenager, she'd learned to take child-raising advice from other people, but never from a man. A man who knew nothing about her son. "Then what qualifies you?" She tapped her chest. "I'm his—"

"*Mamm*." He slanted his brows. "Are you finished?"

She glared a moment, then straightened her shoulders. "*Jah*. I think I made *mei* point."

"I wasn't trying to undermine your authority as the *bu's mamm*. God only knows why you're so . . ."

"Defensive," she acknowledged with a nod.

"I was going to say insecure." He broke eye contact with her and turned his gaze toward the setting sun. "I have work to do and very few hours left in the day to get it done." He bent down, picked up the leather strap he'd just unbuckled, and refastened it under the horse's girth.

Jonica stood off to the side as he realigned the Clydesdale to the plow. She took a few steps toward the fence, then spun around to face him. "I'm *nett* insecure."

He tapped the reins, grinning as though her explanation had proven his point. An insecure person would feel compelled to defend herself. Yet even knowing that, she couldn't stop from adding, "I'm a *gut mamm* to *mei sohn*."

Caleb stopped the horse. "Do you need to get anything else off your chest before I get back to plowing?"

Goaded by his pacifying tone, she let out an exasperated huff. "*Nay,* I think I'm done talking to you." Now that she'd made a complete fool of herself.

"Then please get off the wheat."

Jonica looked down at the freshly turned-over soil and winced. But before she could apologize for disturbing his crop, Caleb tapped the reins and moved on.

The fresh scent of tea tree oil clung to Caleb all afternoon. He had worked the field past dark but failed to get the entire acreage planted. "I don't even know why I'm worrying about getting the field planted if Edna's selling the farm," he told the gelding as he unhitched him from the plow. "The winter wheat won't head out until August."

He clipped a lead rope to the horse's halter and walked him

toward the barn. "Don't you agree, Anchor? Edna should have said something before I invested in seed." Anchor tossed his head up and down as if he understood. Caleb patted the gelding's thick neck. Lately, his horses had become his sounding board. He could talk about the deep-seated pain he hadn't shared with anyone out in the middle of the field with Anchor.

"It's *nett* just the cost of the seed." He rubbed the horse between the ears. "If I'm *nett* farming, what else will I do? Definitely *nett* construction." The only time he planned to swing a hammer again was if his mother needed another nail to hang her pot holders, and that wasn't likely since she had plenty for herself and no daughters to help in the kitchen.

Caleb shook his head. He'd given the matter way too much thought. All afternoon he'd pondered Jonica's words. Edna was selling the farm. For all he knew he was making a mountain out of a molehill. Perhaps Jonica had misconstrued something in Edna's letter. If only it was as simple as that, but the way Edna's thought process was slipping—

Stop! Lord, I can't let this continue to consume my thoughts. You know why I can't go back to construction work. Why I need Edna's fields. I need to make a living—regain mei daed's *respect somehow.*

He led Anchor into the stall, then fed him from the supply of hay and oats he'd brought from home. It was easier to bed the young gelding down in Edna's barn instead of walking him another half mile home only to call upon his strength again at the crack of dawn. After filling the water trough and placing a blanket over Anchor, Caleb left the barn, his shoulder muscles aching after a long day.

Once outside, he caught sight of Jonica standing in front of the kitchen sink, probably *reddying-up* the kitchen after supper.

The woman was certainly a spitfire. Protective of her son. He'd been wrong to provoke her by calling her insecure—even though he sensed that insecurity dictated her actions. For some reason, Jonica wanted him to believe she was a good mother. Perhaps she was sensitive because her child wasn't ill but apathetic. Laziness went against the Amish way, and negative traits tended to reflect on the mother's upbringing. But most mothers probably resembled a wild bear when they or their offspring felt threatened. Even though Caleb was thirty years of age, his mother still defended him, especially to his father.

Caleb headed toward the house to talk with Edna but stopped again as something about the way Jonica was staring out the window tugged at his heart. It was too dark for her to see past the porch steps, so she wasn't looking at him. A flicker of sadness showed in her downturned lips. The boy was probably in bed, and she certainly didn't appear to be rushing through dishes. Maybe she wanted some alone time.

Caleb changed directions and crossed the yard to where he'd left Nutmeg in the corral. A sharp whistle brought the mare to the fence. He hitched the horse to the buggy, then took one last look at the kitchen window before he climbed onto the bench. When Jonica used her shoulder to rub her cheek, an unexpected heaviness filled his chest. He couldn't help but wonder if it was tears she was drying.

His stomach growled, a sharp reminder that he'd only eaten a peanut butter sandwich all day. Hopefully his mother made something good for supper. Caleb turned the buggy around in the driveway, taking another glimpse at the house. Jonica had disappeared from the window. He continued to the end of the driveway and turned onto the main road.

He hadn't noticed the temperature had dropped until he was almost home. Wind flapped against the buggy canvas, and cold air entered through the door trim crevasses. He wasn't ready for winter. Dread settled in his bones as the idea of having to spend longer periods of time indoors crossed his mind. Working Edna's fields had not only given him something constructive to do with his hands, but it gave him a place to go to avoid his father—avoid the pain Caleb had caused.

He pushed the thoughts aside. Winter wasn't something he could change, and neither was his father's cold heart.

Dim lights shone from the kitchen and sitting room windows as he pulled into the driveway. His father was probably reading the Scriptures as he faithfully did every evening. His mother was most likely tidying up the kitchen, waiting, wondering why Caleb hadn't come home for supper. He bedded Nutmeg down in the barn, then ambled toward the house.

Spying his father in his chair, the Bible open on his lap, Caleb drew a deep breath. "Hello, *Daed*." Caleb removed his coat and hat.

"You're late for supper." *Daed* didn't look up from the Bible.

"Sorry." He would have liked to have sat and talked with his father about farming, but instead, Caleb removed his work boots, placed them next to the wall, then went into the kitchen, where his mother sat at the table, a pile of mending in a basket at her feet. "Sorry I'm late, *Mamm*."

She set her sewing aside and stood. "You've had a long day. Wash, and I'll heat up your meal."

Caleb rolled up his sleeves and soaped up at the sink as his mother scurried around the room. The tantalizing aroma overpowering his senses, he hurried through rinsing, then grabbed a clean dish towel from the drawer to dry his hands. "Something smells *gut*." He sniffed, catching the scent of oregano and ground beef. "Meat loaf?"

"*Jah*." *Mamm* smiled, her fleeting joy only lasting a few seconds before despair shrouded her expression once again.

He hadn't seen her smile in months, at least not one that

didn't appear forced. His younger brother's death had cast a dark veil over his family—forever changing them all. His father had withdrawn from everyone, spending long hours in the barn. When *Daed* was inside, he showed no emotion and spoke very little. While *Mamm* didn't speak of Peter's death, she cried a lot. Caleb had found her in the kitchen multiple times with her head buried in her hands, sobbing.

Several months after the accident, as if realizing she had to display strength and move past the tragedy, she unearthed the ability to hide her emotions. She resumed normal activities around the house and attended sewing frolics and get-togethers with the womenfolk in the district, but Caleb wasn't fooled. His mother still suffered deeply, both for the son she had lost and for the husband who had grown distant.

And Caleb shouldered the guilt.

He glanced over her shoulder at the green beans warming. "Need help?"

"*Nay*, sit. Please." She removed a plate from the overhead cabinet and utensils from the drawer.

To satisfy his rumbling stomach, Caleb snatched a yeast roll from the basket, then took a seat at the table. The bread practically melted in his mouth.

She placed the plate of food before him, then poured him a glass of milk. "Were you able to finish planting the fields?"

He shook his head. "I had a few setbacks."

She set the glass of milk on the table and sat in the chair opposite him. "Nothing with Anchor, I hope? He's young and would probably do better paired with— Well." She picked up the sock she'd been darning and pulled her needle through. "I suppose I'm *nett* the one who should be handing out farming advice."

"Anchor did well, and your advice is appreciated." He took

a bite of meat loaf and readied another forkful as he chewed. "Have you heard anything about Edna planning to sell her farm?"

"*Nay*. Did she tell you she was? Where would she go?"

He shrugged. "Maybe to the U.P. I don't know." Jonica hadn't mentioned what Edna's plans were once she sold the farm. "Her niece—"

A knock at the front door claimed his mother's attention and she left the room.

Caleb took another bite, then hearing Darleen's voice in the other room, washed the food down with a gulp of milk.

"He is eating supper *nau*," *Mamm* said. "Can you *kumm* back tomorrow?"

Caleb pushed away from the table, grabbing his napkin to wipe his face on the way to the door. It wasn't like Darleen to go out after dark, especially alone. "This is a nice surprise. What brings you over?"

She glanced toward his mother, then lowered her head.

"Don't forget your food," *Mamm* said on her way back to the kitchen. "It'll get *kalt* if you leave it too long."

He'd eaten plenty of cold meat loaf sandwiches from the leftovers for lunch and could eat green beans cold too, so when he replied, "Okay," it was only to appease his mother. He waited until she was back in the kitchen, then turned his attention to Darleen. "Do you want to *kumm* inside?"

"*Nay*, will you *kumm* out here?" She stepped back, giving him space to swing the door open.

The moment he stepped onto the porch, coldness penetrated his socked feet. He should have grabbed his boots and coat on the way out the door. He crossed his arms but it did nothing to block the night air. "What's on your mind?"

She glanced toward the kitchen window as if checking to see if his mother was spying on them, then motioned for him to follow her to the other end of the porch. The soft yellow glow from the lantern in the sitting room lit her face enough that he noticed the worry lines stretched across her forehead. "What's wrong, Darleen?"

"I need to know where you and I stand. You've been distant ever since Peter died."

His stomach clenched at the mention of his brother's name. The old house wasn't airtight and if his *daed* was still sitting in his chair . . . Caleb glimpsed in the window and breathed easier finding his father's chair vacant. "It's been difficult." He wanted to leave it at that and not have to explain how Peter's death had fractured his family. "It's only been a few months since Peter . . . went on to be with the Lord. It takes time to . . ." *forgive and forget.*

"*Jah*, I know, and I understand that. Really, I do. But I need to know about *us*. Have things changed?"

She was searching for a deeper commitment from him, something he was incapable of giving at the moment.

"Is there still an *us*?" she continued without giving him time to respond, her words running together. "I don't know where I stand in your life, and quite honestly, I'm growing weary of waiting. I want to get married," she blurted, not showing the slightest shame in her boldness. "I want a husband and *kinner*. I want what *mei* friends all have."

He lowered his head. In their district most couples married after courting a year, and they were nearing that time period. But things had changed—he had changed. "I'm *nett* the same person I was a few months ago."

"Peter's death wasn't your fault."

He looked down at his feet, his toes curled under in his socks. She didn't know the whole story—he'd take that to his grave.

Darleen pulled her cloak tighter to her chest. "Is there a rea-son for me to continue waiting for you?"

Hearing the crack in her voice, he lifted his gaze. Tears glossed her eyes as she waited for his answer. "I don't have any-thing to offer you," he replied. The old Victorian house he'd been restoring now sat boarded up. "You said you want what your friends have, but what I have would never be enough."

"*Jah*, it is." She moved closer, placing her palms against his chest. "I promise it'll be enough."

He leaned down and kissed her forehead. Darleen had a tendency to be overzealous and certainly forthright when she wanted something. But he wasn't sure he liked her competitive nature, especially when it came to marriage. Just because her friends had found husbands didn't mean he and Darleen had to rush to the altar.

"We'll be able to afford our own place when you start up your construction company again."

He stepped back. "I told you that I wasn't ever going back to building."

She frowned. "I know *nett* right away."

"*Nett* ever." Frustration elevated his voice. He rubbed the back of his neck. Why couldn't she accept that he'd closed the business? He wasn't a builder.

Darleen remained silent a moment, then lifted her face up-ward and pinned him with a composed smile. "Will you be coming over for supper tomorrow *nacht*? It's *mei* birthday and *Mamm* wants to plan accordingly."

He reached for her hands and gave them a gentle squeeze. "I didn't forget about your birthday. Tell your *mamm* I'll be there."

"At six?"

He nodded. "I won't miss it."

"Then I'll see you tomorrow." She sashayed away only to pause at the porch steps to look over her shoulder. "Think about our conversation. I won't wait forever, Caleb Schulmann."

Chapter 5

"M*amm*?" Stephen cried out.

Jonica lit the lantern, slipped into her robe, then quickly tiptoed across the hall and into her son's room.

Stephen sat up. "*Mamm*?"

"I'm right here, sweetie." She placed the lantern on the night-stand and sat next to him on the bed, her palm instinctively going to his forehead. "Did you have a bad dream?"

"*Jah*, I saw a car coming straight toward me." He tossed off the bedcovers, crawled up on her lap, and rested his head on her shoulder, mumbling something about the man who had saved him.

"I'm here *nau*." She rubbed his back, hoping a little reassurance that she was nearby would help him fall back asleep. Nightmares had plagued him since the accident to the point where lack of sleep had weakened his body. His fever had broken but his forehead felt clammy. Since he was unfamiliar with his surroundings, she should have anticipated he'd wake up in a panic and fixed a place on the floor next to his bed for her to sleep.

Jonica rocked her son in her arms, humming softly "Jesus Loves Me." Her eyes stung with tears as memories of her mother's sweet voice invaded her thoughts. *Mamm* had sung the same song to Jonica every time she'd been rocked as a child. It wasn't long before Stephen's body relaxed and then went limp.

Unwilling to put him down just yet, she savored the serene moment. Life was too short, too unpredictable, to waste this precious time. Her *boppli* was growing up so fast. A heaviness settled in her chest as her gaze moved from the dusting of freckles on his nose to his long lashes grazing his cheek. So much like his father, how could they not . . . ?

Jonica hugged Stephen closer and rested her cheek against his head, her thoughts taking her back to how elated she'd been to hold him for the first time. Before her mother had taken him to clean him up and wrap him in a blanket, Jonica had counted his fingers and toes, awed with love for her newborn son and petrified at the same time.

She held Stephen a few minutes longer, then eased him down on the mattress and tucked the covers around him. The sun would be up soon, so there wasn't much sense for her to try to go back to sleep now. She returned to her bedroom and removed a pen and paper from her belongings. Now was as good a time as any to keep the promise she'd made to Ephraim and send word they had arrived in Posen.

> Dear Ephraim,
>   I hope this letter finds you and the children well.
> I wanted to let you know that Stephen and I made it to
> Posen safely. The trip was overly long, making several
> stops along the way. The excitement of riding the big bus
> wore Stephen out . . .

She skipped the part about Stephen not sleeping through the night. Ephraim was convinced the boy needed more structure in order to overcome the trauma associated with losing his grandparents. But Ephraim's structured discipline with his own children often involved a stern hand.

A firm approach wasn't Jonica's way—not at a time like this. Stephen had been very close to her parents, his grandfather in particular. Her son needed love and reassurance over discipline, and if she spoiled him a little, so be it. God would understand that children grieved too.

> It was so nice to see *Aenti* Edna again. I'm looking forward to spending time with her . . .

Jonica tapped the pen against the paper. It shouldn't be this hard to write a letter to her prospective husband, should it?

> Please be sure to tell the children hello from us.
> Sincerely,
> Jonica

She set the pen down. Perhaps she would have more to talk about in the next letter. Ephraim's marriage proposition replayed in her mind as she folded the letter and stuffed it in the envelope.

"I have four youngsters and nay fraa *. . . and you have no one* nau." Jonica lingered on the last part of Ephraim's comment with a heavy-laden heart. Was it his intent to disregard Stephen? She didn't know Ephraim well enough to settle the questions swirling in her mind. He couldn't know much about her either. She hadn't told anyone about her past. Plus, they hadn't even courted properly, and he was asking for her hand in marriage. But maybe courtship wasn't necessary since they wouldn't have a real marriage. Their arrangement would be more of a contract to raise his *kinner*, so to speak, and in turn, she would have someone to rely on.

With her father's lumberyard closed for the winter and having to dip into her savings to purchase bus tickets, she and Stephen would face an uphill battle to make ends meet without emptying her savings completely. More stores in Cedar Ridge had agreed to sell her rugs on consignment, but she wasn't holding her breath she would see any money until next spring when tourism picked up.

Jonica placed a stamp on the envelope. Ephraim needed her, or at least his children needed someone to balance out their father's strong hand with love. Most importantly, Stephen would have siblings and a father. She had prayed he wouldn't grow up an only child, that she would find an Amish husband who would raise Stephen as his own.

It was her duty to provide stability for Stephen. Even if it meant marrying someone who wasn't in love with her—nor she with him.

She turned the envelope over, ready to pull it back out and add another line stating she would accept his proposal, but a burning sensation rose in the back of her throat. Nay *rash decisions—think it through.* She needed wisdom. Jonica knelt beside the bed and folded her hands.

"Lord, is it Your will that I marry Ephraim? He's a respected man, a minister in the district. Give me wisdom to do Your will, Lord. Amen."

Feeling better about her decision to wait on the Lord, Jonica stood. If God's plan for her life included marrying Ephraim, God would also give him a heart of patience.

Chilled from kneeling on the floor, she tied the belt of her robe securely around her waist, then went downstairs to stoke the woodstove. She might as well ready the cookstove for breakfast.

The cold floors in the old, drafty house reminded Jonica of the middle of winter. She glanced out the front window, half expecting snow on the ground. Instead of a vision in white, she gazed over the beautiful array of red, orange, and golden leaves that carpeted the lawn. Childhood memories of her father raking the lawn while she played in the piled leaves engulfed her thoughts.

Jonica turned away from the window. Reminiscing was dangerous. She had severed ties with Posen years ago, and she couldn't let emotions rule her now.

She grabbed the last piece of wood from the crate, tossed it on the embers, then adjusted the damper. The place should warm up soon. Next, she journeyed into the kitchen. The ashes were cold in the cookstove, and the ash pan looked as though it hadn't been emptied in weeks. It was beginning to make sense why her aunt wanted to sell the place. She just couldn't keep up with things.

Jonica slipped her feet into a pair of mud boots she found by the back door and wrapped a shawl around her shoulders. She removed the ash pan from the bottom of the stove, careful not to spill the cinders and soot as she carried it outside. Ashes were good for the garden in that the wood residue provided minerals, such as potassium, calcium, magnesium, and phosphorus, to the soil. But the garden area was full of weeds. Overgrown after years of neglect.

When her family lived on the farm, she, her mother, and *Aenti* put in a large garden every spring, spending the entire summer and fall canning everything harvested. At the time Jonica hadn't fully appreciated all the hard work it took to prepare for winter. Now, she would give anything to spend one more day in the kitchen working with her mother.

Jonica flung the ashes. As the fine particles of dust fluttered toward the ground, a sudden swift breeze blew the soot back in her face. She coughed hard to clear her lungs.

"It'd probably be wise to test the wind direction before you empty the pan," Caleb said from behind her.

Jonica turned toward him, clutching the empty ash pan against her chest. "What are you doing here?"

He crooked his brow and grinned.

"I mean, what are you doing here so early?" She scanned the yard, spotting his buggy for the first time parked under the lean-to.

"I wanted to get an early start in case it rains."

She followed his gaze to the sky. Dark-gray clouds hung low on the horizon, blocking a good share of the morning sun.

Caleb reached for the pan. "Let me carry that to the *haus* for you."

"*Nay!*" She took a step back as embarrassment heated her face. No worthwhile woman should ever be caught in her state of undress, but here she was, standing before a man with her hair down and wearing a robe. "*Danki*, though." She stumbled over the clunky mud boots as she sped toward the house.

Surely, if the bishop discovered her parading in front of Caleb dressed this way, she would be run out of the district. A disgrace to her father's good name, and after *Daed* worked so hard and suffered so much to keep Jonica in good standing with the community, she'd do everything in her power to keep her father's name pure.

Caleb watched Jonica dart across the lawn and up the porch steps. What was she doing outside, dressed like that, on a chilly day like today? Or any day for that matter. Pneumonia would be knocking on her door if she wasn't careful.

She was a beauty. Her dark hair swept side to side across her

RUTH REID

waistline as she ran. Caleb shook his head. *Get the image out of your head.* He was practically engaged—if Darleen had her way.

Caleb released his buggy mare into the corral, then went inside the barn to get Anchor. "It's going to be a long day, *bu.*" The young Clydesdale had proven yesterday that he had plenty of endurance. He patted the horse's neck. "I hope you're up for another hard one."

He led Anchor out of the stall and over to the support post that held the tackle. As he harnessed the horse, his thoughts returned to Jonica. He didn't know much about the folks in Cedar Ridge, but it seemed reasonable to believe she'd be in trouble with her bishop if she was seen scantily dressed in her district. Unless she was no longer Old Order Amish but instead belonged to one of the new-order versions. That idea was difficult to digest since her father had been one of the ministers before he pulled up roots and moved his family to the Upper Peninsula. Even so, women were supposed to dress modestly—and when they didn't, it was his duty to rebuke unclean thoughts.

A thumping noise outside drew Caleb's attention. He left the barn and, rounding the corner of the building, spotted Jonica restacking firewood against the shed wall. She was dressed more appropriately in an evergreen-colored dress, black apron, and bonnet, so he approached.

"I would ask if you need help, but I'm sure you would decline." He bent down and picked up several pieces of wood.

"You think you know me that well, do you?"

"Just a guess." He placed the logs on the pile. "I'm sorry I embarrassed you earlier."

Her cheeks reddened, giving her face a warm glow. "I humiliated myself. I don't normally—"

He held up his hand to stop her explanation. "We don't have to speak of it." Lord knows, it would be difficult explaining this

morning's interaction to Darleen if someone should have happened to drive by and seen him with Jonica. News in the district, both good and bad, spread like butter on a hot day.

Jonica's eyes dulled. She turned and began collecting pieces
of firewood from the pile.

Caleb groaned. He'd embarrassed her again. He loaded his
arms with heavier pieces of oak, then willing himself not to
speak, followed her to the house.

Jonica shifted the wood in her arms to turn the knob and
used her hip to nudge the door open. She dropped the wood
into the crate. "*Danki* for the help." She dusted bark bits off her
hands.

"I'll bring in more."

"I think this is enough."

They both knew it wasn't enough to last the day, but he
didn't argue the point. Once he finished planting the field, he
would make sure to fill the crate before he went home.

Jonica added a log to the fire. "Can I make you a mug of
kaffi?"

Hot coffee sounded good, but he needed to get to work. He
didn't want his first year of farming to be a failure. As it was, his
crop should have been in last month. The rule of thumb with
winter wheat was to have it in the ground by October first at the
latest, and he was already past that marker. "*Nay, danki*. I better
get out in the field."

Caleb stepped outside and focused on the work at hand. As
long as he didn't get sidetracked again, he should be finished
planting in plenty of time to go home, change into clean clothes,
and make it to Darleen's birthday supper.

Chapter 6

Jonica dodged sputtering bacon grease as she flipped the eggs in the cast-iron pan. She gave them a minute longer to cook, then slid the pan to a cooler area of the woodstove to keep the food warm while she sliced the bread.

Aenti Edna walked into the kitchen and stopped abruptly, putting her hands on her hips. "What are you doing?"

"Making breakfast. I hope you're *hungahrich*." She removed a mug from the cabinet. "Do you still like sugar in your *kaffi*?"

The wrinkles across Edna's forehead deepened, and her face pinched as though straining to think. She looked at Jonica with a stare that went straight through her.

"*Aenti*, is everything okay?"

"Of course it is." Her aunt's shoulders straightened. "Why do you ask?"

Jonica shook her head. "*Nay* reason." She had heard that people with memory issues were often easily frustrated, and she didn't want to upset her aunt further. Jonica motioned to the table. "Why don't you take a seat. I'll bring your breakfast and *kaffi* to the table."

Edna lumbered over to a chair. "I like *mei kaffi* sweet."

"*Jah*, I thought so." Jonica filled a mug with coffee, but instead

of guessing the amount of sugar to add, she set the sugar bowl
and a spoon on the table in front of her aunt.

"*Danki*. Where's the *bu*?"

"Stephen is still in bed." Jonica plated the eggs and bacon.

"You've got a *faul* one on your hands."

Jonica's spine stiffened. Her son wasn't lazy—he was tired.
But she resisted the urge to correct her aunt.

Edna took a sip of coffee, her face puckering as she swallowed hard. "This isn't sweet."

"I'm sorry, I wasn't sure how much sugar to add." Jonica
reached for the spoon inside the sugar bowl. "How much would
you like?"

"I can do it myself. I'm *nett* a *kind*."

"Of course you're *nett*," Jonica said, though her aunt's behavior suggested she wasn't acting her age, or maybe this
childlike conduct was a facet of aging. She'd heard that some
people with memory issues often reverted back to their childhood, which Edna had clearly demonstrated yesterday when she
pointed her finger at Jonica and threatened to tell their parents
if she didn't do the dishes. Even so, what happened to *Aenti*'s
sweet nature? Was this change in personality another facet of
her aging brain?

Jonica handed *Aenti* Edna the spoon, then stood. "I'm going
to check on Stephen."

Aenti's empty stare told Jonica she was trying to piece together who Stephen was, but this time Jonica knew better than
to ask if she was all right. "I'm going to check on *mei sohn*. I'll be
right back," she said, reassuringly.

When Jonica entered the bedroom, Stephen was standing
at the window with his shirt untucked and only one clip of his
suspenders attached to the waistband of his pants. "What are
you looking at, sweetie?"

"A man." He turned away from the window.

Jonica removed a pair of socks from the dresser. "Have a seat."

Stephen plopped down on the bed. "Can I *geh* outside and play?"

"You know Caleb is *working* in the field, right?"

"Like *Daadi*."

Jonica nodded, even though her father wasn't a wheat farmer. He planted trees that would one day be sold for lumber. But Stephen needed to understand that he couldn't disturb Caleb. "Like *Daadi*." She slipped the sock onto his left foot. "Caleb is very busy. He can't have you running around the field while he's trying to work."

"Okay, but can I still *geh* outside and play?"

"We'll talk about it after you've eaten breakfast." She put his other sock on, then tucked in his shirt and fastened his suspenders. Taking him by the hand, she led him down the stairs and into the kitchen.

"*Guder mariye, Aenti* Edna," Stephen said as he climbed onto the chair.

"Did you sleep well?"

"*Jah*." Stephen picked up his fork.

"Glad to hear." *Aenti* lifted her mug. "This *kaffi* tastes like syrup."

Jonica picked up the sugar bowl. Empty. No wonder it tasted so sweet. There had to have been a quarter cup of sugar in that container. "I'll pour you a fresh mug." She refilled the sugar bowl, but this time she added the sweetener herself to the new mug. "Hopefully this one is better."

Edna sampled the drink, then set the mug on the table. "This is just how I like it, *danki*."

"I'm glad." Jonica would be sure to do the measuring for her next time.

Stephen dragged a piece of bread over his plate, soaking up the last of the egg yolk. Jonica was pleased his appetite had returned and she didn't have to plead with him once.

"Done." Stephen set his empty milk glass on the table with a thump. "Can I *geh* outside *nau*?"

"I'll take you outside as soon as we *reddy-up* the kitchen." She motioned to the dirty dishes. "Can you help clear the table, please?"

Stephen nodded enthusiastically and started collecting the utensils.

"If you don't mind, I think I'll lie down a bit." Edna pushed off the chair. "I think I've eaten too much." She ambled out of the room, rubbing her stomach.

"That much sugar would give anyone a bellyache," Jonica muttered. She stacked the dirty plates and carried them to the sink, while Stephen brought over a fistful of silverware he dropped into the basin. Jonica drizzled dish soap over the dishes as Stephen pushed one of the kitchen chairs over to the sink.

"Wait." She stopped him from climbing onto the chair. "Let me pour the hot water first." Using pot holders to pick up the steaming pot of water she'd left on the stove to heat while they ate, she eased it over to the sink, made sure Stephen wasn't within splash range, then dumped it over the dishes. "Okay, you can climb up."

She washed the plates first, dipping each one into the rinse water, then staggered them on a towel-lined counter to cool. Stephen waited, towel in hand, for her okay to rub them dry. The cups and silverware were next.

Stephen leaned closer to the sink and peered into the basin. "Are we done?"

"Almost. You can put the chair back, then *geh* put your boots on while I finish up." The cast-iron skillet was no longer hot, but she didn't want Stephen in the way when she emptied the bacon grease into the container to be rendered. Otherwise she might have a mess on her hands.

He pushed the chair back to the table, making a high-pitched scraping sound on the floor as he went. Stephen ran full speed out of the room and seconds later riffled through the shoes at the front door.

Jonica wiped the seasoned cast-iron skillet clean with the dishrag, gave it a quick rinse, then placed it back on the stove to heat dry. As she removed her apron, the front door opened.

"*Ich geh* outside *nau*, bye."

Jonica raced to the front door but couldn't catch Stephen before he darted outside. She opened the door. "Stephen, *kumm* back inside and put your coat on."

"I'm *nett kalt*." He hid behind the large maple. "Find me."

"Stephen Muller, if I have to tell you again . . ."

"Here I am." He ran back to the house, rosy cheeked and teeth chattering.

"Why did you go outside when I told you to wait, and without your coat?" She had half a mind to face him in the corner, giving him opportunity to reflect on his actions.

Stephen bowed his head. "Sorry."

A lesson learned without consequences? At least he appeared sincere. Perhaps the scolding had been sufficient. Jonica motioned to the house. "*Geh* inside."

This time Stephen didn't run the opposite direction but listened to her instruction. He paused on the landing of the steps. "I'm really sorry, *Mamm*."

"It's very important that you listen to what I tell you."

"Okay, I promise I will." His bottom lip trembled.

As she held the door open for Stephen, a discussion she had with Ephraim over parenting came to mind. "*It's* nett gut *to be too easy on him all the time,"* Ephraim warned. *"Children learn by correction and consequences, and lack of discipline will* nett *teach them anything."*

Jonica pushed the memory to the back of her mind. If Ephraim were here, he would have plenty to say about her allowing this playtime when there were chores to do, but a growing boy needed fresh air and exercise, and so did she. After all, life wasn't all about work. Besides, Stephen didn't have other children to play with, she reasoned, helping her son into his coat. She wrapped a knitted scarf around his neck and pulled his hat down over his ears.

Guilt needled her as she put her own cloak and scarf on, but she dismissed the thoughts. *Aenti's* house hadn't been deep cleaned in years, so putting it off a little while longer wouldn't make a difference in the grand scheme of things. "Ready?"

Stephen nodded.

Once they were back outside, they chased each other around the yard, playing tag until they were both breathless, until they needed a short break. Jonica found a leaf rake in the shed, and just as her *daed* had done when she was growing up, she raked the leaves into large piles for Stephen to jump in. He tossed leaves in the air and tried to catch them as they fluttered to the ground. His ringing laughter warmed Jonica's heart.

She leaned the rake against the porch banister, then joined him in the pile, gathering an armful of leaves and flinging them as high as she could. She pulled Stephen into a hug and fell backward into the pile, both of them giggling. No longer strapped with guilt because she'd left the dusting undone, Jonica knew these moments were meant to be treasured.

A loud crash coming from the house drew her attention and she pushed off the ground. "I need to check on *Aenti* Edna. I'll be right back."

Jonica found Edna kneeling on the kitchen floor picking up pieces of glass. She squatted next to her aunt and helped to clean up the mess.

"I dropped the dish I was going to use to make egg salad. I need to prepare lunch before everyone arrives."

Everyone in an Amish district usually meant someone was hosting Sunday service and the meal following, but this wasn't Sunday. Jonica sucked in a breath. What if Edna had arranged for a few of the women to come for a visit? *Lord, I'm* nett *ready to be interrogated.* She glanced at the wall clock. Noon. If people were invited, they would be arriving soon. "Are you expecting a large group for lunch, *Aenti?*"

Her aunt continued combing the floor for small pieces of glass as if she hadn't heard the question.

Instead of asking again, Jonica pushed off the floor. "I'll clean the rest up with the broom." She grabbed the broom and dustpan from the closet and swept up the glass fragments. From the corner of her eye, she spotted Edna climbing onto the chair that was next to the dish cabinet. *"Ach, Aenti."* Jonica paused to calm her voice. "I could use your help watching over Stephen. Would you mind checking on him for me? He's outside playing in the leaves."

"Sure." Edna wobbled as she climbed down from the chair. She wasn't always stable standing on the floor much less on a chair. Tasked with something new, she ambled out of the room.

Jonica swept the broken glass into the dustpan, then emptied it in the trash container. If she hurried, she could have lunch prepared by the time Stephen and Edna came back inside. Edna had mentioned making egg salad, but she must not have realized the last of the eggs had been used for breakfast.

Jonica went down to the basement, searched shelves full

of canned goods, and selected enough jars of stewed tomatoes to make a large batch of goulash and cornbread, even though something told her nobody was invited and they would be eating leftovers for the next several meals.

As Jonica popped the seal on the first jar, she glanced out the window and spotted Stephen sitting on the top rail of the horse corral, talking to a redheaded *Englischer* pointing out something in the pasture. Jonica pulled the pot off the stove, then fled the house, lunch forgotten.

"Stephen." Panic laced her tone. Not waiting for him to answer, she sped across the yard and slipped between the fence rails. "Stephen," she repeated in a more controlled tone. "It's time to *kumm* inside."

"We're surveying the land." Stephen gazed up at the forty-something man standing beside him and smiled. "Isn't that right, Mr. Jordan?"

"It's certainly a substantial piece of property to take in." The man's shoulders raised as he drew in a breath, filling out his chest cavity. Releasing the air from his lungs, his amber eyes bored into hers. "And don't you just love the scent of the leaves this time of year?"

"*Jah*, autumn is—" A chill juddered along her spine. Had the stranger been spying on her and Stephen when they were playing in the leaves earlier? Jonica redirected her attention to her son. "We should *geh* inside." Where was *Aenti*? She scanned the yard, the porch, the corral without success. Had *Aenti* wandered into the barn or maybe down the road?

"Edna went inside," the redheaded man said as if reading her mind. "She was eager to get lunch ready."

A shiver cascaded down Jonica's spine at the thought of her aunt leaving Stephen in the yard alone with this stranger.

"Edna went in the back door about the same time you were coming out the front." He stepped forward and extended his hand. "You must be Jonica."

Despite the man's gentle demeanor, she placed a protective arm around Stephen's shoulder and pulled him closer. "How do you know *mei* name?"

"Edna mentioned you were coming for a visit." His gaze connected with something beyond Jonica, filling his face with a smile. "Here she comes now."

Jonica turned to find her aunt ambling toward them.

"Here you are," *Aenti* wheezed. "I went inside . . ." She came up beside them, hand on her chest, lips pursed, and taking short, laborious breaths.

Jonica placed her hand on her aunt's bony back. "You're looking a little washed out, *Aenti* Edna. Are you okay?"

"I will be." She took a moment to catch her breath. "Mr. Jordan, I see you've met Jonica, *mei* niece and Stephen's *mamm*." *Aenti* turned to Jonica. "Mr. Jordan's a handy man to have around."

"I started to introduce myself a moment ago. It's nice to meet you, Jonica."

This time when the man extended his hand, she had no choice but to shake it. *Too soft for a handyman.* "It's nice to meet you too." Jonica shifted her attention to her aunt. "We should get back inside. I need to check on the cornbread in the oven."

"*Ach*, we can't let the cornbread burn."

The bread wasn't at risk of burning. It still had plenty of time. But Jonica used the opportunity to grasp Stephen's hand and direct him and *Aenti* back to the house.

Aenti stopped after taking a few steps and glanced over her shoulder. "Mr. Jordan. You're still planning to join us for lunch, aren't you?"

"I wouldn't miss some of your cornbread, Edna."

Jonica swallowed a gasp. *Aenti* had mentioned she'd invited guests for lunch, but an *Englischer*? Jonica decided it best to wait until she and her aunt were alone to approach the topic. Once inside, she helped Stephen out of his coat, hat, and boots, then sent him into the sitting room to play until the meal was ready. She followed Edna into the kitchen. "I'm *nett* sure inviting a stranger to eat with us was wise."

"Mr. Jordan is *nett* a stranger. You met him."

"He's an *Englischer.*" Jonica lifted her brows to stress the point.

"Well, I know that." Edna chuckled. "I haven't lost *mei* mind completely."

Not completely, but what was to stop her aunt from making riskier decisions? Sharing meals with *Englischers* was frowned upon in most Amish districts, and Posen was no different. The bishop and elders would have something to say about that situation.

Jonica checked the cornbread. Just as she expected, it wasn't ready. She had time—time enough to enlist help. She untied, then removed her apron but was slow to loop it over the wall hook. Asking Caleb to join them for lunch could open a can of worms. Stephen had already taken a liking to him, and sharing a meal with a Schulmann went against every fiber within her. Still, the greater risk—Edna's thought process wasn't as keen as it once had been—was that she'd invited an *Englischer* to eat with them.

Jonica had no choice but to elicit Caleb's help. "Will you make sure Stephen stays in the *haus*? I have something urgent I need to do."

Caleb set his sight on the large oak at the top of the hill and urged Anchor to keep the steady pace. A scattering of dark clouds had moved in front of the sun, dropping the temperature a few degrees. The freezing rain mixed with snow forecasted for later in the week might just make an appearance today, making this year's almanac prediction of an early frost accurate.

The weather had been the topic of the men's conversation on Sunday. And while the other men were concerned if they had adequate wood supplies to last a long winter and with covering the windows with plastic wind barriers to block the cold draft, Caleb was preoccupied with the crop he hadn't finished planting and weighing the risk of seed gone to waste. If it was permissible, he would have skipped the after-service meal to work in the field, but working on Sundays, beyond milking cows and feeding livestock, wasn't allowed.

"Let's go, Anchor." Caleb tapped the reins as they started up the hilly incline. He couldn't lose his seed investment and give his father yet another reason to be disappointed in him.

His stomach rumbled, a nagging reminder that the biscuit he'd smothered with blackberry jam for breakfast hadn't held him over. The equipment chains rattled with Anchor's jerking uphill stride. "*Gut bu*, Anchor. Almost there." He pushed the gelding hard in order to maintain a steady pace. Stop-and-go on an uphill climb was always more strenuous.

At the top of the hill, Caleb pulled back on the reins. No matter how much he needed to get the fields planted, he needed to keep his horse healthy even more. This was a good place to rest Anchor and to satisfy his stomach with a bite to eat. He tied the gelding to a low-hanging limb, then plopped down, resting his back against the tree trunk. He removed the thermos of coffee from the haversack, filled the cup lid with the steaming brew, and inhaled the pungent aroma. As he peeled back the tinfoil wrapping from his peanut butter sandwich, he spotted Jonica tramping through the field toward him.

"Caleb," she rasped, sounding both winded and frantic. "I need your help."

He pushed off the ground. "What's wrong?"

"I need you to have lunch with us."

He let out a breath. "I thought the *haus* was on fire the way you sounded."

"*Nay*, nothing like that. Will you have lunch with us?"

"*Danki*," he sat back down, "but I brought *mei* lunch." He held up his sandwich, then took a bite.

She picked nervously at her nails. "Surely on a chilly day like today you could use a hot meal. I made a pot of goulash and I have a pan of cornbread in the oven as we speak."

Though tempted by the hot meal, he had too much work to let food sidetrack him. Caleb shook his head. "Sounds *gut*, but this sandwich is enough." He took another bite, then washed it down with a sip of coffee.

She looked over her shoulder toward the barn and heaved a sigh. "Do you know an *Englischer* named Mr. Jordan? He's an older gentleman."

He thought for a moment, then shook his head. "The name isn't familiar."

"Edna has invited him to have lunch with us."

"An *Englischer*?" That was a *narrish* thing to do.

She nodded. "You and I both know that breaking bread with an *Englischer* is frowned upon."

"Highly." He'd tried to warn Jonica that Edna's mind was slipping.

"Inviting a stranger to lunch—into the *haus*—is . . ." Her face pinched with worry. "I have to get back." She turned and sprinted toward the house.

Caleb scrambled to his feet. Jonica was right. Inviting a stranger to have lunch in a house with a child, an elderly woman, and a young, defenseless mother was cause for alarm. He refolded the tinfoil around his sandwich, placed it back in the knapsack, then unfastened Anchor from the tree. He wasn't sure how long he'd be away and there was no sense leaving the gelding tied in the field when he could refuel on hay and water back at the barn.

Chapter 7

"Why did I ever think Caleb would help? Talking to him was a complete waste of time." Jonica chided herself on the way back to the house. Not only was he unconcerned about *Aenti* inviting an *Englisch* stranger to lunch, but he'd practically shooed her away so he could finish his sandwich.

Jonica spotted Mr. Jordan sitting on the chopping stump, whittling a piece of wood as she came out of the field. She shot him a quick wave, a cordial gesture, while continuing toward the house. Inside, the sweet aroma of cornbread met her at the door. The bread had to be done, but she needed to check on Stephen first. Finding him curled up in the rocking chair coloring on a sheet of paper next to the woodstove, she rushed into the kitchen, grabbed a pot holder, and removed the cast-iron skillet from the oven. Her mouth watered as she eyed the golden loaf.

"Go ahead, Caleb. Eat your dry sandwich. I shouldn't have expected anything different from a Schulmann."

"Did you say something, dear?" Edna asked.

Jonica jolted. She'd been in such a hurry to check the cornbread, she hadn't noticed her aunt on the opposite side of the room. "*Ach, Aenti,* you caught me by surprise. I didn't see you standing there."

Edna chuckled as she removed an apron from the wall hook. "I thought I was the only one who talked to myself."

Jonica stifled a laugh. Though her aunt's momentary sense of humor was refreshing, Jonica wanted to end further conversation in regard to *who* she'd been talking to herself about. Otherwise, *Aenti* might inquire about Caleb, someone Jonica had no interest in talking about. She busied herself with slicing bread, then removing dishes from the cabinet and setting the table.

Edna tied the apron around her waist. "The food smells *appeditlich*." She removed a serving spoon from the utensil drawer when the goulash began to sputter.

"Be careful, that's really . . ." *hot*. Jonica clamped her mouth shut, noting how Edna had shifted her stance and shot her a sideways glance that suggested she didn't need a cooking lesson. Still, *Aenti* was bound to get burned using such a short spoon. Jonica removed a wooden spoon from the drawer and handed it to her aunt. "I think you'll find this one easier to use."

Edna exchanged spoons. "There was a time when I was the one worried about you being too close to the stove." She gently stirred the pot. "*Nau*, it seems I'm the one who is in the way."

Jonica placed her hand on the back of her aunt's shoulder and leaned toward her. "You're *nett* in the way. I love that we have this opportunity to work together in the kitchen again."

Edna sniffled. "Your voice is a sweet song in *mei* ear, *kind*."

Jonica gave the frail-boned woman a gentle hug. "It's *gut* to be back, *Aenti*. I've missed you."

They would both be reduced to tears unless Jonica focused on the final meal preparations. She filled a glass with milk for Stephen, then poured two mugs of coffee for herself and Edna. "I wonder what your new friend will want to drink with his meal."

"He isn't picky."

The hairs on Jonica's arms stood on end. Edna would only know the *Englischer* wasn't picky if they had shared other meals together—something Jonica planned to inquire more about over lunch. She removed another mug from the cabinet. "Do you know how he likes his *kaffi*?"

"Cream and a dash of sugar." *Aenti* smiled sheepishly. "In one of *mei* more *forgetful* moments, I served him black *kaffi*. He drank it down and never once brought the blunder to *mei* attention."

"I guess he's truly *nett* picky."

"That's what I just said." *Aenti* winked.

Jonica poured three mugs of coffee. She fixed hers and Edna's the way they liked it but decided to wait on the *Englischer* and let him prepare his *kaffi* to taste. She set the drinks on the table, then checked for anything she'd missed. Four place settings, salt, pepper, sweet and sour pickles, cornbread and butter. Everything seemed in order.

Standing at the stove stirring the goulash, Edna hummed *Das Loblied*, the praise hymn sung during every Sunday service. Jonica should be pleased how well *Aenti* remembered the tune, but instead her stomach pitted with unanswered questions. How much of her aunt's blissfulness had to do with the *Englischer*?

Edna glanced over her shoulder and stopped humming. "Is there something else you need, dear?"

"I was just . . ." Jonica went to the upper cabinet and removed a large bowl. "I think the goulash is ready, don't you think?"

"*Jah*, I believe it is."

Using pot holders to grasp the pot handles, Jonica eased the piping hot mixture of stewed tomatoes, ground beef, and noodles into the bowl. She placed the dish in the center of the table, then wiped her hands on her apron.

"It all looks so *appeditlich*." Edna's gaze swept across the dishes of food. "I haven't had this many people at the table for a meal in a long time," she said in a soft, reminiscent way.

The loneliness in *Aenti*'s tone lodged deep in Jonica's heart. Five years ago when her parents decided to move up north to Cedar Ridge, *Aenti* had refused to join them. She'd been born in the old house and planned to die in it too. But years of loneliness must have changed her mind—why else would she have decided to sell the beloved family farm?

Edna clasped her hands together. "Let's eat."

Jonica motioned to the other room. "I'm going to round up Stephen and help him get washed up." Leaving the kitchen, she discovered Stephen and the *Englischer* in the sitting room, her son holding a small piece of wood. She hadn't heard anyone knock on the door. Did Mr. Jordan let himself in? She cleared her throat. "Lunch is on the table."

"Look what Mr. Jordan gave me." Stephen held up a wood-carved animal. "It's a horse." He trotted the wooden piece along the arm of the sofa, making neighing sounds.

"I hope you thanked Mr. Jordan."

"He did." The *Englischer* tilted his face upward and drew in a breath. "Is that sweet cornbread I smell?"

"*Jah*, I make it with extra sugar."

Stephen slid off the couch. "You can sit by me." He waved the man toward the kitchen.

"*Nett* so fast, Stephen. You know the rules." She pivoted him toward the washroom and gave him a nudge. "First, you clean up."

Stephen handed Jonica the horse, then scurried off to wash his hands.

She turned the whittled piece over, the craftsmanship better than anything she'd ever seen. She glanced back at the man.

His gray, long-sleeve button-down shirt appeared pressed, not something she would expect to find a drifter wearing. His denim overalls were patch free and clean. Nothing like the soiled garment a hardworking Amish man wore. Yet according to *Aenti*, the man fancied himself a handyman.

Catching the man gazing across the room at her, she lifted the horse. "You have quite a woodworking talent."

"A gift from God."

"*Jah*, well." She cleared her throat. "Stephen will be out in a minute, or you can wash up at the kitchen sink if you would like." She motioned with a nod toward the other room where Edna was puttering, moving dishes around the table. Jonica planted her feet. From this angle, she could monitor the goings-on in the kitchen while being nearby to assist Stephen if need be.

"Very well." The man clasped his hands behind his back and meandered into the other room.

Chatter arose from the kitchen with Edna doting on her guest and the stranger complimenting the cornbread's tantalizing aroma. *Don't be easily charmed*, Aenti. *The man is an Englischer after all.*

Stephen came out from the washroom shaking his wet hands.

Jonica frowned. "You couldn't take a moment to dry your hands with a towel?" Normally she would send him back to finish the job, but today she used the front of her apron. "*Gut* enough."

Stephen raced to the table and eagerly climbed onto the chair next to the stranger.

"Jonica, this is Mr. Jordan," *Aenti* said.

"*Jah*, we've—" Jonica drew back, puzzled as to why Mr. Jordan had stood and thrust out his hand.

"It's nice to meet you," he said.

"You too." Shaking his hand, warmth spread to her core. Jonica moved to the opposite side of the table still somewhat dazed. She'd just taken a seat when someone knocked on the front door. Jonica stood, but *Aenti*, who was quicker to respond, insisted on going herself.

A few moments later, Caleb entered the kitchen, straw hat in hand. "The food smells *appeditlich*. I hope I'm *nett* too late."

"*Nay*. We were just sitting down." Jonica sprang to her feet. "What would you like to drink? *Kaffi*? Tea? Milk? Or *wasser*? There's always *wasser*." *Stop rambling.*

"*Kaffi* sounds *gut*." He hung his hat on the wall hook, then made his way over to the sink and turned on the spigot.

Peter wouldn't have stopped what he was doing. Maybe she had misjudged Caleb. He seemed to have a measure of caring qualities about him. She removed a mug. "Sugar, cream, both, or black?" Why couldn't she talk at a normal speed? Her words ran together like someone stuffed with too many sweets.

He chuckled. "How much caffeine have you had today?"

"Me? *Ach!*"

Stephen snickered. She didn't dare turn and face her son, or *Aenti* and the redhead. But holding contact with Caleb's sparkling blue eyes heated her cheeks. She shifted her attention to the utensil drawer, removing a fork, knife, and spoon.

"A splash of cream would be nice," he said.

Jonica nodded without lifting her gaze from the drawer. She fixed his coffee, then took the mug along with the silverware piled on a plate to the table and placed it before him.

"Caleb, I want to introduce you to Mr. Jordan."

Both men stood and Caleb was quick to shake the man's hand. "Are you from around here, Mr. Jordan?"

"Here and there."

"Caleb, would you be so kind as to lead the blessing for the meal?" *Aenti* bowed her head without giving him time to respond.

"Sure." Caleb sat and bowed his head.

Jonica followed by lowering her head. *Lord, thank You for the food we are about to receive. Bless it to the use of our bodies. Danki for changing Caleb's mind about having lunch with us. And please, God, keep us safe in the midst of this stranger at our table.*

Opening her eyes, Jonica spied Caleb still praying. His thick mop of gingerbread-brown hair, sweat-damp curls from wearing his hat, dangled over his ears. He could use a haircut. Then again, she liked the longer hair, the boyishness. He reminded her of . . .

"Amen." Caleb lifted his head. Usually, the head of the house, who blessed the food, would immediately fill his plate, but Caleb waited.

Edna handed the bowl of goulash to the *Englischer.* "Don't be shy, *nau.* Dig in."

"Bless your heart, Edna. But I think this youngster next to me has waited very patiently." Mr. Jordan looked across the table at Jonica. "Do you mind if I serve him first?"

"I don't mind." But she didn't trust the man and wasn't about to take her eyes off of him no matter how kind he seemed.

"How much would you like, son?"

"A lot!"

Jonica shook her head. "A little, and if you're still *hungahrich,* you can have more."

The visitor placed half a ladleful on Stephen's plate, then scooped himself some before he passed the dish to Caleb, who wasn't shy about taking a healthy serving.

Jonica smiled. That peanut butter sandwich he'd packed for lunch must not have filled him up. At least they wouldn't have to eat so many leftovers. Besides adding cheese and turning it into a casserole, there wasn't too much else she could do to make the goulash appetizing night after night. As it was, she'd made enough that they could all have seconds and then some. The cornbread went around the table next, then the butter dish.

"This is mighty tasty," the *Englischer* said.

"I agree." Caleb lifted his fork to Jonica. "Much better than *mei* peanut butter sandwich."

"*Danki.*" It especially pleased Jonica to hear that Caleb was enjoying the meal, even though a little more sugar would have balanced the acidity of the tomatoes better and the ground beef had a pinch too much salt for her taste.

Edna stopped eating. "Oh, goodness. I haven't introduced any of you to Mr. Jordan. He's been helping me out lately."

"You already did that, *Aenti* Edna." Stephen giggled, then covered his mouth with his hand, leaving markings of goulash on his face. He filled his spoon with another helping.

"*Mamm* and I made a big pile of leaves, and we threw them way up in the air." Stephen's hand gesture demonstrated how he had tossed the leaves and he sent a spoonful of noodles flying to the end of the table.

Jonica cleared her throat to get her son's attention, then eyed him hard.

Stephen pushed against the table, jarring his milk glass. "*Ich* get it."

"Wait until after we finish—" Too late. Stephen disappeared under the table. Mortified by her son's disobedience, Jonica leaned against the empty chair beside her and spotted Stephen just as his knee came down on the visitor's foot. "Stephen Muller," she hissed through gritted teeth.

He burst out from under the table at the opposite end, plucked a noodle off the table, and waved it around as if showing off a prize. "Got it. See *Mamm*?" he said before he popped it in his mouth.

Jonica pointed to his vacant chair. "Take your seat, and stay there until you've been dismissed." She buried her embarrassment in a weak smile and avoided eye contact with the others.

"Don't be too upset with the child," the visitor said. "The boy meant no harm."

"He's a handful, that one is," Edna said, buttering a slice of cornbread.

"Show me a *bu* who isn't." Caleb winked at Stephen. "I know *mei bruder* and I gave our *mamm* fits at times. Of course *mei daed* broke us of that behavior." As if realizing he'd given a deep-rooted secret away, Caleb shifted his attention to the food on his plate and filled his fork. When he looked up again, he'd replaced his somber expression with a forced smile, but he couldn't erase the hint of sadness in his eyes.

It was no secret that Caleb's father had ruled his home with a heavy hand when it came to bringing up his sons—the reason Caleb's brother, Peter, had given for ditching the faith, for making the decision to jump the fence.

"More goulash, anyone?" Edna held up the bowl, then set it back down when everyone declined.

The *Englischer* leaned closer to Stephen. "How old are you, child?"

Stephen held up his palm and counted his fingers. "Five."

Jonica's insides churned but not from hunger. The way Caleb's brows knitted together, he was bound to be doing the math—figuring out how Stephen's age correlated with how long ago her family left town: five years, three months, and ten days ago to be exact. Her secret was out.

She set her fork down and folded her hands on her lap. *Lord, please help me turn the conversation around for Stephen's sake. I'm* nett *ready to answer the questions bound to be stirring in Caleb's head.*

Jonica directed her attention to the *Englischer*. "How long have you known *mei aenti* Edna?"

"A few weeks," Edna answered for him. "He's been . . . a kind friend."

Ach! The man had been hanging around the house longer than Jonica had thought. Did his arrival have something to do with Edna's letter about wanting to sell the farm, or was it just coincidence?

Caleb sat up straighter. "So," he said to the stranger, pausing from taking another bite, "you're from this area?"

The man shifted to face Caleb straight on. "My home is not here. I'm just . . . passing through, you might say."

It's nett *wise to trust a drifter.* Yet everything about his calm, gentle demeanor led Jonica to want to believe the best about the man. Still, the warmth his amber eyes displayed could be practiced deception, intended to hoodwink a fool.

"How is your wheat field coming along?"

"I'll have the crop planted by the end of the day." Caleb half shrugged, belying his confident response.

Edna tapped Jonica's arm. "What do we have for dessert, dear?"

"I, um . . ." Jonica stood. "I'll see what's in the *kichlin* jar."

"It's empty," Stephen said. "Remember, *Aenti* Edna? We looked for *kichlin*. There is none."

The redhead pushed back from the table and stood. "Edna, once again your meal was delicious. Thank you for your kindness."

Stephen had gotten down from his chair and was now tugging on Jonica's apron while she was trying hard to eavesdrop on Edna's conversation.

"*Mamm*, will you make some *kichlin*?" Stephen asked. "Please."

"Later." She looked down at Stephen, holding her index

finger over her lips. "Adults are talking, *nau* shush." But it was too late. She'd missed her aunt and Mr. Jordan's conversation, and now they, as well as Caleb, were headed to the front door. Maybe Caleb was listening.

Stephen tugged her apron again. "Then can I have another piece of cornbread?"

"*Jah*, you may. Stay here." She pulled off her apron. "I'll be right back." She draped the apron over the back of the chair and left the room. She rounded the corner and saw Edna and Caleb talking in the foyer, the *Englischer* gone.

"I'm so glad you were able to have lunch with us," *Aenti* told Caleb.

Caleb glanced at Jonica and smiled, then continued the conversation with Edna. "A hot meal is nice on a *kalt* day like today."

"*Jah*, it is *kalt*." *Aenti* rubbed her arms. "It's supposed to snow. At least that's what Mr. Jordon said earlier."

"I don't like to hear that." Caleb donned his hat. "I better get back out in the field." He turned to Jonica. "*Danki* for inviting me."

His line of vision shot to something beyond her just as she felt a tug on her dress. Stephen peeked around her backside, then ducked back.

Caleb leaned slightly. "I see you, Stephen."

The hair on Jonica's arms stood on end recalling how surprised Caleb was to learn her son's age. "Stephen, stay with *Aenti*. I'm going to walk Caleb out." She grabbed her cloak from the wall hook and tugged it on. She followed him out the door but held her tongue until they were alone. "You seemed surprised by Stephen's age."

"I thought he was younger. Three, maybe four." He shrugged. "I'm *nett* any *gut* at guessing ages. Although most three- and four-year-olds don't know any *Englisch*, and he's doing well."

Bile rose to the back of her throat and she tried to swallow it down. "He has the Muller name." *Don't ask about Stephen's daed.*

"I know." He took a few steps toward the barn and turned back. "Why are you confessing this to me?"

Jonica froze. "For the life of me, I don't know." But she did. She wanted to beg him to keep the information to himself. She wasn't ready to face gossip, and Stephen did know enough *Englisch* that blabbermouths could destroy his innocence.

Jonica lowered her head to compose her words, then steeled herself and lifted her gaze. "Did you recognize the *Englischer*?"

"*Nay.*"

"So, you've never seen him around here before?"

"*Nay,* but he seems nice." He tugged on his coat collar, bringing it up higher on his neck. "I need to get back to work. *Danki* for lunch." He turned and headed toward the barn.

"*Jah,* I agree." She caught up with Caleb. "The man did seem nice."

"But . . . ?"

"But that isn't any reason to blindly trust him. He's an *Englischer*—a stranger." She reached for Caleb's arm and stopped him from going inside the barn. "He's either homeless, or wants something, or both. Why else would he be hanging around *mei aenti's* farm? For *weeks,* I might add. And at the same time he formed a friendship with *Aenti,* he's also managed to keep himself hidden from you. Why is that?"

"That's a *gut* point." Caleb glanced down at her hand gripping his arm. "I know you're worried about Edna and, trust me, I am too. But right *nau,* I need to get back in the field so I can beat the rain. With the temperature dropping, the rain will turn to sleet."

He smiled, but that did little to reassure Jonica. She had

Stephen to think about. It wasn't until he looked again at his arm that she realized she hadn't let go. "Sorry. I uh . . ."

"I'm glad you had the forethought to come get me when you did. I'll definitely talk with the other members of the district. A man with his bright-red hair is bound to stand out. Maybe someone in town knows about him."

Jonica nodded though she didn't hold out much hope. Mr. Jordan might stand out in a crowd, but something told her he was more a loner—a recluse—which was why Caleb had never noticed him before today.

A gust of wind shook the branches, creating a free fall of leaves fluttering to the ground. She pulled her cloak tighter around her neck. "I can't help but think that *Aenti* befriending the stranger has something to do with her sudden decision to sell the farm."

Color drained from Caleb's face. "Why do you think that?"

"Jonica!" *Aenti* shouted from the front door. "*Kumm* quick! It's Stephen."

Chapter 8

The momentary delay it took Caleb to register why Edna was waving frantically calling for help put him several steps behind Jonica who had bolted immediately. Something was wrong with Stephen, which was enough to propel him faster. He reached the porch steps at the same time as Jonica.

"Hurry. Inside." Edna held the door open.

"Stephen!" Jonica bellowed loud enough to carry throughout the house.

"I'll check the kitchen," Caleb said as Jonica poked her head into the sitting room. He rounded the corner and found the boy crouched next to the kitchen sink, holding a bloody dish towel over his hand and tears streaming down his face. "Jonica, in here."

"I'm sorry," Stephen cried. "*Ich* wanted another piece of cornbread."

"It's okay." Caleb knelt beside him and gingerly lifted the towel. Blood surged from the gash on his palm. He reapplied pressure. "Let's take a better gander at it while we're washing it off."

"Stephen!" Jonica rushed to her son's side, her eyes widening. "What happened?"

"He said he wanted another piece of cornbread." Caleb hoisted

Stephen up on the counter next to the sink, then turned on the tap. "*Kalt* water might help stop the bleeding."

"Let me take a peek." She unraveled the towel and gasped.

Stephen yelped when the cold water struck his hand. Rinsing didn't help. Blood gushed in such a way Caleb couldn't see the extent of the wound well enough. He reapplied pressure, then leaned closer to Jonica and lowered his voice so he didn't alarm Stephen. "I think he needs stitches."

"Let's try dipping his hand in flour." Jonica removed a tin canister from the top shelf of the cupboard, then used the measuring cup inside to scoop out the flour. She dumped some on a plate, then held it while Caleb helped Stephen coat his hand with the white powder.

"It stings—stop." Stephen cried harder.

"We have to stop the bleeding, sweetie." Teary-eyed, she gazed up at Caleb. "It's *nett* working."

Edna bustled into the room, her arms loaded with what appeared to be a white sheet cut into strips. "I brought you some clean rags and peroxide." Edna set the supplies on the table, then leaned in closer between Jonica and Caleb. "*Ach!* He's still bleeding. It must be deep."

"Should we try *kaffi*?" Jonica asked.

Flour hadn't slowed the bleeding. Caleb doubted another home remedy would do anything, but locking eyes with Jonica's desperate gaze, he had to do something. He grabbed the jar of ground coffee and sprinkled some over the boy's open palm.

Stephen jerked his hand away and pressed it against his chest, marring his white shirt with bright-red bloodstains mixed with flour gore.

Stephen cried harder.

With further inspection Caleb determined the cut was probably not going to stop bleeding on its own. "We need to take him into town." He wiped his wet hands on the side of his pants.

Jonica nodded, then pressed the sobbing child to her chest and kissed the top of his head. "It's going to be all right, sweetie."

"I'll get the buggy ready. Keep pressure on the cut." He showed Jonica how to hold Stephen's hand to slow the bleeding, then dashed out of the house and sprinted to the barn. He had Nutmeg harnessed within minutes. As he pulled the buggy up next to the porch, Edna held the door open and Jonica came out of the house carrying Stephen.

Caleb climbed out of the buggy. "Let me hold him while you get in."

Surprisingly, Stephen didn't object when his mother passed him to Caleb. Once Jonica was situated on the seat, he lowered the boy onto her lap.

"*Danki*," she said, her voice quivering. "Do you think Sadie might be able to stop the bleeding?"

"We'll stop at her place first." The midwife handled most of the first-aid emergencies in the district, but she wasn't often home, with so many expectant mothers. He tapped the reins, pushing Nutmeg faster. "Still bleeding?"

"I think so."

Caleb slowed the mare as they approached the junction of Leer and Mud Lake Roads. Hitting an unavoidable pothole jostled them on the bench and he winged out his arm to help steady Stephen. When they turned into Sadie's driveway, the wheels sank into soft ground. His gaze combed the pasture, keenly in search of the midwife's horse, but disappointment settled like a tossed rock in the river when he didn't find the trotter grazing in the field. Caleb stopped the buggy and set the brake. "I'll see if Sadie is home before you get out."

In a couple of quick strides, Caleb was at the door and knocking. Meanwhile, he scanned the area for any sign of activity. This time of year, people were usually busy raking in their yards or getting everything put up for winter. But Sadie's buggy wasn't parked under the lean-to. She was probably out on a visitation. He looked back at Jonica, who was gently rocking the child in her lap.

Come on, Sadie. Be home. Caleb knocked again, this time harder. No answer. He waited a few more minutes. The midwife kept odd hours, so maybe she was taking a nap. But he finally gave up and returned to the buggy.

Caleb noticed Stephen had bled through the second layer of bandages. "It's probably best if he's looked over by a *doktah* anyway."

Jonica nodded and continued to soothe Stephen by rubbing his back. She rested her cheek on top of her son's head and closed her eyes, no doubt praying.

Leaving Sadie's driveway, Caleb turned the mare and tapped the reins. As they neared the outskirts of town, Stephen's sobs had turned into soft whimpers. Resting in his mother's arms, the boy appeared smaller and more fragile than ever. Shadows inside the buggy gave the child's complexion a grayish cast.

When they reached the clinic, Caleb tied the horse to a low-hanging tree branch on the side of the building, then went around the passenger side and took Stephen into his arms. He carried the lethargic boy into the office.

"*Mei sohn* cut his hand," Jonica informed the receptionist. "He needs to see the *doktah*."

The young woman at the desk poised her fingers over the keyboard. "What's his name and date of birth?"

"Stephen—Stephen Muller."

She typed a few keys. "Stephen's date of birth?"

"Is that necessary?" Jonica motioned to Caleb who stood beside her holding Stephen asleep in his arms. "*Mei sohn*'s hand is bleeding."

The woman looked up from the computer. "I need to register him for treatment. Besides, the doctor and nurse are both with other patients." She pinned Jonica with a slanted-brow stare. "Can we continue?"

"January eleventh," Jonica said barely above a whisper. Then, prompted by the woman's nod and hands paused over the keyboard, Jonica repeated the date to include the year.

"Your name and relationship?"

"Jonica Muller. I'm his mother."

"Father's name?"

Jonica's hands trembled as she pushed a few stray hairs under her *kapp*. "I'm a single mother."

Although her voice remained calm, her feet shifted awkwardly as if trying to stand up in a rowboat. Now wasn't the time to prod for personal information about the boy's father. Caleb leaned forward. "They're from out of town. Stephen won't be in your computer system."

Jonica's shame-filled gaze flicked to Caleb, but she lowered her head immediately. He wanted to reach for her hand and somehow encourage her to be strong. She didn't need to hide in shame—not around him. He understood too well how it felt to disappoint the people around him, to live ashamed.

"Gotcha," the woman behind the desk said. She handed Jonica a clipboard and pen. "Fill out these forms and return them to me. Also, I'll need a copy of your driver's license."

"I don't have one."

"Sorry." She thumped her forehead with the heel of her hand. "Duh. You're Amish. You don't need a driver's license to operate a horse and buggy." She rolled her eyes. "You'll have to forgive me. I'm new here."

"Dr. Mallory usually works out a payment plan with members from our district." Caleb hoped the charge wouldn't be enormously different for someone out of the area.

The woman's brows rose. "I take it you don't have health insurance."

"*Nay*, I don't."

"I'll find out about the fee while you're filling out the paperwork."

Caleb placed his hand on Jonica's shoulder and directed her to a section of vacant chairs lined up against the wall.

"We probably should have waited for Sadie," Jonica muttered before she started to write on the forms.

"Don't worry about the money. Dr. Mallory is very reasonable." He gently shifted Stephen to his other arm without waking him. "I'm sorry the woman put you on the spot with so many . . . personal questions."

Jonica stopped writing. "You mean about me being a single mother? *Nett* that it's any of your business, but there is someone in Cedar Ridge who wants to marry me."

"I didn't mean to pry." Now he was the one putting her on the spot. He clamped his mouth closed. Anything more he said would only make things worse.

True, an Amish woman having a child out of wedlock was considered disgraceful. But even that indiscretion shouldn't mar someone's reputation for life. From what he'd seen, she was a *gut* mother. Raising a child alone was no easy task, but the boy seemed well balanced and bright. Stephen hadn't suffered— yet. Hopefully the members of the district would look beyond Jonica's past and embrace her and Stephen while they were in town.

Caleb gazed down at the child sleeping in his arms, a sense of protectiveness rising within him. *I'm going to watch over you—and your* mamm.

She finished filling out the forms and walked the clipboard back to the receptionist.

"Thank you. Have a seat in the lobby. I've already let the nurse know you're here. It shouldn't be long before she calls you back."

The moment Jonica sat down, Stephen opened his eyes. He blinked a few times, then peered up at Caleb, his lips trembling as though he was about to cry.

"I'm right here, sweetie," Jonica said.

Stephen climbed onto his mother's lap and, wrapping his bandaged arm around her neck, laid his head on her shoulder and stared at Caleb. The boy's eyelids closed, then opened again as if fighting to stay awake. His complexion hadn't changed. He still had a grayish hue under the fluorescent ceiling lights. Caleb had never seen someone this sickly for just having a cut on his hand.

Caleb rested his elbows on his knees and lowered his chin into his cupped hands. The office had been redecorated since he'd last been in to the doctor a few years back for pneumonia. The blue-flower-wallpapered walls were now covered with pine paneling, and the old indoor-outdoor carpeting had been replaced with wood-like laminate, which didn't look anything like real wood but did offer a timely distraction to find the repeating wood-grain pattern.

When he grew bored staring at the floor, he studied the paintings on the walls, each depicting a different season. The tree-lined landscape offered a peaceful escape from the real reason it was necessary to see the doctor. At least Stephen's condition wasn't serious. He would probably need a tetanus shot and antibiotics to ward off infection, but once the doctor stitched him up, the boy would be fine.

The door leading to the back hallway opened, and a woman dressed in blue scrubs called Stephen's name.

Caleb hesitated to stand, unsure if Jonica would want him to wait in the lobby or go with them to the examination room. He cleared his throat. "Do you want me to *geh* with you or should I stay—?"

"*Nay*, I mean, *jah*."

Puzzlement must have shown in his expression because she motioned with a nod toward the nurse standing in the doorway, her eyes pleading with his. "*Kumm* with us, Caleb. Please." She waited for him to stand, then muttered, "I'm *nett* sure how things will *geh* when the *doktah* . . ." She wiggled her brows and glanced at her son.

Caleb nodded, understanding that he might be needed to help hold Stephen down when it came time to stitch his hand.

"My name is Tammy. I'm Dr. Mallory's nurse," the woman said as she led them down the hall.

Another patient door opened on Caleb's right, and Hazel Lantz, Darleen's best friend, nearly plowed into him. Her face flushed. "Caleb, what are you doing here?" She looked beyond him, her brows arching in puzzlement. "Jonica Muller, is that you?"

Jonica stiffened like someone had stabbed a pitchfork in her back. She turned and faced Hazel. "Hello, Hazel."

"I'm Hazel Lantz *nau*, Jacob's *fraa*. You remember Jacob Lantz, don't you?" Hazel didn't give Jonica a chance to respond before redirecting her attention to Caleb. "I hope you didn't forget it's Darleen's birthday today."

"I didn't forget." He stepped aside to allow a worker to pass by. "We shouldn't crowd the hallway."

"And don't tell her you saw me here." Hazel placed her hand on her belly. "I want Jacob to hear the news first."

"*Nay* need for worry." He had no plans to tell Darleen anything. Caleb turned just in time to see Jonica being led into a room, two doors down. As he headed to join them, he sensed Hazel still watching him. Tongues would wag within hours. Hopefully, he'd have time to explain to Darleen before distorted speculations reached her ears.

Caleb knocked on the open door as he entered. "Sorry to interrupt."

"That's no problem," the nurse said from behind a computer.

He glanced at Jonica, but her focus remained on Stephen trying to get off the paper-lined table. Caleb stood on the opposite side of the exam bench to block the boy. "Stay still, Stephen."

The boy looked up at Caleb and blinked, releasing a string of tears. "*Ich bang.*"

"I know." Any child would be afraid in his situation. Caleb placed his hand on Stephen's leg. "Your *mamm* and I are *nett* going to leave your side."

Stephen wiped away his tears with his bandaged hand. "You promise?"

Caleb nodded. "For sure."

The nurse continued. "Can you tell me what happened?"

"He cut his hand on a knife," Jonica replied.

The nurse frowned, no doubt wondering why a boy his age had access to a knife. "When did it happen?"

Jonica glanced at the wall clock. "I'd say it's been an hour."

"More like two." Caleb took into account the time it took to harness the horse and time spent at Sadie's.

"Any known allergies?" Tammy continued.

"*Nay.*"

The nurse typed Jonica's response into the computer, then asked if Stephen was up-to-date on his shots. When the nurse finished gathering information about his medical history, she washed her hands at the sink, then approached Stephen. "Can I examine your hand?"

Stephen turned away from the nurse and reached for his mother.

"Stephen, sweetie." Jonica combed her fingers through her son's hair, sweeping it away from his face. "Be a *gut bu* and let her take a look at your hand."

Though reluctant at first, Stephen finally extended his injured hand toward the nurse.

Tammy carefully unraveled the blood-soaked rags and set them aside.

"The white powder is flour," Jonica explained. "When the flour didn't stop the bleeding, we tried *kaffi*, but it didn't work either."

The nurse went over to the sink and turned on the water. "I've heard of people using flour on cuts but coffee is a new one." She filled a basin with water and removed some paper towels from the dispenser. "I'm going to wash your hand so the doctor can take a look, okay?"

Stephen nodded. His bottom lip puckered and his eyes welled with tears. "Will it hurt?"

"It might a little. But I'll be as gentle as possible, and when we're all done, I'll let you pick out a sticker."

"Stephen is a brave young *bu*," Caleb said. "Isn't that right, Stephen?"

The boy nodded.

The nurse wiped the area clean, exposing the reddened area around the wound, which had finally stopped bleeding.

Jonica leaned forward. "How bad do you think it is?"

"I've seen worse." Tammy emptied the wash pan in the sink, then went to the door. "The doctor will be in to see you shortly."

Stephen sat up the moment the nurse left the room. "Can we *geh*? Mr. Jordan said he would let me watch him whittle."

Jonica leaned down to Stephen's level. "I won't hear of it. You already know what happens when you play with knives."

Caleb rolled the stool around to Jonica's side of the table so she could sit.

"Mr. Jordan gave Stephen a horse he'd whittled out of a piece of wood," Jonica explained.

Stephen pulled it out of his pocket and handed the wooden object to Caleb.

Caleb inspected the carving. The proportions were accurate, the horse's muscle structure correct. It was not a simple piece merely whittled with a pocketknife. The oak was smooth. "His work is exceptional."

Jonica frowned. "I wonder how long he's been working on it."

Caleb shared her concern. Something with this much detail must have taken days to complete. The sanding alone would have taken several hours to get it this smooth. Caleb turned the piece over in his hand, then handed it back to Stephen. "You should put it back in your pocket so you don't lose it."

"I don't want you hanging around him," Jonica said.

"Why? He's *nett* a stranger," Stephen said.

"Stephen."

She held up her hand, but it didn't stop the boy from adding, "I've seen him before . . ." He lowered his head and muttered, "In *mei* dreams."

For half a second Jonica stood with her mouth agape.

"He's an *Englischer*," Caleb attempted to explain. "*Nett* that all *Englischers* have hidden agendas . . . but some do." The boy's puzzled expression revealed his lack of understanding. "It's best that you listen to your *mamm*."

A few minutes later, Dr. Mallory came into the room along with the nurse. He examined Stephen's hand but seemed more concerned over the blood-saturated rags than the cut itself. "Did you apply pressure?"

"*Jah*, but it just kept on bleeding," Jonica replied.

Dr. Mallory continued the exam. "Is there any history of bleeding disorders in the family?"

Jonica appeared deep in thought and looked at Caleb as if staring straight through him. Then without further prompting from anyone, she seemed to shake off whatever she was thinking. "Bleeding problems? None that I know of."

The doctor was giving the nurse instructions about the suture tray, but Caleb was more interested in why Jonica was picking at the thin paper lining the table. What was she so nervous about? Hearing the doctor and nurse discuss needle size must have made her green around the gills. Her forehead beaded with perspiration and she licked her lips as though her mouth had gone dry. Caleb positioned himself to catch her should she faint.

"Does he bruise easily?" Dr. Mallory asked.

"Easily?" Jonica echoed.

Her dazed, vacant stare warned Caleb she needed support before she leaned against his arm. He placed his hand around her waist. "Do you need to sit down?"

She shook her head but immediately squeezed her eyes closed. Clearly, she was having problems standing on her own.

Caleb eased her onto the stool and rolled her into the corner out of the way.

"*Mamm?*" Stephen's uninjured arm flailed.

"*Mamm* isn't feeling *gut*." Caleb took Jonica's place at the boy's side. "I'm here with you, Stephen. You're going to be okay."

"I would like to do a brief physical while the nurse gets everything else ready." He examined Stephen's mouth, nose, and ears, then tapped his abdomen in several places, touched his neck and armpits, then listened to his heart.

It all seemed routine to Caleb and the doctor didn't reveal any of his thoughts.

The nurse rolled a stainless-steel tray over to the table, then adjusted the overhead light so it was aimed at Stephen's hand.

"This is going to sting a little," Dr. Mallory said as he injected the numbing medicine in the tissue surrounding the wound.

Caleb held Stephen's uninjured hand. "Tell me something you like to do."

Stephen squeezed Caleb's hand as the doctor made the first stitch.

"Do you like to go fishing?"

"*Jah, mei daadi* used to take me."

Caleb was determined to keep Stephen's attention off what the doctor was doing. "Maybe we can go fishing sometime."

"Today?"

Caleb liked the boy's enthusiasm. October wasn't an ideal month for fishing, and his mother had made it clear they weren't staying in town long, so waiting for the pond to harden over with ice was out. "We'll go when your hand is better. I promise."

Jonica stood and wiped her forehead with her dress sleeve. She mouthed "thank you" to Caleb as he stepped aside.

"*Mamm* too?"

Jonica's brows pinched together. "*Mamm* too? What are we talking about?"

Caleb smiled. "Stephen and I are planning a day to go fishing."

"In October?"

Caleb winked. "We needed a distraction."

"But you promised," Stephen said.

"So I did." Caleb shrugged at Jonica. "I can't break *mei* promise."

The doctor finished the stitches and wrapped Stephen's hand with gauze. "You'll have to keep your bandage dry, so I think you and your dad will have to postpone the fishing trip a few days."

Stephen frowned.

"Tammy, would you please take Stephen out to the nurse's desk and find this brave young man a sticker? I would like a few minutes to speak with his parents."

Caleb glanced at Jonica, but she seemed oblivious to what the doctor had said about needing to talk with Stephen's parents. Caleb held his tongue. If Jonica wasn't going to correct the doctor, neither would he.

The nurse helped Stephen down from the table, then took him by the hand. "I think we can find two stickers."

After the door shut behind the pair, Dr. Mallory got right to the point. "I would like Stephen to have some blood work done."

"What's wrong with him?" Jonica's voice cracked.

"Most cuts like Stephen's stop bleeding with a little pressure. His didn't. He lost more blood than he should, which leads me to suspect a possible clotting disorder or some form of auto-immune disease. Does he get sick easily?"

Her face contorted. "He's been overly tired lately. He's had a lot of nightmares since *mei* parents were killed in an accident. Do you think lack of sleep might have something to do with it?"

"I don't want to alarm you before the tests come back. It might be just something we need to keep an eye on."

Jonica's complexion paled and she swayed like she might pass out.

Caleb came up beside her. "You should sit and rest a minute."

She shook her head. "I want to know what's wrong with *mei sohn.*"

As she began to shake with sobs, Caleb turned her into his arms, offering both emotional and physical support. "It might *nett* be anything," he whispered in her ear. "We're going to pray it isn't."

Her body tense in his arms, he half expected Jonica to push out of his hold. Instead, she buried her face in the crook of his neck. Holding her wasn't a big deal—she needed someone.

Dr. Mallory jotted something on a prescription pad, then tore off the top sheet. "Give this to the outpatient department at the hospital."

Caleb took the piece of paper. "Once the blood work is done, how long before we know something?"

"We should know something by Monday or Tuesday," Dr. Mallory said.

Jonica pushed off his chest, breathing heavily and staring like she was confused.

"That's only a couple of days away, Jonica," Caleb said.

"*Jah*, this is Friday. I know." She turned to the doctor. "Tell me, *Doktah*, what do I need to prepare for?"

"That will depend on a number of things. But again, let's wait and cross that bridge if and when it comes. For now, it's a waiting game. Hopefully the results will prove negative."

"But what if they're *nett* negative? I don't understand . . ." Her words were lost in another wave of sobs. "Are you thinking it's something bad? Something incurable?"

"There are a number of things it can be. Does anyone on either side of your family have a blood disorder? Such as hemophilia, thalassemia, or sickle cell? It could also be leukemia, which is a form of blood cancer. I can't rule anything out at this point."

Caleb waited for Jonica to respond, but she didn't. She just stared. The doctor's attention shifted to him, but he didn't have any information to share. Nothing about the father's side of the family. "I don't know about the family history. Jonica's parents were killed in an accident."

"Cancer?" she gasped. "You think he has . . . ?"

Watching her body tremble uncontrollably, Caleb fought the urge to gather her into his arms again. Instead, he placed his hand on her shoulder. *Lord, please strengthen Jonica with Your presence. Give her peace.*

The doctor grimaced but in a flash the concern was gone. Accustomed to being the bearer of bad news, he gave them a moment before he replied. "There is a possibility, but I'd like to discuss that more after the blood work comes back and we have a better idea of what we're dealing with. For now, have the blood drawn. Do you have a contact number listed so I can reach you once the test results are back?"

"I . . . ah." Jonica turned to Caleb. "Do you know Beverly Drombroski's phone number?"

He shook his head. "I have it written down at home."

"You can give my receptionist the information later to update your file. In the meantime watch him for signs of bleeding—in his stool, even if his gums bleed when he's brushing his teeth. If you see any bleeding at all, bring him in right away. Also, if he complains of joint pain or runs a fever, don't hesitate to bring him in."

Jonica nodded, tears rolling down her cheeks.

It almost seemed like a moot point in light of everything else, but Caleb asked anyway. "What about the stitches? When should they be removed?"

"Stop at the desk and the receptionist will set up an appointment."

Caleb plucked a couple of tissues from a box on the counter and gave them to Jonica. Why hadn't she told Dr. Mallory about Stephen's fever the other day?

Chapter 9

Jonica removed the pamphlet she'd received at the doctor's office from her handbag and read about bleeding disorders as Stephen slept on her lap for the ride home. She didn't get beyond the first page before tears welled, blurring the words—*genetic disorder*.

"Stephen is going to be okay," Caleb said, breaking the silence.

"You don't know that." *Get control. Breathe.* She took a moment to calm herself. Caleb didn't deserve the clipped response. He'd been nothing but kind to her and Stephen. She dried her face with the back of her hand. "I shouldn't have snapped at you just *nau*. I'm sorry."

"It's okay." A comforting smile touched his lips.

"*Nay*, it isn't." She swallowed the lump rebuilding in her throat. "I shouldn't take it out on you. None of this is your fault."

"It isn't yours either."

"I'm his *mamm*. I should have known something was wrong." She continued reading, stumbling over a majority of the information. "I don't know what all these words mean." She glossed over the scientific jargon about the different clotting factors and their functions, and skipped to the list of signs and symptoms.

"We don't know for certain that *anything* is wrong. Even the *doktah* isn't sure."

She gazed down at Stephen sleeping peacefully. "He's always had pasty skin color. I thought it was because he didn't get much sun. He tires easily . . ." Her lungs burned pulling in a hitched breath. Recalling all the times she'd forced Stephen out of bed when he begged to sleep longer muddled her thoughts.

"What else does the pamphlet list as things to watch for?"

Jonica shrugged. She didn't want to admit that she could see in Stephen everything she'd read so far. "Do you know anyone with blood cancer?"

"*Nay*. But a lot of people are easily tired. I'm that way."

"What about hemophilia or leukemia? Do you know anyone?"

"*Nay*, I don't know anyone." He was quiet a long moment. "Do you think you should tell—" He glanced at Stephen, then mouthed, "his father?"

She shook her head. "We never stayed in contact." Peter had whisked her off her feet and sweet-talked her until he'd taken what he'd wanted. Afterward, embarrassed beyond repair, they both agreed never to mention what had happened. Her moment of weakness changed her life forever.

"Did you tell him about . . . ?"

"That I was pregnant? *Jah*, but that didn't change his mind. He didn't want to stay Amish. He still chose the world—to live as an outsider." She'd already said more than she'd told anyone. Even her closest friend, Faith, didn't know the reason they moved away. Nor could anyone know of the meaningless, one-night stand.

Jonica peered down at her son. "I can't talk about this *nau*."

"I understand."

She appreciated Caleb trying to be encouraging in a horrible situation, but Stephen's medical condition wasn't his problem.

She had given birth as a single mother, and she would walk through this crisis alone. She missed her parents, especially her mother. A mixture of anger and loneliness overtook her emotions and she cried harder. Her world was crumbling.

Caleb split his attention between her and the road but remained silent. Either he found himself at a loss for words or sensed she needed space. Either way, she was grateful for not having to explain the nightmare she'd been fighting in her head.

The sun was low on the horizon, filling the landscape with a golden glow, when Caleb pulled into the driveway and parked next to the porch. "Wait just a minute." He jumped out, looped the reins over the hitching post, then raced around to her side of the buggy.

Caleb held out his arms to take Stephen. Feeling drained, Jonica didn't object.

Aenti met them at the door. "How is Stephen? You've been gone such a long time, and I've been worried sick."

"He's sleeping," Jonica whispered. She wasn't ready to go into a long explanation of everything that had transpired at the doctor's office. Jonica motioned to the staircase. "Will you bring him upstairs to his room, please?"

Caleb nodded for Jonica to head up the stairs to Stephen's room. Asleep in Caleb's strong arms, her son seemed small. Inside the room she pulled the bedcovers back and stepped aside to give Caleb space to lower Stephen onto the mattress.

Stephen opened his eyes. "Are we still going fishing?"

"I promised, didn't I?"

Stephen smiled, then closed his eyes.

Jonica rushed out of the room, then sank against the hallway wall. She buried her face in her hands. What if something was wrong with Stephen? What if she lost him too? There'd be no reason to live. None.

She glanced up as Caleb slipped out of the bedroom. He squatted beside her, his strength soothing her in ways too familiar of his brother.

"I know the next couple of days will be hard to get through, but that *bu* is going to need you to be strong."

"You're right." Jonica pushed off the floor. "I'm all Stephen has." That reality had sunk in at her parents' funerals. They only had each other. She took a deep breath. "We'll get through this." *Alone.*

"Supper," *Aenti* called from downstairs.

"Coming." Jonica headed toward the staircase. Not that she was hungry, but she needed distance from Caleb, from finding comfort from a Schulmann.

Caleb trailed down the steps behind her, but he stopped near the front door. "I'll help any way I can."

She opened her mouth to thank him, but *Aenti* Edna's footsteps behind her caused her to turn and greet her aunt with a forced smile.

Aenti dried her hands on her apron. "Did Stephen need stitches?"

"Just a few," Jonica said.

"Poor *kind*. He shouldn't have tried cutting his own piece of cornbread." She ambled toward the kitchen, mumbling something about being hungry.

"I meant what I said about helping you." Caleb brushed his cheek with his shoulder, and when he looked at her with red-rimmed eyes, she believed him.

"Can I speak with you in private? Outside," she said, opening the door. Nerves tightened her throat, but she would persevere and say what should've been said long before now.

"What do you want to talk about?" Caleb asked once they were on the porch.

Aenti's hearing wasn't the keenest, but Jonica didn't want to take a chance talking on the porch. She moved to the driveway before she replied. "I don't want anyone to know about Stephen's condition. *Nett Aenti—nett* . . . your family—*nett* anyone in the district."

"May I ask why? We all support each other, and you need—"

"What I need is your promise that you won't say anything." She lowered her head, unable to look him in the eyes, and pushed a stone around with the tip of her shoe. When he didn't say anything immediately, she continued. "I came back to Posen with the sole intention of doing whatever paperwork *mei aenti* needed and leaving before anyone found out I was in town."

"Why?" Caleb shifted his stance. "What—or *who*—are you hiding from?"

Caleb studied her a moment. The unyielding glare in her eyes hid fear. If he was going to keep Jonica's secrets, he should at least know what she was hiding.

"People have too much to say in this district," Jonica finally volunteered. "I don't want *mei sohn* the topic." She motioned to the bloodstain on his shirt. "You'll need to *geh* home and change your clothes before you go to Darleen's birthday celebration."

He crossed his arms. "How did you know?"

"I overheard Hazel reminding you at the *doktah*'s office." She motioned to his buggy. "You should go. I don't want to keep you."

"You're *nett*." Celebrating a birthday, even Darleen's, seemed trivial in comparison to dealing with the news Jonica received at the doctor's office today. She was in turmoil. Attending a birthday celebration was the last thing he wanted to do at the moment. He didn't want to leave Jonica alone. "I want to be here."

"I, ah . . ." She took a step backward, increasing the distance between them. "I feel bad that you weren't able to finish planting your winter wheat."

He'd made her nervous. Caleb shrugged, hoping a carefree approach would relax her sudden unease. "The field work will be there tomorrow."

"Still, I don't want you to miss . . ."

"Jonica," he said, "why are you changing the subject? There's something more behind your *nett* wanting me to tell anyone about Stephen."

She scowled.

After several seconds, he groaned under his breath. "I'll keep your secret."

"*Danki.*" She turned and headed back to the house.

"Wait a minute. Our conversation isn't over."

"*Gut nacht*, Caleb," she said without looking back. "I'll see you *meiya*."

Jah, *Jonica, you will see me tomorrow, and we're going to pick up the conversation where you left it.*

Caleb took a few steps toward his buggy, but remembering he hadn't fed or watered Anchor since he'd put him up in the barn at lunchtime, he turned and headed to the barn. He tossed some hay into the stall and filled the bucket with clean water. Usually, he liked to spend more time with the young gelding, rubbing him down after a hard day. But he was already late for supper at Darleen's house, and he still needed to go home to change his clothes.

Coming out of the barn, Caleb glanced at the house as he headed toward his buggy. If he could talk to Jonica again, let her know she wasn't alone, maybe . . . Light shone from the kitchen window, but he didn't see Jonica. "Lord, please let the blood tests come back negative, and please, God, comfort Jonica. Give her peace."

He couldn't stop thinking about Jonica on the drive home. About how frightened she'd been in the doctor's office, and the brave face she'd put on in front of her son at the hospital when he was having his blood drawn. It broke Caleb's heart to watch the child endure first stitches, then more needles to draw the blood. He'd only known Stephen a few days, but there was an unexplainable connection to the child. A connection that went deep.

Parking the buggy next to the house, he jumped out and hurried inside.

His mother looked up from her writing tablet and gasped. "What happened?" She dropped the pen and stood.

Caleb followed her gaze to the stain on his shirt. "It's nothing."

"That's blood." Panic filled her eyes.

"Don't worry. I'm *nett* hurt." He'd been so preoccupied with thoughts of Jonica when he came inside, he'd forgotten about his bloody shirt or that it might remind her of Peter, when they found him lying in a pool of his own blood.

"Then how did you get blood on you?"

"Edna's great-*bruderskind* cut himself with a knife. Can I tell you about it later?" He tugged at his shirt.

"*Jah*, *geh* change." She shooed him out of the kitchen. "I'll warm up the spaghetti and meatballs."

"I thought I told you. It's Darleen's birthday. Her *mamm* invited me to have supper at their place."

His mother frowned. "Abigail Yoder is *nett* a *gut* cook, and from what I've tried of Darleen's cooking at the church meeting meals, she doesn't have much to woo *mei sohn* with."

"*Mamm*, be nice."

She scowled. "I know you fancy yourself as . . . having feelings for the *maedel*, but I'm warning you right *nau*, if you marry her, you'll be *hungahrich* the rest of your life."

Caleb had eaten plenty of food Darleen had prepared for various fellowship meals and he hadn't been disappointed once. But he wasn't about to get into that debate with his mother, who needed to feel important, and that meant being the best cook. Caleb glanced at the wall clock over the table. "I have to go."

He peeled off his shirt on the way to his bedroom and slipped into his Sunday clothes without washing up. Caleb removed Darleen's gift, a wooden box he'd made to hold her straight pins, from where he'd stashed it in his sock drawer. It needed a twine-tied bow but there wasn't time for that now. Going back downstairs, he poked his head in the kitchen. "I'm going, *Mamm*. Save me a plate, and I'll heat it up when I get home."

Mamm smiled. "I'll be sure to save a *gut*-size portion."

He donned his hat and grabbed his nicer Sunday coat on the way out the door. The Yoder's farm was only a few miles up the road. Hopefully he wouldn't be too late. Birthday celebrations at his house consisted of his mother cooking the birthday person's favorite meal, and the family—no guests—having cake afterward.

The turnout for Darleen's special supper looked more like a gathering for a Sunday meeting. Counting the number of buggies parked along the fence as he drew closer to the farm, Caleb figured out quickly that he was the last to arrive. He had no idea so many had been invited. Before knocking on the door, Caleb sniffed his armpits. He wished now that he'd taken a few extra minutes to wash up.

Darleen answered, relief flooding her face. "I thought you forgot."

"I'm sorry I'm late."

She stepped aside, allowing him to enter. "Well, *kumm* in. *Nay* sense in you standing on the porch when everyone is waiting to eat."

Caleb removed his hat as he stepped inside. Supper was set up buffet style with a stack of plates and a basket of silverware on one end of the counter. The Yoders were a large family, with Darleen being the youngest of ten. Her brothers and sisters were all married and had children of their own, making any family get-together a little overwhelming for an outsider like himself. Caleb greeted a few of her brothers, who milled around the sitting room. Laughter rang out from one of the bedrooms where the children had been sent to play.

"I'll tell *Mamm* that you're here." Darleen disappeared into the kitchen, leaving him in the sitting room with her *daed* and *bruders*.

Caleb didn't recognize all the men. A couple of her brothers, who lived in Mio, he'd only met one other time.

"Did you finish getting your wheat planted?" David, Darleen's oldest brother, asked.

"Still working on it." He sat next to James, who was married to Ellen, Darleen's second-to-oldest sister.

Melvin Yoder, Darleen's *daed*, shook his head. "We're supposed to get snow tonight. That's what most of *mei* customers said when they came into the store to pick up supplies."

"*Jah*, that has me worried too," Caleb said. No one was saying it outright, but everyone knew he'd messed up by not getting the seed into the ground before now.

James elbowed Caleb in the ribs. "I thought you only had twenty acres to work. What's the holdup been?"

"The field needed more prep than I anticipated and the long rainy season didn't help. Plus, I have a young gelding." Most of the members in his district, including James and David, owned mule teams to do the work. Six mules could easily cover more ground in less time than one Clydesdale. But Caleb wouldn't let a little friendly ribbing get him riled up. He was used to his father harping on him.

"You want me to bring *mei* mules over?" David asked.

Perhaps pride stood in Caleb's way and maybe he'd later regret turning down the help, but he wanted to prove to himself, his father—and now, Darleen's family—that he could plant and harvest the fields on his own. "*Danki*, but I'll manage. Besides, I wouldn't want your team to stumble or something to happen to your equipment. The field hasn't been worked in years. I'm still picking stones as I go."

David nodded as though he understood. "Let me know if you change your mind."

"I will."

James changed the subject and the conversation turned to potatoes and the enormous beetle population that ruined many of the crops.

Caleb didn't know much about potatoes other than what he'd heard from some of the others in the district.

"Even with all the pesticides the *Englischers* use, they've had problems with the beetles this year too," Melvin added.

Caleb had considered putting in potatoes next planting season because the soil was so good in this area for growing them, but listening to the problems the farmers were having this year, he thought he'd better stick with soybeans or corn. Thankfully, he didn't have to make the decision tonight. He had the winter to figure out what to plant, if anything at all, depending on what Edna did with her farm.

His thoughts shifted to the redheaded *Englischer*. Jonica mentioned she believed Edna's decision to sell the farm had something to do with the stranger. Something about the timing of the two didn't seem right.

James elbowed him again. "You falling asleep, Caleb?"

"*Nay.*" He rubbed his side. "Someone remind me *nett* to sit by James at the next get-together."

"I was just trying to get your attention." James moved his elbow like he was about to nudge him again, but Caleb scooted closer to the arm of the couch.

The men laughed.

"Okay," Caleb said, laughing along with them. "Without jabbing me in the ribs, what did you want?"

James shrugged. "I forgot."

This time, Caleb jabbed James.

"I had asked if you were still building," Luke said. "I know of two men in our district who are looking to put up barns."

Caleb shook his head. "I gave up the business."

"Why?" Luke drew back in puzzlement. "To become a farmer?"

"Why does that surprise you? Farming is our way of life." Many families in the area had struggled after two years in a row of widespread crop loss, and this year's prolonged rainy season placed an even heavier burden on the farmers. As a result some families left the area while others sought alternative means of income outside of farming.

"Your construction business was *gut*, or at least that's what I heard. For someone who has other options, farming seems too risky."

"I needed to do something different." Caleb suspected Darleen had something to do with the conversation he was having with her brothers and father. She'd been pressing him to reopen his construction business. But this wasn't the time or the place to discuss his decision to give up building. Luke hadn't lived in Posen in years and probably hadn't heard about his brother passing away, and Caleb wasn't going to put a damper on the family gathering by bringing it up. Instead, he changed the subject, directing his question to Melvin. "Have you seen any red-headed *Englischers kumm* into your store lately? A man in his forties?"

Melvin shook his head. "Why do you ask?"

"I met someone who's been . . ." Caleb lost everyone's attention when Darleen came into the room and announced the meal was ready. It was just as well. He should have waited to speak with her father when he was at the market. Maybe one of his other workers would remember the man based on his description. Caleb stood but let the others go first.

Darleen leaned closer to Caleb. "How are you getting along with *mei daed* and *bruders*?"

"*Gut,* I think." He rubbed his side again. "But James has a mean jab. He got me with his elbow a couple of times."

"They're just treating you like you are part of the family."

"Is that so?"

Darleen smiled sheepishly. "I hope one day *soon* you'll think of them as your family."

The children came bursting out of the bedroom and stampeding into the sitting room. "Is it time to eat?" one of the boys asked.

Caleb's thoughts flicked to Stephen. The two boys would be similar in age. Only, Stephen was much smaller—a sickly looking child with washed-out skin tone.

"You *kinner* go find your *mamms*." Darleen shooed all eight of them into the kitchen. "They get too loud when they're all together."

Caleb hadn't given it much thought, but he liked the sound of children laughing. It was too quiet—too dismal—at home. With Peter gone Caleb was the only one at home. His oldest brother, George, had moved to Wisconsin with his wife's family several years ago, much to his mother's displeasure. Caleb smiled as the sound of laughter and the chatter of multiple conversations all happening at once filled his soul.

They made their way into the kitchen, where her father blessed the food. Caleb lined up with the men. Everything smelled and looked delicious. He selected a piece of fried chicken, green beans, mashed potatoes, a large spoonful of creamed corn, and a sourdough roll lathered in butter.

"I hope you're saving room for birthday cake," Darleen teased.

Caleb smiled. "I always have room for cake."

He waited for Darleen to go through the line, then followed her to a vacant chair in the dining room. Despite what his mother had said about Darleen and her mother's cooking, he liked everything he ate. Even though he was stuffed like a Thanksgiving turkey, he still managed to eat a piece of chocolate cake.

When it came time to leave, Darleen walked him outside.

He removed the wooden box from his coat pocket and handed it to her. "Happy birthday. I hope you like it."

"It's beautiful," she said, admiring it in the lantern light.

Something in the way she was studying the box led him to think she might be disappointed. "I thought you could put your straight pins in it for safekeeping."

"*Jah*, that's a *gut* idea." She was silent a long moment. "Have you given any thought to our conversation the other *nacht*?"

He shook his head. "Dar-leen . . ."

"Don't drag out *mei* name like that."

"Like what?" It was late and he wasn't in the mood for one of her overdramatized fits, which always reminded him of the eight-year age gap between them.

"Just don't—" She took a step backward, lifting up her hand when he started to follow. "You're pitying me and I don't like it."

"I'm sorry." Nothing had changed since the topic of marriage had first come up a year ago. He still couldn't afford a house. How could he support a *fraa*? She was used to having everything she needed and more. Her own horse and buggy, dresses in every color. She'd never once worn out a pair of shoes. As the youngest of her siblings, she'd been spoiled.

"I think you should go," she said.

"I didn't mean to ruin your birthday."

Darleen turned her back to him and sniffled. "I don't even like birthdays anymore. They just remind me that I'm getting older."

"Twenty-two isn't old." He was thirty and didn't consider himself ancient.

"*Mei* friends all sit in the married section during Sunday services. All of them."

Caleb sighed. When Darleen made up her mind about something, she was determined to get it. Knowing her, if her friends decided to jump off a cliff, she would climb to a higher ridge to make her jump.

She spun around to face him. "I asked that the whole family *kumm* for *mei* birthday because I was sure you would ask for *mei* hand in marriage."

"I'm sorry I disappointed you."

"We used to talk about getting married."

She'd been the one to talk about marriage. He wasn't so quick to believe she was mature enough yet, and he wasn't about to rush into a lifetime commitment.

"Darleen." He stopped when the door opened and some of her family members came outside.

"Happy birthday, sis." Ellen gave Darleen a hug. "We have to head home and get the *kinner* in bed."

"*Danki* for coming." Darleen gave her niece and nephew a hug good-bye.

"I'll stop by the store and talk with you tomorrow," Ellen said.

"It was nice seeing you again, Caleb," James said.

"*Jah*, you too. I'll see you on Sunday." He waited for them to walk away, then turned to Darleen. "I'm going to get going. It's been a long day. I'll talk with you soon?"

Darleen shook her head. "I can't go on like this. You've changed, Caleb."

"True."

This wasn't the conversation to have at her birthday celebration, but Darleen straightened her shoulders as if determined to air everything out tonight. "You said yourself that you don't know when you'll be ready to get married." She crossed her arms. "You don't want to be a builder anymore, but I wonder." She eyed him hard. "Why haven't you finished planting your field? Do you want to fail?"

"Why are you asking that?"

"You use the excuse that you can't afford a *fraa*. So, tell me, Caleb, when your crop fails—because you never planted it— will I be expected to wait yet another season?" She squared her shoulders. "I don't want to wait any longer—I won't."

After half a second ruminating whether or not to explain the various reasons why his crop wasn't in, he decided against it. Her mind was made up, and it was just as well. He'd never reach her ideal potential now that he wasn't a builder. "I understand."

She turned when another family member came outside and wished her happy birthday.

As Caleb headed to his buggy, it started to rain. Wet and chilled to the bone, he wrapped himself in the blanket he'd given Jonica to use earlier, her tea tree scent swamping his senses. On the ride home icy sleet slapped at his windshield, washing away his dreams of yielding a profitable crop like summer dust.

Chapter 10

J onica added an extra spoonful of coffee to the percolator. She needed a heavy boost of caffeine to start her day after being awake most of the night, conjuring up a multitude of reasons why Stephen's hand bled so much. Had she aggravated the cut somehow by dousing his hand in flour? Jonica took a coffee cup from the shelf and leaned back against the countertop. She scanned the kitchen for the pamphlet from the doctor's office. Though she had already skimmed the information in the buggy, somehow she'd misplaced the pamphlet. Mentally, she ticked off the places she'd already searched—her bedroom, Stephen's room, the sitting room . . . The thing had simply vanished. Jonica couldn't recall if Dr. Mallory had office hours on Saturday, but she would find out when she went into town for groceries.

As the coffee brewed Jonica gazed out the window. The night sky had lifted, filling the horizon with soft shades of pink and blue that illuminated the snow-covered field. She sighed. Lying awake last night, listening to icy rain splatter against her bedroom window, she had worried about Caleb's crop. Farming was hard work and he'd given up time that he could've been planting to help her.

Not wanting him to lose everything, she'd prayed it wouldn't snow—that he would have time to plant his winter wheat. But once again, another prayer went unanswered.

"Why, Lord? Caleb seems like a *gut* man. He stepped in as a *daed* would and calmed Stephen, keeping him from panicking in the *doktah*'s office."

Caleb had a calming effect on her as well. When he placed his hand on her shoulder, she wanted to turn into his arms and melt in his strength. Somehow, with him by her side, she had reason to hope, to believe everything would be all right.

No. He was a Schulmann—Peter's brother. Jonica pushed the thoughts to the recesses of her mind. Her past would always stand in the way.

"Lord . . ." At a loss for words Jonica turned away from the window. She'd been raised not to question God, to accept her lot in life with a thankful heart. After all, God had shown unmerited mercy on her. Still, questions plagued her. Why would it snow earlier than normal? Why had her parents died? She never had the chance to say good-bye to her mother and she'd prayed for her father to survive the accident, only to stand at his grave a few days later.

"Lord, I don't understand. You care for the sparrows but don't care about Caleb's crop?" She clamped her mouth closed, not wanting to verbalize her deepest fear—that God would not answer her prayer that Stephen's blood work would return normal.

Jonica filled a mug with coffee, then took a sip, the hot liquid burning the back of her throat as she swallowed. She set the mug on the table and took a seat. Normally this was when she would read the Bible and spend time meditating on God's Word. But today she sat frozen in thought.

Edna ambled into the kitchen. "*Guder mariye.*"

"*Mariye, Aenti.*" Jonica rose to her feet. "Have a seat and I'll bring you a mug of *kaffi*." She readied the drink with sweetener, then placed the mug before her aunt. "Did you sleep well?"

"Like a *boppli*." Edna blew on the steaming coffee before she took a sip. "This is *gut*, *danki*." She wrapped her hands around the mug as if to draw warmth.

"Are you *kalt*?"

"When you get to be *mei* age and your skin thins, you'll find that you're always *kalt*." *Aenti* chuckled. "God has a sense of humor."

"How's that?"

"During *mei* middle-age years, I complained about hot flashes. *Nau* that He's turned off the heat, I'm *kalt* all the time."

"*Jah*, quite the sense of humor." She buried her sarcasm in a whimsical tone.

"God answered *mei* prayers like He answered the Israelites. When they complained about manna, He gave them so much quail it came out their nose." *Aenti* wagged an arthritic finger at Jonica. "Let that be a lesson to you. Watch what you grumble about."

Ashamed she had started her morning grumbling about the weather—about unanswered prayers—Jonica lowered her head, then changed the topic. "I thought I could make a list of the groceries we need and go into town today." It'd give her a chance to pick up another pamphlet if Dr. Mallory's office was open.

"Put peanut butter on the list. I promised Stephen I would make a batch of *kichlin*. Flour, and we could probably use more sugar."

Jonica removed a piece of paper and pen from the cabinet bottom drawer and jotted down the things *Aenti* mentioned. Thankfully the little red wagon was still in the shed. Otherwise she would need to limit what items she bought since *Aenti* had sold her horse and buggy. It used to take her two hours to walk to town, longer if she stayed off the main roads. Excessive weight in the wagon would slow her down more. Jonica put the pen down. "I think this is a *gut* start." No sense filling the cabinets when she and Stephen would be leaving soon.

Aenti shivered. "You think it's *kalt* in here?"

Heat from the cookstove had warmed the kitchen, but Jonica hadn't fired up the woodstove in the sitting room. "You're probably feeling a draft from the window. It snowed last *nacht*."

Aenti pulled the curtain back and frowned. "We're in for a snowstorm."

Jonica leaned toward the window to get a better look outside. "*Ach!* It's snowing again." The way the snow was coming down in large flakes and sticking to the ground, she might better skip breakfast and hurry into town for supplies now. As it was, with *Aenti's* pantry depleted, they weren't prepared to be housebound any length of time.

Jonica drank the last sip of coffee, then stood. She had a fire to start and wood to bring in before the weather got any worse. It'd be a lot faster if her aunt could watch Stephen while she went into town. "The *haus* should warm up once I get a fire started." She pointed to the notepad. "If you think of anything else we need, jot it down."

The wrinkles around her aunt's eyes deepened. "We'll need canning jars."

"For what?"

"Canning pickles, silly." The kitchen echoed with her aunt's lighthearted laughter. "We can't have all those cucumbers in the garden going to waste."

Jonica sighed. "*Nay*, that wouldn't be *gut*."

Just when Jonica thought her aunt seemed lucid enough to oversee Stephen while she went into town, her aunt's mind slipped into the past. The fallow ground hadn't produced anything but weeds in years. "Write it on the list," Jonica said, even though she had no intention of buying jars when it wasn't canning season. In addition, her aunt must not remember she had shelves full of empty jars in the cellar.

As Jonica padded into the sitting room, she made a mental note to look inside one of the outbuildings for a roll of plastic sheeting to winterize the windows. She recalled one winter in particular when the northeastern wind off Lake Huron brutally whipped across the field. The cold air would have gone through the old house had the windows not been covered with the sheets of plastic film. Jonica squatted next to the woodstove and wadded up a few pages of *The Budget* newspaper to use to start the fire.

Stephen toddled into the room rubbing his eyes with his bandaged hand.

"*Guder mariye, schlofkopp.*" She greeted the sleepyhead with a kiss on his cheek.

He wrapped his arms around her neck in a tight hug. "I'm *hungahrich, Mamm.*"

"We'll eat breakfast soon." She glanced down at his bare feet. "*Geh* back upstairs and put your socks on. The floors are too drafty to be running around the *haus* barefooted."

He wiggled his toes. "I'm *nett kalt.*"

"Maybe *nett*"—she pointed at the stairs—"but do as I say."

"Okay." Stephen turned, took a few steps, then stopped at the window. "If I put socks on, can *Ich geh* outside and play in the snow?"

She drew in a breath and released it slowly. Children rarely thought about chores and duties. But Stephen needed to learn that life wasn't centered around playtime. One day—much sooner than she wanted to think about—Stephen would be the man of his own home and be the one to bear the burden of responsibilities that came with supporting a *fraa* and *kinner.* And without him having a father as a role model, it was her duty to train him up in the Amish way. "We have other things to do today." She prepared to recite the list of tasks if he challenged her.

The corners of Stephen's mouth turned down. As he walked away it broke Jonica's heart to see his shoulders slump and excitement drain from his body. Perhaps a sweet treat from the market would lift his spirits. Not that she wanted to get into a habit of rewarding him for work, but a surprise now and then wouldn't spoil him.

She finished building a teepee of thin slabs of kindling, then touched a match to the paper. The woodbox held only a few logs, not enough to keep a fire going throughout the day, let alone get through the night, but restocking would have to wait until after breakfast. Stephen was hungry, and judging by the sound of a chair scraping against the kitchen floor, *Aenti* must be restless.

So much for going into town early. Maybe if she waited a few hours, the weather would let up. If only the sun would come out and melt the snow. She took another peek out the window. Dismal gray clouds stole her hope. Jonica headed back to the kitchen to get breakfast underway.

"We're out of eggs," *Aenti* said, searching a cabinet from atop the chair.

"*Jah*, I used them up yesterday." Jonica caught the back of the chair as it started to rock and steadied it. "What are you searching for?"

"A jar. It's up here somewhere."

"It might be easier for me to find it since I'm taller." *And sturdier on mei feet.*

"Found it." *Aenti* handed Jonica a Mason jar filled with cash, then climbed down. "We're out of eggs."

"So you said. Where did all this money *kumm* from?"

110

"Some is from selling *mei* knitting and the rest is from your *daed*. He sent money every week." She shrugged. "I don't have much need. I tried to tell him that, but he said I should save it for a rainy day."

Jonica marveled at the discovery. "This is a lot of money, *Aenti*."

"There's another jar or two in the cellar somewhere. I think I hid that one too well." She pointed at the container. "Is that enough for what we need?"

"More than enough." Jonica wasn't sure what to think. Her aunt's cabinets were practically empty, but it wasn't from lack of funds.

"I've been hungry for a big bowl of oatmeal. Does Stephen like oatmeal?"

"*Jah*, he does." Jonica moved the chair back to where it belonged, then prepared a pot of oatmeal, adding a dash of cinnamon and sugar to the mix.

They all sat down to eat, but Stephen lost interest in eating after a few bites and picked at his food.

Jonica studied her son. The pamphlet had listed loss of appetite and weight loss as symptoms. "I thought you were *hungahrich*."

He shrugged.

She tapped his bowl with her spoon. "I'm *nett* taking you with me to the grocery store if you don't eat."

Stephen sat up straighter and dug his spoon into the bowl. He finished the oatmeal in a matter of minutes. "Can we *geh*?"

"Where is everyone going?" *Aenti* asked.

Jonica stood and collected the dirty dishes. "I need to pick up supplies in town. Remember, we made a list of things we need?"

"I buy *mei* eggs from Ida Hosteller, milk from the Kauffmans on Leer Road, and bread from The Amish Table. Faith packages mine in half loaves already sliced . . ."

Her aunt continued, but Jonica only half listened while she filled the sink with water. She planned to buy everything at one place—the *Englisch* grocery store in town. Yoder's was closer, but she didn't mind walking the extra mile if it meant less chance of running into other members of the district. She trusted Caleb to keep her secret. So far he hadn't asked questions, but others in the district would be much more inquisitive about her, about Stephen, and about knowing why her family left the district. She wasn't prepared to answer any of those questions.

". . . and everything else, I put on *mei* account at Yoder's Market." *Aenti* came up beside Jonica at the sink and lowered her empty oatmeal bowl and coffee mug into the sudsy water. "Caleb should be here soon. I'll ask him to give you a ride."

"*Nay*," she said abruptly. "I want the exercise."

Aenti's brows wrinkled as she studied Jonica with a scrutinizing stare. "How will you manage to carry everything? I sold *mei* buggy mare."

"I noticed an old wagon in the shed yesterday when I went in there to find a rake. I'll use that." Up north when the roads iced over and it was too dangerous to take the horses into town, she used a sled. Of course, back then, her mother was home to take care of Stephen.

Jonica crossed off a few items on the list. They didn't need five-pound bags of flour and sugar when they could make do with less. Her aunt's squiggly handwriting was illegible, but assuming it meant canning jars, Jonica scratched that out as well. She gazed out the window. The sun had finally started to melt some of the snow. The pavement would still be wet and most likely the shoulder of the road would be slushy, but the wagon would go through that. And, if necessary, she'd either make multiple trips or maybe wait until later in the week when she could arrange for Beverly, the district's *Englisch* driver, to take her shopping.

Stephen charged into the room holding his coat, hat, and one mitten. "*Ich* ready."

"Leave that stuff on the chair and *geh* get an extra pair of socks from upstairs." His boots were large enough that he could probably wear three layers and still have wiggle room for his toes.

"You'll need a blanket." Edna followed Stephen out of the room.

Jonica pulled the washbasin plug to release the water. She needed heavier leggings to wear under her dress and an extra pair of socks too.

Once they were both dressed like they were going out into a February blizzard, they headed to the garden shed. Shopping list in hand, Jonica cleared a path, repositioning the wheelbarrow, rakes, and shovels in order to drag the wagon out from the back.

"Can I help you with that?" asked the redheaded *Englischer* standing at the door of the shed.

She jumped at his presence, clutching the list to her chest.

"I'm sorry. I didn't mean to frighten you." He came closer.

"I don't need any help. I can do it by myself." She gave the wagon handle a hard jerk but it didn't budge.

"I think the back wheels are stuck." He motioned to the handle. "May I?"

She pulled again. "I can get it." The contraption didn't move.

"Please, let me try." The man's eyes filled with compassion, something Jonica usually despised, but this man oozed a sense of comfort and trust that she couldn't push away. Jonica moved to give him room to work, then signaled Stephen to come stand beside her.

Mr. Jordan stooped, then freed the wagon from a hose that had been looped around the back wheels. The rusted wheels squeaked as he rolled it out. "Where are you two off to?"

"We're going to the store," Stephen said. "Want to *kumm*?"

Jonica cleared her throat. "I'm sure Mr. Jordan has things to do."

"Yes, your mother is right." He produced a small block of wood. "I'm going to turn this into something for you, Stephen."

Stephen's eyes widened. "What will it be?"

Mr. Jordan shrugged. "Anything you want it to be."

"That's very kind of you," Jonica said. "But Stephen doesn't need—"

"Can you make a *hund*? I've always wanted a *hund*."

"Then it's settled. A dog, or *hund* as you say, is what it'll be." Mr. Jordan turned and walked away, not giving Jonica time to object.

She didn't want her son receiving gifts from strangers. The man should have asked her if it was okay. Then again, she was the one who had allowed Stephen to keep the wooden horse.

Stephen climbed into the wagon and held his arms up so Jonica could cover him with the blanket. The small wagon wasn't designed to haul much weight and the rickety wheels wobbled as she dragged it along.

Not even a half mile from the house, her shoulder ached. The washboard gravel road proved tiring. Stephen seemed to enjoy the bumps.

By the time they reached the main road, Jonica had amended her list again, eliminating everything but basic necessities. Although the pavement proved a little easier, one of the back wheels began to give her problems. Several yards down the road, a tinging sound behind them caused her to turn quickly, just as the corner of the wagon hit the ground with a jolt. Searing pain tore through her shoulder as the handle ripped from her hand and hit the pavement.

"*Ach*, Stephen are you *allrecht?*" She held her sore arm to her body as she stooped to check on her son.

"*Jah*, I'm *gut*, but that was scary." He struggled out of the tangled blanket and stood, holding his side. Jonica checked him for injuries the best she could without removing his coat but found none.

"Go stand in the ditch while I try to fix this." She pushed him toward the safe area. "Don't get your feet wet." That was all she needed was for Stephen to catch cold.

Jonica moved back to the wagon and lifted the back end. Without tools, there was little she could do to fix the problem.

"Look up, *Mamm*. It's snowing." Stephen stuck out his tongue to catch the falling snowflakes.

A gust of wind hit her face with a flurry of snow that dissolved into freezing wetness. Going all the way into town was out of the question and *Aenti* Edna's was more than a mile away.

"I'm freezing." Stephen hugged his coat to his body as his chin shivered, his cheeks bright red against the gray pallor of his skin.

"*Mamm*." His voice quivered.

She had no choice but to seek shelter.

"You haven't said how supper went at the Yoder's last *nacht*," Caleb's mother said as he worked on setting up her quilting frame in the sitting room.

Caleb suspected what *Mamm* really wanted to know was if he liked the food Darleen's mother served, but he wanted to avoid talking about last night. His mother would prod him with questions if she found out Darleen had ended things. Replaying last night's conversation over in his mind had given him an odd sense of relief. Darleen was one less person he had to prove himself to. He'd never measure up to her expectations and, surprisingly, he was all right with that truth.

"Caleb, is something wrong?"

"It was crowded. Most of Darleen's *bruders* and *schweschders* were there with their families." Caleb tightened the wing nut on the frame's leg to hold the loom in place.

"*Jah*, the Yoders were blessed with a large family." Her melancholy tone drifted into a forlorn sigh, expressing a haunting sadness that had shrouded her since Peter's death. She forced a smile he'd seen before when she was trying to hide her emotions. "Did you give Darleen the wooden box you made?"

"How did you know about the box?"

"I do your laundry, *sohn*. Your sock drawer was jammed to where I had to pull everything out and reorganize it in order to close it properly." She dusted the lamp table. "I assumed it was a birthday gift."

"*Jah*, I gave it to her."

"You did a *wunderbaar* job on the piece. I hope she appreciated it."

His mother wasn't particularly fond of Darleen, so where was she going with this conversation? Had she already heard Darleen didn't want to court him anymore?

"She doesn't strike me as someone who would be easily satisfied," his *mamm* continued.

Not sure how to respond, he moved to the last leg and adjusted its tightness. "Okay, you're all set up." He stood, checked that the frame sat evenly on the floor, then collected his tools.

"*Danki*, Caleb. What would I do without you?"

"I'm not going anywhere anytime soon." Caleb placed his

tools in his tool bag. "Anything else?" Waking up to snow on the ground, Caleb stayed home to do odd jobs for his mother. *Mamm* must have enjoyed his company because it seemed like she was inventing things to keep him busy just to have him around the house longer.

"There's a large wicker chest in the hall closet. Would you bring it here, please?"

"Sure." Caleb located the container marked *sewing* in the back of the closet and lifted it with a grunt. Not that the basket was overly heavy. He'd been hunched over at an awkward angle causing the muscles between his ribs to spasm. The same spot where he'd been bruised last night from all James's elbowing. He brought the container to his mother. "Is this it?"

"I think so." *Mamm* opened the lid and peered inside. She removed a large piece of plain navy fabric, a roll of cotton batting, and finally a navy-and-white-checkered quilt top big enough to fit a bed. "I've been meaning to quilt this blanket for some time. Would you give me a hand setting it up on the frame, please?"

"Sure." He had helped sandwich the material between the rollers on the frame before, so it wasn't difficult as long as the material wasn't wrinkled. Following his mother's instruction, he guided the different layers between the rollers, then safety-pinned the center of the blanket, the area his mother couldn't reach. He was placing another pin six inches from the first when his father walked through the door.

Daed's full six-foot frame took up the sitting room entryway. Though Caleb's own stature matched his father's, the man still gave off a sense of dominance.

Crossing his arms, *Daed* scowled at Caleb. "You have nothing better to do with your time than sew with a woman?"

"I was helping *Mamm*. She has a hard time reaching the center of the quilt to pin it down." The need to explain his actions

117

churned in his gut. "Did you need help with something? I fed the livestock and the woodbox is full."

His mother stood. "It's been snowing all morning, you must be *kalt*, Abraham. I'll put the kettle on the stove for *kaffi*."

Caleb placed the pins he'd been holding on the lamp table next to his mother's chair. "I have field work over at Edna's I need to do."

"That's what I thought," *Daed* said. "You have a lot invested in that seed."

Jah, and they both knew it'd go to rot if he planted it now. He'd missed the season. Still, he needed to do something productive. Lingering around the house any longer would only irritate his father further.

Caleb grabbed his coat from the wall hook and slipped it on.

His mother's voice drifted from the kitchen. "Stop picking on the *bu*, Abe. Please, for me."

"The *bu* . . ." His father's brows narrowed. "The *bu* is a man, Deborah, and he can't even get a plot of seed in without failing. You've doted on him his whole life . . ."

Caleb quietly closed the door behind him as he stepped outside, cold air stinging his face. "Lord, please show me how to mend *mei* relationship with *mei daed*."

Standing in the yard as the snow fell, he offered up to God once again the burden that refused to lift from his heart. "Jesus, please, forgive me for *mei* words that drove Peter to end his life."

Chapter 11

C aleb heaved the oversize rock into the bed of the wagon, the springs groaning with the added weight. For the last hour, he'd dealt with his frustrations the only way he knew how—hard work. That process cleared two acres of Edna's land that he would plant next spring. Unless she sold the property.

The high-pitched call of the whippoorwill came from the brush. Caleb clapped his hands together to brush off some of the cold mud. He scanned the trees along the edge of the field. Whippoorwills migrated south for winter, and they were nocturnal birds. Strange to hear one call out this time of year. The poor fellow must have been left behind.

He heard the bird again. The accented *whip-poor-will* sounded more distinct. Movement caught his attention, and Caleb stepped toward the thick underbrush. Though most of the leaves had already turned and fallen off, there was enough foliage to make seeing past the first foot or two of woods difficult.

"Hello, Caleb." Mr. Jordan emerged from the thick underbrush, his red hair shining in the late afternoon sun. "Working hard, I see."

"*Jah*, I'm trying to." Caleb bent down and hoisted up another rock in both hands. "What are you doing all the way out here?"

Mr. Jordan smiled. "Checking on you." He looked over the newly cleared field. "You got a lot done today."

"It's too *kalt* to *nett* keep moving." He walked the rock over to the wagon and tossed it in with the others.

The *Englischer* gazed toward the road. "Did you give up on the front field?"

"Had to. I missed the planting season this year." Caleb stared across the field at the patches of snow mixed with the half-frozen muddy ground.

He'd hoped, even prayed, for the snow to melt, and that a hard freeze wouldn't come for a few more weeks—just enough time to get his crop in. But this morning it began to snow and the temperature plummeted. Winter was coming, no doubt about that.

Mr. Jordan peered upward. "All things are possible for those who believe."

"*Jah.*" Caleb picked up another stone and added it to the pile. On God's command a mountain would crumble, but that didn't mean He would command the snow to melt or the wind to change directions for Caleb's sake. Caleb was nothing in the grand scheme of things, a human composed and created from dust, and one who eventually would return to dust.

"But do you really believe that?" Mr. Jordan turned his gaze to Caleb. "Do you believe you can still have a full harvest of wheat come spring?"

"Do I believe?" Did he?

"Yes, do you?"

"I admit, I've failed at many things. I tried to be productive as a farmer, but it just didn't work. And I'll be okay with losing the crop." He'd had to endure losing something much greater—his brother, his father's respect, his family. Losing the crop wouldn't shatter him any more than he was already.

120

"You still didn't answer my question, Caleb. Do. You. Believe?"

"That I'll be able to finish planting and the crop won't fail?" He shook his head. "I can't change the weather or make the sun stand still. Do I believe God can do that? *Jah*, I believe. If it's His will—God can do anything." He grabbed another rock and heaved it over the side of the wagon. "Do I believe I deserve His mercy?" Caleb chuckled. "That's another story." A gust of icy wind stung his raw cheeks. He pulled his coat collar higher up his neck to block the winter squall from going down his back.

Mr. Jordan seemed unaffected by the weather. The man wasn't even wearing a hat or gloves. "You have other things weighing on your mind, don't you, son?"

Caleb wasn't someone who shared personal things with strangers and especially not with *Englischers*, but when he looked intently at Mr. Jordan, a ray of something illuminated the man's eyes with a mesmerizing amber glow. Indescribable warmth traveled down Caleb's spine and rendered him speechless.

"God resists the proud, but He gives grace to the humble." Mr. Jordan's smooth baritone voice held a comforting tone. "Cast all your care upon Him, Caleb, for He cares for you." The man placed his hand on Caleb's shoulder. "So, you see, child. The burden is not yours to carry. All you need to do is allow Him to bear it for you."

Caleb wanted to respond, but the egg-size knot growing in his throat strangled his vocal cords. If only it were that easy. Give his cares away for someone else to carry?

"Do not fear, Caleb. Only believe."

Prompted to lower his head and close his eyes, he silently spoke what was on his heart. *Lord, forgive me for letting anxious thoughts rule me. I am casting* mei *cares upon You. I know You will take care of* Mamm *and* Daed *and heal their brokenness. Lord, I ask that You send Your* engels *to watch over Stephen. Give Jonica peace. She's hurting too, having lost her parents. Please free me from my unbelief.*

As if God was answering his prayers, lifting his burdens, Caleb was inundated with peace he couldn't understand. He stood motionless. Though rendered speechless, he sensed a closeness—spiritual communion with his Savior that he'd never before experienced. Danki, *Father. For Your mercy is steadfast and Your love endures forever.*

At a repeating whippoorwill call, Caleb opened his eyes. The redheaded man was gone and there wasn't a bird in sight.

He stood still for a moment, the cold seeping through his winter clothing. He pulled his coat tight around his throat. The heaviness that had almost overwhelmed him a few minutes ago had faded to almost nothing. Yet he didn't feel abandoned.

"Thank You, God."

Caleb tossed a few more rocks into the back of the wagon, then decided to call it a day. Before grabbing the reins to lead Anchor back to the barn, he rolled his head side to side in an attempt to ease his stiff shoulders, then fisted and unfisted his fingers to try and chase the coldness that had stiffened his hands.

The temperature had dropped even more. His breath froze as he exhaled. His big Clydesdale had no problem pulling the wagon to Edna's barn. At the building he paused to unlatch the doors.

"Caleb."

He turned as Edna rushed toward him without her coat. Alarmed by the elderly woman's distressed expression, he dropped Anchor's reins and met her halfway. "What's wrong?"

"I'm worried about Jonica and Stephen. Have you seen them? They're *nett* here."

"I haven't seen them all day. Where would they *geh*?"

"That's the problem. I don't know." She blew into her fisted hands.

Caleb tied the Clydesdale to the fence. "Let's *geh* inside before you get chilled."

"I didn't think to grab *mei* cloak. I wanted to stop you before you left."

Perhaps Edna was confused. She could have fallen asleep and woken up to what she thought was an empty house. He couldn't imagine Jonica going anywhere with Stephen in this weather. Not on foot anyway. Reaching the front door, he stomped his boots on the mat so he didn't track snow into the house.

"Jonica!" Caleb called the moment he entered the house. He searched the sitting room, then the kitchen. Empty. He went to the foot of the stairs. "Jonica? Stephen?"

"I told you. They're gone."

"She didn't leave a note?" He trailed Edna into the kitchen. "What's that?" He pointed to a pad of paper on the table.

Edna picked up the tablet and turned it toward him. "It was the list of supplies we needed."

"The paper's blank. They must have gone into town."

"*Jah.*" Edna nodded. "To get eggs. I remember *nau.*"

"I'll find them." Were eggs so important that she would risk Stephen or her getting sick? The temperature had dropped steadily over the last couple of hours and the snow didn't look to be letting up anytime soon. Were they dressed warm enough for this weather? He had multiple layers of clothing on plus his winter coat, hat, and gloves, and his face still turned numb in no time.

Leaving the house, Caleb spotted Mr. Jordan hitching Nutmeg to the buggy. Where'd he come from? Caleb sprinted across the yard. Nutmeg was high tempered and didn't respond well when *Englischers* tried to pet her. For that reason Caleb made a practice to keep people away from her as much as possible.

"She's *nett* a very friendly mare." Caleb came to a stop next to his horse, then raised an eyebrow. The mare stood perfectly still as the stranger buckled her girth.

Mr. Jordan looked over the back of the animal. "Edna said you were going into town." He pulled a leather strap into place. "The weather is getting worse. You should get a move on. It could be dangerous out there. And don't worry about your plow horse. I'll take good care of him."

"*Danki.*" Caleb checked the equipment to make sure it'd been properly attached. Not many *Englischers* knew how to harness a horse. He tugged on the straps and found them secure. "I'd rather you leave Anchor where he is. He's a gentle giant, but I wouldn't want him to slip on ice and bring you down with him." Caleb hated leaving Anchor tied to the fence, but the animal had his thick winter coat and should be okay.

As he climbed into the buggy something wedged between the passenger door and floorboard caught his attention. He picked up the pamphlet about blood disorders that the nurse had given Jonica. "That's strange. Where did this *kumm* from?" He hadn't noticed it earlier. Caleb tucked the pamphlet into a pocket. Jonica would need this.

A gust of frigid wind rocked the enclosed buggy. He glanced again at Anchor tied to the fence post. "I'll add an extra serving of oats to your feed, *bu.*" But first, he needed to be sure Jonica and Stephen were safe.

Whiteout conditions decreased Jonica's visibility to almost nothing. Her arms ached. After she abandoned the broken wagon on the side of the road, she'd carried Stephen. A half mile or so since she first started carrying her son, with the wind at her face, she stopped to readjust Stephen to her other hip.

Her hands and feet tingled from the cold. The roar of a semi-truck came behind her. She turned and tried to shield Stephen from the onslaught of slush and ice she knew was coming. The truck sped past them, creating a gust of wind that nearly shook her off her feet and soaked one side of her dress and leggings.

Stephen tightened his grip around her neck and spoke through chattering teeth. "*Ich bang*. What if a car hits us?"

"We're going to be okay. We're almost there." It was a lie, but God would have to forgive her this one time. She needed to keep her son calm.

Even though traffic wasn't heavy, Jonica walked as close to the ditch as possible while avoiding any standing water. At any time a car could slip on a patch of black ice and . . . She tucked Stephen's head under the crook of her neck, holding him tight.

Another car passed. "I wish Mr. Jordan was here. He'd save us." Stephen squeezed her neck a little tighter as he whimpered into her coat collar.

Mr. Jordan? Jonica recalled what Stephen had said in the *doktah*'s office. "*I've seen him before . . . in mei dreams.*" She swallowed hard.

This was a mistake. A terrible mistake. She should have waited until Stephen was down for a nap, then left him home with *Aenti*. Jonica would have made it into town and already be back home by now.

Jonica mentally scratched everything off the list. Grocery shopping would have to wait until another day. The weather was too frigid to stay out in it much longer. Stephen needed a place to warm up. He was shivering and she could barely feel her nose with the wind at her face.

The Amish Table was only a half mile away. Yoder's Market was even closer. But if she had to wait out the storm, she'd rather do it sipping coffee at The Amish Table, and Stephen would enjoy a mug of hot cocoa topped with whipped cream. They could make it to the restaurant.

Pressing herself to an easy jog, Jonica almost laughed out loud when Yoder's Market finally came in sight.

Stephen tapped her on the shoulder. "I have to use the potty."

"Can you hold it a little longer?" She stopped at the end of Yoder's drive.

"I don't think so."

"*Mamm* will get you to a potty. Hang on a few more minutes." Jonica quickly headed toward Yoder's. With her gaze locked on the front door of the store, her foot suddenly dropped down into an icy puddle. Frosty water seeped into her shoes and soaked into the double layers of socks.

"Oh, what else can go wrong today?"

Chapter 12

A s Jonica turned the doorknob to the country store, she
breathed out, "*Danki*, Jesus."

The overhead vent welcomed them with a blast of hot air. She
stomped snow off her shoes on the mat at the door, then headed
straight to the restroom located in the back. Thankfully, they made
it in time.

A few minutes later, Jonica helped Stephen wash and dry his
hands, then put on his coat, gloves, and hat. "Are you warmer?"

"*Jah*, but I don't want to go back outside," he whined. Jonica
should have corrected him, but in truth, she didn't want to go
back outside either. She wanted to ask Melvin Yoder if he had
Beverly Drombroski's phone number. Even in bad weather like
today, the *Englischer* had always been willing to drive her parents
when a need arose.

Jonica and Stephen wove around the bulk dry goods bins,
making their way to the front of the store, their boots squeaking
against the linoleum floor with every step. As they neared the end
of the aisle, chatter erupted from the register area. Focused on
blowing warm air into her fisted hands to get warm, Jonica disregarded the muffled conversation two women were engaged in—
until her name was mentioned.

"He was with Jonica and the *bu* at the *doktah*'s office. I saw them myself."

Jonica froze. She recognized Hazel's voice.

"Together?" the other woman asked.

"*Jah*, I even talked with them," Hazel replied. "I wonder if she's back in Posen for *gut nau* that her parents have passed on."

Approaching footsteps clumped toward her from the opposite end of the aisle. Jonica swiped a box of Froot Loops off the shelf and pretended to read the nutritional label on the side of the box. As the customer neared she shifted her stance, keeping her back to the passerby.

"I guess the rumors were right about why they left town." Hazel patted her belly. "I wouldn't know how to bring up *mei boppli* if I didn't have a husband."

"*Mamm?*" Stephen tapped Jonica's arm. "I'm thirsty."

She reached for Stephen's gloved hand. "Let's *geh*, sweetie." The place had suddenly turned colder than the outdoors.

As they rounded the corner Darleen Yoder turned. "Can I help—?" Her lips formed a straight line.

"We were just leaving." Jonica kept her head down and bustled to the door. Once outside the store, a gust of cold wind pushed her back a step. She gathered Stephen into her arms, then headed in the direction of The Amish Table.

Thankfully the short walk to the restaurant was uneventful. Jonica set Stephen on his feet and pulled open the front door. A bell rang overhead.

"Sit anywhere you—" Faith spoke over her shoulder while carrying a food tray toward a table. She stopped and whirled around, knocking the ketchup bottle off her tray. "Jonica!"

Relief washed over Jonica at the sight of her friend's wide smile. "*Jah*, it's me." She bent down and picked up the bottle. "At least the glass didn't break."

"*Jah*, what a mess that would have been." Faith motioned to the roomful of empty tables. "Please, sit. I'll be with you in just a second."

As Faith served her customers, Jonica led Stephen to a cozy table in the back corner. "Stay here, Stephen. I'm going to grab a booster seat for you." Finding the high chairs and booster seats in the same place stacked against the wall at the waitress station, she grabbed one for Stephen to use. "This should give you some height." She lifted him onto the chair.

Faith set her tray on the empty table, then came over to them. Turning to Jonica with outstretched arms, she greeted her with a warm hug. "I was hoping you would *kumm* to see me. It's so *gut* to see you again."

"It's *gut* to see you too." Jonica hadn't realized how much she missed Faith and her friendship until this moment. Although she had made a few friends in Cedar Ridge, none of those friendships were close like what Jonica had with Faith when she lived in Posen. Faith was more like the sister she never had.

Faith released Jonica. "When did you get back in town?"

"A couple of days ago." Jonica helped Stephen remove his coat, hat, and gloves, then took off her cloak and hung the outer coverings over the back of an empty chair.

Faith touched Stephen's cheek. "Is this your *sohn*?"

"I'm Stephen Muller," he said before Jonica had a chance to answer.

She watched Faith for a sign she'd pass judgment on them for Stephen bearing her father's name and Jonica not being married when he was born, but Faith's expression didn't change—except to smile wider.

"It's nice to meet you, Stephen. I have a *sohn* about your age. His name is Daniel. Maybe one day soon the two of you can play together while your mother and I have *kaffi*."

"Can I, *Mamm*?"

"We'll see." His hand needed to heal first.

Faith studied him a moment, still smiling. Nothing but admiration and love shone on her features. "He has your eyes, Jonica."

"Like the big lake. Right, *Mamm*?"

Jonica nodded to Stephen, then explained to Faith. "On the bus ride here, I told him his eyes were as blue as Lake Huron."

"*Jah*, I agree." Faith winked at Stephen, then shifted her focus to Jonica. "Are you back for *gut*? I hope so. I can use some part-time help here if you have someone to care for Stephen."

"*Nay*. I'll *nett* be staying long." Running into Darleen and Hazel earlier had reminded her of why she wanted to make her visit short, but Faith wasn't anything like the other two. "I'm sorry. I didn't mean to be curt."

"I didn't take it that way." A bell in the kitchen dinged and Faith motioned to the kitchen. "*Mei* order is up. What can I get you two to drink?"

"I'll have *kaffi* and Stephen will have a hot cocoa, please."

"Give me a minute to serve *mei* other table their food, then I'll be right back with your drinks."

Jonica leaned in her chair to see into the kitchen as Faith swung the double doors open and disappeared from the dining area. Faith's mother, Irma, and her cousin Catherine had alternated as cooks when Jonica waitressed at the restaurant, but she couldn't get a look at the cook. And that was a long time ago. She scanned the seating area. Large family-size tables that could seat eight customers were centered in the room with smaller tables along the front windows and back and side walls. She glanced at the wall clock. Three o'clock, no wonder the place was almost empty. The lunch crowd would have left hours ago.

Stephen sneezed, bringing her attention back to him. He held his hands in his armpits and his teeth chattered. She grabbed his coat off the back of the chair. "Let's put your coat back on for a little while."

He pushed one arm at a time through his coat sleeves. "*Ich* tired." He yawned.

Entering a hot building after being outside in the cold often made her sleepy as well, but what she found alarming was his ashen complexion. The pamphlet she'd received from the doctor's office flashed through her mind. Pale skin—check. Tiredness—check. She placed her palm against his forehead. Thankfully, his skin was cool to the touch. At least she didn't have to tick the box marked fever or infection.

"Here you go." Faith set a mug of black coffee in front of Jonica. "Be careful, this is really hot," she told Stephen as she placed his mug of whipped cream–topped cocoa in front of him.

"Give it a minute to cool, Stephen," Jonica said.

Faith posed her pen over the order pad. "What would you like to eat?"

"We'll just share a grilled cheese sandwich, please." Perhaps having something in her stomach besides coffee would give her strength to carry Stephen home. It wasn't so much his weight—he only weighed thirty pounds—but he was lanky and awkward to hold for any length of time.

"Any fries or onion rings?"

Jonica hadn't eaten onion rings since she worked at the restaurant. But she didn't have unlimited funds. She still had to purchase their bus tickets to return to Cedar Ridge. "Just the sandwich for *nau*."

Faith tore the ticket off the pad. "I'll put your order in, then *kumm* back to visit some more. Maybe it'll stay quiet in here and give us a chance to catch up." She placed a hand on Jonica's shoulder. "I want to hear all about Cedar Ridge and everything you've been up to."

She took a few steps toward the kitchen, then spun around, somber faced. "Please, forgive *mei* thoughtlessness." She returned to the table and leaned down to give Jonica a hug. "I'm so sorry for your loss."

"*Danki*. And *danki* for the beautiful card you sent." The lump in her throat caused her voice to strain. "It meant a lot." Jonica used her napkin to dab the corners of her eyes while willing herself not to fall apart.

She glanced at Stephen, but he was too preoccupied eating the whipped cream off his drink with a spoon to notice her eyes tearing up. She had to toughen her emotions for her child's sake.

"I'm sorry, Jonica. I should have known you were still grieving."

Jonica drew in a calming breath. "I'm getting stronger every day. I'm sure it doesn't seem like it at this moment, but I am."

"I wish I could have been there with you."

Jonica smiled. "I know." Faith had always been a true and trustworthy friend. She had gone through a lot herself, finding out at sixteen that her parents were not her biological parents. But the discovery made her stronger in the end.

Faith reached for Jonica's hand and gave it a gentle squeeze. "I better give the cook your order or you won't ever get your food."

"Don't let me keep you." Jonica waited until Faith went into the kitchen, then lifted up a silent prayer. *Lord, I don't want to fall apart every time someone mentions* Mamm *and* Daed. *This world was* nett *their home. I know they are much better off with You. Please, help me to move on. For Stephen's sake.*

The sound of the swinging doors opening drew her from her prayer. "Your sandwich will be out in a minute or two," Faith said, while placing plates filled with roast beef, potatoes and gravy, and some kind of greens in front of the customers across the room.

Faith tucked the tray under her arm and came back to their table. "Do you mind if I sit?"

"I'd love it." Jonica reached over to pull out the chair without their outerwear.

Placing the large, round tray on the empty table behind them, Faith took a seat, then twisted slightly where she could keep an eye on her other customers. "You said you weren't staying long, but you never said how long you'd be in Posen."

"I don't know exactly how long, but we'll go back to Cedar Ridge after I finish doing paperwork for *Aenti* Edna to sell the farm." Jonica decided not to mention that Stephen's blood work might keep her in town longer. She trusted Faith to keep the information to herself, but she didn't want to talk about the possibility of a clotting disorder or, worse, cancer. Not in front of Stephen.

"Is Edna moving to Cedar Ridge to live with you?"

Jonica shrugged. "We haven't had a chance to talk about the details yet, but according to the letter I received, she wants to live with her older *schweschder* in Mio."

"Her *older schweschder*?" Faith's brows rose. "How much older?"

"*Aenti* Mary Anna is in her eighties." Faith's brows had arched the same way they used to when she was unsure of something and wanted to prompt the other person to say more. "Why do you look concerned? What are you thinking?"

Faith shook her head. "I just assumed with her memory declining that she'd live with someone who could care for her if it was no longer safe for her to live alone. And honestly, I assumed that was why you had *kumm* back home."

"I know *mei daed* was worried about something because prior to the accident, he'd made plans to visit *Aenti* once the lumberyard was shut down for the winter." Jonica blinked several times to ward off the developing tears. "To be honest, *Aenti* and I haven't been close ever since . . ." She looked at Stephen, smiled, then cleared her throat and continued.

"Most of *mei* interactions with *Aenti* were simple greetings sent through letters exchanged with *mei mamm*. *Mamm* kept her updated about Stephen, his first words, his first steps, but *Aenti* never seemed . . ." Jonica swallowed her words. Stephen didn't need to hear why her aunt didn't approve of his mother. Besides, Edna had treated them well since their arrival. Perhaps her memory decline had somehow blocked that part of the past.

Jonica sipped her coffee, her thoughts drifting to the letter she'd received from *Aenti* wishing to sell the farm. The letter had been logical—thought-filled. Nothing she'd said indicated mental decline. Even her handwriting had been legible.

"If Edna goes to live with her *schweschder*, I hope you will still *kumm* back to Posen and visit me."

Jonica had no intention of ever coming back in the first place—there were too many bad memories here and too many opportunities to cause her heartbreak—but she didn't want to thwart Faith's hopefulness. Before Jonica could formulate a satisfactory reply, the kitchen bell dinged.

"Sounds like your food is ready." Faith bounded up from the chair.

Stephen pushed his empty mug aside. "*Ich* hot." He slipped his uninjured arm out of his coat but struggled to free his bandaged hand.

"Patience, sweetie." Jonica stood and helped him remove the garment. "Are you warmer *nau*?"

He nodded, causing a lank of his hair to fall into his eyes. Jonica pushed it aside, reminded suddenly of the boy's father. Though she knew there'd never be any relationship between Stephen and his *daed*, the threat of accidently bumping into

Peter in the community—if he still lived around these parts—
was another reason to leave the district as quickly as possible.

Faith approached with the food, serving Stephen and Jonica
both full sandwiches and a large basket of onion rings. "This is
mei treat." She winked at Stephen. "Onion rings were always your
mamm's favorite when she worked here."

"*Danki*, Faith. You're so sweet." Jonica tapped Stephen's hand.
"What do you say, *sohn*?"

"*Danki!*" He reached for the largest ring.

"*Ach!*" Faith's eyes enlarged. "What did you do to your hand?"

With Stephen busy chewing his food, Jonica answered, "He
tried to cut a piece of cornbread when I wasn't around." She
picked up the ketchup container and squeezed a dollop onto her
plate.

"That must have hurt," Faith said.

Jonica nodded as she dipped an onion ring in the ketchup.
"He needed a few stitches but I hope it'll heal quickly."

"*Jah*, it hurt really bad," Stephen mumbled, then piped up
with excitement. "But I'm going fishing."

Jonica grabbed her coffee mug and gulped the hot liquid,
pushing down a mouthful of food, but the clump of fried onion
rings didn't mix well with the acid churning in her stomach. The
burning sensation in the back of her throat prevented her from
finding her voice to hush Stephen.

"Caleb's taking me."

Too late.

Faith's eyebrows rose, then she seemed to push aside her
surprise and replaced it with the same all-knowing smile she'd
had when they were growing up. "That's nice."

Jonica motioned to the food. "This is a nice treat. I forgot
how much I liked onion rings. What do you think, Stephen, do
you like them?"

"*Jah*, it's *gut*."

"Here." Jonica slid her plate forward. "Try one dipped in ketchup." She glanced at Faith who seemed to be waiting for a response to the elephant in the room. "Caleb Schulmann was at *Aenti* Edna's *haus* when the accident happened. He took us to the *doktah*'s office. He's putting in a crop of winter wheat on *Aenti*'s acreage." Enough explanation. Focus on eating—on leaving.

"*Nau* it all makes sense. When Hazel Lantz was here earlier, she mentioned running into you in town."

"*Mentioned*, you say?" She could certainly read between those lines.

Faith glanced at Stephen as if to measure his interest in the conversation, then leaned closer to Jonica. "We can talk more later."

Jonica shook her head. "You don't have to say anything. Hazel's at Yoder's Market probably still running her mouth. I just came from there." This was exactly why she didn't want anyone to know she was in town. Rumors had a way of swirling with the wind. She picked up her sandwich and opened her mouth to take a bite.

"Was she talking to Darleen?"

Jonica nodded. "I guess Stephen and I are big news." No longer hungry, she set the sandwich back down. She'd take the leftovers home to eat later, or maybe *Aenti* Edna would want the food if Jonica reheated it.

"Darleen is sweet on Caleb. She's been somewhat vocal about their courting, but I've never gotten the impression his mother approves."

"Oh, dear. Caleb was probably late for her birthday celebration because of me." No wonder Darleen had shot daggers at her in the store.

"According to Hazel, Darleen's been working on a proposal since before—" Faith craned her neck and nodded to someone across the room. "Coming."

Jonica glanced over her shoulder and glimpsed the customer seated at a table near the window lift his coffee mug.

Faith stood. "That's *mei* cue to make another round with the *kaffi* pot." She eyed Jonica's mug. "Looks like you're ready for a refill too."

Jonica waited until Faith walked away, then leaned forward. "Stephen, finish your sandwich." They needed to leave. Gossip had already spread throughout the community, and she didn't want Stephen exposed to any of those comments. When Faith returned with the coffeepot, Jonica declined. "We need to get back home before *Aenti* starts to worry."

"*Mamm*, it takes so long. Can't we stay longer? It's too *kalt*."

"Stephen, eat." She shifted her attention to Faith. "He's a little whiny because he missed his nap. We came into town for groceries, but one of the wheels on the wagon broke, so I had to leave it on the side of the road. Needless to say, it's been a long, *kalt* day." Jonica motioned to her plate. "May I have a to-go box for *mei* sandwich?"

"Oh, Jonica, look at the weather. It's gotten worse since you've been inside. You can't walk home in this." Faith motioned toward the front-facing windows.

Snow now blew across the parking lot and swirled in little tornadic whirls. Walking home in this weather would be foolish, let alone trying to carry Stephen.

"Wait here, and I'll try to find a driver to get you home."

"That would be great. Would you call Beverly for me?"

"She's out of town for her *bruderskind*'s wedding this week, but don't worry. It shouldn't be hard to find someone at Yoder's to give you a ride." Faith started to walk away.

"*Nay*," Jonica said, stopping her friend. "I can't stay." But could she leave?

⁂

Yoder's Market was the last place Caleb wanted to go. After last night, he didn't want to face Darleen, her father, or anyone else in her family for that matter. But not finding Jonica and Stephen on the way into town meant they were probably inside the store waiting out the storm. He drew a deep breath, the cold air triggering a cough.

It didn't make sense why the first snowfall of the season always felt colder, but it did. He pushed his hat down lower to cover his ears, then flipped up the collar on his coat as he headed to the front door.

Entering the building, he spotted Darleen with a customer. He looped around to the back of the store, checking each aisle he passed, but didn't find Jonica or her son. Lately, Edna's memory hadn't been reliable, but when she found the supply list was missing, she had seemed certain that Jonica and Stephen had gone to town. He'd assumed since it was snowing and Yoder's was close by that they would have come here for their supplies. Then again, she had made him promise not to tell anyone they were in town. Maybe she foolishly walked an extra mile to shop somewhere else.

"What can I do for you, Caleb?"

He flinched at the iciness in Darleen's tone, then lowering his head, he turned to face her. "Hello, Darleen. How are you?"

"I've been better. What do you need?"

She had a way of making him feel like dung collected on the bottom of boots. "I'm sorry."

"You are? Is that why you're here?"

"I'd like for us to be friends," he said, then when her expression remained hardened, he added, "I'm looking for Jonica Muller and her *sohn*. Edna thought they were headed into town. I thought they might have stopped here."

"So, what I heard was true. She is back, and you two were at the *doktah*'s office together—on *mei* birthday. That's why you were late for supper. You were with her."

"Don't listen to gossip. Her *sohn* cut his hand and needed stitches. I gave them a ride. And *jah*, that was why I was late for your get-together." And why he didn't get his crop planted on time. Her eyes, he once thought so kind, locked with his, making him feel small. "Like I said last *nacht*, I didn't mean to ruin your birthday." He turned and walked away.

"Caleb."

His spine stiffened. He didn't want to discuss why he was late to her birthday—not now, and especially not in her father's store.

"Jonica was here."

He turned. "How long ago?"

Darleen shrugged. "I don't know. It's been a while. She didn't buy anything. Her *sohn* used the restroom and they left."

"*Danki*." He left the store uncertain where to look next. She might have continued into town, or maybe she'd gone home taking another route with less traffic. He untied Nutmeg from the hitching post, then climbed inside the buggy. The wind had picked up, blowing snow in a horizontal direction. He needed to find them.

He turned onto the road, the snow covering the line dividing the lanes, making it difficult to see his side. She'd been a fool to go anywhere with this amount of snow falling.

Chapter 13

I have *gut* news." Faith handed Jonica a Styrofoam container for her leftovers. "Lois arrived early for work, so I'm free to give you and Stephen a ride home."

"That's *wunderbaar*. Are you sure it isn't a problem if you leave?"

Faith chuckled. "There's *nay* threat to losing *mei* job when I own the restaurant." She looked around the dining room. "Besides, it's *nett* like we have an abundance of customers. The *kalt* weather has kept people away."

Jonica wished she had never ventured out today as well.

"There's a couple of things I need to do in the kitchen before we *geh*, but it shouldn't take long. Would you like more *kaffi* while you wait?"

"Maybe half a cup."

"Me too?" Stephen picked up his hot chocolate mug and tipped it to show Faith and Jonica it was empty.

"If your *mamm* says it's okay."

"Can I?"

Her son's boyish smile was hard to resist. "*Jah*," Jonica finally said. "But only half a cup." She loaded the to-go container with the uneaten food.

A few moments later, Faith returned with the coffeepot and another mug of cocoa topped with extra whipped cream.

"*Danki*," Jonica said when the volume of coffee Faith was pouring reached half a mug.

The two *Englischers* seated at the table next to the window stood, and Faith met them at the register.

As the customers left the building, Jonica shuddered at the rush of cold air entering the building. She reached for her cloak and placed it over her shoulders. "Are you *kalt*, Stephen?"

"Nope." He took a drink, then licked the ring of cream from around his mouth.

"I think it's gotten colder outside," she muttered. "Thankfully, the Lord has graciously provided a ride home for us."

"Yep." He continued to drink his hot chocolate.

After a few minutes, Faith came out of the kitchen carrying a wooden crate. "I'm ready to go if you are."

Stephen tipped his mug to get the last drop, then wiped his mouth with the napkin. "All done."

Jonica helped Stephen into his coat, then put her own cloak on properly. Frigid air caught in her lungs as they stepped outside. At least an inch of new snow covered the sidewalk, making it slippery to walk on. "I really appreciate you giving us a ride home."

"I'm happy to do it." Faith led them to the back of the building where her buggy was parked under an oak. She set the crate on the ground long enough to open the buggy's back door, then she placed it inside.

Jonica situated Stephen on the bench, then climbed in beside him as Faith untethered the horse from the post.

"This must be a record snowfall for this time of the year." Faith sat on the driver's side of the bench. She picked up the reins and clicked her tongue. "I don't know about you, but I'm *nett* ready for winter."

"Me either," Jonica said.

"I like snow." Stephen expelled white puffs of breath as he spoke. "When can I play with your *sohn*?"

Faith glanced both ways before turning onto the main road. "What do you think, Jonica? Maybe one day next week we can arrange to all get together?"

Her son's smile heaped guilt onto Jonica's shoulders. "That would be nice." If need be, she would come up with an excuse later. She didn't want to deny Stephen playtime, but everything depended on the results of his blood work.

"You'll be able to meet Daniel tomorrow. Sunday service is at the bishop's *haus* this week."

Jonica merely nodded. After running into Hazel and Darleen at the market and overhearing their discussion, she didn't want to repeat that experience in front of a larger crowd. Word traveled fast in tight circles. She had to protect Stephen.

"Would you mind pulling over?" Jonica asked when they neared the area where she had abandoned the wagon. "Our wagon should be in the ditch. There." She pointed to the opposite side of the road. "I think I left it there."

Once Faith stopped the buggy, Jonica jumped out, crossed the road, and searched the ditch. The wagon was gone. Snow had covered their tracks, but she was sure she'd left it in this very spot. Jonica returned to the buggy. "It's gone."

"Oh, I'm sorry," Faith said.

"The wheel was broken and it was old. I just didn't want to leave it on the side of the road for it to rust away." Stephen shivered and Jonica placed her arm around him. The cold air getting in and out of the buggy had caused him to shake uncontrollably.

As they came up on *Aenti*'s house, Jonica glimpsed a man working in the front field. Why was Caleb planting now—in the snow? Shouldn't he know it'd be a waste of time and seed?

Nothing would grow in this weather. Even winter wheat needed to establish its roots before frost.

She climbed out of the buggy when Faith brought the horse to a stop. She lifted Stephen off the bench. His clothes damp from snow, he was shivering. "*Danki* again for the ride."

"Anytime. It's great having you back." Faith jumped out and rounded the buggy to the backside. "I almost forgot." She opened the hatch. "I put together a box of some basic things you might need. Bread, milk, eggs, butter, macaroni . . ." She winked at Stephen. "And peanut butter cookies."

He giggled. "For me?"

"I happen to know that your *mamm* loves peanut butter cookies too, so I think you'll have to share with her."

"And *Aenti* Edna," he said.

"*Jah.*" Faith nodded. "*Aenti* Edna too."

"Faith." Jonica's voice choked with emotion. "I'd give you a hug if *mei* hands weren't full. *Danki*, so much."

"It's the least I can do. You mentioned that you'd come to town for groceries, but I didn't see that you had any bags." Faith followed them up the porch steps.

"When the wagon wheel broke, I realized I wouldn't be able to carry Stephen and the groceries." She opened the door and stepped aside so Faith could enter.

Aenti Edna shuffled into the foyer from the sitting room, knitting needles in hand. "Finally, you're home. I've been worried sick about you."

Jonica lowered Stephen to the floor. "I'm sorry you were worried, *Aenti*. The weather turned bad, and Stephen and I went to The Amish Table to have something warm to eat and drink." Jonica lifted the Styrofoam container. "Have you eaten?"

"*Jah*, Mr. Jordan and I had soup."

Jonica grimaced. "You had lunch with him again?"

"The man has been hard at work in the field."

"*Hiya*, Edna," Faith spoke loudly.

"I'm *nett* deaf." Edna squinted at Faith. "Do I know you? You don't look familiar."

"I'm Faith Rohrer. Gideon's *fraa* and Irma and Mordecai's *dochder.*"

"Faith," Edna repeated, continuing to eye the other woman like she was trying to put her name together with her face. "*Nay*, I don't know you." She turned and ambled toward the sitting room.

"I'm sorry." Jonica spoke as she removed Stephen's coat. "The other day she thought I was her *schweschder* and we were still living at home with our parents." She hung the garment on the wall hook, then motioned to the kitchen. "Would you like a cup of tea or *kaffi?*"

"Tea sounds *gut.*"

Noticing her son shivering, Jonica turned Stephen's shoulders, aiming him at the stairs. "*Geh* upstairs and put on some dry clothes."

"Okay."

"Make sure you change your socks too," she called as he scurried up the stairs. "He gets distracted easily," she told Faith as they headed into the kitchen. Jonica filled the kettle with water and placed it on the stove, then helped Faith unpack the wooden crate.

"Edna has never *nett* known me." Faith removed a loaf of bread. "The restaurant keeps me busy, so I don't get to many of the sewing frolics."

"She has *gut* and bad days—moments even. In a few minutes she will probably ask you all about your parents and how the restaurant is doing. You just never know." Jonica placed a restaurant-size ten-pound bag of uncooked macaroni in the cabinet. "Have you heard of a Mr. Jordan? He's an *Englischer* in his forties, has red hair."

"He doesn't sound familiar. That's the man she had lunch with?"

"*Jah*, and he was here yesterday for lunch too. I thought maybe you've seen him around town or maybe he's *kumm* into your restaurant."

Faith shook her head. "I'll ask Gideon when I get home if he's seen him, and I'll ask about him when I go into work on Monday. How long has she known him?"

Jonica shrugged. "According to Mr. Jordan, a couple of weeks. But Caleb has been working the field and he met the *Englischer* yesterday for the first time."

Faith frowned. "That's strange."

"*Jah*, it is."

"You need to be extra careful."

Jonica's thoughts drifted to earlier when the redheaded man had helped her get the wagon out of the shed. He knew she and Stephen were heading into town and would have known *Aenti* was alone. Had he used the opportunity to persuade *Aenti* to invite him into the house?

"So." Faith interrupted Jonica's thoughts. "Tell me about Cedar Ridge. What's it like?"

"It isn't much different than here. Other than the growing season is shorter. Our soil is mostly clay based and drainage isn't *gut*, which made gardening a challenge. I don't know how many times *Mamm* and I tried to plant corn. Our stalks never reached knee high by the fourth of July."

The teakettle whistled. Jonica placed a tea bag in each cup, then added the hot water. She and Faith sat at the table with their drinks. Talking with her friend felt like old times. "How many *kinner* do you have?"

"Just Daniel so far. He turned three last summer." She sipped the tea. "How old is Stephen? He knows more *Englisch* words than *mei* Daniel."

Jonica looked down at her tea. "He's five." Not giving Faith a chance to comment, Jonica continued. "He's small for his age. Everyone always thinks he's younger."

"I was going to say he's very smart."

"*Danki*." She drew in a deep breath and let it ease out. News would reach Faith's ears soon enough. Jonica might as well get everything out in the open. "The rumors are true," she blurted, then covered her mouth with her hand and glanced around to make sure they were still alone.

Jonica leaned closer and lowered her voice. "We moved to Cedar Ridge because I was pregnant. I wanted to write to you. I really did. But I was too ashamed."

Faith reached for Jonica's hand. "I'm glad you told me, and for whatever it's worth, I don't think any less of you. You will always be like a *schweschder* to me. And I know *mei* Daniel will be excited to meet your Stephen. They'll be able to play after service tomorrow."

Jonica smiled, hoping to fool her friend. It was one thing to trust Faith with her shameful past, but she couldn't trust that tongues wouldn't wag tomorrow if she attended service.

"God is rich in mercy," Faith said. "His forgiveness redeems and sets us free of our past."

Jonica nodded. Over the years, God had certainly shown her mercy and blessed her with a friend who couldn't be easily fooled by a masked smile.

Faith slid her chair closer. "What else is troubling you?"

"When Stephen cut his hand, it didn't stop bleeding right away. The *doktah* was concerned and ordered blood work." She made sure Stephen wasn't nearby, then leaned forward. "He doesn't know but there might be something wrong. I didn't tell *Aenti* Edna either. Other than you, Caleb is the only one who knows, and that's because he was in the room when I received the news."

"Oh, Jonica, I'm so sorry. When will you know more?"

"Monday, hopefully. Although *Doktah* Mallory said it might *nett* be until Tuesday before he gets the test results." She sipped the tea in an attempt to ease some of the pressure building in her throat. It didn't help. Her skin was tingling, her vision dimming. She closed her eyes, willing the light-headedness to go away. *Relax. Stay strong. Focus on God—He's in control.*

"Jonica?"

She looked down, vaguely aware Faith was tapping her arm. Lifting her gaze to meet her friend's, the room began to spin.

"What does the *doktah* think is wrong with Stephen's blood?"

Jonica pointed to the faucet, unable to speak.

"Would you like a drink of *wasser*?"

She gave a slow nod.

Faith went to the sink, filled a glass with water, then handed it to Jonica. "Here."

After several sips, Jonica set the glass on the table. "That helped, *danki*."

Stephen darted into the kitchen with his shirt untucked and wearing only one sock. "Can you do this?" He held up his other sock.

"Let me help you," Faith said.

Stephen climbed up on the kitchen chair beside Faith and placed his foot on her lap. "Can I have a *kichlin*? Can I, *Mamm*, please?"

"One." She pushed off the chair, removed a peanut butter cookie from the bakery box, then handed it to him. Jonica didn't usually allow him to eat sweets before supper, but given that she hadn't started to prepare the meal, she would make an exception. She didn't even stop him when he took off running into the other room.

Jonica closed up the box. "It might be cancer," she said, not finding the strength to turn around.

"I'm sorry, Jonica. I'm so sorry." Faith came up beside her and wrapped her in a hug. "We serve a mighty God, and Stephen is in His hands."

Although Jonica struggled to believe God wanted to help someone like her, the words were comforting. "The information I read said some blood disorders are caused from some sort of a genetic mutation." The matter-of-fact tone rang eerie to her own ears.

"What does that mean?"

"I might have been the one who passed a bad gene to *mei sohn*." She plucked a tissue from the box on the counter and blotted her eyes. "It's *mei* fault."

"*Nay*." Faith shook her head. "Don't blame yourself."

A knock sounded at the front door, forcing Jonica to pull herself together. She dabbed the wadded tissue against her eyes once more, then rounded the corner as Stephen was opening the door.

"Caleb!" Stephen squealed. "Are you here to take me fishing?"

Caleb knelt on one knee. "I haven't forgotten about *mei* promise, but *nau* that it's snowing, we have to wait for the pond to freeze over."

"Do you want a *kichlin*?" Stephen showed off his half-eaten treat. "It's peanut butter."

Caleb's gaze lifted to hers and he stood. "Maybe later, Stephen. I need to talk with your *mamm*."

⌒✑⌒

Caleb's initial relief at finding Jonica and Stephen home morphed into renewed concern once he noticed Jonica's puffy, red-rimmed eyes. Had she received bad news from the *doktah*? He closed the distance between them. "What's wrong?"

She shook her head.

The wadded-up tissue she was holding told him otherwise. He turned to Stephen. "Will you get me one of those cookies?" Once Stephen tore off to the kitchen, he redirected his focus on Jonica. "I went into town to find you."

"You did?"

"*Jah*, I was worried." *Still am.*

"Jonica, did you give Stephen permission—?" Faith rounded the corner and took in a sharp gasp when she spotted them to-gether. Her brows arched as she looked at him, then Jonica, then back to him.

Caleb took a step back, his mind searching for something to say. Darleen and Faith hadn't been close friends, not that it should matter since Darleen was the one who ended their courtship, but he was quite certain by Faith's expression that he'd somehow overstepped his bounds with Jonica. Perhaps his wanting to comfort her was written on his face.

Stephen returned and thrust the cookie at him. "You like peanut butter?"

"I certainly do. *Danki*." Caleb accepted the cookie, grateful he had a reason not to have to talk. He took a bite.

"You like it?" Stephen asked.

Caleb shielded his mouth with his hand to hide the food he was chewing. "It's the best."

Faith moved toward the door. "It's getting late and I need to get supper on the stove."

Jonica followed. "*Danki* again for the ride home."

Faith smiled. "I'll see you soon?"

"Drive safe." Jonica closed the door, but she took a few seconds to turn around.

Was she praying? Crying? Caleb's throat dried and he had to swallow hard to push the cookie down.

When she did finally face him, her eyes were dry and she appeared composed. She rubbed her arms. "Burr. It's getting colder out."

"That was nice of Faith to bring you home."

"*Jah*, we would probably still be walking had she not—"

"Did you get bad news from the *doktah* while you were in town?" He eased closer.

She sidestepped him, moving farther away.

"Something's wrong. You've been crying. Unless you were peeling onions."

"I haven't heard anything more. I was planning to go to the *doktah*'s office while we were in town, but the weather turned bad. I didn't make it there to inquire."

"I went by the office to look for you, but the sign on the door said they were closed. Apparently, they're only open until noon on Saturdays."

"I'll keep that in mind."

"You don't have to walk the next time. I'll be happy to take you into town for *doktah*'s appointments, groceries, for anything."

Her lips formed a thin line in an unreadable expression. "Who was working your field?"

Jonica was good at changing the subject. "I cleared some rocks earlier in the back field."

"That wasn't you in the wheat field?"

"*Nay*, the seed wouldn't survive if I planted it *nau*."

Her brows crinkled. "It was your horse."

Nay, Anchor was . . . tied to the fence. He'd been in such a hurry to find out if Jonica and Stephen made it home that he hadn't even checked on Anchor. "You saw *mei* horse in the *front* field?"

"*Jah*. You need to check on your plow horse and make sure everything is okay." Jonica practically shooed him out of the house.

"*Danki* for the *kichlin*." Caleb snapped off a bite on his way out the door. As he trekked across the snow-covered yard, he replayed the conversation he'd had earlier with Mr. Jordan when he'd offered to put Anchor in the barn.

Caleb increased his pace. Entering the barn, he rushed to the stall. Wearing his winter blanket, Anchor had been bedded down for the night, his water trough full, and plenty of hay in the feeder. Out of curiosity, he checked the area of the barn where he stored his seed. The bags were gone.

Chapter 14

J onica placed the last supper plate on the drying rack. She untied her apron and hung it on its designated hook. The ache in the soles of her feet crept up her calves. It had been a long day.

She walked into the sitting room to find Stephen curled up on the couch asleep and *Aenti* snoring in the rocking chair. "*Aenti* Edna, it's time for bed." Jonica touched her aunt's shoulder to wake her up.

Aenti put her knitting in the basket next to her chair and stood. "Tell your *onkel* to hurry to bed." The older woman left the room while Jonica stared. Uncle Bob had been dead ten years. Maybe *Aenti* was dreaming.

Maybe—it was something more.

Jonica drew in a deep breath and released it slowly. As soon as she got the results of Stephen's tests, she'd insist *Aenti* go for a physical. Maybe a doctor would be able to prescribe something to help her memory or suggest dietary changes that would improve her brain.

She picked up Stephen, carried him upstairs to his bedroom, and gently laid him on the bed.

The boy stirred and rubbed his eyes. "I like Caleb," he murmured, half awake as she helped him into his pajamas. "He's going to take me fishing."

"*Jah,* I know what he said." She wished Caleb hadn't made a promise he couldn't keep. Spring was a long time away to keep a boy waiting, and Stephen wasn't about to forget. For some reason Caleb had made a big impression on her son. Jonica couldn't help but wonder how much different their life would have been if Peter had wanted to stay Amish—wanted them.

Stephen crawled under the covers. "Do you like Caleb?"

"Close your eyes and *geh* to sleep."

"But do you?"

"*Jah*, of course I do." Maybe more than she should. Maybe more than she had any right to. She liked the concern Caleb had shown when he'd realized she'd been crying. And how he'd searched town for them. But mostly, she liked his kindhearted nature toward her son.

Stephen's eyes closed. Seconds later, he was asleep again. Jonica pushed his hair from his forehead. He looked so much like his father.

Her thoughts drifted to the day she'd shared the news about the pregnancy with Peter. He'd been mucking out the horse stall when she slipped into the Schulmann barn. The pungent aroma of manure had never bothered her before, but the moment she entered the stall, her stomach roiled.

Peter jumped when he finally noticed her. He removed his earbuds, boisterous music continuing to play. "What brings you here?"

"I, ah . . ." A wave of queasiness washed over her. Her mouth watered as remnants of undigested breakfast filled her throat. She fled the stall, making it to the compost pile outside the building before she emptied her stomach. Bacon grease coated the back of her throat and no amount of swallowing would rid her of the vile taste.

Peter leaned against the stall post and crossed his arms. "What's wrong with you?"

"The scent of manure got to me." She swiped her mouth with her sleeve. Lately, nothing agreed with her stomach.

Peter chuckled. "Never knew you had such a weak stomach." He pushed off the post and resumed shoveling.

"*Jah*, lately, certain aromas and food bother me because . . . I'm pregnant."

It took him a long moment before he turned to face her. "You're what?"

"I'm—*we're*—going to have a *boppli*."

His Adam's apple dropped to the base of his neck and he cringed.

Jonica nodded. "I took one of those tests you buy at the drug-store."

He shook his head.

"The test was positive, Peter."

Silence.

She cleared her throat. "I thought—"

"That I would marry you? *We*." He gestured with his hand to her, then to himself. "You and I agreed. That *nacht* was a mistake."

"I know."

Peter removed his hat and ran his hand across his forehead, leaving a smear of dirt. "What are you going to do?"

Jonica shrugged. Hopes of him doing the right thing evap-orated like morning dew.

"I'm leaving Posen," he said. "I don't want to join the church—I don't want to be Amish." Frustration hardened his tone. "I was honest with you, Jonica. I told you about leaving before—"

"I know." She shifted her attention to the straw-matted floor. *Lord, what am I going to do?*

Five years seemed an eternity ago. She peered down at Stephen and smiled. Motherhood was worth every moment.

Jonica tiptoed out of Stephen's room. She went downstairs

and added a few more logs to the fire, then adjusted the damper on the woodstove so the slabs of oak would burn slowly throughout the night. Taking the lantern with her, she made her way upstairs to her bedroom, exhaustion causing each step to feel like a weight was attached to her ankles.

The lantern dimly lit her bedroom. Jonica undressed and slipped into bed. The cold sheets chilled her. She closed her eyes for a moment, then opened them. She'd forgotten to pray. Maybe God would forgive her for praying in bed tonight.

No, God had been too good to her. She flipped back the covers and knelt next to her bed.

"Lord, thank You for this day. Thank You for watching over me and Stephen. Please keep *Aenti* Edna under Your protective wing. Don't let Mr. Jordan take advantage of her kindness." Caleb's kind blue eyes came to mind. "I also thank You for Caleb and ask that You bless him."

Jonica climbed into bed, then extinguished the lantern flame. Though she tried to fall asleep, images of Caleb kept her awake. He seemed grounded in his faith—nothing like his brother. Should she tell him that Stephen was his *bruderskind*?

After several minutes of tossing and turning, she sat up and relit the lamp. Then she removed a tablet of paper from the drawer of the bedside stand and started a letter to Ephraim.

Ephraim,

How are you? The weather turned bad today. We got more snow than I've ever seen for this time of year. Did it snow in Cedar Ridge too?

We had a bit of a rough time. My return trip will be delayed. First, Stephen cut his hand on a knife and needed stitches. The bleeding was profuse—even with holding pressure on the wound. I didn't think it would stop. He had blood work done, and I need to wait for the results. The *doktah* will discuss treatment, if any, after he reviews the labs. Stephen will also need his stitches removed in a few days. I still haven't taken care of the paperwork for my *Aenti* Edna to sell the farm. I'm not even sure how to *geh* about it yet. Because of all these things, I cannot say when I might return. I hope this delay does not cause you much difficulty.

Please tell the *kinner hiya* for us.

Jonica lifted the pen to her lips. *Love, Jonica* didn't seem like the right way to close the letter. *Thinking of you* wasn't exactly the truth either.

Her thoughts had been scattered for sure—her son, her aunt, the farm, Caleb, even the redheaded man . . . but the one thing she hadn't thought about was Ephraim. She signed the letter *Sincerely, Jonica* and folded the paper. But even as she addressed the envelope, it was Caleb who was on her mind—interrupting her thoughts like a rude child.

Caleb led Nutmeg into the barn stall and removed her halter. He filled a beat-up, old coffee can with oats, emptied it into the feed trough, then filled the other feeder with hay. He took the bucket outside, tossed the murky water, then headed to the well. The iron pump handle squawked as he thrust down with more force than needed. Water gushed from the spigot, filling the pail with a few hard cranks. Careful not to slosh water over the sides of the bucket, he returned to the barn. Once the mare was fed and watered, he grabbed an old towel from the wall peg and wiped down the horse, something he did every night as she ate.

Nutmeg lifted her head. Her ears perked and she whinnied.

Caleb patted Nutmeg's neck. "Easy, girl."

Daed came up to the stall and rested his arms on the half door. "You going to be around on Monday?"

Caleb hesitated. He'd already planned to take Jonica into town. If she were to receive bad news from the doctor, he wanted to be with her. She didn't need to be alone.

"Did you hear *mei* question, Caleb?" Impatience coated *Daed's* tongue.

"*Jah,* I'll be around. What do you need help with?"

"Your fieldwork is finished, then?"

"I still have a few acres over at Edna's to clear before . . ." *Winter.* His father compressed his mouth into a narrow line. He'd made it clear he wasn't really interested in Caleb's farming attempt. *Daed* firmly believed in developing other trades. His parents had moved from Pennsylvania where land was expensive and scarce, and though his father farmed enough to feed their own livestock, he thought farming for resale was too risky.

Daed had pushed Caleb at an early age to become a builder and wanted Peter to fit that same mold. His father had been right about the many pitfalls in farming. Unpredictable weather this season had ruined Caleb's winter wheat.

"Jack Pulloski is bringing his truck and trailer over on Monday to pick up some of the cattle for the auction." Though *Daed* hated farming land, he continued to raise cattle. Easy money, according to him. "With the ground covered in snow, I can't afford to keep them all."

Thinning the herd every fall was a way to cut down on the cost of winter feed. This year, with the ground snow-covered earlier than normal, it would be difficult enough to keep the horses, milk cows, and yearlings fed.

Caleb folded the dirty part of the towel to the inside and

moved to Nutmeg's opposite side. He rubbed her neck. "What time is Jack coming?"

"Shortly after daybreak."

"Okay." Growing up, Peter had always been the one who looked forward to helping *Daed* round up the cattle from the back pasture. Six years younger, his brother had begged to help at an early age. Riding and roping came naturally for Peter. During his *rumspringa*, he spent a good share of his time helping at the livestock auction house where his skills came into use. A job *Daed* still blamed as the reason Peter extended his *rumspringa* to the point where the bishop and elders came to discuss their concerns with *Daed*.

Caleb moved down the horse's back with the towel, massaging her muscles in a circular direction. After a few moments of silence, he glanced toward the half door, assuming his father had said what he needed and left the barn. But *Daed* was still standing in the same spot, staring up at the rafters as if searching for understanding.

Caleb stopped rubbing the horse and studied his father's aging features. His pure white beard washed out his complexion, and his hooded eyes were void of the optimistic hope he once had. Years of working in the sun had wrinkled his face, and now, for a man in his fifties, he looked haggard and frail, wallowing in grief he shouldn't have to face.

Peter had taken more than his own life—he'd taken the hearts of those who loved him.

When *Daed* caught Caleb watching him, he cleared his throat. "Let's make sure we have the herd ready. I don't want to keep Jack waiting any longer than necessary." He turned and walked away.

Last year Peter had overslept and they were late getting the herd trailered. His brother complained about feeling tired all morning. But Caleb dealt with Peter's grumbling on a regular basis when he worked on Caleb's construction crew. Not a day went by that Caleb didn't have to nudge him for something. Caleb figured Peter's lack of interest had something to do with his discontent with the Amish way.

After living in the world for a time, Peter returned home. He followed through with baptism and joined the church, but he never married or fully embraced the plain life, always talking about saving enough money to leave. Caleb suspected Peter had a girlfriend outside of the district, but Caleb didn't make it his business to find out. He respected Peter's privacy and figured when he was ready, he would share the news.

Caleb covered Nutmeg with a winter blanket to block the draft. He secured the barn door and headed toward the house. The scent of supper met him at the mudroom door. He breathed in the tasty aroma of the beef, tomato sauce, and noodle mixture as he kicked off his boots.

"*Yummasetti* will be ready in a few minutes," *Mamm* called from the kitchen.

He removed his coat. "Smells *gut*."

"*Danki*, I made a large pan so we'll have leftovers."

As Caleb stepped farther into the room, another scent caught his attention. He eyed the apple pie with the sugar-sprinkled crust sitting on the cooling rack.

"Don't even think about it," she said. "I baked the pie to take to the fellowship meal tomorrow."

He frowned. "You didn't make an extra one for tonight?"

"I didn't have enough apples. You'll have to be satisfied with bread pudding."

Caleb would rather have cake, cookies, or pie over bread pudding any day, but he wouldn't complain. One of *Daed*'s favorite desserts was *Mamm*'s cinnamon bread pudding with vanilla sauce.

159

"Your *daed* is reading the newspaper in the other room. It'd be nice if you two would spend some time together before the meal."

"We were just talking out in the barn. I doubt he has anything else to say." Caleb wanted to remind his mother that *Daed* was a man of few words, especially when it came to having a conversation with Caleb, but he kept his thoughts to himself.

"Do it for me."

His mother's efforts to bring their family together wouldn't fail because of him. Becoming a tight-knit family like other families in the district was next to impossible. But he would try to make peace with his *daed*—again.

Caleb poured a mug of coffee, then took it into the sitting room. His father was seated in the chair next to the window, *The Budget* held high and tipped toward the glow from the lantern. The weekly paper supplied news from various Amish and Mennonite communities throughout the United States and was often a means of keeping up with long-distant relatives. *Mamm* was the paper's community reporter. She gathered information, be it gardening and weather conditions, or news about marriages, deaths, baby arrivals, and out-of-town visitors, then compiled the data for print. Except she omitted sending news about Peter's death. Caleb assumed she hadn't wanted to explain his cause of death to people outside their district.

Caleb took the empty chair flanking the small reading table next to *Daed*. "Anything interesting in *The Budget* this week?"

"Michigan districts are all predicting a hard winter." He turned the page. "I'd venture to guess there isn't anyone still planting winter wheat this late in the season—except for *mei sohn*."

Caleb groaned under his breath, choosing his next words carefully. "It is a risk to plant in this weather."

Daed peered up from his paper, his eyes narrowed. "Bishop

Zook went by Edna's place earlier today and noticed you were planting the front field—in the snowstorm." He shook his head. "What were you thinking? Nothing will grow *nau*. It makes you look foolish and wasteful, but it wouldn't be the first time, would it?"

His father took the opportunity to get a jab in about Caleb letting his last construction project sit boarded up—unfinished. Caleb agreed; he probably did look like a fool and the seed would go to waste. But how would he explain that an *Englischer* took it upon himself to plant the field, using Caleb's plow horse? *Daed* wouldn't understand.

And neither did Caleb. But it was done. The seed was in the ground and Anchor was in the barn. Safe.

"You should stick to construction," his father snipped. "That is your talent." He went back to reading his paper.

Caleb stared at the newsprint. *Daed* thought he had a talent in construction? Peter had been the talented brother. Caleb was . . . well, foolish and wasteful summed it up.

Chapter 15

G uilt gnawed at Jonica as she cleared the breakfast dishes from the table. She glanced at the wall clock. Sunday service would be underway, the congregation singing songs from the *Ausbund*.

It was just as well that they missed the church meeting. More snow had fallen during the night, and if the roads were icy, *Aenti* might slip and fall. Stephen could catch a *kalt*. Besides, *Aenti* hadn't even remembered that today was Sunday.

Jonica lowered the stack of plates into the basin. Posen was no longer her district, so the bishop shouldn't frown upon her absence. In addition, if she stayed out of Hazel and Darleen's sight, maybe she would also stay off their minds as well. Surely Caleb would be relieved not to have Stephen pestering him about fishing or drawing unnecessary attention from others. Plus, where would she and Stephen sit? On one of the back pews with the other unmarried women?

Coward.

No matter how hard she tried to justify her actions, nothing settled the unease feeding her thoughts—she had disappointed God. Again.

You know the truth, God. Avoiding church service today had nothing to do with the amount of snow on the ground or the distance we would have to walk. I am a coward. What if someone recognized the similarity between Stephen and Peter? What if . . . ?

Jonica's stomach roiled at the mere thought of Stephen's father. His last words to her had been so cruel, so—heartless.

Jonica had written to him after Stephen was born. She named their son after him in hopes he would love them—accept them. Stephen—his *daed's* middle name. But to no avail. He'd been given every opportunity to contact her—five years to inquire about his son—and he'd chosen not to care.

Peter Stephen Schulmann abandoned them both.

Besides, by now Peter could have returned to the Amish way. He may have grown tired of the world . . . He could be married— have other children . . . No, she couldn't come face-to-face with him.

"Jonica?"

Aenti's voice pierced the silence. Jonica glanced over her shoulder. "I'm sorry, did you say something?"

"I asked if you were finished with your *kaffi?*"

"You can leave *mei* mug on the table. I'm going to have more after the dishes are done." Jonica focused on scrubbing maple syrup off a plate.

Aenti came up beside Jonica with a clean dishrag she had removed from the drawer. "Would you mind wetting this for Stephen? He's going to wipe the table."

"Sure." Jonica dipped the cloth in the warm water, wrung out the excess, then handed it back to Edna, who walked it over to Stephen.

With them all working together, it didn't take long to *reddy-up* the kitchen.

Stephen tugged on her apron. "Can I go play with *mei* wooden horse?"

"*Jah*, for a little while." Jonica placed the kettle on the stove to make another pot of coffee. Then noticing the table was still sticky in some spots, she washed off the syrup that Stephen had missed.

"What do you think?" Edna brought the pink afghan she'd been working on into the kitchen and spread it out on the table.

Jonica inspected the crib-size blanket. The soft spun pastel-pink yarn was offset by alternating rows of white. "You've done a beautiful job." She ran her fingers over the soft, fur-like texture. "Are you making this to sell?"

"*Nay. Mei* needlework isn't suitable for the shop." She sat at the end of the table and situated the piece on her lap, then began knitting. "I missed a few stitches here and there."

Jonica looked at the blanket again. "The dropped stitches are *nett* obvious to me. I think it's perfect."

"You're very kind." *Aenti*'s hands shook as she worked the yarn and needles.

"*Mamm* used to say, 'The flaws give it character' about *mei* needlework. *Mei* stitches were never as even as they should be." Jonica shrugged.

"*Mei* mother always said, 'Practice makes perfect.'" Edna chuckled. "And I've been practicing seventy-some years *nau* and I'm still *nett* perfect."

"The blanket is perfect to me." Jonica filled two mugs with coffee, gave one to *Aenti*, then settled back in the chair. "Will you tell me a story about *mei daed*?"

Aenti thought for a moment, almost as if she were reliving a moment in time, then a smile broadened her face, and she laughed softly to herself. "Your *daed* was eight years younger than I but incredibly wise and composed for his age. He was always whittling something. And he was good at it. One time he made a whistle out of a piece of oak. When he blew it, it made a horrible screeching noise that agitated the *hunds*. They would go to howling and get the neighbor *hunds* howling until it sounded like coyotes lamenting all over the countryside.

"Your father liked to embellish the story and say that he could rile up a pack of coyotes on command." Edna picked up her ball of yarn, unwound a few feet, then set the ball and needles on her lap long enough to take a sip of her drink. "He was a character. *Mamm* was always harping on him to stop blowing that whistle in the *haus*. I think she disliked the sound more than the *hunds*. He eventually honed his whistle-blowing skills to various animal calls. He'd call up a flock of turkeys or a buck at almost any time of the year." Edna smiled. "We sure didn't *geh hungahrich* after he made that silly whistle."

"I love that story." Jonica blew on her coffee before she took a sip. *Aenti*'s mind was keen today. Though she would love to listen to more tales, especially about her father, she needed to talk to Edna about the farm while her mind was sharp. "You have so many *gut* memories here. Are you sure you want to sell the farm?"

Aenti looked up from her afghan, and for a moment, she appeared lost in thought. "You take your memories with you wherever you *geh*."

"True." There were so many special times on the homestead Jonica would always hold dear to her heart too. "As long as you're sure." She took another drink of coffee, intentionally giving her aunt more time to think about the decision.

"It's the right thing to do," Edna said, though her downcast gaze seemed to say something else. "I told the man I would."

"What man did you tell?"

Aenti shrugged.

Jonica leaned forward. "Is the man from our district?"

Her aunt's vacant stare sent a shudder down Jonica's spine. Amish farms were *nett* usually sold. Ownership was often transferred to the next generation. Aging relatives moved into the *daudi haus* and the pattern repeated throughout time. This would be a new process for both of them.

Edna's brows creased as though she was puzzled. "I asked if you wanted the place, didn't I? I don't remember everything Mr. Jordan said in the letter."

"Mr. Jordan?"

"He wrote the letter for me." She held out her hand. "*Mei* hands shake so that I was afraid you wouldn't be able to make out *mei* penmanship."

Jonica recalled her aunt's scribbly writing on the supply list. It was starting to make sense why Mr. Jordan was always around the farm, having meals with Edna. He'd wormed his way into her life.

Jonica cleared her throat. "I have *mei* parents' *haus* in Cedar Ridge." The house was situated in the middle of their lumber-yard, and she hadn't given much thought about the business. Without her father to run the sawmill . . .

"I see." Edna set the ball of yarn on the table. "I think I'll give *mei* hands a rest."

"*Aenti*," Jonica said as her aunt started to stand. "Do you think you could hold off the sale for a while longer?"

"Why? I thought you were in a hurry to *geh* back to . . ." She pressed her fingers against her forehead.

"Cedar Ridge. And I do want to get home as soon as possible. It's just . . ." She didn't want to sign off paperwork without knowing more about the sale. "I thought Stephen and I would extend our visit. Is it okay if we stay longer?"

"I would like that very much." Edna stood, then walked her empty mug to the sink. "If you don't mind, I'm going to lie down for a bit."

"Are you feeling *allrecht*?"

"Just tired." She shuffled a few steps, then turned. "Jonica, this is your home too. It always has been, my dear. Since I have no *kinner*, I always thought of you as *mei* own. I hope you know that you're welcome to stay as long as you wish."

"*Danki, Aenti.*" Jonica stood and hugged her aunt. Holding her small frame reminded Jonica of the last time she'd hugged her mother. "Get some rest. We'll talk more later."

As her aunt ambled down the hallway toward her bedroom, Jonica went into the sitting room to check on Stephen, who was on the floor playing with the wooden horse.

"Have you thought of a name for your horse yet?"

"Nutmeg." He pretended to jump the horse over a stick of kindling he must have removed from the box of firewood.

"Like Caleb's?"

"Yup."

Stephen had become attached in a short time almost as if he knew they were family. But he didn't know—no one alive knew Stephen was a Schulmann—and it would stay that way.

She opened the side of the woodstove and fed the flames another log. Stephen came to the woodbox and pulled out a handful of small kindling. "When can I play with Daniel?" He sat back on the floor and started to stack the pieces of wood like log walls.

"I'll talk with Faith again soon. I'm going outside to bring in more wood. Would you like to help?"

"Sure." He placed the wooden horse on the lamp table, then went to the front door where he plopped onto the floor to put on his boots.

Once they were both wearing their winter garments, they went outside. Stephen took off toward the woodshed, slipping and sliding on iced-over puddles in the driveway.

"Careful, sweetie." Keeping her head down, Jonica eased over the slippery surface, snow crunching under her boots with every step. At least it had stopped snowing and the wind had died down some since yesterday.

Hearing Stephen's laughter, Jonica glanced up to find her son talking with someone bundled up in an oversize winter coat, his face covered by a scarf. As she drew closer, Jonica recognized Mr. Jordan's voice.

"It's a whippoorwill." Mr. Jordan opened his coat pocket for Stephen to see the bird. "He was too weak to fly south for the winter with his family."

Stephen studied the animal. "I've never seen one before."

"Hello, Jonica." Mr. Jordan turned toward her. "Would you like to see what the fuss is all about? I'm taking care of a wounded whippoorwill."

She eyed the tiny bird. "He's awfully small. Will he make it through the winter?"

"God is in control, but I have faith that it will."

The man's gentle nature erased some of Jonica's earlier concern. Then she noted the knitted scarf he had on. It wasn't store-bought. The rows were uneven, and she spotted several places where double stitches were taken. "That's a nice scarf you're wearing."

"Thank you. It's a gift from Edna. She was concerned about the weather changing." He touched the material. "Your aunt is very thoughtful."

"What will the bird eat?" Stephen interrupted.

Mr. Jordan shifted his focus to Stephen. "Whatever God provides."

What Edna provides was probably more accurate.

"Did you want to say something, Jonica?"

She shook her head, guilt heating her cheeks. Jonica turned and faced the woodpile. Squeezing her eyes shut, she refocused her thoughts. *Forgive me, Father. It's You who provides for us all,*

including the birds. Including this stranger. Help me see him through
Your eyes. Help me know what his motives are and if he's truly helping
Aenti *or if he has another purpose.*

Hearing the bird chirp, Jonica opened her eyes. "Stephen,
you need to be careful *nett* to frighten the bird. Let the bird rest
nau."

Stephen frowned. "Okay." He turned to Mr. Jordan. "Will I
be able to see him again?"

"Absolutely. I'll keep him until he's strong enough to fly,
then I'll set him free. You can visit him anytime."

Stephen smiled. "Did you hear that, *Mamm*?"

"*Jah*, I did." She looked beyond her son at the small saucer
sled hanging by a rope on the wall. She sidestepped the pair in
order to reach the sled, then removed it from the wall. "This
should work perfect to stack wood on."

Mr. Jordan and Stephen helped load the sled with wood.

"*Danki* for your help, Mr. Jordan." Jonica picked up the rope
and gave it a tug. "Ready Stephen?"

"Bye, Mr. Jordan." Stephen took hold of a portion of the rope
and helped Jonica pull the load of wood back to the house.

A rock skidded past Jonica and she looked back as she reached
the porch steps. Mr. Jordan followed close behind with his arms
full of split logs.

"Stephen, start taking the wood inside the house. Be sure
to shut the door to keep the heat inside." Once he was out of
earshot, Jonica turned to Mr. Jordan. "There's something I need
to ask you."

He stacked the wood on the porch. "Ask away."

"I understand that you wrote the letter to me about the sale
of the farm on *mei aenti*'s behalf."

"I did. She was concerned you wouldn't be able to read her
handwriting. So, I offered to help."

"That was nice of you. Were you also the one interested in buying the farm?"

"It's a beautiful piece of property." He scanned the area, then brought his focus back on her. "I know Edna struggled with her decision to put the house on the market. Selling is a good thing, don't you think?"

"*Nay*, I don't think under the circumstances it is." Jonica squared her shoulders. "In fact, I've decided to stay." She took in a sharp breath, stunned by her own words. Edna clearly needed more than Mr. Jordan's guidance. She needed family. Someone who truly had her best interest at heart. After all, this was the place where her *daed*, his sisters, and Jonica had all grown up. The place she had wanted to raise her offspring.

"I thought you didn't want to move back to Posen."

She didn't. But she didn't want the farm going to a stranger either. "I've changed *mei* mind about leaving so soon. I might even stay through winter." If it meant protecting her aunt, Jonica had no choice.

"It is going to be a difficult season. A test of wills you might say."

"Exactly why Edna needs me here." Jonica wasn't sure what had come over her, but as she made the statement, she felt an odd sense of peace with the decision.

Chapter 16

As the bishop dismissed the congregation at the end of service, Caleb scanned the crowd once more for Jonica. He had looked for her prior to the start of service, then several times while everyone was singing, but he didn't see anyone from Edna's house.

Disappointment clouded his thoughts. Last night Jonica had been distant. He couldn't put his finger on what had changed, but something was different. Caleb spotted Faith leaving the barn with the other married women and took a few steps in their direction. Surely she would know if Stephen was ill.

Someone came up behind Caleb and clapped his shoulder, and he turned to find Darleen's brother David.

"How's everything going, Caleb?"

Even though the Yoders were a tight-knit family, Caleb doubted Darleen would have said anything so soon about ending their courtship. Especially to one of her brothers. "Everything's fine."

"I feel bad. Your *daed* said you didn't get your winter wheat planted in time."

"*Jah*, I waited too long. I'm learning." Caleb noticed his *daed* standing with the bishop and Melvin Yoder. He lowered his head. Why did his father have to tell everyone about his failures?

"You should have let me help."

171

Pride had a way of bringing a man to his knees. Determination to prove to himself and his father that he could do something other than construction had caused him to fail. Miserably.

Caleb cleared his throat and raised his gaze back to David. "I underestimated the amount of rocks that needed to be cleared before I could till the ground."

"A new field always takes longer to prepare."

"*Jah*," Caleb said half-heartedly. "Lesson learned."

"There's always next year. Keep the seed dry."

"The seed is already—"

A commotion outside the door between a group of young boys caught David's attention. "I better put a stop to them throwing snowballs before someone spooks the horses." He marched out the door just as the cast-iron bell clanged to signal mealtime.

Caleb migrated toward the bishop's house with the other men, his stomach growling. But once inside, his hunger pangs waned when he glimpsed Darleen's glare from across the room. He looked away, but his gaze happened to land on one of her friends, who held a similar expression of wrath. He needed to come up with a reason to leave. Quick. He should've known better, known it was too soon.

Gideon Rohrer came up beside Caleb. "Are you in line?"

"*Nay*, go ahead. I'm thinking I might *nett* stay."

Gideon leaned back. "You feeling under the weather?"

Caleb shook his head.

"Something wrong?"

Everything was wrong. Darleen and most of the women in the district were upset with him, but his primary thought was Jonica and why she wasn't at the service today. When she mentioned not wanting people to know she was in town, he didn't think she would also avoid God. Besides, if she really wanted to hide, she wouldn't have gone into Yoder's Market, where members of their district regularly shopped. Plus, she reconnected with Faith.

"Caleb?" Gideon's brows pinched together.

"Sorry, *mei* mind was . . . elsewhere." He shrugged. "I didn't sleep well." Hopefully, that was enough explanation. Gideon would find out more soon enough. Based on the scowls Caleb had received from the women's side of the room, the news about him and Darleen had already spread.

Still, he refused to talk about the situation here, even though he trusted his longtime friend. When Caleb had been filled with grief over Peter's death, Gideon had been his sounding board. His friend was quick to listen and slow to speak and offered wisdom beyond his years. But this was different. Jonica had invaded his thoughts. How could he talk about something he didn't understand himself?

Faith came up beside her husband and smiled warmly. Her expression lacked the judgmental demeanor of the other women. "*Hiya*, Caleb."

"*Hiya*, Faith." He backed up. "I should be . . ."

"Caleb isn't planning to stay for the meal," Gideon said. "Would you mind making him a plate to take?"

Caleb backed up another half step. "That's okay. I'll make a sandwich when I get—"

"It's *nett* a problem. I'll be right back." Faith walked away.

"You seem in a rush to leave."

His friend would be too if he was despised by the women in the room. "Let's change the subject."

Gideon smiled. "What about this weather? I think the snow surprised everyone."

Was this Gideon's attempt to lessen Caleb's farming failure? *Daed* had probably given him an earful about Caleb's crops. "*Jah*, this will be a long winter. It's been many years since we had this much snow this early in the season. How did your apples do this year?"

"I've had better years."

Gideon went on to explain the problems he had with insects, but Caleb only half listened. He needed to find out if something was wrong with Jonica and put an end to this all-consuming distraction—the sooner the better.

Faith returned with multiple containers of food. "I wonder if you'd be so kind as to take some food to Jonica, Stephen, and Edna on your way home?"

Caleb glanced at Gideon. He didn't appear confused or surprised at the mention of Jonica or Stephen. Faith must have told him about Jonica being back in town. Either that or the rumors had already reached his friend's ears. "Sure." Caleb reached for the containers.

"When I gave Jonica and Stephen a ride home from town, I made sure to tell her that today's service would be held at Bishop Zook's *haus*." Faith looked up at her husband. "I even volunteered to pick them up so they wouldn't have to walk in the snow, but Jonica refused. She didn't want us to drive out of our way . . . I should have insisted."

"Next time," Gideon said.

Faith nodded. "Stephen was so excited to meet our Daniel." She grasped her husband's forearm. "What if something's wrong? Stephen looked a little peaked at the restaurant."

"I've actually had the same worries. I'm leaving *nau*," Caleb said as an image of Stephen flashed before his mind's eye. "I'll go straight to Edna's to make sure everything is *allrecht*." He nodded good-bye and rushed out the door. What if Stephen was sick? Or Edna fell? Or Jonica was in trouble? Caleb still didn't know anything about Mr. Jordan. What if . . . ?

"Lord, I haven't stopped thinking about Jonica all morning.

Have You laid her on *mei* heart for a reason? Is something wrong? Please, protect them from danger."

Caleb secured the food on the back seat and climbed into his buggy. He turned Nutmeg toward Edna's house. As his high-spirited mare often did in cooler temperatures, she responded by increasing her pace. Caleb didn't hold back on the reins.

Without much traffic on the road, it didn't take long to reach Edna's place. But somewhere along the way the containers had slipped off the back seat. Thankfully, the lids stayed intact. He grabbed the containers off the floor and hiked up the porch steps.

"Caleb." Jonica's brows rose in surprise. "I—*we*—weren't expecting you. It's Sunday—*kumm* in. It's *kalt* outside." She opened the door wider and stepped aside, giving him room to enter.

"Faith sent over food from the fellowship meal." He lifted the containers.

"That was kind of her. We haven't eaten yet."

"Is everything okay?" He leaned slightly toward the sitting room entrance to get a better view but didn't see anyone.

"Everything is fine." She motioned to the kitchen. "I just made a pot of *kaffi*. Would you like a mug?"

"*Jah*, sure." He stomped his boots on the rug, then followed her into the empty kitchen. "Where is everyone?"

"Stephen is in his room playing with the wooden horse Mr. Jordan made for him and *Aenti* Edna is searching for another skein of yarn in one of the back bedrooms." She removed a mug from an upper cabinet and placed it on the counter. "Did the service end early?"

"*Nay.*" *I was worried about you.* Caleb pulled a kitchen chair out from the table and sat without taking his eyes off Jonica. This was the Lord's day yet she appeared to have no concern about missing service?

She placed a steaming mug of coffee on the table before him but didn't take a seat. Wiping her hands on her apron, she backed away, then when their gazes connected, she spun her back to him and busied herself with opening the containers of food.

He stood and, telling himself he was interested in finding out how the food traveled, he came up beside her. "The containers slid off the buggy bench on *mei* way here." He noticed mashed potatoes on top of something that resembled meatloaf.

"You already told me and that's *nett* a problem."

But there was a problem with her not attending service—at least for him. "Is everything okay with Stephen?"

"*Jah*, he's doing *gut*. No bleeding issues."

Doubts about her relationship with God invaded his mind. She'd been made aware of the service location, was offered a ride, yet seemed indifferent about missing church—same as someone who was outside of fellowship. Without the boy having a father, she was the spiritual leader in her family. Why, was she out of fellowship? "And Edna. Is she okay?"

"She's fine."

Caleb waited for Jonica to say something—anything—about missing church, but she didn't. A knot formed in his stomach. Missing church was never taken lightly, and she'd said nothing had been wrong with any of them. Why wasn't she following their Amish way? Didn't she believe Stephen should be in church?

Caleb's mouth dried. He'd realized today sitting in service that he'd developed feelings for Jonica and her son. But what if the woman who had captured his attention was not in good standing with her church district because she wasn't in good standing with God?

He couldn't wait any longer to find out. "Why weren't you

at service today? Faith said she offered to *kumm* by and pick you up."

"*Jah*, she did."

As she reached for a plate from the cabinet, Caleb caught her arm. "Please don't avoid the subject. Are you in right standing with God?"

Chapter 17

In right standing with God?" Jonica echoed Caleb's words even though she understood his question.

"*Jah*," Caleb said, holding eye contact that penetrated her every fiber. "Are you?"

Edna walked into the kitchen, knitting needles and yarn in hand. "It took a few minutes but I finally found what I was looking for." She held up the forest-green skein of yarn. "I'm going to make Stephen a scarf. He said green is his favorite color." She smiled at Caleb. "*Hiya*, Caleb. I didn't hear you *kumm* in."

"He brought us some mashed potatoes, gravy, and meat loaf." Jonica flipped open the other container. "And yeast rolls."

"It was Faith who put the food together. From the fellowship meal."

Aenti stared at Caleb a long moment. "When did you—?" *Aenti* stopped herself. "I already asked when you got here, didn't I?"

Caleb smiled. "I just arrived, Edna. I came straight from Sunday service. I thought maybe you weren't feeling well when you missed service."

"Oh, dear. Today is Sunday?"

Guilt threaded Jonica's veins the moment *Aenti's* attention turned to her. Her selfish—no, cowardly—decision not to attend service imprinted upon her heart. Even if she didn't want to go, she'd been wrong not to make arrangements for Faith to pick up *Aenti*. Wrong not to remind her aunt that today was Sunday, and wrong to keep Stephen from hearing today's important Bible teachings. Now Caleb questioned her standing with God. Her aunt was probably wondering too. Would they understand if she told them the truth?

Jonica pushed away from the counter. "Would you like me to pour you a mug of *kaffi, Aenti* Edna?"

"*Jah, kaffi* sounds *gut.*" *Aenti* moved to the counter and inspected the different containers of food. "This all looks *appeditlich.*" She turned to Caleb. "Will you join us for lunch?"

"He probably already ate."

"*Nay,* I haven't eaten yet," he told Jonica, then shifted to address *Aenti.* "I would love to stay for lunch, Edna. That'll give Jonica and me time to finish our earlier conversation." He motioned to the table. "Shall we sit?" He pulled out a chair for *Aenti*, then helped guide her into the seat.

Jonica couldn't help but admire his patience. He had a gentle way about him, with her aunt, her son . . . Caleb was nothing like his brother.

As Jonica poured Edna's coffee, Caleb came up beside her. "I really am interested in hearing your answer."

"Later." She wanted to tell him the truth of why she missed church, but not at this moment. Jonica handed Caleb mugs of coffee for him and *Aenti*, then went about reheating the food.

A short time later, Stephen bounded into the room, his nose held high taking in the tasty aroma of meatloaf. "I'm *hungahrich.*"

"I'm glad to hear that," Jonica said, removing the pan from the oven. "Give me a minute and I'll help you wash up."

"I can do it." Stephen grabbed a chair from the table and started to push it over to the sink, making a scratching sound against the floor.

"Let me help you." Caleb picked up the chair, set it next to the sink, then hoisted Stephen up onto the chair.

"Don't get your bandage wet." She didn't have more gauze to change the dressing and he needed to keep what he had on clean and dry. At least until tomorrow. She wanted him to be presentable at the doctor's office.

"I'll make sure he's careful." Caleb turned on the faucet. He helped Stephen wash his uninjured hand, then soaped his own.

Jonica removed a clean dish towel from the drawer and handed it to Caleb. "*Danki.*"

"Anytime." Caleb returned the chair to its place at the table and helped Stephen onto the chair next to him.

"Where's Mr. Jordan?" Stephen asked as Jonica set the warm dish of meat loaf in the center of the table. "Isn't he going to eat with us?"

Jonica glanced at her aunt, assuming she would answer. But *Aenti* looked as interested in the answer as Stephen. "There's plenty of food. We'll save him some for later." She took her place at the table next to her aunt.

"How many fish are in the river?" Stephen asked between bites of mashed potatoes.

"Too many to count," Caleb replied.

Stephen skipped to the next topic. "Know what I named *mei* horse?"

Caleb's brows rose and Jonica explained. "He's talking about the wooden horse that Mr. Jordan gave him."

"Ah." Caleb nodded. "Is it a boy or girl's name?"

"I don't know." Stephen giggled. "His name is Nutmeg."

Caleb smiled. "That's *mei* horse's name too."

"I know." Stephen stabbed his fork into a chunk of meat loaf and popped it into his mouth.

Jonica figured her son's healthy appetite had something to do with Caleb eating with them, but she was pleased that he finished his meal just the same. She picked up the bowl of potatoes. "Would you like more, sweetie?"

"*Nay*," Stephen rubbed his tummy. "I'm done."

"Me too," *Aenti* said.

"Caleb?"

"Sure." He took the bowl and spooned more on his plate.

Stephen pushed his dish forward and plopped his elbows on the table. "Do I have to take a nap today?"

"*Jah*," Jonica said. "And please remove your elbows from the table."

Stephen groaned but did as told. After sitting patiently for everyone to finish with their meal, he asked to be excused.

"I'll be up in a minute to tuck you into bed." Jonica gathered the dirty dishes.

"I want Caleb to. Please."

Jonica's thoughts scrambled for a reason to say no without flagging more questions. Stephen had already formed a bond with Caleb, but she didn't want her child to obligate him. He had other things to do. Sunday was a day to rest.

Caleb took one last drink of coffee, then stood. "I suppose you want a horseback ride up to your room too."

Stephen raised his arms and waited for Caleb to scoop him up.

Jonica followed them out of the kitchen. A shudder passed down her spine watching them go up the stairs. Stephen with his arms wrapped around Caleb's neck, laughing as Caleb put more bounce in each step. Her son was loving every second—exactly how it should have been between his father and him. Would

Ephraim have the same patience? The same loving relationship with Stephen?

"They seem very fond of each other," Edna said. "I think Caleb has developed a soft spot in his heart for you as well."

"He doesn't know me." Jonica went back to *reddying-up* the kitchen. Her aunt must not know that Caleb was courting Darleen Yoder.

"There's a resemblance between them. They both have blue eyes and they share the same jawline."

"Stephen's eyes are the same color as mine."

Aenti studied Jonica. "*Jah*, but your jaw isn't square." She spread tinfoil over the dish of leftovers. "You should think about finding a husband. Stephen needs a *daed*."

Jonica grimaced. Of all times for her aunt to be in her right mind to carry a conversation, this was the worst. Caleb would be downstairs any minute, and with *Aenti's* unpredictable mind, she might ask him to weigh in on the topic and embarrass them both.

Once Stephen closed his eyes, Caleb eased toward the door. He only made it a few steps before Stephen's small voice said, "Will you be here when I wake up?"

Caleb turned to face Stephen. "I'm *nett* sure, but I'll see you tomorrow."

Stephen lifted up on his elbow. "Are we going fishing tomorrow?"

Caleb hated disappointing the boy. "Remember what the *doktah* said about your hand?"

"*Jah*." Stephen protruded his bottom lip.

"Your hand needs time to heal. Plus, your *mamm* would be upset if you get your bandage wet. So, we have to wait." He hoped the boy and his mother would stay through winter. Once the pond froze over they could drill a hole through the ice and drop a line.

"Okay." Stephen lay back down.

"Get some sleep." Caleb slipped out of the room. He'd never liked ice fishing, but he wished the pond would hurry up and freeze over so he could keep the promise he made Stephen. Caleb went down the stairs and into the kitchen.

Standing at the sink with her hands submerged in sudsy water, Jonica glanced over her shoulder. "Did Stephen try to talk you out of the nap?"

"*Nay*, he was *gut*." He leaned one shoulder against the wall and crossed his arms. "But he's expecting me to take him fishing soon."

Jonica frowned. "I hope you're *nett* still encouraging him."

He smiled sheepishly.

"Caleb, I don't think the fish bite in this weather." She scrubbed a plate, then lowered it into the rinse water.

"True. We won't catch anything."

"*Jah*, you will. You'll both catch a *kalt*."

"We'll dress warm." Caleb wished he hadn't made the promise, but he had, and Stephen wouldn't let him forget it. "I gave him *mei* word, Jonica. We wouldn't have to stay long. Enough for him to get a taste of fishing."

She shook her head. "He could fall in the river."

Caleb glanced at Edna as she dried the dishes, a large smile stretched across her face. "What do you think, Edna? Am I trustworthy enough to watch over Stephen?"

"You should take Jonica too. That way if . . ." Edna placed her hand against her chest and blew out a few quick breaths.

"*Aenti*, what's wrong?"

"It's nothing."

Jonica placed her hand on the small of her aunt's back. "You need to sit and rest."

Edna handed Caleb the dish towel. "I hate to leave you all the work, but *mei* legs are feeling wobbly." She steadied herself with the countertop. "Help Jonica *reddy-up* the kitchen for me."

Noticing tiny beads of sweat along Edna's brow, Caleb reached for her elbow. "First, let us help you to a chair."

Jonica helped Caleb lead Edna to the table, then pulled out a chair.

Aenti waved off the offer to sit. "I'd rather rest in the other room where it's more comfortable." She ambled toward the sitting room with Caleb on one side of her and Jonica on the other. They guided her into her favorite chair, settled her in, and covered her with a light-blue afghan.

Jonica took a half step closer to Caleb, and he resisted the urge to put his arm around her as she twisted her hands in front of her. "Can I get you anything? A glass of *wasser*? Your knitting needles and yarn?"

"I'm fine for the moment." Edna shooed them away. "I just need a few minutes to rest."

Jonica didn't move.

Caleb touched Jonica's elbow, then stepped back a couple steps but stayed in the room. Just the other day Edna was climbing the kitchen chair to dust cobwebs; today she appeared frail.

Edna opened her eyes. "Don't stand there staring at me. I'm *nett* going to die." When they didn't leave immediately, she started to push herself up. "If you two aren't going to finish the dishes, then I will."

Caleb held up his hand. "*Please,* stay put. Jonica and I will leave you alone and finish *reddying-up* the kitchen."

Jonica glanced at Caleb, fear etched in her features. "Are you sure you're okay?"

Edna's head dropped back. "I said so, didn't I? *Nau*, shoo." She waved her hand toward them.

"Holler if you need something," Jonica added.

Caleb motioned with a nod toward the doorway, and he and Jonica left the room. He picked up the dish towel and went to the sink.

"You don't have to stay, Caleb. I can handle this by myself."

"I want to help." He picked up a plate and dried it with the cloth.

Jonica moved to the sink and began to wash and rinse the remaining dishes. "Earlier, you asked if I was in right standing with God." She kept her head down as she spoke. "The truth of the matter is, I—I don't know that I am."

Caleb stopped washing dishes and turned toward her. "Why is that?"

She wiped her cheek against her shoulder, and her elbow brushed his arm. "I don't know. Lots of little reasons and some big ones too. My life has not been easy, and I know that's due to my own poor choices, but still, I'm tired." She sniffled. "I'm tired of being alone, tired of *nett* knowing my future, tired of fighting to keep Stephen safe. And I'm not even twenty-five yet. Worst of all, there's a huge part of me that is still angry about the accident that took *mei* parents from me—from Stephen. I'm *nett* ready to be alone. It's just *nett* right—*nett* fair."

"I know the feeling of life *nett* being fair." *Too well.* "But, Jonica, God understands your pain. He created our emotions, so He understands when we're angry or tired or lonely. But He loves us and *nett* only expects us to turn our sorrow over to Him, but desires that we give Him our burdens."

She nodded. A single tear trailed down her cheek as she washed a plate. "It's so hard."

"I know. It's difficult. I've had *mei* own issues giving my

185

problems over to God." He let a few moments of silence linger between them. "Is that why you didn't *geh* to service today?"

Her shoulders lifted as she drew in a breath, then slumped again with her exhale. "I remember how easily rumors spread around here. I don't want to make trouble for anyone."

"What are you talking about?"

"During the snowstorm, I stopped at Yoder's Market. Darleen and Hazel were talking about . . ." Jonica shook her head. "It doesn't matter."

"I'm sorry for whatever they said. If Darleen lashed out at you, it's most likely because she's upset with me. As for Hazel, she's been known to exaggerate, making up something out of nothing."

"She didn't make any of it up. It was all true. They were talking about me having a *boppli* out of wedlock. I expected people to gossip, but what upset me was their total disregard for Stephen being within earshot."

No wonder she didn't want to attend service today. "Do you think Stephen understood what they were talking about?"

"I hope *nett*." She squared her shoulders. "I'm *nett* willing to chance another run-in, and if that means *nett* attending service, then so be it."

He went to reach for her elbow, but she took a step back the moment he touched her.

"Faith told me that you and Darleen are courting." Jonica squeezed out the excess water from the dishrag, then faced him. "If you two are courting, what are you doing here—with me? This is exactly how rumors get started."

"I'm sorry, Jonica. This is all *mei* fault." Caleb groaned under his breath. He never meant for his breakup with Darleen to cause Jonica pain. "Darleen isn't a bad person, but she's spoiled and right *nau* she's angry because she didn't get her way."

"I'm *nett* following."

"We had been courting a little over a year. She decided she wanted to get married—*nau*. Mainly because her friends are all married and she doesn't want to feel left out."

Jonica's mouth dropped open, and her stare took on a fierce look.

Caleb held up his hands. "Oh, we're *nett* getting married. We're no longer courting." Saying the words out loud was almost refreshing, freeing. Hearing the way Hazel and Darleen gossiped about a child in front of him and his mother confirmed what he'd already known. The inner conflict he'd had about Darleen was right—he could never marry someone like her—even if Jonica hadn't come to town.

Jonica grimaced. "It's *nett* because you were late to her birthday party, is it?"

He shook his head. "That had nothing to do with it. It was me. Things just fell apart after *mei* brother's death, and—"

She gasped. "What did you say?"

Caleb stopped drying the dish. "I changed after *mei* brother's death."

Jonica turned pale and stumbled backward until she hit the table.

"Are you *allrecht*?" Caleb rushed to her side and pulled a chair out so she could sit down before she fell down, but she grasped the edge of the table instead.

Her gaze flickered. "Peter's . . . dead?"

Chapter *18*

He ... died?" Stunned, Jonica's chest tightened until she could hardly pull in a breath.

Caleb lowered his head a moment. When he looked up, murkiness filled his gaze. "A few months ago."

Memories of Peter's jovial smile, his hearty laughter, his careless nature, flashed before her. He'd been worldly and restless and adventurous—everything she thought she'd wanted on her *rumspringa* . . .

And he was gone.

Forever.

Caleb motioned to the chair. "Are you sure you don't want to sit?"

She blinked tears off her lashes. "What happened?"

Caleb flinched. He touched his throat as his Adam's apple moved down his neck. Obviously struggling to speak.

She held up her hand to stop him. "I'm sorry. I shouldn't have—"

"Suicide," he blurted.

She stared blankly.

He half shrugged. "Peter, ah . . . he didn't leave a note."

Jonica's lungs tightened. She hadn't realized she'd been swaying until Caleb's hands steadied her shoulders. Neither of them spoke for a long moment as unrestrained tears streamed down her face. She cupped her face in her hands as she cried for Peter, for Caleb, for their parents, and for Stephen. Oh, Stephen. The smidgen of hope she had held on to over the past five years, that one day Peter would want to know his son, vaporized like a drop of water on a hot cast-iron stove.

Peter had lofty dreams that didn't include remaining Amish, but what would have driven him to take his own life?

Lord, I don't understand.

A high-pitched ringing filled Jonica's ears while at the same time her peripheral vision darkened as if she were looking through a narrowing tunnel. Her knees buckled. About to go down, she reached for the countertop, but Caleb's strong, comforting, consoling arms encircled her.

He pulled her to him, cradling her against his chest. And though the voice inside her head was warning her to move away—that it wasn't right, not her place—she didn't object. She needed him, wanted him to comfort her. Instead of pushing away, she leaned closer, wrapped her arms around his waist, and held him tighter.

After a moment, Jonica's light-headedness eased. The buzzing din replaced with the rhythmic *lub-dub* timbre of Caleb's beating heart, which lulled her deeper into his arms.

He rubbed her back in circular motions. "I'm sorry," he whispered. "I should have been mindful of your situation."

Her body stiffened. Had he known all along that Stephen was Peter's son? Fully aware of their closeness, of Caleb's warm breaths on the back of her neck, she moved out of his embrace. Jonica's heart raced as she adjusted her *kapp*.

"I'm sorry if I made you feel uncomfortable."

"You didn't." It wasn't Caleb's fault. She should have heeded the warning and kept her distance. Truth was, he hadn't made her feel uncomfortable at all, but rather the opposite. Snug in his arms, she found refuge. A feeling she hadn't experienced in a long time—if ever.

Caleb's brows drew together as his analyzing gaze explored what felt like every inch of her. "I thought you might pass out there for a minute."

She shifted her focus to a small wrinkle on her apron. "It was the first I had heard about your *bruder*. Peter was so young." She hand-pressed a small wrinkle on her apron, debating if this was a good time to tell Caleb that his brother was Stephen's father.

"*Mei* mother kept his . . . passing out of *The Budget*. *Mamm* is the one who sends in the district updates to the paper every week, and she—" He grimaced. "We all took his death very hard."

"What did you mean when you said you should have been mindful of *mei* situation?" She held her breath.

"Your parents' recent deaths. I know how hard it can be to hear about another person's death when you're still struggling with the same form of grief. At least that's the way it is for me. I haven't been able to talk about his death. It triggers too much . . . unresolved—"

"Pain," she said.

Caleb nodded. "None of us have been the same." His usually strong voice came out weak and almost frightened.

"It had to have been a shock for sure, especially for your *mamm*." Losing her parents in the accident had been devastating, but at least she was comforted knowing that they both had lived for the Lord up until their last breath. If Peter had jumped the fence, left his Amish upbringing . . . ?

Lumped emotion pressed against Jonica's throat making it

difficult to talk. She swallowed hard, relieving some of the pressure. She couldn't help but ask the question. "Peter jumped the fence, didn't he?" Caleb's eyes flickered closed, and she reached for his arm. "You don't have to answer. Trust me when I say, the last thing I want to do is overrun you with questions that cause more pain."

She didn't need Caleb to say what she already knew—Peter didn't want to stay Amish. He never hid that fact. Nothing would have changed his mind. She lowered her head, recalling Peter's words when she'd told him about the pregnancy. *"I can't take care of a* fraa *and* kind. *I'm* nett *joining the church. I'm leaving the fold—jumping the fence. Is that clear?"*

"Crystal clear," she muttered, not realizing her thoughts were audible until Caleb leaned down to glimpse her staring at her wool socks.

"What's crystal clear?"

Jonica swallowed hard. "Peter," she said, her throat hoarse. "He'd decided to stay on *rumspringa* . . . indefinitely."

"He returned, eventually."

The air left her lungs. "He did?"

Caleb nodded. "As soon as he came back, he wanted to be baptized and join the church."

Her stomach clenched. "Then why did he—?" Nett *tell her?* Had Peter only led her to believe he wasn't planning to stay Amish in order to avoid marrying her? He'd seemed so sure of himself—of his *Englisch* plans.

"I don't want to talk any more about Peter," Caleb snapped, his tone guttural, a strong indication that a raw nerve had been struck. He tilted his head upward, but it didn't stop tears from rolling down his cheeks and landing on his shoulders.

Before Jonica could process the meaning behind Caleb's words or explore the depth of pain unmasked in his pitch,

Stephen darted into the kitchen filled with renewed energy after his nap.

❧

Caleb turned toward the sink as Stephen captured Jonica's attention. He turned on the faucet and splashed cold water on his face, attempting to relieve the sting. Usually, he guarded his emotions better. Another reason not to talk about Peter. If she knew the truth . . .

Jonica nudged his arm with a dish towel as he turned off the water. He couldn't decipher if it was concern, sadness, or pity in her eyes, but he couldn't hold her gaze any longer. "*Danki*." He buried his face in the towel.

"Can I, please?" Stephen pleaded.

Jonica redirected her attention. "Can you what, sweetie?"

"Have a *kichlin*. I slept *gut*."

"Would you like a *kichlin* too, Caleb?" Jonica opened the jar and removed a cookie that she handed to Stephen.

"*Nay, danki*." His eyes still stung. He placed the towel on the counter. "I'm going to check on Edna." He needed a reason to leave the room before his emotions bubbled to the surface once more. Leaning around the wall of the sitting room, he spotted Edna sitting in the rocking chair knitting. He stepped away from the entrance, not ready to face anyone.

Jonica came out of the kitchen. "Is everything okay?"

"Edna's fine. She's knitting."

"With you?"

He didn't deserve her concern.

She cleared her throat. "If it's okay . . . I'd like to talk more about Peter."

"Jonica." He cocked his head. "I can't talk about how he

died—why he died—or him. I just can't." What would she think if she knew he'd been the one who'd egged his brother on—he didn't physically push him, but his words were what pushed Peter to his death. He couldn't bear her knowing that mean-spirited part of him. Not now, not ever.

"I didn't mean to make you sad. I know how much you must miss your *bruder.*"

Caleb forced a smile. *Lord, she deserves to know everything.* He'd squelched Darleen's curiosity surrounding Peter's death by distancing himself, but Jonica was different. He wanted to share everything with her—he just couldn't. Still, he couldn't have her thinking she'd inflicted this pain. "Your questions were the same as everyone else's in the district."

"Still, I shouldn't have—"

He held up his hand signaling her to stop. "It was *gut* to talk about it," he lied.

Her lip-pressed smile suggested she didn't believe him.

The silence between them prompted Caleb to continue. "I'll admit it's been rough," he said, finding courage to share. "For everyone. *Mei daed* has more or less closed himself off from *mei mamm* and me, and *Mamm* has become clingy." He shrugged. "I guess she's afraid she's going to lose me too."

"As a *mamm* I understand." Jonica placed her hand on her heart. "I don't know what I would do if something happened to Stephen."

"Sometimes she cries when she thinks no one is around. It rips me apart to hear it." Caleb sighed. "I don't know why I'm rambling so much." He did know why. Jonica was a *gut* listener. He'd shown more weakness in the last few minutes in front of her than he had to Darleen during the entire time they had courted.

"You're *nett* rambling. It's nice to see this side of you."

"And *nett* the cantankerous man who told you to get off his wheat."

She chuckled. "Or the person who referred to me as a package to be picked up." Her expression sobered again. "I know what you're going through. And I won't press you to talk about Peter, unless you—"

Stephen came around the corner of the kitchen, a cookie in each hand. "Can I *geh* out to the barn to see Mr. Jordan's bird? I want to feed it."

Jonica's eyes narrowed. "How do you know the bird is in the barn?"

"Because Mr. Jordan is in the barn, and he's protecting the bird in his coat pocket."

Jonica pointed to her son's hand. "You can't feed a *boppli* bird those." She placed her hands on her hips. "And who gave you permission to get into the *kichlin* jar?"

Stephen's bottom lip protruded. "No one."

Jonica groaned. "I don't want you going outside alone."

Caleb placed his hand on Stephen's shoulder. "The *kichlin* could make the bird very sick, and you wouldn't want that to happen, would you?"

Stephen shook his head.

"I didn't think so." Noticing the disappointment in the boy's expression, Caleb turned to Jonica. "Would you like me to take Stephen out to see the bird?" He stopped short of mentioning how much time the boy spent indoors.

Stephen's face beamed with excitement. "Can he, please, *Mamm*, please?"

"Mr. Jordan might not be around."

"He is," Stephen insisted. "He's in the barn."

Jonica frowned.

"I'll make sure he's supervised." Caleb would also make a

point to talk to Stephen about minding his mother. Something told him the boy had been out to the barn by himself at least once today.

"Are you sure you don't have more important things to do?"

Caleb glanced down at Stephen and smiled. Suddenly nothing was more important than spending time with Jonica and her son. "I'm sure." He sensed her hesitation. "You can *kumm* with us."

"*Danki*. Maybe next time. I should go spend some time with *Aenti* Edna." Jonica bundled Stephen up in his winter garments, then squatted to help him into his boots. She held his coat lapels and forced him to look at her. "You listen to everything Caleb tells you, and be careful around the bird."

"I will."

Caleb reached for Stephen's gloved hand and opened the door. "Don't worry, *Mamm*. I'll keep a watchful eye on him." He winked at Jonica but found himself instantly taken by the pink hue coloring her cheeks.

"*Geh*," she shooed. "You two are letting in all the *kalt* air."

The wind whipping at his ears sent a chill straight to Caleb's core. The late afternoon sun cast long, spindly shadows of nearby tree branches over the snow.

This was a good day to stay inside—with Jonica. He liked her smile and the rosy glow in her cheeks. She'd gone through so much losing her parents. She deserved happiness. *Lord, please give her the desire of her heart.*

"I'll race you." Stephen sprinted ahead.

Caleb caught up to the boy with a few long strides but dropped back as they neared the barn so Stephen could win.

"I beat you," Stephen said, panting hard.

"*Jah*, you did." Caleb opened the barn door and as Stephen went inside, Caleb glanced at the front windows in the house. He shot Jonica a quick wave, then disappeared inside the barn.

"Mr. Jordan?" Stephen called as he ran through the barn.

They checked the empty stalls, the feed storage area, and even climbed up the wooden ladder leading to the hayloft and searched the area. Neither Mr. Jordan nor his bird was anywhere around.

"Sorry, buddy," Caleb said. "Mr. Jordan isn't here."

Stephen looked at the cookies he'd been holding, made a half shrug, then handed one to Caleb.

Caleb took a bite. "*Jah*, I don't think it'd be wise to feed this to the bird." He sat on a mound of hay. "It tastes way too *gut*."

"*Jah*, way too *gut*." After a few minutes of nibbling on his cookie, Stephen asked, "Is something wrong with me?"

"Because you like too many *kichlin*?" Caleb shook his head. "Nothing wrong with that."

"*Nay*," he said, his staid expression haunting. "Because *Mamm* cries all the time. That's like what she did when *Daadi* was in the hospital."

Caleb swallowed the glob of cookie he'd been chewing as heaviness filled his chest. His plan to lecture the child about obeying his mother faded. It was more important to listen.

"*Mamm* sits on the side of *mei* bed, and sometimes, I hear her praying when she thinks I'm asleep." He looked point-blank at Caleb, and with an eerie candor far beyond his years asked, "Am I dying?"

"You're *nett* dying." He swallowed hard, this time to push down stomach acid that had coated the back of his throat. "You know how God placed Mr. Jordan in charge of caring for the whippoorwill who wasn't strong enough to fly south with his family?"

"*Jah*."

"There's a verse in the Bible that says, 'Look at the birds of the air; they do not sow or reap or store away in barns, and yet your heavenly Father feeds them. Are you not much more valuable than they?'"

"But what does that mean?"

"That you are very important to God. He's watching over you."

"And *Mamm*?"

The tremble in Stephen's voice tugged at Caleb's heart. He pulled the child into a hug. "God doesn't want you worrying. He's watching over your *mamm* too."

They finished their cookies, then spent some time exploring the barn. "I want to have a horse one day," Stephen said. "A real horse, *nett* just a wooden one like Mr. Jordan gave me."

"You'll have to learn how to take care of him. Horses need to be fed and watered, and their hooves cleaned and trimmed. They get into the brier bush and get burs tangled in their manes and tails. You'll have to brush them every day."

"I'll do all that."

"I'm sure when you get a horse, you'll take *gut* care of him." Caleb recalled how his father had taught him how to take care of his first horse. Goose bumps spread over his arms as he realized he wanted to do the same for Stephen. He wanted to be the one who taught him how to not only groom the horse but harness and drive a buggy. But that wouldn't be possible. When Jonica and Stephen returned to Cedar Ridge, he might never see them again.

Caleb stood and removed pieces of hay that had stuck to his pant legs. In the process of sweeping hay dust from his coat, the pamphlet about blood disorders he'd found in his buggy fell out of his pocket. He picked it up. "We should go back inside. I don't want your *mamm* worrying." It'd be horrible if Stephen caught a bug because they had stayed in the drafty barn too long.

Stephen's lip curled as though he was about to protest, then he stood without a fuss.

Caleb closed up the barn. He started to tuck the pamphlet into his pocket, then decided to hold it for fear he'd forget to give it to Jonica. She would want to be prepared for tomorrow, although the information he'd read about might keep her awake.

"Do you think I'll be able to see the bird tomorrow?" Stephen asked.

"We'll have to see if Mr. Jordan is around." Caleb didn't want to disappoint Stephen, but he didn't expect Mr. Jordan would hang around much longer, now that the weather had changed.

They climbed the steps, and upon entering the house, Stephen called for his mother, who came bursting around the corner.

"The bird is gone," Stephen said, peeling off his coat.

Jonica glanced at Caleb. "Did something happen to it?"

He shrugged. "Mr. Jordan wasn't anywhere to be found either."

"Maybe that's a *gut* thing," she muttered.

Caleb nodded. Mr. Jordan seemed like a nice person, but they didn't know anything about him. Only that he was an *Englischer* and a friend of Edna's.

Jonica hung Stephen's winter clothes on the hook. "*Geh* in the bathroom and wash your hands."

"*Mei* hands aren't dirty. See?" Stephen lifted his palms.

"You've been out in the barn." She pointed down the hallway. "*Geh nau*, and do as I said." As Stephen padded down the hall, she turned back to Caleb. "Would you like to stay for *kaffi*?"

Caleb wanted to accept the offer, but he still needed to tend to his horses and talk with his *daed* about what time he wanted to get started in the morning. "I should *geh*. I have chores to do before it gets too late." He reached for the doorknob, then turned back around. "I almost forgot. I have to help *mei daed* in the morning, but as soon as I'm done, I'll take you and Stephen into town to see the *doktah*."

She shook her head. "I can't disrupt your life any more than I already have."

"You're *nett*."

"Caleb . . ."

The way she ground out his name between her teeth made him cringe. "Jonica, I've come to care very much for Stephen. Don't you think that I'm also very interested in finding out the results of his lab work?"

She released a sharp exhale. "And what will people—Darleen— think if we're seen together again?"

"I told you, Darleen and I are no longer courting. And don't worry what others might think. You shouldn't be alone when you hear the news."

"You think it's going to be bad news, don't you?" She held his gaze a half second, then tilted her face toward the ceiling.

Had his doubts been that apparent? "*Gut* or bad, I want to be there with you."

After a moment, her attention shifted back to him, but she looked away. Her brows narrowed when her gaze landed on his hand.

"Oh, I found this in *mei* buggy." He handed her the pamphlet. "It's the one from the *doktah*'s office. You must have dropped it."

"*Jah*, I've been searching for this."

A few more seconds of silence passed between them. Caleb cleared his throat. "How much of it did you have the chance to read in the buggy?"

"*Nett* much."

"Maybe it'd be better to wait until we have more information. He's *nett* going to have all those diseases." But all of them listed required lifelong treatments, many with no cure. Stephen's question in the barn, "Am I dying?" replayed in Caleb's mind.

"I'm scared," she whispered.

He drew her into his arms as a means to comfort her and himself. "That's why I don't want you going to the *doktah*'s office alone."

They held each other a long moment, neither in a hurry to let go. Then Jonica pulled back all flustered, as if realizing for the first time she'd completely let her guard down.

She looked around the room, nervously adjusting her prayer *kapp*. "You need to go home."

"Wait for me, okay? I promise I'll try to hurry." He held her gaze until she finally smiled.

"*Jah*, I'll wait for you."

Chapter 19

The sun was beginning to set as Caleb left Jonica's house Sunday evening. A mix of charged emotions flowed through his veins that he couldn't sort out. From friendly concern to something way more devoted than he cared to admit.

"Lord, I didn't even know I could care so deeply. Am I just worried Stephen could have a disease that could take his life? I can't be around Jonica without wanting to hold her. Please place a watch before *mei* tongue. Guide *mei* actions. I shouldn't have taken her into *mei* arms. I should have been able to restrain myself. Yet I want her to know that she can lean on me. She can depend on me. Lord, I don't know what tomorrow will bring . . . but I ask that You spare Stephen's life. Whatever condition he has, please don't take him from Jonica. Give her strength to get through this. Help me to be a better man. A man after Your heart."

Caleb continued to pray the entire way home and while he fed and watered the horses. When he entered the house, his mother met him at the back door.

"Where have you been all afternoon?" *Mamm* crossed her arms. "Darleen said you left the fellowship meal early. Where did you go?"

"I took food over to Edna Muller, whose niece and great-*bruderskind* are visiting. They weren't able to make it to service." He removed his coat, hat, and boots at the door.

"That's a bit odd. Why would they ask you to bring them food when it'd be a more fitting task for one of the womenfolk?"

"*They* didn't ask. Faith put together some containers of food and I volunteered."

"Hmm . . ."

Caleb ignored his mother's way of weighing her thoughts out loud. Usually it was her way of coaxing more information out of him.

"Darleen moped through the meal setup and all during the cleanup. Her friends were all doting on her. I wondered if you were aware."

His mother was fishing. So obvious. What happened to respecting someone's privacy? His privacy. Holding back information he suspected she already knew would only antagonize his mother. Besides, he didn't have anything to hide.

"Darleen and I have decided to stop courting." He expected the corners of her mouth to twitch downward into a forced frown. This time she genuinely appeared saddened, maybe even a little stunned, by the news. "I thought that's what you wanted. At least, you've never spoken favorably about Darleen in the past."

"Perhaps I was wrong."

Where did that sudden revelation come from? Caleb shook his head. "*Nay, Mamm,* I think you were right all along." He wasn't just trying to ease his mother's guilty, meddling conscience. He believed the breakup was for the best, for both Darleen and him.

Mamm huffed. "So, the scuttlebutt is true. You've been spending time with Jonica Muller—and her *kind.*"

"His name is Stephen." He left the room, checked the sitting room for his father, then returned to the kitchen. "Have you seen

Daed? I need to find out what time he wants to get started loading cattle in the morning."

"Her *kind* was born out of wedlock. It's easy enough to figure out; she and the *bu* have her family name. I don't think she's
someone—"

"*Mamm*, stop."

She crossed her arms. "You're jeopardizing your *gut* name
spending so much time over there. You are a baptized member
of the church, and no one knows if she's confessed her sins."

Caleb groaned. "Do you know where *Daed* is or *nett*?"

She glowered several seconds, then finally spoke when he
turned to leave the room. "He said something about taking hay
out to the back pasture to feed the cattle before it got dark." *Mamm*
glanced out the window facing the barn, then turned back to him.
"Maybe you should check on him. He's been gone a long while."

A sense of impending doom cloaked Caleb. The same dismal sensation he'd felt when his mother sent him to find Peter.

Jonica fixed leftover meat loaf sandwiches for supper, but after
taking the first bite, she decided she wasn't hungry. Her stomach was queasy, her nerves rattled. Caleb had a way of turning
her entire thought processes upside down. He'd comforted her
before, but this time felt different. Maybe because she wasn't
sobbing uncontrollably, or perhaps it had something to do with
knowing he was no longer courting Darleen. Before, he seemed
merely interested in calming her down during a spurt of hyste-
ria. This time she sensed he cared very deeply. For Stephen. He
admitted he'd been worried about the test results too.

"Neither of you are eating. Is something wrong with the food?"
Aenti glanced at Jonica, then Stephen, then back to Jonica.

"I'm *nett hungahrich*." Her knotted stomach would revolt if she took another bite. She motioned to Stephen's untouched sandwich. "Why aren't you eating, sweetie?"

He shrugged.

Edna furrowed her brows. "Too many *kichlin*?"

He shrugged again.

It wouldn't surprise Jonica if Stephen had a stomachache. No telling how many cookies he'd taken out of the jar. He'd left the house with two and came back with none after not finding Mr. Jordan. Plus, he'd already eaten at least one other. "Try to eat at least one more bite." She turned to *Aenti*. "How is your knitting coming along?"

"Finished four rows." She beamed with pride.

"That's *wunderbaar*." Jonica picked up her water glass and took a drink.

"It was nice of Caleb to bring food over today," *Aenti* said. "He must really like you."

Jonica choked on the mouthful of water and had to put the glass down to grab her napkin.

"There's nothing wrong with that," *Aenti* continued despite Jonica's glare. "He'd make a fine husband. Someone you should consider."

"*Aenti*, please." She motioned with her eyes across the table at Stephen, playing with his food. "Little ears hear everything."

"Can I have a horse?" Stephen blurted. "A real horse. One that I can feed and water and brush out the burs every day. I'll take *gut* care of him. Please."

"We'll talk about getting you a horse when you're a little older." Jonica would much rather talk about horses than if Caleb would make a good husband or she a good wife. Things were not that simple.

Jonica stood and took her plate and glass to the sink. "Unless you're feeling too tired, I thought we could read a few passages from the Bible tonight."

"I would enjoy that." *Aenti* rose from her seat. "I'll get the Bible."

"If you don't mind, I'd like to use *mei mamm*'s. I have it upstairs in *mei* room."

"Then Stephen and I will clean off the table while you run up and get it." *Aenti* picked up her plate and glass, then directed Stephen to do the same.

Jonica hurried up the steps and grabbed the Bible sitting on her nightstand. She'd always found a sense of comfort reading from her mother's Bible. Not that the words were different; the High German Bibles were the same. But Jonica liked that her mother had underlined different verses throughout the pages. Verses that spoke to her heart on different occasions. Now those same underlined passages came alive to Jonica as well.

With all of them seated around the table, Jonica opened to the book of Deuteronomy and began reading where she had left off the night before. She slowed down when she came to an underlined area. "'It is the Lord who goes before you. He will be with you; he will not leave you or forsake you. Do not fear or be dismayed.'" Jonica paused, allowing time for the words to soak in.

"This was nice," *Aenti* said. "I hope we can do it again tomorrow."

Jonica hadn't planned on stopping just yet, but *Aenti* had already stood and Stephen was yawning. She placed a cloth ribbon between the pages and closed the Bible. This would be a good verse to mediate on as she fell asleep. "I think it's time for bed, Stephen."

"I'm heading that way myself," *Aenti* said. *"Gut nacht."*

"Sweet dreams, *Aenti* Edna." Jonica gave her aunt a hug, then she and Stephen went upstairs to their rooms.

"Can you read the story about all the animals tomorrow?" He climbed into bed.

"The one about Noah building the ark?"

"*Jah*, I like that one." Stephen laid his head on the pillow and was asleep before they finished their nightly prayers.

Jonica watched him sleep a few minutes, then tiptoed out of the room. She changed into her nightdress, then sat on the edge of the bed, blood disorder pamphlet in hand. Would she learn anything new if she read it again, or would the information kindle more unnecessary trepidation? The debate continued several moments. Finally, she placed it on the nightstand, choosing to spend her time pondering the message God wanted her to receive from reading His Word.

"Lord, Your Word is a light onto *mei* path. You go before me. I will *nett* fear or be dismayed. You know the beginning from the end, and I will put *mei* trust in You. Please help me stand on faith."

"*Daed!*" Caleb lifted the lantern higher, but the flame wasn't strong enough to reach beyond a few feet. He trekked across the open field, toward the distant sound of mooing steer. It wasn't like his father to be out after dark. Hovering snow clouds blocked most of the moonlight, making it impossible to spot let alone track footprints in the snow. The coyotes would surely be on the hunt tonight. Probably the reason *Daed* had for moving the cattle closer to the house. Why hadn't his father waited until Caleb was home to help?

He reached the hay wagon where the Herefords were milling around both sides, chewing their cud. If the docile beasts noticed Caleb approach, they didn't seem to care about him or the lantern he held.

He'd seen before where hungry cattle charged the wagon. If his father somehow got in the herd's direct path, they might have stampeded over him, unless he had the forethought to roll under the wagon bed. Caleb had dived for cover once or twice himself when the cattle spooked and came too close.

He went to the front of the wagon, dropped to his knees, and shone the light under the bed. "*Daed?* Can you hear me?"

No answer.

Snow soaked into the knees of his pants. His father would freeze if he wasn't found soon. He searched the immediate area. *Daed*'s plow horse, Big Red, was tethered to the gate separating the back pasture from the front. Why was the gate still open? The purpose for moving the cattle was to separate them from the back acreage so it'd be easier to round them up in the morning. *Daed* would never risk leaving Big Red tied to the gate unattended. The old horse would have no defense against a pack of coyotes. In addition, black bears didn't usually enter their winter den this early, so they'd be another potential threat. Did his father think to bring a rifle?

Caleb continued the search, growing more anxious by the minute. At what point should he stop searching and go after help? According to *Mamm*, it'd already been several hours since *Daed* had gone out to feed the livestock.

"Lord, what am I supposed to do? I'll never find him on *mei* own. I need Your help. Where is he?" Caleb continued to comb the area as he prayed. "Please, God, let him see the glow from the lamp and signal me." Caleb called, "*Daed!*" again but received no answer.

Without wearing multiple layers of clothing, it'd be tough for anyone to survive the night. Not without getting frostbitten. Caleb had no choice. He had to get help. As he untied Big Red from the post, he considered his options. To the north Yoder's farm was the closest, and Bishop Zook's place was about the same distance to the south. All he needed to tell was one person, who in turn would spread word throughout the district. He'd have everyone here within a matter of minutes and they could team up and take different sections.

Caleb tugged on Big Red's reins to get him to walk faster, but the clumsy, old Clydesdale only plugged along. Caleb would make better time if he cut through the woods, and Big Red could find the barn on his own. Caleb tied the reins around the horse's neck so he wouldn't trip on them, then gave Big Red a hard pat on the hindquarters to send the horse on his way. Caleb headed for the woods.

Chapter 20

B y the time Caleb reached the Yoder's farm, he was starting to lose feeling in his face, fingers, and feet. At least his body wasn't completely numb. Knocking on the door sent a prickling sensation from his hand down to his elbow.

Darleen answered on the first knock. "Caleb, what are you doing here?"

"I need your *daed*'s help," he said, through chattering teeth. "It's . . . emergency."

"*Kumm* inside. You look like you're freezing."

"I am." He extinguished the lantern flame to conserve kerosene, then left it on the porch. Even after he entered the house, he couldn't stop shivering. The heat radiating from the cookstove was a welcome relief, but he wouldn't have time to completely thaw before having to go back out.

"Take a seat by the stove while I fetch *mei daed*." Darleen pushed one of the kitchen chairs next to the cookstove, then disappeared into the other room.

A few moments later, Melvin came into the kitchen. "Darleen said there's an emergency?"

"*Mei daed* is missing. He went out to feed the cattle and didn't come back."

Darleen returned with a lap quilt she wrapped around Caleb's shoulders. "Can I make you something hot to drink?"

"*Nay, danki.* I have to get back home and resume the search." He noticed the puddle on the floor his boots had made. "Sorry about the melted snow. I cut through the woods to get here on foot. I didn't want to take time to go back to the barn and hitch the buggy."

Melvin removed his coat from where it hung on the wall with several other coats and cloaks. "How long has Abraham been missing?"

"I'm *nett* sure. Long enough to catch pneumonia. *Mamm* said he went out to the back pasture to feed the cattle before dark." Caleb pulled the quilt higher up his neck wishing he could crawl under it completely. One of them was bound to ask why his father went out alone—why Caleb hadn't fed the livestock or at least gone with his father. If only he'd left Edna's house sooner . . .

Melvin headed to the door and stopped Caleb as he started to follow. "Stay here where it's warm while I hitch the buggy. I'll drop you off at home, then go tell the others."

"Is there something I can do to help, Caleb?" Darleen asked.

He shook his head. Not being familiar with the lay of his father's land, she might get lost herself. "*Danki* though."

"*Jah*, anytime."

Awkward silence hung in the air.

She was the first to speak. "I noticed you left without eating today."

No, Darleen. This was not the time to discuss their breakup, not after she and Hazel had gossiped about Stephen with him in earshot.

She continued. "I hope you weren't feeling sick?"

"*Nay*." He stared out the window toward the barn. "Nothing like that."

"I would say you missed some really *gut* food, but I heard Faith Rohrer fixed you a plate."

"I think I see your *daed.*" He removed the quilt from around his shoulders. "*Danki* for letting me use the blanket."

"Take it with you. It will help keep you warm. Plus, when you find your *daed*, you'll have something to put around him."

"*Danki*, that's very thoughtful of you."

"You can bring it back to me tomorrow." She smiled. "I'll be home all day."

Caleb suspected she had a hidden motive behind her suggestion but kept it to himself. "Thanks again." Holding the blanket tight around his neck, he opened the door.

Melvin wasn't finished harnessing the horse, but he didn't want to keep him waiting. At least that was what he told himself. Truth was, he had to leave the house before Darleen probed him with questions about Jonica. Darleen had to know the food Faith had sent home with him from the fellowship meal would be delivered to Edna's house. He didn't want to hurt Darleen any more than he had already, and he'd be as tactful as possible if she pressed for information, but he'd developed feelings for Jonica—feelings he couldn't explain.

When Melvin led his horse out of the barn, Caleb grabbed his lantern from where he'd left it on the porch and met him at his buggy. "I appreciate your help."

"Your *daed* would do the same for me." Melvin backed up the gelding, aligning him to the front of the buggy.

Caleb went around to the opposite side and fastened the harness to the shaft. His fingers trembled working the leather straps through the rings. The wind wasn't as strong, but he'd started shivering uncontrollably again. Wet pants from kneeling in the snow made things worse. He needed to move to generate heat.

Neither spoke on the ride home. Caleb suspected Melvin had heard about Darleen and him and her father had nothing good to say. Just as well. In order to keep his teeth from chattering, Caleb had clamped his mouth closed.

Melvin stopped the buggy next to the house. "I'll wait here if you want to run inside and check if your *daed* made it back home."

Caleb left the quilt on the bench and climbed out. "It'll only take me a minute." He whispered a prayer that he would find *Daed* sitting in his chair, as he did every night, reading the Bible.

Mamm met him at the door. "Did you find him?"

"*Nett* yet. I was hoping he'd be here." Caleb turned around. "Melvin Yoder will tell the others so we can form a search party."

"Be careful," she said as he was leaving the house.

"He's *nett* home yet," Caleb told Melvin.

"Then I'll round up a crew and return as soon as possible."

"*Danki*. The hay wagon is parked between the front forty and back eighty acres. I'll be somewhere around there." He waited for Melvin's buggy to roll forward, then turned toward the darkness.

Big Red whinnied from the corral fence. He'd found his way home. Caleb put the horse in his stall, removed the bridle and harness, then tossed a handful of hay to tide Red over until he could feed and water him properly. "I won't be long." *I hope.*

He lit the lantern and adjusted the flame to the highest setting. Times like this were when he wished his district allowed the use of flashlights. Caleb hiked out to the pasture, telling himself not to dwell on the bitter cold stinging his face or his wet pants chafing his legs. A beard would have helped shield his face and neck.

The thought of growing a beard one day—of getting married—came out of nowhere. It wasn't Darleen who came to mind as his *fraa*, but Jonica. That unsolicited moment of introspection should shake him in his boots, but instead, it gave him a little bounce in his step.

Warmth filled Caleb's chest. He thought about eating cookies in the hayloft with Stephen and how the boy talked about wanting a horse. Jonica was a good, loving mother who was patient and tender, but boys needed to learn from their father as well. Only, Stephen didn't have that opportunity. According to Jonica, the boy's father wanted nothing to do with his son. He'd left Jonica to raise the child on her own.

A short time later, he spotted several lights flickering in the distance. *Daed*'s name echoed as the group of men neared. He met them at the edge of the woods.

"*Danki* all for coming to help," Caleb said, relieved to see so many. Not wanting to waste any more time, he got straight to the point. "I've searched this section off to *mei* right and along the far fence line."

"I can start at the back and work *mei* way forward," Gideon offered.

"*Jah*, that will help." Caleb kneaded the back of his neck.

Bishop Zook came up beside Caleb. "How are you holding up?"

"Much better *nau* that I have help. I'm worried *Daed* has been out here too long. He's got to be *kalt*." Or injured.

"We're going to find him." Bishop Zook clapped Caleb's shoulder. "I know it's difficult but try *nett* to worry."

Gideon organized the group and split the men up. Caleb continued searching the wooded side of the field.

His father's name was called repeatedly from every direction. Surely someone would find him. Caleb canvassed a long stretch of land before he stopped. His father wouldn't have come this far. Unless he had a good reason to leave his horse . . .

Something rustled in the brush a few feet away. Caleb inched closer. "*Daed?*" He lifted the lantern higher.

Nothing.

Caleb turned, then stopped when he heard what sounded like a faint moan. "*Daed?*"

"Caleb?"

"*Jah*, it's me. Where are you?" Caleb whirled around, shining the light in every direction. Nothing. Where was he? Caleb was sure he'd heard his name. Then again, the wind could be playing a trick on his ears. "*Daed*, if you can hear me, let me know where you are. Make some noise."

A stick snapped a few feet away.

Caleb swung the lantern in the opposite direction and spotted his *daed* lying on the ground. "I found him," he yelled, repeating the news multiple times. He raced over to him and fell on his knees. "*Daed*, are you hurt? Are you okay?"

His *daed* tried to rise on his own but dropped back down.

"No sense moving just yet. Stay still until the others arrive." Caleb looked as best he could in the limited light for any obvious injury but didn't find anything. "What happened? I've been searching for you awhile *nau*. How did you end up in the woods?"

"I don't know." *Daed* placed a hand on the side of his head. "*Mei* head was hurting and I got disoriented . . . Red . . ." His voice drifted off.

"Big Red is okay. He's in the barn."

"*Nay*, the man who . . . ah." He winced. "*Mei* head is pounding."

"Help is on the way." Caleb pushed off the ground, stumbled through the brush to reach the edge of the pasture, and yelled again, "I found him. Over here!" He waved his lantern and repeated the call until he got someone's attention.

"Is he hurt?" Melvin, the first to arrive, asked.

"I'm *nett* sure. He's talking." Caleb led Melvin and a few of the others through the brush.

With men on all sides of his father, they gently lifted him off the ground and carried him out of the woods where the remaining men caught up with them. Together, they carried *Daed* back to the house.

Darleen and the bishop's wife stood at the same time his mother did when Caleb and the other men carried *Daed* through the kitchen door. *Mamm* led them into the sitting room where she instructed them to lower him onto the couch.

Daed clutched the side of his rib cage as though the movement had caused pain. He moaned as *Mamm* shoved a pillow under his head. "Just relax, Abraham," she said as she unlaced his boots.

Caleb retrieved an afghan from the rocking chair and placed it over his father. He would need more blankets and probably something hot to drink before he started to feel warm. Caleb went to the woodbox and selected a few small pieces that would burn fast and generate more heat.

Darleen came up beside Caleb. "I was worried about your *mamm* being alone."

"*Danki*, I'm sure she was pleased to have company." He tossed the slabs of wood on the burning embers.

"The bishop and Alice arrived a short time later, but your *mamm* encouraged me to stay."

Caleb motioned to the hallway. "I need to find a heavier blanket." Thankfully, she didn't follow him down the hall. He went into what used to be Peter's bedroom, removed the wool blanket from his bed, then took it to *Daed*.

The house had thinned of most of the searchers. Left were a few stragglers, and Darleen. *Mamm* had managed to get *Daed*'s boots off and with help from Bishop Zook was in the process of removing his winter coat.

Caleb waited until they had the winter garments removed, then lowered the wool blanket over his father, who was shaking miserably. "Maybe you should see a *doktah*. I can take you to the hospital."

"*Nay*, I'll be fine. The dizziness has already passed. I'm feeling better."

With the other searchers heading out the door, Alice Zook went into the kitchen to put the teakettle on the stove, and his mother went to the bedroom to get *Daed* dry socks. It left Darleen and Caleb alone with his father, who had burrowed deeper under the cover.

"Do you think he'll be *allrecht*?" Darleen asked.

"I hope so." The extreme cold had probably numbed his pain, at least the intensity. But the way *Daed* held his side and moaned when they lowered him onto the couch and flinched when *Mamm* removed his coat, he was sore from something—or injured. Caleb recalled what his father had said in the woods. His head hurt. He'd been disoriented . . .

Caleb headed toward the door. He needed to fetch the district midwife. Sadie would know if *Daed* needed to go to the hospital. "I left your quilt in your *daed*'s buggy. *Danki* again for letting me use it," he said over his shoulder.

Darleen followed him outside. "Caleb do you have a few minutes so we can talk?"

"Sorry, but I don't." He continued toward the barn. "I didn't want to say anything in front of *mei daed*, but I'm leaving to get Sadie. He needs to be checked over."

"I could ride along and keep you company."

"It's getting late, Darleen. You need to go home." He increased his pace. Even if Darleen wanted to start courting again, he didn't.

Within minutes Caleb had Nutmeg hitched to the buggy and was heading to Sadie's place. Thankfully the midwife wasn't on a house call and was able to grab her medical bag and leave immediately. En route, he relayed what his father had said happened. "Maybe he slipped and hit his head," Caleb said. "He didn't seem to remember much."

"But what he's saying makes sense?"

"*Jah*, his words aren't slurring like someone who's had a stroke if that's what you mean."

Sadie's queries continued, though many he couldn't answer. *Daed* wasn't someone who talked freely about personal matters, especially about his health.

Caleb stopped the buggy next to the porch and Sadie climbed out, taking her medical bag with her. He tied Nutmeg to the hitching post. He wanted the horse ready in case he had to go down the road to their *Englisch* neighbor's house and call for an ambulance.

Entering through the back door, he overheard *Daed* fussing about all the attention. *Mamm* was insisting he let Sadie look him over. Caleb put the kettle on the stove. Going into the sitting room now would only agitate his father more since he'd been the one to fetch Sadie.

It wasn't long before Sadie and his mother came into the kitchen.

Caleb stood. "How is *Daed*?"

"His blood pressure is somewhat elevated," Sadie said. "But more alarming was how low his sugar has dropped."

Mamm poured a large glassful of milk. "Is this too much?"

"*Nay*, that's *gut*," Sadie said. "I'd give him a *kichlin* and maybe some nuts if you have them."

Caleb removed a cookie from the jar as his mother searched for nuts in the cabinet. "Do you think his blood sugar dropping was what caused him to black out?"

"I'm sure it made him disoriented and dizzy. He might have blacked out from falling and hitting his head."

"Sadie thinks he might have a concussion," *Mamm* added.

"What does that mean? Should we take him to the hospital?"

"He won't *geh*," *Mamm* said over her shoulder as she left the kitchen with the snacks.

Sadie pulled a chair out from the table and sat. "After he's eaten, I'll recheck his sugar and we'll go from there."

"What about the concussion?"

"You'll need to monitor him throughout the *nacht* to check for any mental change in his condition. If his headache worsens, you should get him to the *doktah*."

Chapter 21

Caleb yawned as he poured a mug of morning coffee. He and his mother had spent the night taking turns waking up his father every few hours to make sure he was okay. None of them got much sleep.

Daed lumbered into the kitchen, his hair matted and the area under his eyes darkened and puffy from lack of sleep.

"How are you feeling, *Daed*?"

"Better." He turned to his side and coughed into his fist, then took a half second longer to steel his pinched expression before he turned back to Caleb.

"You look like you could use this." Caleb handed him the mug of coffee he'd just poured.

"*Danki*." *Daed* took a seat at the table.

Caleb filled another mug and joined his father. "How many head of cattle do you want separated from the herd?"

"At least a dozen. That should help lower the feed bill over the winter. We'll keep the calves, their *mamms*, and most of the two- and three-year-olds. The older ones can *geh*. They weigh the most so they'll also bring in the most money at auction."

"True." Caleb took a drink. "Are you able to recall what happened last *nacht*?"

"You waking me up every minute to ask what month it is?"

"Before that. What happened in the pasture?"

"I was coaxing the herd in from the back pasture with a load of hay when Red started to limp. I had to move him away from the cattle in order to inspect his hooves. I started to get dizzy and—" *Daed* shrugged. "I must have bent down too fast."

"Sadie said your blood sugar was low. I think you blacked out. I found you at the edge of the woods. In the bushes."

Daed stood and took his mug to the sink. "Are you going to sit and drink *kaffi* all day or help me bring in the herd?"

"Are you sure you feel up to it today?"

"It's gotta be done."

Caleb had learned years ago not to argue with his father. He slugged the remainder of his coffee in a couple of gulps as he went to the sink. To chase the burning sensation, he filled the mug with cold tap water and chugged that as well.

Daed put on his boots. He'd said he wanted to get going early, but that was before everything happened last night. He was moving around stiffly and yet seemed to be in more of a rush than usual.

Caleb shoved his foot into his boot and laced it up. "Are you sure you're feeling up to doing this?"

"I've already made arrangements with Jack. I can't cancel *nau.*"

"We don't have to cancel. I can bring them in from the field and get them loaded. You don't have to—"

"You're *nett*—"

"Peter. I know. Every day I'm reminded. I'm *nett* Peter." Caleb swiped his coat off the hook. "I'll be out in the barn."

Caleb strode across the yard. "I'll never be enough. I don't know why I try." He entered the barn and grabbed a bridle and saddle from the tack room. It wasn't until he finished spouting off every ill thought he'd stored since his brother's death, that he finally realized he just needed to pray.

"This is all out of *mei* hands, Lord. I guess all this time You've been waiting for me to admit the truth. I'll never measure up to Peter in *mei daed*'s eyes. Help me to accept that and move forward. Help me understand what he's going through. He lost his *sohn* . . . Peter took his own life—the very breath You gave him."

Caleb slumped against a nearby post. "It's so hard *nett* knowing if he's with You. When he came back home, I thought he'd changed, that he'd given his heart to serving You."

Light flooded the area as *Daed* entered the barn. He went into the equipment room and grabbed the other saddle.

Caleb took his gear into the stall and began to saddle Jet, Peter's roping horse that he'd trained himself. Jet was a spitfire, and coupled with not being ridden in a while, he would be a handful to control. But Caleb was determined—admittedly for the wrong reason. He wanted to prove himself to his father.

Daed stopped in front of the stall Caleb was in. "You going to ride him?"

"No reason *nett* to." He tightened the quarter horse's cinch. "The horse will get fat and lazy if he isn't exercised." Besides, Peter wasn't coming back. The horse needed to either be used or sold.

Daed continued into the adjoining stall, mumbling something about a pounding headache and the need to get the roundup over.

With the cattle already moved to the front pasture, Caleb decided he could bring them into the corral alone. He led Jet out from the barn, mounted him, and reined him toward the pasture. Once through the gate, Caleb increased knee pressure into the horse's sides, urging Jet into a gallop.

The cutting horse assumed his role without much direction from Caleb. It didn't take much effort to get the herd moving toward the barn. Peter had been a better horse trainer than people had given him credit for. Of course, when *Daed* recognized his talent, he pushed him toward training buggy horses and opening a blacksmith shop, which Peter wasn't interested in doing. He had returned home though he still talked about leaving Posen. *Daed* and Peter's blacksmith disagreement was how Peter ended up in construction working for Caleb.

In hindsight the biggest mistake Caleb made was hiring his brother. It was dangerous enough to be on a metal roof or suspended multiple stories high working off homemade scaffolding, but putting one's trust in a disgruntled laborer was a disaster waiting to happen, which Caleb discovered the hard way.

Daed galloped his horse toward Caleb. "I'll take the right and you come in from the center and we'll separate the herd." He immediately galloped away, cracking the bullwhip and sending part of the herd stampeding a different direction for Caleb to work.

Caleb found the use of a bullwhip unnecessary. A stampeding herd was more unpredictable and therefore more dangerous, but he couldn't convince his father that waving his hat and making noise worked just as well. With the older cattle split from the herd, he drove them into the corral.

Jack, the *Englisch* livestock hauler, was in the process of backing the trailer up to the gate. Between *Daed* cracking the bullwhip and Jack's backup alarm, the cattle grew increasingly agitated, moving in circles.

"Watch the fence, Caleb!" *Daed* yelled.

Some of the steers had rammed themselves up against the rail and the entire structure was bending. Caleb heeled Jet and the horse leapt into action. Riding alongside the fence, Caleb spotted a young calf, who'd gotten separated from his mother, caught between the bars, bawling. With the calf about to get trampled by the larger steers, Caleb wedged Jet between them.

Then another sharp crack of the bullwhip spooked the herd and they shifted suddenly. Jet's abrupt sidestepping motion threw Caleb off balance. Hurled from the saddle, he landed first on the back of a steer, then onto the ground.

"Caleb!"

His foot lost traction in the mud as he tried to stand. It all happened in a matter of seconds. Moving hooves were everywhere he looked. He noticed a break in the herd, then the legs of *Daed*'s horse.

Caleb scrambled to his feet, and shooting pain from his knee to hip almost brought him back down. He took a chance and dove for the fence. Landing hard on his ribs, it was all he could do to push himself over the rail. He dropped on the ground outside the corral and lay still a moment, taking inventory of what muscles and bones hurt.

A shredding sensation tore at Caleb's leg and sharp stabs stole his breath. He let out a cry as he pushed off the ground. Feeling a bit disoriented, he didn't put together what was happening. Why was Jack waving the herd toward the other side of the corral?

Daed?

Caleb vaulted toward his father, who was slumped over in his saddle, his face the color of snow.

"*Mei* chest," *Daed* said. "Pressure."

"Hold on." He led his father's horse to the gate, gently lifted him out of the saddle, and carried him outside the pen.

"I'm sorry, *sohn*," *Daed* said as Caleb lowered him to the ground.

His phone to his ear, Jack jogged back to the gate. "I dialed 911." He handed the phone to Caleb. "They need the address."

Caleb gave the woman their address and his father's name and age. "I can't talk any more. *Mei* father is *nett* responding."

Chapter 22

J onica placed the Mason jar of split pea soup in the cabinet with the other homemade soups. While waiting for Caleb to arrive to take her and Stephen into town, she had kept herself busy in the kitchen. She had cleaned out every cabinet, taken inventory of what canned goods her aunt had, and reorganized the contents in the cabinets. It passed the time. Too much time according to the wall clock.

Two more hours had passed since they'd eaten lunch and still no Caleb. He had something he needed to do for his father, but shouldn't he have given her an idea of how many hours the chore would take?

How long was she expected to wait?

The doctor's office would close in a few hours. She glanced out the window. With the sun shining brightly, the snow appeared to be melting. A typical fall day. Cool but not cold. If Stephen dressed in multiple layers, he should be able to stay warm, even if the wind picked up. She would need to carry him most of the trip. He'd coughed all morning, and his forehead was hot when she put him down for his nap. Another reason to see the doctor or keep him inside where it was warm and wait for Caleb.

She'd come to rely on Caleb for his emotional support, his

friendship. A mistake. She should have known not to count on a Schulmann. She thought Caleb was different. That when Caleb gave his word, he kept it.

She took a deep breath and exhaled slowly, but it did nothing to calm her anxious thoughts. Until she learned the results of Stephen's tests, she would wear out the planks on the kitchen floor pacing, fretting, overwhelming her mind with endless possibilities.

Where are you, Caleb?

Lord, I don't want to be alone when I receive the news. What if it's bad news? How will Stephen and I manage? Jonica missed her parents, especially her mother who helped Jonica get through her pregnancy and delivery. When her entire world was falling to pieces, her mother had been there. Now Jonica had to be strong for Stephen. She was all her *sohn* had.

Her morning devotional came to mind. *"Seek the LORD and his strength, seek his presence continually."* God's strength would get them both through this time. She was wrong to count on Caleb. Just as she'd been wrong to think Peter would change. *Lord, I will seek Your strength—Your presence continually.* Jonica recited the passage again, this time meditating on each word.

Someone knocked on the front door.

Caleb! Jonica raced to the entry and swung the door open. "Ida." She forced a smile, hoping to mask her disappointment. "How are you?"

"*Guder mariye*, Jonica. I heard you were in town." Ida Hosteller lifted the wicker basket she was holding. "I brought eggs."

"Please, *kumm* in." She stepped aside, making room for Ida to pass. "*Aenti* Edna is in the sitting room." Jonica closed the door. "I'll let her know she has a visitor."

"Did I hear someone at the door?" *Aenti* rounded the corner to the entry. Her face brightened. "Ida, it's *gut* to see you."

"I heard you had company staying with you." She followed

Edna into the kitchen. "So I thought you could use more eggs. I'm sure you're thrilled having your *bruderskind* in town."

"I am." Edna smiled at Jonica. "*Mei bruderskind* is a big help around here."

"I'm sure." Ida removed the towel surrounding the eggs and transferred the eggs from her basket into a basket *Aenti* kept on the counter. "How long do you plan to stay, Jonica?"

"I haven't decided yet." She couldn't help but think Ida was here to collect tidbits of news to tell the other curious women in the district, namely her best friend, Deborah Schulmann, Caleb's mother. Had news also spread about Stephen?

Aenti removed a jar stuffed with cash from the cabinet and pulled out a few bills she gave to Ida. "Jonica, would you mind making a fresh pot of *kaffi?*"

"Don't make any on *mei* account. I have a few other deliveries to make." Ida looked at Jonica with a scrutinizing eye. "You'll have to plan to bring Edna to the upcoming sewing frolic. It's in a couple of weeks. I'm sure everyone would love to see you again."

"I don't get out much anymore," Edna said.

Gut *excuse,* Aenti. Jonica smiled, relieved she was off the hook.

"But I'm sure Jonica would enjoy attending the get-together. Wouldn't you?"

"We'll see when the time is closer. I have to *geh* back to Cedar Ridge sometime." Even if she didn't mind being cornered by a bunch of well-wishing women, she couldn't make any plans without knowing if something was wrong with her son. If he had any of the bleeding disorders described in the pamphlet.

"If you're *nett* able to *kumm* to the frolic, I hope to see you the Sunday after next at the Yoders' *haus*. Melvin and Abigail are hosting the next Sunday meeting."

"We'll be there," her aunt said. "I'll be sure to mark the date on *mei* calendar so we don't miss out."

Jonica stayed in the kitchen while *Aenti* Edna walked Ida to the door. The moment she heard the location for the next Sunday service, she'd decided against attending. She'd figure out an excuse, some reason to avoid Darleen's parents' *haus*.

"Seek the LORD . . . Seek his presence continually."

Conviction closed Jonica's eyes. *I'm sorry, Lord. I'm more worried what people will say, how Stephen will be treated . . . being an outsider. Forgive me, God. I've already lost focus on You.*

A few minutes after Ida had left and *Aenti* returned to her knitting in the sitting room, Stephen shuffled into the kitchen rubbing his eyes. "*Ich* slept *gut*."

Jonica smiled at the way he automatically answered before she had the chance to ask about his sleep.

"I'm *dorstig*."

Jonica removed a small glass from the cabinet and filled it halfway with water. "It's nice outside," she said, handing him the glass. "I thought we would walk into town."

He drained the glass and handed it back. "Can Caleb go with us?"

"He's busy today."

"What about *Aenti* Edna?"

"I'll find out if she's up to making the trip while you use the restroom." She didn't want to have to stop at Yoder's Market again to use their facilities. Especially after learning Caleb and Darleen were no longer courting. Her mother had always said it was best to keep trouble at arm's length.

Jonica sighed. Being back on the farm made her miss her parents even more. She had yet to provide her father's death certificate to the courthouse in order to change ownership on the farm deed—the reason she'd returned to Posen.

Jonica found *Aenti* in the sitting room working on her knitting project. "Stephen and I are going to walk into town. Do you feel up to joining us? I thought once I get into town I would arrange for an *Englisch* driver to take us to the courthouse in Rogers City to take care of the paperwork."

"Let's do that another day. You did say you wanted to stay longer, *jah*?"

"Yes, but—"

Aenti lifted her finger. "I'm *nett* feeling up to doing any paperwork." She lowered her knitting needles and picked up her mug. "Would you be a dear and add a little more *kaffi* to *mei* cup before you leave?"

"*Jah*, no problem."

"Mr. Jordan would like some too. He takes cream in his."

Jonica glanced around the room, half expecting to find him sitting in the corner. But the *Englischer* wasn't nearby. Had her aunt's mind slipped to the point of seeing people? Was she imagining the redheaded stranger in the room? "Have you . . . talked with Mr. Jordan?"

"We talk all the time."

"And he told you that he wanted *kaffi*?" Jonica swept the room with her gaze again.

"If you're looking for Mr. Jordan, he's *nett* here." *Aenti* Edna chuckled. "You must think *mei* mind has really slipped."

Jonica set the mug on the lamp table, then knelt beside her aunt's rocker and reached for her hand. "Can I ask you a question?"

"Anything, dear."

"Does Mr. Jordan have anything to do with your decision to sell the farm? Is he the one who wants to buy it? Because he's been awfully interested in the property."

Aenti shook her head. "As he would tell you himself if he was here, Posen is *nett* his home. He's just passing through."

"Then who's the man who wants to buy the farm?"

Aenti lowered her head. "I received a letter in the mail from someone who buys houses. I hadn't contacted them, but I thought if you had a reason to *kumm* home . . . you might . . . stay. I know I was wrong. Will you forgive me?"

"I'll forgive you, but you need to tell Caleb. He's been worried too. He put time and money into the fields. And what about your going to live with *Aenti* Mary Anna?"

"That was true. She needs help. But . . ." *Aenti's* eyes turned watery. "I know *mei* mind isn't what it used to be. I'm forgetting things. I wouldn't be much help."

"You're a help to me with Stephen." Jonica gave her aunt's hand a squeeze, then reached for the hankie on the lamp table and handed it to her. "If I make you an appointment with Dr. Mallory, would you go? Maybe he can prescribe medicine or recommend things you can do to help your memory."

"It's part of aging. Something I have to accept."

"I'm still going to make you an appointment." Before her aunt could object, Jonica grabbed her mug from the table and went into the kitchen.

Stephen tottered into the kitchen. "I'm ready." His coat wasn't fastened and his boots were on the wrong feet.

"Wait for me at the door," she said, refilling *Aenti's* mug. "I'll only be a minute." Jonica prepared a mug for Mr. Jordan to appease her aunt but left it in the kitchen. She set *Aenti's* mug on a wooden coaster on the table next to her chair. "Mr. Jordan's mug is on the kitchen counter." Where it would probably still be when she returned.

"*Danki*, dear. I'll see you when you get back from town."

"We shouldn't be too long." Jonica went to the door and chuckled when she discovered Stephen putting his mittens on the wrong hands. "Let me help." She switched the mittens, his boots, fastened his coat, then readied herself for going outside.

As they stepped onto the porch, she spotted Mr. Jordan

pulling a little red wagon. She eyed what appeared to be the same wagon she'd left along the side of the road. The one with a broken wheel. "Is that . . . ?"

Mr. Jordan nodded. "I thought you might want it back."

"How did you know where I'd left it? I looked for it on *mei* way home from town, but it was gone." She inspected the wagon. "You fixed the wheel?"

"It wasn't difficult."

Stephen tugged on Jonica's cloak. "Can I ride in it?"

Mr. Jordan offered her the handle. "I think you'll find it easier to pull. I made a few adjustments."

Jonica was still confused. Had Mr. Jordan been following her into town? How else would he have known where she'd left the wagon?

"Can I, *Mamm*?"

"I believe young Stephen is ready to go," Mr. Jordan said.

This wasn't the time to debate, even with herself, how the man had come upon the wagon—or the parts to fix the wheel. She needed to get into town before the doctor's office closed. "*Jah*, Stephen, go ahead and get in. You can ride." Jonica looked over at the *Englischer*, his amber eyes flickering in the sunlight. "*Danki*, Mr. Jordan."

He nodded. "My pleasure."

Jonica pulled the wagon a few feet immediately noticing the difference. The wheels went through the soft ground without a problem, and she couldn't even tell Stephen was in the wagon, though it wasn't as though he weighed a lot. Excited with the changes Mr. Jordan had made, she turned the wagon around and went back to where the *Englischer* was standing. "I'm *nett* sure what adjustments you made"—she rolled the wagon back and forth—"but you definitely made it easier to pull. *Danki* again."

"My pleasure. And, Jonica, don't be discouraged when

you're at the doctor's office. Remember what the Word of the Lord teaches. 'Seek the LORD and his strength, seek his presence continually.'"

Dumbfounded that Mr. Jordan had recited the exact verse she had read earlier during her morning devotions, she simply nodded.

"Go in peace," he said.

"And you as well." She headed toward town. Her thoughts twisted. She hadn't even told her aunt why she was going into town. How did Mr. Jordan know about the doctor?

Jonica signed Stephen in at the front desk, then took a seat in the doctor's lobby.

"*Mamm.*" Tears collected on Stephen's long lashes. "Is it going to hurt?"

"*Nay*, I think Dr. Mallory is only going to look at your hand and make sure it's healing."

Stephen fidgeted on the chair. "Why didn't Caleb *kumm* with us?"

"I don't know, sweetie. I'm sure he would be here with you if he could."

The door to the exam area opened and the nurse called Stephen's name. Jonica reached down and took her son's hand.

"I'm scared," Stephen whimpered.

She gathered him into her arms. *Lord, please, calm our fear like You calmed the stormy sea.* Jonica followed the nurse into the examination room and sat on the chair with Stephen on her lap.

The nurse motioned to Stephen's hand. "Are we seeing Stephen for a dressing change today?"

Jonica nodded. "He also had blood work drawn on Friday,

231

and I was told the results might be in today. Also, before I forget, can I make an appointment for *mei aenti*? She's having problems with her memory."

"I'll let the desk clerk check for availability for your aunt while I see if the results are in for Stephen. But first, let's get your temperature." She asked Stephen general questions about his hand pain as she swiped his forehead with the digital thermometer.

Jonica waited until the nurse entered the information in the computer. "Does Stephen have a fever? He was warm earlier when I put him down for his nap."

"What was his temperature?"

Jonica shook her head. "He wasn't boiling up, so I didn't take it."

"It's a little elevated: 100.3. Let's take a look at your hand."

Jonica came up beside the nurse as she unwrapped the bandage. The stitched area was red. "Does it look infected to you?"

"I think it's healing nicely." She tossed the old bandage in the trash can. "Dr. Mallory will be in shortly to check him out."

Stephen rotated his hand. "It doesn't hurt."

"That's *gut* news." Jonica combed her fingers through his thick brown hair. Now all she needed to hear was that her worry had been for nothing. That her boy's blood tests were normal and everything was fine.

"Am I going to get a treat?" Stephen asked.

"After the *doktah* checks you over."

Stephen coughed, then touched his hand to his throat, and made a face when he swallowed.

"Does your throat hurt?"

He shrugged, which told her it did. Hopefully the office visit wouldn't take long and they could get back home before the sun went down. She glanced at the clock on the wall. Four o'clock. It didn't give them much time. It was getting dark around six.

Jonica was busy planning out the supper meal in her mind when Dr. Mallory entered the room.

"Hello." Dr. Mallory smiled. "How is our young man doing today?"

"*Gut*," Stephen said. "Can I *geh nau*?"

"You haven't given me a chance to check your hand yet. What's the hurry?"

"I'm going to get a treat." Stephen peered up at Jonica. "Right, *Mamm*?"

"After Dr. Mallory is done."

"Then we'd better get right to it." The doctor examined Stephen's hand, then turned to Jonica. "I think his hand looks great. He'll have a scar, but that's unavoidable."

"What kind of a scar?" Stephen asked.

"Just a small one. It'll fade with time."

Jonica wasn't concerned about scarring. "So, it's *nett* infected?"

"No, the redness is normal. It'll start to scab over in the next day or two. Unless it starts weeping, and I don't expect it to, I wouldn't worry about it. Continue to keep it clean. Limit the amount of activity, but you should be able to leave the bandage off."

"What about the blood tests? Have the results *kumm* back?"

Dr. Mallory motioned to Tammy, his nurse. "Would you take Stephen to the nurse's desk and let him pick out a sticker?"

Jonica's heart pounded hard against her chest. Was the news bad—life-threatening? Why else would Dr. Mallory send Stephen out of the room? *Stay calm. Deep breath in—and out.* Her lungs were still tight. Suffocating. Self-talk wasn't helping either. The bushel of questions feeding her mind was creating a whirlwind of panic.

"Can I, *Mamm*?"

"What?" She shook her head to dislodge the negative thoughts.

"I'm sorry, sweetie. I wasn't listening." Her son was sick—possibly dying—and she wasn't listening. Great mother.

"Pick out a sticker?" He reached for her hand. "Can I?"

"Dr. Mallory and I need a few minutes to talk." *Lord, don't let Stephen see me upset. I don't want to frighten him.* She cleared her throat. "*Jah*, sweetie, it's okay." She lifted him off the examination bench and was about to set him down when he sneezed. Blood sprayed her face, the front of her dress.

"*Mamm*! What's wrong with me?" Clots of blood gushed from both nostrils, running down his face, neck, and soaking into his shirt.

"Let's get him back on the bench," Dr. Mallory said. "Tammy, I'll need a silver nitrate stick."

Stephen wrapped his arms around her neck and clung tightly. Sobbing hysterically, he refused to let go.

"The *doktor* needs to take a look at you." Jonica steeled her voice when she wanted to break down and cry right along with him. "What's wrong with *mei sohn*? Why is he bleeding like this?"

Chapter 23

J onica's world fragmented into a million pieces when Dr. Mallory couldn't stop Stephen's bleeding in the office. It all happened in a blur. An ambulance was called to shuttle him to the hospital, then when they arrived, a team of nurses held him down as another staff member gave him a sedative—then something unexpected happened. Stephen's eyes rolled back into his head.

Blood was everywhere.

Jonica stood at the head of the stretcher, machines beeping around her. "What's wrong with *mei sohn*? Stephen, talk to me!"

Overhead pages summoned others for help. Within seconds Jonica was crowded away from Stephen, to the corner of the room. Still dazed, she didn't notice someone putting their arms around her shoulders or being turned toward the door.

"We'll take good care of him," one of the trauma nurses said as she guided Jonica out of the examination room.

The door closed, separating her from Stephen. She should have fought to stay in the room. Her son needed her.

A woman dressed in gray slacks and a frilly rose-colored blouse approached Jonica with a clipboard.

The woman's mouth was moving, but Jonica couldn't hear anything but garbled words. Focusing on the woman's lips, everything else blurred. Her ears rang. As if things were happening in slow motion, someone helped her into a wheelchair.

She pointed at the room. "*Mei sohn.*"

"The doctor is with him."

"I have to—" She pushed up from the wheelchair too fast, and the high-pitched winding noise in her ears returned. She sat back down.

"I'll have someone update you on your son's progress as soon as possible. But for now, let's give them a few more minutes to work on him, okay?"

Jonica nodded.

The worker held out the clipboard. "I have some paperwork for you to review and sign if everything is correct." She went on to explain each consent form as Jonica scrawled her name on the blank lines.

"How long before I can see *mei sohn*?"

"I'll see what I can find out." The woman handed Jonica a piece of paper. "This is your copy of the Healthcare Information Privacy Act."

The office worker went on to explain what patient information they could and could not share, but Jonica wasn't listening. Her only concern was Stephen.

"If you'll follow me, I'll show you where the lobby is located." The woman motioned to a door on her left marked Exit.

"I should stay nearby in case Stephen needs me."

"He's in good hands, Ms. Muller. The doctor will know to find you in the waiting room. We have to keep the hallway cleared."

Questions loomed. How could a simple nosebleed escalate to an ER visit? And why did the nurse want to send her out of the room?

The woman cleared her throat, and when she obtained Jonica's attention, she politely motioned to the door again. Jonica followed her to the lobby, where multiple clusters of seating areas made up the large room. She sat the farthest away from the television on a vinyl chair that had lost its firmness.

Like a pot that never boiled, staring at the wall clock didn't move the minute hand. Jonica prayed, watched the clock, then prayed some more.

What seemed like hours later, a forty-something man wearing black scrubs and a long, white medical coat strode into the room. Jonica stood as he neared, then shook his hand.

"I'm Dr. Rumflin, the ER physician taking care of your son."

"How is Stephen?"

"I was able to cauterize the bleeding. He's stable at the moment."

"At the moment? Do you think if Stephen sneezes he will start bleeding again?"

"There's a possibility. I've arranged for him to be admitted, and for Dr. Yarbrough, a hematologist, to consult. Your son's blood counts are low, which could indicate a deeper problem. Has he had any recent injuries, falls?"

"*Nay*."

"What about blood in his urine or stools?"

"*Nay*."

"I've ordered a pint of blood to be administered; however, he may require a second."

"Will that make him better?" Her body trembled. She clasped her hands on her lap, but even holding them tight didn't stop the quavering rocking her body.

"Are you all right, Ms. Muller? Can I get you some water?"

"*Nay*, thank you." She looked up to meet the doctor's gaze. "The blood you are giving him, will it make him well?"

"It isn't a cure. Blood replacement is more of a temporary fix. It provides more time to find the underlying problem. Dr.

Yarbrough will be able to tell you more once he's had the chance to review Stephen's chart and examine him."

"Can I see him?"

"Yes, I'll take you to him."

As they went through a set of doors marked For Authorized Personnel Only, the doctor explained, "His nose will be sore. I've ordered Tylenol for discomfort. The nurse will let you know when a room has been assigned. At that time he will be moved upstairs, and Dr. Yarbrough will take over care."

"Dr. Mallory in Posen ordered lab work last Friday." She should have remembered sooner, but she'd been rushed out of the room so quickly that it hadn't crossed her mind.

"I believe Dr. Yarbrough has been in touch with Dr. Mallory, but you might want to mention it to Dr. Yarbrough when you see him." He paused outside Stephen's room. "Don't be alarmed if he's still groggy. He had to be sedated in order for me to cauterize his nose."

Jonica hurried to the side of the stretcher and reached for her son's hand. "Stephen." Her voice cracked. "It's *Mamm*. Can you hear me?"

Stephen's eyelids barely opened, and his only reply was a whimper.

"Stephen, sweetie, are you in pain?"

His eyes closed.

Caleb sat opposite his mother next to his father's hospital bed, where he'd been the last few hours, riddled with uncertainty and uselessness. He wrung his hands. He should have insisted on loading the cattle alone, especially after *Daed*'s dizzy episode last night. He should have seen that *Daed* wasn't in good enough condition to be on horseback let alone working cattle. Caleb should have asked Gideon to help in his father's place. But his father was set in his ways—ruled by stubbornness and pride.

One of the machines at the head of the bed beeped repeatedly. A nurse came into the room, pressed a few buttons, and the noise stopped. She replaced the empty bag that hung on the IV pole with another bag, then checked the monitor that was recording his heart activity.

"How is he?" *Mamm* asked.

"His blood pressure and heart rate are within normal range, and the rhythm of his heart is stable. The medicine the doctor ordered seems to be working."

Mamm blotted her eyes with a hankie. "Why isn't he waking up?"

"He's sedated. It's important for his body to rest, especially over the next twenty-four hours." The nurse repeated what the doctor had told them earlier. That even though Caleb's father had suffered a mild heart attack, he wasn't out of danger.

The nurse smiled warmly at his mother. "It's also important for the family members to rest as well. The cafeteria is open and if you're interested, there's a chapel on the first floor."

Mamm nodded, though Caleb doubted she would leave his father's bedside any time soon. And understandably so, since they had never spent a day apart in the last thirty-some years. Still, there was nothing either of them could do—except wait. Caleb didn't think she would heed the nurse's suggestion, but maybe she would his. "*Mamm*, why don't you take a break."

She shook her head. "I'd rather stay. You *geh*." She reached into her handbag and pulled out her change purse. "Would you bring me back a cup of *kaffi*, please?"

"Sure." Every muscle fiber in his body screamed as he stood, reminding him of the time he'd carried enough lumber to cover fifteen-hundred square feet of floors up two flights of stairs.

"What's wrong, Caleb?"

"I'm just stiff from sitting too long." He went to stretch but recoiled as muscle spasms around his ribs sucked the wind out of him. Placing his hand against his rib cage, he buried a groan, then straightened to his full height. Aware he was under his mother's watchful eye, he pivoted to face the door. "Do you want anything to eat?"

"*Nay*, just *kaffi*. Are you sure you're *allrecht*, Caleb? You're limping."

"I'm fine." He wasn't going to tell her about falling off the horse or having to dive under the fence rail to avoid being trampled. Doing so would only add unnecessary stress to the situation. She didn't need to concern herself with him. Not when his father had come close to dying.

He lumbered out of the room, his entire right side throbbing with each step he took. Caleb pressed the button on the elevator, his thoughts flying a million directions. He needed to make arrangements for someone to tend to the livestock, but more importantly, he needed to get word to Jonica about why he never showed up. He'd ask the person at the information desk in the lobby where a pay phone was located and call Beverly, their *Englisch* driver, to deliver the messages.

The elevator door opened, and without lifting his head Caleb stepped forward.

A faint scent of tea tree oil caught his attention at the same time a male voice asked, "Going up?"

Realizing he was about to get into the wrong elevator, Caleb looked up. Jonica stood in the corner with her head down. "Jonica," he said, catching the closing door with his arm. He entered the elevator car. "What are you doing—?" He noticed

Stephen lying on the stretcher, and every hair on his arms stood up. "What happened?"

"Stephen's nose started bleeding," she whispered, then glanced at her sleeping son. "He's being admitted. The *doktah* doesn't know . . ." Her voice trailed off.

Caleb wanted to pull her into his arms but restrained the urge. Her sagged shoulders and red-rimmed eyes tugged at his heart. She had to be disappointed with him. Stephen had another bleed and he hadn't been there. "I'm sorry I wasn't there when it happened. Is there anything I can do *nau*?"

She shook her head.

The elevator stopped on the fourth floor and he exited with Jonica and the man pushing Stephen's stretcher. She seemed indifferent to Caleb tagging along. He understood. She'd needed him and he'd let her down.

A ponytailed nurse followed them into the room. "Hi, I'm Massy. I'll be Stephen's nurse today."

Stephen opened his eyes briefly as the nurse and transporter moved him from the stretcher to the bed, but he closed his eyes again before Caleb had a chance to greet him. He studied the boy; his washed-out complexion gave him a gaunt appearance.

"He's still sleepy," Jonica explained.

Caleb nodded, though he feared Jonica was either in denial or trying to make light of something much more serious. The blood loss had to have been greater than when he cut his hand. Otherwise, why would he be admitted to the hospital? The bleeding had stopped. At least, the nose bandage wasn't blood soaked. Jonica's solemnness worried him more than if she'd been pacing or crying or panic stricken. She didn't even appear on the verge of tears.

"Can you tell me why Stephen is being admitted?" the nurse asked.

"His nose wouldn't stop bleeding," Jonica said. "The *doktah* wants to keep him overnight. He said something about giving him blood and Stephen might need more, depending on his labs. I don't remember everything the *doktah* said."

Her doleful tone meant fatigue had set in. Caleb leaned closer to Jonica and lowered his voice. "Are you doing okay?" Stupid question. Of course she wasn't okay. Her son was in the hospital.

"*Jah*," she said, but her forlorn gaze at her sleeping son suggested otherwise.

The nurse continued to question Jonica, asking about Stephen's past medical history, until her pager buzzed, summoning her out of the room.

Silence hung between Jonica and Caleb several seconds too long for him. He cleared his throat. "Did Stephen fall or bump his nose on something that started the bleeding?"

She shook her head. "He sneezed."

"Sneezed?"

Jonica moved over to the window and wrapped her arms in a self-hug as she stared outside at the parking lot.

Caleb came up beside her and placed his hand on her back. Her body tensed, yet she didn't attempt to move. "I know *nett* knowing what's going on with Stephen is difficult, and seeing him in the hospital bed is painful."

"I waited for you."

"I'm sorry, Jonica. Please, forgive me. If I could change what happened to Stephen . . . or this morning's events—"

"You can't."

His throat dried.

"Neither can I," she muttered.

He pressed his hand on her back a little harder and she turned into his arms. Holding her close as she cried, he wished he could wipe every tear away. *Lord, please have mercy on Jonica.*

Heal her sohn. Give him a long, fulfilled life. Lord, show me how I can help.

After a long moment, Jonica pushed back from his embrace and wiped her face with her hands. "I can't keep doing this."

"Doing what?"

"Falling to pieces. I can't keep . . ." She made a hand gesture at Caleb. "Doing that—I have to be strong."

"*Doing that* as in, letting someone comfort you?"

"You, Caleb. I can't let *you* comfort me."

Her words punched him in the stomach. He wanted to be the one she leaned on, someone she could depend on. Caleb noticed a box of tissues on the bedside stand and lumbered across the room to retrieve it. "You don't have to go through this alone." He offered her the box. "I care . . . deeply for you—and Stephen."

She plucked a tissue from the box and used it to dab her eyes. "Why are you limping?"

What? Was she really asking about his leg when he'd just poured out his heart? He exhaled his pent-up breath. She didn't want his comfort. Didn't want to know he cared—*deeply*. Why did he admit that? Obviously she didn't feel the same.

"Did you do something to your leg this morning?"

"It's nothing. I got pinned by a steer." He needed some distance, a few minutes to think, to regroup. Jonica had set new boundaries, or reestablished ones that had been there all along and he'd ignored.

"*There's a man in Cedar Ridge who wants to marry me.*" Recalling what she had said in the doctor's office, he took a step backward. He would respect her wishes. "I, um." He motioned to the door. "I should check on *mei daed*. He had a heart attack earlier."

"*Ach!* I didn't know." Jonica's forehead wrinkled with concern. "How is he doing?"

243

"The *doktah* said it was mild." He shrugged. "He was still sedated when I left his intensive care unit. I was on *mei* way to find a pay phone to call Beverly. I need to get word to Bishop Zook and make arrangements for the horses and livestock to be fed and watered." He rubbed the back of his neck. "I also wanted Beverly to stop at Edna's so you would know what happened. I thought maybe she could take you and Stephen into town if you hadn't gone already."

She lowered her head. "I was too anxious to wait."

"And it's *gut* you didn't. Otherwise, Stephen—" Caleb couldn't say out loud what they both had to be thinking. Stephen might have bled out.

"I'm glad we ran into each other," she said. "But you should be with your *daed*. He might wake up and need you."

Caleb nodded, though he'd come to accept that his father would never need him. On the off chance that he did, his father would be too stubborn to admit it. More importantly, did Jonica need him?

Chapter 24

C aleb had only been gone a few minutes and Jonica already felt his absence. She sank into the chair next to Stephen's bed. The limited amount of window light cast long shadows in the room, but she didn't want to turn on the overhead light for fear of disturbing Stephen. He needed rest.

She leaned her head back against the cushion and closed her eyes. But she couldn't sleep with Caleb's words replaying in her mind.

"You don't have to go through this alone . . . I care deeply . . ."

Jonica didn't dare admit how much she'd come to care for Caleb or how dependent she'd become on his support. His wisdom. His kind nature. Not only toward her. Caleb treated Stephen good. Better than good. He treated Stephen as his own.

She should have noticed him limping sooner. When he'd gotten on the elevator or while walking beside him down the hall. She'd been too self-absorbed in her own problems. He'd pushed the injury off as though he was fine, but was he?

Light from the hallway entered the room as the door opened. Jonica shot up from the chair when someone flipped on the overhead light. It took a half second for her eyes to adjust, but when they did, she saw that a tall, thinly built man with a close-shaved, salt-and-pepper beard had entered the room.

"Hi, I'm Dr. Yarbrough." The man extended his hand. "Are you Stephen's mother?"

"*Jah.*" She shook his hand. "I'm Jonica Muller."

"*Mamm?*" Stephen woke up, startled.

"I'm right here, sweetie." She went to the head of the bed and reached for his hand.

"You must be Stephen." The doctor approached the other side of the bed. "I'm Dr. Yarbrough. How are you feeling?"

Stephen squinted, then rubbed his eyes.

"I just want to take a look at you. It will only take a few minutes, and I promise it won't hurt."

Stephen rolled Jonica's direction and lifted his arms. "*Mamm!*"

"I'll be right here. I'm *nett* leaving." Jonica held Stephen's hand, then nodded at the doctor.

Dr. Yarbrough removed his stethoscope from around his neck, inserted the earpieces, then listened to Stephen's heart, lungs, and abdomen, then he tapped his fingers over several places just below his rib cage on his right side.

"How is he?"

"His heart and lungs sound normal. His liver doesn't appear to be enlarged." Dr. Yarbrough replaced Stephen's bedcovers. "You did well, Stephen. Thank you."

"*Welkum.*"

"Now, I would like to talk with your mother a few minutes in the hall."

Stephen's eyes widened. "*Mamm*, don't leave me."

"I won't be long." Jonica kept her voice as even as possible to hide the fear setting up camp within her.

"Promise?"

"*Jah*, I promise." She kissed his forehead, then followed Dr. Yarbrough out the door. "How bad is he?"

The doctor pointed to a small alcove of chairs in a waiting area. "Maybe you should sit down."

Jonica had waited days to find out what was wrong with her son, and now, studying the doctor's long face, his subdued manner, something told her she didn't want to hear the news. She eased into the chair and folded her hands on her lap.

"Stephen has an abnormal bleeding condition called von Willebrand disease. It's a clotting disorder. That's why it took so long for his nose to stop bleeding and when he'd cut his hand."

"What does that—?" She clutched her chest as sharpness seized her breath. "What does that mean? Is *mei sohn* going to—?"

"There is no cure for von Willebrand disease."

Jonica shook her head. She was overly tired. Dreaming. This wasn't happening . . . it couldn't be happening. But even as her mind searched for reason not to believe, she could hear the doctor's voice drone in the background, albeit, muffled. No wonder Dr. Yarbrough wanted her to sit down.

"I noted several bruises on his arms and legs. Based on the yellow-green coloration, they are old bruises, and I don't believe they pose a threat . . ."

Dr. Yarbrough's voice droned on, his words blending into the background of Jonica's subconscious. Should she take Stephen to a different doctor? Someone who would run better tests, offer more hope? Someone who would . . . "*It is the* LORD *who goes before you. He will be with you; he will not leave you or forsake you. Do not fear or be dismayed.*"

Jonica buried her head in her hands. "Lord, I can't lose *mei sohn!*"

Dr. Yarbrough stopped talking. "Having this disease doesn't mean Stephen cannot live a full life."

She sat up straighter. "It doesn't?"

"Your son's clotting disorder can be managed. He won't be able to play contact sports like football or rugby. You'll have to monitor him closely for bleeding, and he will need regular lab work to make sure his hemoglobin, hematocrit, and platelet counts are adequate. He might require occasional blood transfusions, and should he need surgery, special medicine will be needed to help him clot."

"But Stephen will live. Is that what you're telling me?"

Dr. Yarbrough nodded. "With close monitoring and ongoing care. You'll need to make sure others involved with his care, such as babysitters, daycare workers, schoolteachers, are informed about his condition and know how to handle an emergency."

Tears of joy streamed down her face. *Thank You, Lord, for the mercy You've shown me.* Danki, *God.*

"Since von Willebrand is a hereditary disease, you should have the other members of the family tested. Unless a major trauma occurs, it could go years undiagnosed. This condition doesn't always present with symptoms. Stephen's siblings are at risk."

"Stephen is *mei* only child." She brushed away more tears to clear her vision. "Can he go home?"

"I want to make sure he doesn't start bleeding again. One of the dangers of losing too much blood is not having enough iron in your system. Iron carries oxygen, and low levels of oxygen can lead to numerous issues, including organ damage. I also want to run a few more tests that will measure how his clotting factors function in greater detail."

"Do you think his organs have been damaged?"

"At this point nothing leads me to suspect any serious problems. As I already mentioned, his heart, lungs, and abdomen all sound normal. His liver doesn't appear to be enlarged. I don't believe we will find anything more conclusive by doing the additional tests, but the results will represent a baseline should we need a comparison at a later date. Something you'll need to keep in mind and monitor regularly are bruises. It's important they don't go unchecked. Otherwise, he could hemorrhage internally, essentially bleed to death if his organs become damaged." He paused. "Do you have any questions for me?"

Jonica shook her head, her throat too constricted to speak.

"If you think of anything, you can have the nurse page me. I'll see you and Stephen again tomorrow."

"Okay, thank you, *Doktah*." Jonica sat in the alcove several minutes. She didn't want Stephen to see that she'd been crying. She wanted to find a better time, when Stephen was fully awake, to talk about his condition. He would have to learn to be mindful in everything he did and report any signs of bruising.

But her son would live. "*Danki,* God. It is You who goes before me. You will be with me. *Danki,* Father, for your mercy."

The entire time Caleb sat at his father's bedside, his thoughts were on Jonica, alone with a sick child. But if he were sitting with Jonica, his mother would be alone. Caleb was torn.

Mamm patted Caleb's leg with her hand. "You're tapping again."

He hadn't been aware he'd been tapping his boot against the floor. "Sorry." He stood, walked to the sink on the far wall, and splashed a handful of cold water on his face.

"Maybe you should go home and get some sleep," *Mamm* said.

Sleep wouldn't help. He needed to know how Stephen was doing. If Jonica had heard anything from the doctor yet.

"The *doktah* said your *daed* is going to be okay."

"*Jah*, I know." He sat back down. He debated on telling his mother about Stephen. She hadn't been thrilled to learn he'd spent time with Jonica. But Stephen needed everyone's prayers. "It isn't just *Daed* I'm worried about. Stephen Muller is a patient in the pediatric unit."

"Who?"

His mother knew very well *who* Stephen was. But since she was exhausted, he gave her the benefit of doubt. "Stephen is Jonica's *sohn*. Jonica Muller."

"What's wrong with him?"

"Jonica doesn't know. His nose started bleeding and—"

"She brought him to the hospital for a nosebleed?" *Mamm* made a *tsk-tsk* sound. "That will cost a pretty penny."

"I don't think she's concerned about money when her *sohn* is lying in a hospital bed." He'd never known his mother to be this inconsiderate.

"Peter used to have nosebleeds," she said reflectively. "That's why we had multiple pans of water on the woodstove. Steam helped."

"That's a *gut* suggestion. I'll pass that information on for Jonica to try," he said, grateful that, in her way, she was attempting to help.

"A *mamm* figures those things out. She also figures out how to stop bleeding. If I ran Peter to the *doktah* every time something happened . . . Well, she's a . . . *young mamm*."

Enough. Caleb stood again. "I'm going to get another cup of *kaffi*. Would you like me to bring you back some?"

"Are you really going for *kaffi*, or are you going to see . . . that *maedel*?"

"Both." He wouldn't hide his feelings any longer. "Jonica is alone. She needs me."

His mother popped up from the chair like a kernel of heated

corn. "I need you." She clutched her chest. "Your *daed* is lying on that hospital bed with all sorts of tubes in him. Don't you think your *daed* needs you to be here too?"

"*Mamm*, I'm praying. That's all I can do—all either of us can do. I'll bring you a cup of *kaffi* when I return." Caleb stopped at the door. "I'll also be praying that God places Stephen on your heart so you'll start praying for him. We're instructed to pray for others, and he's sick."

Jonica noticed Stephen's smile widen before she noticed Caleb tiptoeing into the room, one hand behind his back.

"Caleb!" Stephen pushed the button on the bed remote and raised the head. "You came to see me."

"I had to check on *mei* buddy." He held up a stuffed dog he'd been hiding behind his back. "I think this *hund* is looking for a friend."

"I'll be his friend." Stephen took the toy and hugged it.

"That's very nice of Caleb," Jonica said. "What do you say, Stephen?"

"*Danki*, Caleb."

"You're *welkum*."

As Stephen played with the stuffed toy, Jonica stepped away from the bed, motioning Caleb with a nod to follow her over to the window. "He might go home tomorrow."

"Did the *doktah* say what's wrong?"

"He has von Willebrand disease. It causes abnormal bleeding due to missing or damaged clotting factors. I don't know all the particulars of the disease, only that Dr. Yarbrough said Stephen could live an active life. He just needs to be careful." She grabbed Caleb's hands without thinking and gave them a squeeze. "Can you believe what God has done! He answered *mei* prayer."

"That's *wunderbaar* news."

She followed his gaze to their hands, then pulled hers back. "I'm sorry. I, um . . . was overly excited."

"Don't be sorry." He took her hands into his. "I want you to celebrate your *gut* news with me. What God has done. It's a blessing for me too." His eyes glossed over and he clamped his lips together.

Watching Caleb's reaction, Jonica's emotions bubbled to the surface. There was no one she'd rather share the news with, celebrate with, than Caleb.

Stephen giggled.

Jonica jerked her hands free from Caleb's. Heat rushed up her neck to her face. She didn't need to ask her son what he was giggling about; he'd been watching them.

Caleb crossed the room and sat on the corner of Stephen's bed. "Have you decided on a name for your pup?"

"Rusty."

"That's a *gut* name."

"Do you like *mei mamm*?"

"Stephen!" Jonica rasped. "That isn't something you—I apologize."

Caleb chuckled. "I like your *mamm* a lot, Stephen. Is that okay with you?"

Stephen nodded. "Can I get a real dog?"

"That's something you'll have to ask your *mamm*." He stood. "I need to go. I promised to bring *mei mamm* a cup of *kaffi*. I am very glad to see you are doing better. You take care of Rusty."

Jonica followed Caleb to the door and lowered her voice. "You know he's going to needle me about getting a dog *nau*."

Caleb grinned. "I know where we can get him a puppy."

Jonica furrowed her brows and pinned him with the sternest glare she could muster despite his adorable lopsided smirk. "*Nay.*"

"Hmm. I suppose that's a topic for another time."

Jonica laughed. She loved that she and Caleb could joke around. It felt good to laugh again.

"Caleb," Stephen said, stopping him as he turned to leave. "Will you *kumm* back to see me again?"

"Absolutely." Caleb winked at Jonica. "As long as *Mamm* is agreeable."

"You're putting me on the spot again, aren't you?"

Caleb nodded. "Absolutely."

Chapter 25

Jonica hadn't seen Caleb since Stephen was discharged from the hospital. Three days ago. She understood he had extra chores to do at home with his father still on the mend, but knowing that didn't stop her from missing him or constantly looking out the window in hopes of seeing his horse and buggy pull into the driveway.

Edna shuffled into the kitchen. "Is Stephen's condition contagious?"

"*Nay*. He has a blood disease." Jonica gave the abbreviated version. She'd already explained to her aunt, in great detail, what the doctor had said—multiple times.

"A boy his age shouldn't be cooped up in the *haus* all day. He should be outside playing."

"*Jah*, I agree, but he's still recovering."

"How long does it take to recover from a nosebleed?" Her aunt lifted her brows. "He isn't wearing a bandage on his hand or his nose for that matter. The cut looks to be healed."

Jonica nodded. "You're right. He does need some fresh air."

"*Gut.*" *Aenti* Edna stepped around the corner to the entryway. "You can go."

Go. Who was Aenti *talking to? Stephen?* The front door opened and closed before Jonica could move the pan of sliced onions she'd been sautéing in butter off the stove and get to the front entry.

"He'll be *allrecht*," *Aenti* said. "He promised to stay in the yard."

Jonica scanned the wall hooks for Stephen's coat and the mat on the floor for his boots. Both were gone. "How did he dress so quickly?"

Her aunt ignored the question and swept her hand over her apron as if something had spilled on it.

"*Aenti*," Jonica scolded.

"I helped him. But he didn't go outside until you agreed about him needing fresh air. You'll stunt that boy's growth if he doesn't get some exercise."

Jonica disagreed but remained silent. She yanked the door and stuck her head outside. Stephen was going down the porch steps, his forearm stretched across the railing, removing the newly fallen snow as he went. "Stephen," she said. "Stay where I can see you."

"Okay." He bent down, scooped a handful of snow, and packed it with his hands.

"And don't throw snowballs at the *haus*."

"Okay." He continued to shape the snow into a ball.

The scent of caramelizing onions sent Jonica hurrying back into the kitchen. She gave the translucent onions a stir in the brown butter, the pungent aroma filling her senses, reminding her of the meals she'd made with her mother. Following her mother's recipe, she removed the onions from the pan and placed them in a bowl to add later. Next, she dipped the thinly sliced pieces of liver in buttermilk, then coated them with biscuit mix. Liver and onions had always been one of her favorite meals, but she'd based the meal decision on Stephen. Liver was a good source of iron, something he'd been low on in the hospital.

Jonica placed a pot of peeled potatoes on the stove and tossed in a generous pinch of salt. Then she added a few tablespoons of lard to the buttery pan she used to cook the onions. She added the meat to the splattering grease, and soon smoke drifted upward.

Jonica opened the kitchen window as much to filter out some of the smoke as to keep an ear on Stephen. She stood at the window a moment, watching Stephen who was on his knees rolling a tire-size snowball that was matted with dead leaves. He needed a friend. As an only child herself, she'd often felt alone, isolated on the farm. Though she had her parents, her grandparents, and *Aenti* Edna growing up, she longed for sewing frolics and get-togethers where she'd be around other children her age.

When Faith suggested getting the boys together, Jonica had squelched the idea for selfish reasons. Now, something told her Faith's Daniel would be a perfect playmate for Stephen. The boys were close enough in age, and Stephen needed a friend.

Sputtering grease pulled Jonica away from the window. She flipped the meat over in the pan to fry the other side.

"I don't know." Stephen's voice filtered through the open window.

"You could make a snow fort," the man said.

Caleb? Excitement bubbled up within Jonica, then fizzled just as fast when she spotted Mr. Jordan outside the window.

The older man went down on his knees. "Can I help?"

"*Jah!*"

Jonica watched the two of them stacking snow together several minutes. She wished it were Caleb and Stephen working together.

"Do you still have the bird?" Stephen asked.

The *Englischer* removed the small feathered bird from his coat pocket. "He's getting bigger, isn't he?"

"Does he miss his *mamm* and *daed*?"

"He will see them again in the spring. Until then, it's my job to watch over him."

"I wish I had a *daed*." Stephen picked a leaf off the mound of snow and twirled it around by its stem. "I asked God for one."

"Your Father in heaven has heard your prayers. Who do you think planted that desire in your heart? It was God."

"So I'm going to get one?"

"All things work together for His purpose."

Jonica pushed away from the counter and marched to the door. She couldn't let Mr. Jordan encourage Stephen to hang his hope on the impossible. In the end Stephen could become angry with God. She didn't want her son confusing the *Englischer's* words. Just because Stephen desired a *daed*, didn't mean that would happen. He had a father—his heavenly Father.

"Don't leave yet," *Mamm* said as Caleb reached for the doorknob. "I have some things I need you to do."

Caleb took a second to take a deep breath and let it out slowly. *Mamm* had kept him busy around the house the last few days, and now she was finding something else to prevent him from seeing Jonica. "What do you need me to do?"

"The garbage needs to go out to the burn pile. The bucket of scraps next to the sink can be taken out and fed to the pigs . . ." She twisted her lips. Probably thinking of more little projects to tie up his time.

"The horse stalls should be mucked out. Your *daed* cleans them out at least once a week."

"I've already done them." He grabbed the half-filled bag of trash from the canister with one hand and the scrap bucket in the other. Before she found more things to add to the never-ending to-do list, he headed to the door.

"I also need you to pick up pumpkins from the Millers."

He drew another deep breath and let it out.

"Unless you don't want pumpkin pie for Thanksgiving."

"*Jah*, okay." He took another step toward the door and stopped. "I know what you're doing."

"Oh?"

"You're intentionally finding things to keep me busy around the *haus*. Why?" He figured it had something to do with Jonica, but maybe if she admitted her role in preoccupying his time, she would realize how silly it all was.

"Is it wrong for me to want a few things done around the *haus*?"

"*Nay*." He lifted the trash bag and gave it a light shake. "Taking out a half-full bag seems wasteful to me."

"Well, I don't want it stinking up the *haus*."

"I think you don't want me visiting Jonica and Stephen."

"You said Stephen was released from the hospital. So, he's better." She turned, picked up the dishrag, and wiped down the area of the counter where the bucket had been.

"He has a bleeding disorder. Von Willebrand disease. I want to check on him."

"And his mother."

"*Jah*, Jonica too." His mother had interfered with him courting Darleen, but not to this extent. Her shoulders were shaking and she was weeping. He set the bucket and trash bag on the floor and joined her at the sink. "*Mamm*, I'll do everything I can to help around the *haus*. But I also need . . . space."

She nodded. "I know you'll do everything you can. You've always been *mei* thoughtful *sohn*."

He smiled. She meant well, but his mother had a way of

heaping guilt on him. Standing in front of the sink, Caleb glimpsed a buggy pulling into the driveway. "Someone's here to visit *Daed*."

Mamm dried her eyes. "Go see who it is."

Once again, Caleb grabbed the items his mother wanted discarded. He wanted no reason to come back into the house. After he took out the trash and fed the pigs, he planned to see Jonica. Maybe she and Stephen would like to go with him to pick up pumpkins.

"Hello, Caleb." Bishop Zook walked toward him as Melvin Yoder tied the horse to the hitching post. "How is your *daed*?"

"He's getting stronger every day." He motioned to the *haus*. "*Daed*'s resting in the sitting room, and I'm sure *Mamm* has a fresh kettle of *kaffi* on the stove."

Bishop Zook stepped forward. "We've *kumm* to talk with you, Caleb."

A "we need to talk" visitation from the bishop was bad enough, but when he brought along a church elder, something was serious. Caleb had nothing to hide.

"I'm heading out to the barn to feed the hogs if you'd like to tag along."

The bishop nodded. "That'll be fine."

Melvin said nothing, though Caleb understood the custom. The elder served as witness when accusations were made, when reprimands were given, or when someone was shunned. But Caleb hadn't done anything wrong.

Caleb placed the rubbish in the burn barrel, then headed to the barn.

Bishop Zook held the door open. "How did your *daed* do with the cattle he sold?"

"He didn't get the price he'd wanted, but considering the early snow and talk of a hard winter . . ." Caleb shrugged. "I think selling them was the right decision." He tossed the slop over the fence. "Is that what you wanted to talk about?"

"As you said yourself, it's probably going to be a hard winter," Bishop Zook said.

"*Jah*," Caleb agreed.

"Your *daed* will need help."

Caleb nodded. He still wasn't sure what this talk was all about.

"*Nett* just around the farm. He will need help financially for medical bills and general living expenses," Bishop Zook said.

The tightness in Caleb's chest eased. His father had a tendency to be prideful when it came to accepting handouts. Even when his crops failed last year along with everyone else's, he refused to take money from the district fund. Instead, his father gave what money he had so that no one went without. It'd been a struggle and his family had eaten a lot of meatless meals, but his father was grateful they hadn't burdened the system more.

"I want to offer you a job," Melvin said. "More than a job. Part ownership of the market."

It made no sense. Why would Melvin give away part of his store?

"I've always thought you would be a *gut* asset to the business, and if you and Darleen marry—"

"She didn't tell you?"

"I'm well aware that you two are no longer courting." Melvin crossed his arms. "It's admirable that you didn't want to get married without having means to support a *fraa* and *kinner*. I'm offering you that ability."

"Does Darleen know about this . . . arrangement?"

Melvin shook his head. "She doesn't always know what's best for her, which is why I'm making this arrangement for her.

At twenty-two she should be settling down, and you two have been courting for a while *nau*."

Stomach acid burned its way up the back of Caleb's throat, but he remained calm and maintained an even tone. "So, this is a marriage of convenience?"

"We don't have to look at it that way." Bishop Zook placed his hand on Caleb's shoulder. "You will be happy with Darleen. She's an upstanding member of our district, comes from a *gut*, God-fearing family, and will make a fine *fraa*."

For someone else.

"Think about it," Melvin said. "It's in the best interest of everyone. You'll have a *gut*—indoor—job with enough income to support Darleen, *kinner,* and have money left over to help your parents. They won't have to worry about their future."

"Nor should they have to worry at their age," Bishop Zook said.

Caleb had always liked and respected Darleen's father. He'd built a steady business but had spoiled his youngest daughter. Caleb just didn't want to be the toy at the bottom of the cereal box.

Chapter 26

A horse's neigh caught Jonica by surprise as she was loading her arms with firewood. Turning, she noticed Caleb's buggy pulling into the yard. Excitement fluttered. She hadn't realized how much she'd missed spending time with him until she couldn't control her quivering nerves and the tingling sensations the sight of him brought on.

"Hello, stranger." Caleb strode toward her, favoring his right side.

She smiled. "Hello, yourself." She motioned to his leg. "You're still limping."

He shrugged. "It's getting better." He gathered pieces of wood from the pile. "How's Stephen feeling?"

"He's doing great." But something was troubling Caleb. She hadn't known him long, but he seemed different and she couldn't put her finger on why.

"*Nay* more bleeding?"

"Thank the Lord, *nay*. How is your *daed*? I've been praying for him."

"*Danki* for praying. *Daed*'s finding it difficult to rest. Some days he overdoes it and ends up a little winded, but overall his health is improving."

"That's *gut* to hear." She picked up another slab of wood, and when she glanced at Caleb, he was gazing toward the wheat field with a quiet eeriness that told her something was heavy on his mind. "Everything *allrecht*?"

His attention flicked back to her. "What?"

"You had that far-off look in your eyes . . . as if the weight of the world had been placed on your shoulders."

"First, I'm *nett* that strong." He smiled.

"And second?"

His smile broadened. "Second, carrying the weight of the world is God's job."

"That doesn't mean people don't try."

"And you speak from experience?" He lifted his brows.

"*Jah*, I think that's a flaw of mine, and apparently *nett* just me." She picked up another slab of wood, the weight heavy in her arms. "Would you like to *kumm* inside for *kaffi*? Stephen should be waking up from his nap soon. I'm sure he will want to see you."

"Sounds *gut*." He grabbed a few more slabs, the bundle high in his arms, blocking most of his face.

"Are you sure you can carry that much?"

"First you compliment *mei* strength and capability to carry the weight of the world on *mei* shoulders, then you insult *mei* ability to tote an armload of wood." He chuckled. "That's a woman. Always changing her mind about something."

She pretended to scowl but was unable to hold the stern expression long. She laughed along with Caleb, wishing this moment could go on forever.

Finding *Aenti* asleep in the rocking chair, Jonica gently placed the wood into the box, then helped unload the stack Caleb held. She motioned for him to follow her to the kitchen. As she prepared the coffeepot, Caleb removed two mugs from the cabinet.

He set the mugs on the counter. "What's it like in Cedar Ridge?"

"It's a nice community. Touristy in the summer and early fall. Most of the businesses close for winter, so during those months it can feel even more isolated. But everyone stocks up on food and supplies and prepares for snowbound days or sometimes weeks. It goes with living in the Upper Peninsula."

"It sounds like you like it there."

She poured the coffee into the mugs, not sure how to answer him. "I'll admit, I didn't mind the isolation. Our sawmill was situated between state and federal land, so our nearest Amish neighbor was like from here to town with only trees in between." As an unwed pregnant teen, the more remote the better. Her parents had never indicated that was how they thought, but she often wondered if that was part of the reason they chose the business in the middle of nowhere. Jonica handed him a mug and took hers to the table.

"Without your parents . . ."

"*Jah*, it's lonely." She wasn't looking forward to spending a winter at the sawmill alone. She and Stephen had enough supplies to last several winters, but isolation would take on a different meaning now that her son had a bleeding disorder. She stood and took the sugar container over to the counter. It didn't need filling, but she needed something to do. Jonica removed the bag from the cabinet and poured more sugar into the smaller container.

Caleb came up behind her. "Maybe you should consider staying here."

She nodded without turning around.

"Edna would love the company," he said.

Edna. Nothing about him. "Did I tell you that *Aenti* isn't selling the farm?"

"I thought Mr. Jordan was interested."

She shook her head. "*Aenti* said he was never interested."

"And she was . . . in her right mind?"

"I think so."

Caleb smiled. "That's great news!"

Jonica rubbed her arms. "I thought Stephen would be up from his nap by *nau*."

"He probably needs his sleep."

"I don't want to keep you from your work. I'm sure with everything that's happened, you must be behind in whatever construction project you have going on. You won't have much more time before winter—do you even work in the winter?"

"I'm *nett* doing construction any longer." Sadness filled his eyes. "I was remodeling a *haus* with plans to sell it and use the money to purchase a large plot of land . . ."

"It never sold?"

Caleb shook his head. "It was never finished." Tears collected on his long lashes and he used the back of his hand to swipe them away. "That's where I found Peter. Lying in a pool of blood. Dead."

Jonica's throat tightened. A mix of emotions warred within her. Sorrow, sadness, and anger toward Peter for what he'd done to his brother, to his family—to her and Stephen.

She placed her hand on Caleb's arm. "I'm sorry," she whispered.

He attempted to smile, then rested his hands on her shoulders. The strength of his touch sent a shiver through her. He pulled her close, pressing her to his chest, his warm breaths sending tingling sensations down her neck.

Move away. Don't give your heart to him.

When he looked up, something had replaced the sadness. Her heart hammered as he studied every inch of her gaze. His fingers caressed her jaw, lifting her face to his.

Caleb was different. He wasn't self-serving. He wasn't Peter.

She closed her eyes as his lips came down on hers. His kiss was slow and tender. She raised to her toes in an effort to be closer—bonded. Her surroundings blurred as he pressed her even tighter against his chest and deepened the kiss.

Thump, thump, thump echoed from the stairs, jolting her back to reality.

༉

Caleb ignored the racket Stephen was making jumping down the stairs one step at a time. *Thump.* The average staircase had twelve steps, that was five, *Thump.* Six . . .

Jonica broke from the kiss but not from his embrace. "Caleb. That's Stephen."

When her baby blue eyes peered up at him, he disregarded every warning alarm firing through his body and kissed her once again.

The thumping stopped—Stephen had reached the landing. "*Mamm?*"

Jonica gently pressed Caleb away from her. "In the kitchen." She cleared her throat. "Sweetie." Jonica eyed Caleb. "Look what you've done to me. I can't even talk." She turned to face the counter, hands gripping the edge of the laminate as if holding on for support.

Caleb smiled. Under her pushed-up sleeves, her arms resembled a plucked chicken skin. He took a step away from Jonica just as Stephen ran into the room.

"Caleb!"

He scooped the youngster into his arms. "How are you, Stephen?"

"I'm all better, right *Mamm?*"

Jonica turned and leaned against the counter, a laid-back

smile displaying slightly swollen lips. "You look rested. How was your nap?"

She might have fooled her son with her composure, but not him. She was still rattled. He liked her off-kilter. The moment she made eye contact with him, he winked. Her sheepish reaction of looking down and rubbing her arms sent hot irons down his spine.

Caleb turned his attention to Stephen. "I thought maybe you and your *mamm* would like to go with me to pick out some pumpkins."

Stephen's eyes widened. "Can we *Mamm*? Please? I want to go." His eager gaze locked with Caleb's. "Can I bring Rusty?"

"Absolutely." Caleb lowered Stephen to the floor. "Go get your *hund*." He waited for Stephen to leave the kitchen before he faced Jonica. "Sorry, I should have waited for your permission."

She crossed her arms. "You don't wait for permission about a lot of things."

Caleb grinned. "Should I apologize for kissing you?" He inched closer. "It would be a lie though. I'm not sorry, and I definitely want to do it again." He slid his hand around the back of her neck, the silkiness of her dark hair caressing his fingers, then leaned to kiss her lightly on the forehead. "And again." He gently moved his touch to lift her chin and kissed her lips.

"Caleb, we can't do this." She sidestepped him, then adjusted her *kapp*.

Stephen returned, waving his stuffed toy in the air. "Got him. Can we go *nau*?"

For the split second that he studied Jonica, Caleb half expected her to cancel the outing. This time she appeared more than ruffled by his kiss. Something was wrong.

"Let's get your coat and boots on." She took Stephen by the hand.

"I'll get the buggy ready." He grabbed his coat on the way out the door. He had Nutmeg unhitched and the buggy aimed toward the road when Jonica and Stephen came out of the house. She kept her attention on her son going down the porch steps, then hoisted him into the buggy, planting Stephen between them on the bench.

Message received. He'd follow her rules and respect the distance. Caleb clicked his tongue and Nutmeg pitched forward. The sun had melted any trace of snow on the pavement. He took Leer Road to the end and turned right onto US-23. Taking the long way gave him more time with Jonica, plus the roads were all paved. Until he reached the Millers' entrance. The buggy wheels bogged down in the soft ground. The heavy rains they'd received earlier in the year had exposed a network of tree roots that sprawled across the long driveway.

Stephen laughed as the bumps lifted him off the bench. He'd chatted the entire trip about what size pumpkin he wanted to pick out, and now his neck was stretched looking toward the crop.

Caleb stopped the buggy near the oak tree at the corner of the flagged-off parking area. Several cars and trucks took up an entire row. The Millers' patch was the largest in the area, and people came from all over the county to select pumpkins.

He tied Nutmeg to a low-hanging limb as Jonica helped Stephen down from the bench. Caleb's boots sank into the soft ground. He bent down and picked up Stephen. "I'll let you down once we get out of the muddy area."

"I think I like the snow better." Jonica came up alongside Caleb, arms teetering.

His mother's friend Agnes Miller was sitting at the picnic table collecting money from a customer, while her husband, Clyde, was busy in the field helping other customers. Caleb headed toward Agnes. Once he reached dry ground, he lowered Stephen.

"Hello, Caleb." Agnes peered over her glasses. "And who is this cutie?"

"This is Stephen." Caleb placed his hand on the boy's shoulder. "He's a little distracted by all the pumpkins." He motioned to Jonica. "Do you remember Edna's niece, Jonica?"

"*Hiya*, Jonica. How long will you be visiting?"

"I'm *nett* sure." She redirected her attention to Stephen who had wandered toward the patch. "Stephen, you need to wait for me." She glanced apologetically at Agnes. "I don't want to come across rude, but I should be with him."

"I understand, dear." Agnes smiled. "He's excited. *Geh.*"

Caleb followed Jonica with his gaze.

"Your mother's pumpkins are in the crates under the tarp." Agnes pointed at the garden shed. "She always buys *mei* odd-size ones at the end of the season."

"*Jah*, I'm looking forward to her making pumpkin pie." Caleb wasn't in a hurry to load the crates. He wanted to observe Jonica interact with her son. She was a good mother. Gentle and patient and everything he wanted in a *fraa*.

Caleb swallowed hard. He'd never thought that way about any woman. The notion didn't put him on edge as he'd been when Darleen hounded him about marriage. He assumed the combination of Peter's death, lack of finances, and the uncertainty of his future had uncovered a fear of commitment. But now it seemed deep down he had sensed something was missing between Darleen and him. Kissing Jonica had healed his heart. He wanted to spend time with her and Stephen. Every minute of every day.

But money was still an issue. His parents needed help. And he'd proven he wasn't much of a farmer. What could he offer Jonica and Stephen except a broken man?

"Caleb." Stephen pointed to the vines at his feet. "I found a big one. *Kumm see.*"

"Sounds like the *bu* has found the one he wants." Agnes handed Caleb a knife. "Save Clyde some time, if you will, and cut the *bu's* pumpkin vine for him."

Caleb met Jonica and Stephen in the field. "That's a big pumpkin. Are you sure that's the one you want?"

Stephen nodded.

Jonica took him by the hand. "Let's stand back so we're *nett* in Caleb's way."

Caleb chopped the vine and hoisted the pumpkin into his arms.

Stephen's mouth gaped. "*Mamm*, look at it."

"You picked out a *gut* one." Jonica smiled. "It'll make a couple loaves of bread and at least one pie."

"Pumpkin pie is *mei* favorite," Caleb said.

Jonica chuckled. "You're invited."

"Exactly what I wanted to hear." Caleb lifted the pumpkin. "I'll take this one up to the table. Stephen, help your *mamm* find another pumpkin." He winked at Jonica. "The more pies the better."

Caleb paid for the pumpkins, then loaded his mother's crates and Jonica's pumpkins in the back of the buggy. The small amount of activity in the pumpkin patch had worn Stephen out. He crawled up on his mother's lap on the ride home and laid his head on her shoulder.

"He had a fun time." Jonica combed her fingers through Stephen's hair.

"What about you?"

"*Jah*, it was nice to get out of the *haus*. *Danki*."

"About what happened in the kitchen," he said. "I should have asked."

"I would have said *nay*," she said, softly.

As if he'd been seared with a blacksmith's iron and pounded into another shape, he ached all over. He'd messed up. *Apologize.*

A lovely pink blush colored her cheeks. "I'm glad you didn't . . . ask."

"You're *nett* upset with me then?"

Jonica shook her head, then motioned to the mailbox coming up on the right. "Will you stop so I can get the mail, please?"

He'd do anything for her. Caleb pulled back on the reins, then set the brake and jumped out. He snatched the only envelope in the box.

A letter addressed to Jonica Muller. Sent from someone named Ephraim King in Cedar Ridge.

Caleb's stomach knotted.

Chapter 27

Jonica turned Ephraim's letter over in her hand. She wished she hadn't asked Caleb to get the mail. The letter had put a damper on both their moods, and she hadn't even opened it yet.

"Is that the man who—?"

"*Jah.*" Hopefully her sharp reply sent a strong enough message. She wasn't going to discuss Ephraim around Stephen. Her son wasn't aware of the marriage proposal. He'd been praying for a father without knowing someone in Cedar Ridge had already offered to take on that responsibility.

Caleb signaled his horse and focused making the turn into the driveway. His jaw muscles twitched.

Stephen yawned, then sat up straighter. He pointed at the horse and buggy next to the house. "Who's here?"

"Maybe one of *Aenti* Edna's friends have *kumm* for a visit."

"That's Gideon and Faith's horse," Caleb said, not hiding the disappointment in his tone.

Stephen wiggled on Jonica's lap. "Did Daniel *kumm* to play with me?"

"I don't know, sweetie."

Stephen scrambled to get out of the buggy the moment Caleb set the brake. He hurried up the steps ahead of them.

Caleb reached for Jonica's arm and stopped her at the foot of the porch steps. "Are you going back to Cedar Ridge soon?"

Was he asking her to stay? "Stephen has a follow-up appointment and more blood work scheduled." It wasn't the answer he was looking for, but it was all she could give at the moment.

"*Mamm*," Stephen said, working the doorknob with mitten hands. "I can't get the door to open."

Caleb released her arm. "I'll unload your pumpkins."

Jonica continued up the steps. When she opened the door, heat from the woodstove warmed her face.

Stephen peeled off his coat and handed it to Jonica to place on the hook. He sat on the floor and was pulling his boot off when a curly-haired child came around the corner.

"I'm Daniel." He pointed at his chest. The child had Faith's blue eyes and Gideon's slightly oversize ears.

"I'm Stephen. Want to play with *mei* horse?"

"Let me help you with your boots first." Jonica gave the muddy boots a yank and took Stephen's sock off at the same time. "Wait," she said as he started to stand. "You have to wear your socks." She slipped it back on his foot. "*Nay* roughhousing."

As the boys scurried into the sitting room to play, Jonica removed her winter cloak and winter bonnet, then kicked off her boots and shoved them against the wall.

Caleb came to the door holding both pumpkins in his arms. He stomped his boots on the mat.

"Don't worry about removing your boots," she said. "I'll mop later."

Caleb winced. "*Jah*, I wasn't planning to stay. I need to get the other pumpkins home to *mei mamm*." He headed into the kitchen. "*Hiya*, Faith, Edna." He set the pumpkins on the counter, then turned to leave.

Jonica followed him to the door. "*Danki* again for the pumpkins. I hope you will still plan to *kumm* over for pie."

"I'll try. *Mei mamm* has been keeping me busy around the *haus*." He opened the door and paused. "I'll see you later."

Unexplainable heaviness filled Jonica's heart when Caleb left. She watched his buggy leave before going into the kitchen to join Faith and *Aenti* Edna.

Aenti motioned to a basket on the counter. "Faith brought us some baked goods. Isn't that sweet of her?"

"It isn't much," Faith said.

"That is very sweet of you. *Danki*." Jonica poured a mug of coffee.

Aenti stood. "I'll keep a watchful eye on the boys while you two catch up."

"They should be fine," Jonica said. "You don't have to leave."

"I'm eager to finish the scarf I've been working on. You two enjoy your time." She shuffled into the other room.

As if Faith had been waiting on pins and needles for *Aenti* to leave the room, she leaned forward. "So, you and Caleb went out picking pumpkins together. Hmm . . ."

"He thought Stephen would enjoy getting out of the *haus*."

Faith shook her head. "He's interested in Stephen's *mamm*. It's written all over his face. I see it in his eyes when he looks at you."

Jonica lowered her head. "He kissed me today."

"And?"

"And it would never work. Caleb doesn't know his *bruder* . . . Peter is Stephen's father."

Faith's jaw dropped. "I didn't know."

"I never told anyone, except *mei* parents and Peter, but they're all . . . no longer with us." She touched her throat as she swallowed and closed her eyes a moment. "Peter and I were on *rumspringa.* It just . . . happened. I thought—" She shook her head. "I was a fool. He was planning to jump the fence—for good. Even after I told him that I was . . . It wasn't some wild attempt to snare him."

"You could have told me. We would have remained friends."

"I was so embarrassed. Ashamed. Plus, you were still dealing with your own issues, finding out about your biological parents."

Faith nodded. "I was sort of lost in *mei* own crumbling world back then. But things worked out okay for both of us, *jah*?"

Did it all work out? She wouldn't have lost her parents had they not moved. Jonica removed the hankie she kept stashed up her dress sleeve. "Peter had a change of heart once the news soaked in. Well, sort of. Of course, he'd been guilt ridden when he said he'd do the right thing and marry me—but he wanted me to jump the fence with him. He refused to live by our Amish way. And I refused to leave *mei* family, *mei* beliefs—leave God. I had the chance to rectify *mei* wrongs . . . but the cost was too great."

"Peter was a troubled soul and I'm glad you didn't leave the faith with him. But Caleb is different." Faith took Jonica's hands in hers. "You have to tell him."

"He's still very torn up about his *bruder*'s death. He won't want anything to do with me. I can't blame him. It'd be impossible for anyone." Except for Ephraim, who needed someone to care for his children.

"Caleb is nothing like Peter. Tell him."

Jonica nodded. Her friend was right, especially now that Caleb had kissed her. She couldn't withhold that information. But how did one begin that type of conversation? She'd been ashamed of her waywardness and had worried about what others thought of her for so long, it'd become normal. But Caleb had treated her different. He'd shown respect and hadn't even asked about Stephen's father—why?

ced̮

It'd been a week since Caleb had seen Jonica—a week since she'd received the letter from the man who wanted to marry her. At first Caleb didn't balk when his mother gave him a list of chores that kept his days and nights busy. He needed time to get his head together. He wasn't the jealous type—until he thought her heart belonged to someone else. The conversation after their kiss repeated in his mind.

"I should have asked."

"I would have said nay." Her initial response had caught him off guard. When she added, "I'm glad you didn't ask," he believed her.

"Caleb." His mother's voice interrupted his thoughts. "You need to finish your pancakes. I need you to take your *daed* into town for his follow-up *doktah*'s appointment." She placed her hand on his shoulder. "I won't be able to catch him if he falls."

Daed entered the kitchen grumbling that he'd heard her. "I'm *nett* going to fall."

"Until the *doktah* says you're strong enough, you need to accept help from others." She turned back to Caleb. "You don't have anything else to do today, do you?"

Only miscellaneous things you find for me to do.

Daed grunted putting on his boots. "I'm perfectly capable of driving *mei* own buggy."

"I don't mind," Caleb said. "I have a few things to do in town anyway."

"At Yoder's Market?" *Mamm*'s brows arched, and there was no mistaking the smile. She wanted him to go to the market.

"Why do you ask?" If she needed something picked up, he'd stop at the *Englisch* grocery store.

"I thought you might be ready to accept Melvin's job offer."

It wasn't just a job proposition, but something told him she was well aware of the arrangement. "*Nay*, I need to talk with Luke at the hardware store." Caleb shoved the last bite of food in his mouth, washed it down with milk, then stood. "I'll hitch the horse."

He rushed out of the house before his mother pelted him with more questions. He planned to help them with the medical bills, but not by being strong-armed into marriage. Even if Jonica went back up north.

Daed ambled out of the house, leaning more on *Mamm* for support than what his father would admit. He was breathless and needed Caleb's help to get onto the buggy bench.

"Are you coming, *Mamm*?" Caleb asked, surprised she'd turned back to the house.

"It's only a checkup," *Daed* said. "Your *mamm* has other things she needs to do."

What "other things" were more important than going with her husband to his *doktah*'s appointment? His parents were acting odd.

"Don't be late," his mother said.

Caleb climbed into the buggy. "She's acting strange."

"The women's sewing frolic location was moved to our *haus*. She has a lot to prepare before Friday."

Caleb wasn't sure what would need to be done between now and Friday, but something told him it would involve his help. "And you're *allrecht* with a houseful of women while you're still recovering?"

Daed stared straight ahead. "If it's important to your *mamm*, it's important to me."

His father's near-death experience must have changed him. Either that, or he was worried his heart would give out again.

"Watch the pothole," *Daed* said.

Too late. Caleb didn't veer the horse to the other side of the road in time and the wagon wheel came down hard, giving the buggy a jolt.

"That's hard on the horse. Hard on the buggy. You could have damaged one of the wheels. You need to be more mindful of where you're going."

"*Jah*, I'll try." So much for believing his father had changed. "Just relax. You don't want your blood pressure soaring."

"How can I relax when you're all over the road?"

Caleb allowed his mind to drift to a better place. Jonica had kissed him back. She responded. He pictured Stephen's smile as he pointed to the pumpkin he'd selected. The more time he spent away from them, the more he missed them. Focusing his thoughts on Jonica and Stephen, Caleb was able to block out everything else. His father's crankiness, his mother's constant clinginess, his shattered family. The bishop and Melvin's visit. The marriage arrangement. He had to see Jonica—today.

Pulling into the doctor's office parking lot, all of the places were filled. He dropped *Daed* off at the front door, then looked for a spot in the back of the building to tie his mare.

Stabbing pain shot up Caleb's leg as he lumbered toward the front of the building. The lobby was full of patients. *Daed* was standing at the front desk, jotting his name on the sign-in log. Caleb waited until he finished, then walked him to an empty seat, standing close by as he sat in case he needed assistance.

"Didn't you say you had errands to run?" his father said the moment Caleb sat.

"It can wait." His leg was hurting and the thought of walking to the back of the building again made him inwardly cringe.

"*Nay*," *Daed* said. "Do what you have to do. No sense in both of us sitting in the lobby doing nothing."

"Are you sure you'll be okay?"

"It's just a checkup."

Caleb didn't like leaving *Daed* alone, but he also didn't want to agitate him more by staying. He scanned the room, counting to himself how many patients were waiting to be seen. "I'll probably be back by the time your name is called."

"Don't rush. Take your time."

Caleb left the office and climbed into his buggy, more confused than ever—until he passed Yoder's Market on the way to the lumberyard. Then it hit him like a shovel to the head. His father must have thought he was going to the market to accept Melvin's arrangement. To propose to Darleen.

"Lord, I need help. I need a job." He pulled into the hardware/lumberyard, tied Nutmeg to the post, and went into the office, doing his best not to favor his leg.

"How's it going, Caleb?" Luke stood from behind the desk and came around to the customer side of the counter of the small office.

"I'm *gut*. You?"

After a few minutes of small talk about the new county building codes, Luke asked, "What brings you in today?"

"I'm looking for a job. You know *mei* background in construction. I can be a help to you and your customers."

"You would be a great asset. But you know how it is around here in the winter. Construction comes to a halt. People may do some minor indoor home improvements, but, for the most part, the lumber and building materials sit in storage."

Caleb nodded. Even when he was in construction, he did very little during the winter.

"I can use you in the spring if you want to check back. I

know that's several months away, but"—he shrugged—"I barely keep the doors open during the winter as it is."

"Thanks anyways."

"If you want to post a handyman sign on the board, I could probably snag you a few customers. I'll give you a good reference. With all the lumber and supplies you've purchased over the years, I've never heard one disgruntled customer of yours, and I hear it all. The people around here have only good things to say about your company."

"*Danki.* I'll keep the handyman idea in mind." Caleb hung his head as he left the building. Disappointed in himself—in God. "You know how much I need a job. If I posted a handyman sign, how would people get in touch with me without a phone or phone shanty in the district?"

He prayed for wisdom as he climbed into the buggy, then pulled out of the parking lot and prayed even harder as Yoder's Market came into view. "Lord, I need help. *Please*, give me wisdom. I might have found happiness with Darleen had Jonica *nett kumm* back to town."

A driver behind him wailed on his horn as Caleb waited for traffic to clear before he made the left-hand turn into the doctor's office. He didn't trust impatient drivers, especially ones who thought nothing of blowing their horns. Once the road was safe, he tapped the reins. He parked in the same spot and tied Nutmeg to the commercial-size trash container. The moment he set his foot on the ground, pain shot up his leg again. As a result of trying to disguise his limp at the lumber store, he'd inadvertently made it worse.

His father wasn't sitting in the lobby. "I'm Abraham Schulmann's *sohn.*"

"The nurse just took him back, sir," the receptionist said. "I'll buzz you in."

Caleb waited for the door to unlock between the lobby and the hallway to the exam rooms, then waited to be directed to his father's room.

"What happened to your leg?" one of the nurses asked.

"I got pinned between a herd of cattle and the fence. I think the fence won."

She chuckled. "I guess that's better than a bull."

"*Jah.*" He probably wouldn't be walking at all if one of the steers had stepped on him.

"I'm sure Dr. Mallory will take a look at it. How long ago did it happen?"

"A couple weeks ago. I injured *mei* leg the same day *mei daed* had a heart attack."

"You shouldn't still be limping. You might have a hairline fracture."

Caleb shook his head. "I don't want to hear that."

She opened the first door on her right and flipped on the light.

Caleb hesitated. "This isn't *mei daed*'s room."

"You need to have your leg checked. I can tell by a person's expression when they're in pain. You're hurting." She motioned to the table. "Have a seat and I'll let Dr. Mallory know you're here."

"I can't afford this. Just take care of *mei daed.* I'll be fine."

"You don't have to worry about your father. We'll take care of him. But you need to let Dr. Mallory determine if you're fine." She smiled. "I happen to know Mrs. Mallory would like some flower boxes built. I'm guessing you can negotiate, and between you and me, her birthday is coming up."

Caleb still hesitated. His leg was swollen and stiff, but he could get around.

"You can't afford not to have your leg checked out. It could be something serious."

❧

A buggy pulled into the yard, and Jonica's heart raced. She sped to the door expecting Caleb but was taken aback by his mother.

"*Hiya*, Jonica. May I *kumm* in?"

"Sure." She stood aside and waited for Deborah Schulmann to pass. "I'll let *Aenti* Edna know you're here."

"I've *kumm* to see you. Shall we sit somewhere?"

Jonica's stomach dropped. Did she know about Stephen being Peter's son? Surely Faith wouldn't have said anything.

Jonica motioned to the kitchen. "I'll put the *kaffi* pot on."

Her secret would be discovered sooner or later. She just wished she'd been more prepared. Jonica led Deborah into the kitchen.

"I can't stay long." Looking around, Deborah's gaze seemed to stop on Stephen's pumpkin sitting on the counter. Her eyes narrowed.

Jonica pretended not to notice and busied herself preparing the coffeepot with fresh grounds.

"I'm *nett* sure if you've heard." Deborah began the conversation. "The women are having a sewing frolic."

Jonica breathed easier. Perhaps this was a friendly visit.

"Friday, from noon to three at *mei* place. Everyone is bringing a dish to pass."

"*Danki* for letting us know." She poured two mugs of coffee. "I'll be sure to pass along the news to *mei aenti*." She forced a smile as she placed Deborah's mug and a spoon on the table.

"It's been a while since you've been in town. Has it been four or five years?"

"Five and a half." His mother was much harder than she'd remembered. Caleb had said that Peter's death had changed his *mamm* and *daed*, and Jonica sympathized with their loss. Her parents' deaths had changed her too.

Deborah added a spoonful of sugar and stirred the coffee. "A lot of things have changed."

"I heard about Peter. I'm very sorry for your loss."

Deborah's stirring stopped. "I didn't *kumm* here to talk about Peter."

Jonica turned away from the table and disguised her relief in a cough.

"Caleb has the chance to become part owner of Yoder's Market. It's an opportunity he needs to . . . make the most of."

Stephen zipped into the kitchen, his stuffed dog in his hand. "Can I have a *kichlin*?"

"Maybe later. We have a guest."

Stephen faced Deborah. "Want to see *mei* horse?" Before she had a chance to answer, Stephen sidled up on the chair beside her. "See."

"That's a nice-looking horse you have." Deborah shifted away from him.

Stephen tugged her dress sleeve. "Want to see *mei* wooden horse?"

"Stephen, sweetie, you're being rude." Jonica needed to come up with something to occupy him while Deborah was here. "I think *Aenti* Edna is looking for you."

"Nope. She's sleeping."

"Maybe you should check on her." Jonica popped up from the chair. "Here, take *Aenti* a *kichlin*." She handed him two pumpkin-spice cookies.

"For me?"

Jonica held up one finger. "One for you and one for *Aenti*."

"What about her?" He pointed to Deborah.

"*Nay danki*." Deborah shook her head. "I don't snack between meals."

Stephen took the cookies and went into the sitting room.

"He doesn't seem sick to me." Deborah sipped her drink.

"He's much better."

"What exactly is wrong with him? I heard it has something to do with his blood."

"He has von Willebrand disease." If she thought Deborah was concerned, she would share more about the condition, but she seemed disinterested, which was ironically uplifting. But if this visit had nothing to do with Peter and nothing to do with Stephen, then why was she here?

"He has a *doktah*'s appointment at the same time as the sewing frolic, so I don't think I'll make it to the get-together."

Deborah smiled as she took another sip. "As I was saying, as part owner of the market, Caleb can do well."

Stephen zoomed back into the kitchen, startling Deborah and making her spill some of her coffee.

"Stephen, stop running in the *haus*." Jonica stood to get the dishrag.

"This is Nutmeg." Stephen climbed up beside Deborah and held up his wooden horse.

The older woman's brows quirked. "What's his name?"

"Nutmeg. Like Caleb's horse. Only mine is a *bu* horse." He trotted the horse on the table, making neighing sounds that sprayed spit everywhere.

Jonica wiped up the mess. "I apologize. He's *nett* always this way."

"Nothing a stern hand couldn't correct."

Deborah's singsong tone didn't fool Jonica. It was a dig at her parenting ability.

"I don't suppose he has a *daed* to—"

"I will have," Stephen interrupted. "Mr. Jordan said so."

Deborah's brows rose to a new height, and she shifted in her chair to face Stephen. "Is this Mr. Jordan going to be your *daed*?"

"*Nay*, silly. He's an *engel*."

"He's *nett* an *engel*. He's an *Englischer*." Jonica walked around the table and picked Stephen up from his chair. "It's time for your nap." She carried him to the staircase, then lowered him onto the first step. "I'll be up in a minute."

"Your *sohn* has quite the imagination."

"Sometimes he does." Though calling Mr. Jordan an angel was new to her. She'd have a talk with Stephen about that once they were alone. "As for Caleb, if he wants to become a store owner, I'm happy for him."

Deborah smiled. "I'm pleased to hear that you support Caleb's decision to marry Darleen Yoder. She is a *gut* match for him."

Chapter 28

T ell me that again," Caleb said, not fully following Dr. Mallory's
explanation. "*Mei* muscles are bleeding?"

"You have a muscle tear, which has damaged some of the surrounding tissue and vessels. I believe the damaged vessels are
bleeding into the muscle and is what's causing the extensive bruising, swelling, and pain."

Caleb raked his fingers through his hair. "Why do you think I
have a bleeding disorder?"

"You have the same signs and symptoms as someone with
von Willebrand disease. Same as Stephen, the child you brought
in to see me. There are different types of von Willebrand and not
everyone responds the same. That's why the blood tests to determine how much clotting factor you have are important."

Caleb tried to remember what Jonica had said about the disorder. Knowing Stephen could live an active life was all that had
mattered at the moment. He couldn't wrap his mind around it all.
"And I've got this disease, how?"

"The condition is inherited, which means your siblings have a
high likelihood of also having the disease. You need to make family members aware. Many people don't know they have a problem

until they have a problem like you and Stephen. Had your leg injury been an open wound, you might have bled to death."

Caleb shook his head. Nothing the doctor was saying made sense. He pointed to his leg. "This is from falling off a horse and being nearly trampled by a herd of cattle. Besides, it wasn't like I cut myself and couldn't stop the bleeding. I didn't bleed. At all. Wouldn't this type of injury, bruised ribs, muscle tear, be expected?"

"The injury makes sense, but the amount of swelling and bruising is another thing. You'll need to see a blood specialist and a surgeon. And like your son, you'll have to take a lot of precautions from now on."

Dr. Mallory had mistaken him for Stephen's father before when he'd brought Jonica and the boy into the clinic, and Caleb never corrected him then. But this was altogether different. He and Stephen couldn't share the same disease unless . . .

"You said siblings could have the same issues? So *mei bruder* could've had von Willebrand disease too?"

"Yes, the mutated gene is passed from parent to child."

Peter. A knot formed in his stomach. He recalled Jonica's words. *"Do you know anyone with blood cancer? What about hemophilia or leukemia?"* She seemed desperate to know if he *knew* anyone.

Peter was Stephen's father.

Caleb tasted bile in the back of his throat, but he held it down. In the background of his ruminating, the doctor droned on. It wasn't until the doctor said something about referring him to a specialist that Caleb snapped back to the present. "You want me to do what?"

"Only a surgeon can determine if you need surgery."

He still tried to piece things together. "How common is von Willebrand? Do you have a lot of Amish patients with clotting problems?"

"Stephen was my first, which was why I wanted to wait for the blood test results before saying anything. We'll run the blood tests on you as well, but I'm 99 percent sure you have the same disorder. You're probably the one who passed the mutated gene to your son. And as I told your wife, if you have other children, they should be tested. Have you been taking anything for the pain?"

"A few ibuprofen tablets is all. The pain is somewhat tolerable."

"If your leg keeps swelling, it won't stay that way. But taking ibuprofen can worsen your bleeding. You need to stop."

A knock sounded on the door, and the nurse poked her head in the room. "Dr. Yarbrough doesn't have an opening available until after Thanksgiving, and the surgery center is closed today. I can try again tomorrow to make Caleb an appointment."

"Yes, please do." Dr. Mallory sighed.

"Why do I need to see a surgeon if it's a bleeding problem?"

"Only a surgeon will be able to determine if your muscle tear will heal without surgery. Also, there's a possibility you'll need a drain."

"Isn't that something you can do here?" This medical care was going to cost him more than building a few flower boxes.

Dr. Mallory removed a paper tape measure from a drawer. "I'm going to need you to measure your leg at least four times a day. Record the measurements on a piece of paper and make sure you bring it with you each day."

"Each day?"

"Caleb, this could be serious. If you have an active bleed and the swelling continues, you could lose your leg. So until we get you in to see a specialist, I'll monitor you. *Each day.*"

His medical care would cost a fortune. "There's no other way?"

"We can't risk it."

Caleb sighed. "Okay."

"It's important that your leg feels warm like the uninjured

one. If it becomes hot or cold, you must go to the emergency room immediately." The doctor placed two fingers on the top of Caleb's foot, then directed him to do the same. "Do you feel the pulse?"

"*Jah.*"

"It's important that you check your foot pulse every day. If it becomes hard to find or feels faint, you must go to the emergency room." Dr. Mallory paused. "Will you be able to do all these things?"

Caleb nodded.

"I'm going to write you a prescription for an antibiotic, and you can take Tylenol for pain. If your pain increases, it will most likely mean the swelling has increased. Make sure you measure your leg. If swelling happens—"

"I know. Go to the emergency room," Caleb said.

"Immediately."

Caleb nodded. "I will."

"Don't forget to bring your measurement log when you come in tomorrow. We will discuss the next step after we get in touch with the surgical center."

"Okay."

"Any questions?"

None for the doctor—only Jonica. "I can't think of anything at the moment."

Dr. Mallory jotted some numbers on a piece of paper and handed it to him. "This is my personal cell number. Call me if you have any problems, and stay away from cattle until you're healed."

"Thank you." Caleb went to the desk, made an appointment for the next day, then joined his father in the lobby.

"What did the *doktah* say about your heart?" Caleb asked as they left the office.

"Everything is *gut.*" *Daed* ambled toward the buggy, huffing with every step. "You get everything taken care of in town?"

"Everything I needed to do." Caleb helped his father onto the bench.

Daed talked very little on the ride home, exhausted from the outing and the energy it required getting in and out of the buggy. Caleb had a mound of questions—all about his and Stephen's disease. And why Jonica withheld the truth.

Jonica spread a freshly laundered dress over the back of the kitchen chair, then pushed the chair closer to the cookstove so the wet garment would dry. She pulled a pair of Stephen's pants out of the basket and hung them over another chair.

A knock sounded on the door.

After her unexpected visit from Deborah Schulmann, Jonica wasn't in the mood for more visitors.

The visitor knocked again, this time harder.

Jonica hurried to the door, so the rapping didn't wake Stephen up. Caleb stood with his hat in his hands. A strange expression masked his usually kind features. "Caleb. What are you doing—?"

"We need to talk." He moved past her and entered the house but didn't leave the foyer. "Where's Stephen?"

"He's taking a nap."

"Edna?"

"In the sitting room. What's this about?" Her heart dropped in her chest. Was he finally going to tell her about his plans to marry Darleen? Oh, Lord, could she bear the heartbreak again?

He shifted his stance as though favoring his right leg. "Maybe we should talk outside." He grabbed her cloak off the wall hook and handed it to her. "I'll meet you on the porch." Without giving her a chance to agree or object, he exited the house.

Guilt had him rattled. It was the only logical explanation

she could come up with for his on-edge behavior. It'd been a while since she'd seen Caleb, since they kissed, and he was overwhelmed with remorse. He'd probably already confessed to Darleen, which most likely had something to do with his mother's sudden involvement.

Jonica took her time putting on her cloak, her boots, then her winter bonnet. She had half a notion to leave him on the porch and go back to hanging clothes. She'd already spent too much time sobbing on and off as she took her anger and frustration out scrubbing dirty clothes against the washboard.

She glanced out the window in the door. He was pacing and favoring his right leg as he limped back and forth. She had to put him out of his misery. And finally set herself straight that she and Caleb had no future together.

Jonica opened the door and stepped outside. "You don't have to feel guilty. I forgive you."

"Me?" His brows furrowed. "You forgive me?"

She winced at the harshness in his tone. "I figured you came over to apologize for kissing me—but obviously, I was wrong."

He turned and held on to the porch banister.

The silence between them was suffocating. "It's okay." She came up beside him. "The kiss just happened. I'll be gone soon, and you can . . . go on with your life."

Facing her, anger flared his nostrils. "Is that what you told Peter?"

Jonica stared, the breath in her chest frozen like the wind blowing her cape. "What I told Peter when?"

"He's Stephen's *daed*, isn't he? I'm Stephen's *onkel*?"

He was standing so close, every word he spoke grazed her ear. "I wanted to tell you. I was going to tell you," she whispered.

"When?"

Mustering every iota of courage within her, Jonica turned and faced him nose-to-nose. "When you were interested enough to ask. And by the way." She stiffened her spine, standing to her full height. "You're *nett* much different than your *bruder*. You took advantage of *mei* vulnerability and you . . ." *Were in love with someone else.*

Feeling herself start to wither, she flipped around and, facing the house, leaned her forehead against the door. She'd gone through Peter's rejection and survived. She would get over Caleb too—once she left town.

"Did Peter know?"

"*Jah*, I told him when I found out and I told him when Stephen was born. We wanted different things. He made that clear." This was exactly why she had wanted to keep her secret.

Judgment.

"Caleb, please *geh*." She reached for the doorknob.

He held the door closed with his hand for several seconds, then dropped it. His footfalls paced across the porch again. "He knew?"

"*Jah*."

"Why didn't you tell me—or my family?"

She turned to him as he paced by. "For just this reason, Caleb." A tear ran cold down her cheek. "I will not have Stephen known as your *bruder*'s bastard *sohn*. His birth was not his choice; it was mine."

"But I deserved to know. A part of Peter lives on in Stephen. I should have been told."

"*Nay*, Caleb. Don't put this on me. *Nett* only did Peter decide *nett* to tell you or your family, he made the choice to abandon us."

He stopped his pacing, his face downcast. "You should have told me." He turned and walked away, his back stiff with anger.

Jonica went into the house, ran up the stairs, and fell onto her mattress. She sobbed into her pillow. Her life had once again been destroyed by a Schulmann.

Chapter 29

Leg pain had kept Caleb immobile and thoughts of Jonica kept him awake at nights. He hadn't seen her in four days—four miserable days.

Today when the women started arriving for the sewing frolic, he hurried out of the house. He didn't like misleading his mother, but every day that he had gone into town to see the doctor, she assumed he was going into town to see Darleen. *Mamm* didn't come right out and ask, and he didn't make a point to correct any wrong thinking on her part.

He tapped the reins to increase Nutmeg's pace as he passed Edna's farm. His gut was telling him to stop, but he'd stopped listening to his gut. Without clear thought as to where he was headed, he continued down the road several miles. He wasn't sure what had come over him, but he felt compelled to turn down the narrow dirt road leading to the old Victorian house he'd been working on when Peter died.

He stopped the buggy in the driveway and sat for several minutes staring at the place. His once-big dream was now boarded up and abandoned. He climbed out of the buggy and walked the perimeter of the house, trying to gather up the nerve to go inside. After finding Peter's body on the ground, Caleb wanted nothing to do with finishing the house—even driving down the road. Gideon believed that, with time, Caleb would work through his grief and want to complete the project, so taking it upon himself, his friend boarded up the opening to protect the house from weather damage or vandalism.

Caleb came to the spot where he'd found Peter and stopped. He lifted his gaze to the dormer addition jutting out from the second story. The boarded-up window, a horrid reminder of the last day he'd spent with his brother, released a well of tears down Caleb's face. The last conversation he had—would ever have—with Peter played over in his mind as it had a thousand times.

"You messed up the framing, Peter. Nau I have to order a different size window." Caleb gritted his teeth to the point his jaw started to throb. The desire to throw his brother off the job overwhelmed his senses.

"You sound like Daed." Peter's nonchalance added to the welling pressure in Caleb's chest about to explode like a fiery volcano.

"You've cost me extra time and money. It's another mistake that's going to set me back." Caleb measured the opening again. *"This size is a special order. It'll cost twice the amount."*

"It was a mistake. Take it easy."

"Because you weren't paying attention? You can't even swing a hammer or measure a hole. What can you do right, Peter?"

"I guess nothing, so I might as well jump off the roof and end mei life nau." His brother stood.

"Maybe you should. But do it after you clean up the mess you've made. Someone's going to trip over these tools, and I'm tired of cleaning up after you." Caleb jotted down the new measurement on a notepad, then shoved the pencil behind his ear and the paper in his pocket. *"I have to go into town to order the window. Don't do anything else except your cleanup. I can't afford your help. I'll see you at home."*

Caleb rubbed his hand over his face, struggling to get the image out of his mind. His cruel words had pushed Peter to do the unthinkable. As Caleb fell to his knees, pain shot up his injured leg and settled in his hip joint. But that pain didn't compare to the agony of losing his little brother.

"Why did he do it, God? I didn't think he would actually jump." Caleb fell forward, his face in the snow. "Why didn't You stop him? Why didn't You stop me from going into town? Why, God?"

"He didn't die alone," a man from behind Caleb said.

Caleb whirled around to find Mr. Jordan. He scrambled to his feet. "What did you say?"

The *Englischer* looked up toward the roof. "He didn't jump."

"He didn't jump? How do you know?"

Mr. Jordan smiled kindly. "I believe you have an idea of who I am, don't you, Caleb?" He pointed to the dormer. "Peter was stapling a sheet of plastic to the opening in order to protect the house's interior from rain. He got twisted around and lost his balance."

The hair on Caleb's arms stood on end. He'd been the person to find Peter lying in a pool of blood, body twisted and bones exposed.

"If you saw him fall, why didn't you get help?" He pointed toward the road. "The *Englisch* neighbor on the corner has a phone. You could have called an ambulance."

"It is not by my power, but by the will of God, who determines the number of days a man is given. It was Peter's hour to leave this earth. I could not change that."

"I don't understand. If you've known this all along, why didn't you tell me? We've been together multiple times at Edna's house. You even planted my winter wheat. Why am I just *nau* learning this about Peter?"

"Again, it is for God alone to know the reason. Don't concern yourself with discerning why. Trust God. He hasn't left you nor forsaken you. Just the opposite, He's held you in His hand."

"My last conversation with Peter was unforgivable." Caleb spun around and wept, wishing he could take back the harsh words he'd spoken to his brother.

Mr. Jordan placed his hand on Caleb's shoulder. "'The LORD bless you and keep you; the LORD make his face shine upon you and be gracious to you; the LORD lift up his countenance upon you and give you peace.'"

Heat penetrated from the top of Caleb's head to his toes. He stood enthralled by the stillness surrounding him, the peace that passed all understanding filling him.

"God is working in ways you cannot see, and things hidden will come to light. But you must trust Him. He loves and cares for you, Caleb. Therefore, do not be troubled or dismayed. God, who formed you in your mother's womb, knows your deepest thoughts, your deepest pain, your deepest desires. And just as you have received forgiveness, you also must forgive."

Caleb remained in a peace-filled state, soaking in the unseen presence of the Holy Spirit for several minutes. When he looked up, the redheaded man was gone.

He bowed his head. "Lord, thank You for Your forgiveness. I pray that You will soften Jonica's heart so she can accept *mei* apology. Help me to know what to say to *Daed* so he can begin to heal, and Father, guide me to be what Stephen needs—an *onkel*, a friend, or a *daed*. I also ask that You direct *mei* steps. Give me wisdom to know what to do about this *haus*. Open *mei* eyes that I might see You. Open *mei* ears that I might hear Your voice. I want to follow You the rest of *mei* days. In Jesus' name, amen."

Caleb eyed the house, spotting new potential. With inner strength he could only obtain from God, he went inside. He walked through the darkened house making a mental list of things that still needed to be done. When he got to the room with the dormer, he cried again.

Peter's tools were still stacked in one corner.

As Caleb bent to pick up his brother's hammer, he noticed a small notebook sticking out of the pocket of the tool belt. Flipping through the pages, he came to the beginnings of a letter—to Jonica.

∼�∼

Caleb urged Nutmeg into a faster trot. He couldn't wait another minute to make amends with Jonica. He'd been wrong to say what he did. And probably wrong to read the letter Peter had started, but hopefully, she would accept his apology.

He turned into Edna's driveway and stopped the buggy next to the house. As he climbed out of the buggy, Stephen ran up to him.

"Caleb, I missed you." Stephen wrapped his arms around Caleb's bad leg and squeezed.

"I missed you too, buddy. Are you playing in the snow?"

"*Kumm* see what I made." Stephen grasped Caleb's hand with his snowy mitten and gave it a tug.

Caleb went with Stephen around the side of the house and stopped in front of three snow angels.

"They're a family." He pointed to each one. "That one is the *daed*, that one is the *mamm*, and that one is me!"

Caleb smiled. "Did you make them all by yourself?"

"*Nay*, Mr. Jordan helped."

A car pulled into the driveway and stopped. Caleb walked toward the car as the man was asking the driver to wait until he found out if this was the right house.

"Can I help you?"

The Amish man turned. "Is this Edna Muller's house?"

"*Jah*," Caleb said. The man wasn't from their district. The rim of his hat was wider.

He sent the driver on his way, then held out his hand to Caleb. "I'm Ephraim King from Cedar Ridge."

He was the one who wrote Jonica the letter, the one who wanted to marry her. Caleb's stomach soured.

The man looked more than twice Jonica's age. "I've actually *kumm* to see Jonica, *nett* Edna."

Of course he had.

"It's a surprise." The out-of-towner must have spotted Stephen peering around Caleb's leg, because the man sidestepped and leaned down. "*Hiya*, Stephen. Is your *mamm* around?"

Stephen shrugged.

"The *bu* doesn't talk much, does he?" Ephraim's gaze skimmed the area. "Are you the one who's going to buy the farm?"

Caleb shook his head. "I'm Caleb Schulmann, a . . . friend of the family. I believe Jonica is inside." He headed to his buggy, his heart aching. He'd been too late. As Caleb climbed onto the bench, he took one last look at the house.

Jonica was standing at the door, welcoming her future husband inside.

Jonica's jaw dropped. "Ephraim, what are you doing here in Posen?"

"I *kumm* to see you." He removed his hat and held it in his hand.

"What a . . . surprise."

"I hope it's a nice surprise."

"*Jah*, I just can't believe—Here I am blabbering and you've had a long journey. Would you like a cup of *kaffi*?"

"*Jah*, please."

She led him into the kitchen. The mugs clanged together as she nervously removed two from the cabinet. "How are the *kinner*?"

"Busy in *schul*. The youngest, Tommy, has had a *kalt*."

"He's doing better *nau* though, right?"

"*Jah*, he is." He cleared his throat. "But that's one of the reasons why I'm here. Did you get *mei* letter?"

Jonica froze. Was he really here to pressure her into marriage? It wasn't a decision she could make lightly. She didn't know him that well. "I received it, but I haven't had time to reply."

"You know winter is coming upon us. We already have several inches up north, and they're predicting more by Thanksgiving."

"*Jah*, you mentioned you were winterizing your house." She poured the coffee, then realized she didn't even know how he liked it. With cream, without? With sugar? With cream and sugar?

Lord, help me. Stephen's been praying about a daed. *I don't want to deny him a* gut *upbringing.*

"Jonica?"

Aenti Edna's voice interrupted her silent plea for help. "Did you want another cup of *kaffi*, *Aenti*?"

Her aunt handed Jonica an empty mug. "Only half, please." She eyed Ephraim. "Do I know you?"

"This is Ephraim King, *mei* . . . friend from Cedar Ridge." She avoided making eye contact with Ephraim. "This is *mei aenti* Edna."

"You can call me Edna. Are you from around here?"

"*Nay*." He lifted his brows, obviously puzzled, "I'm from Cedar Ridge."

Jonica handed him a coffee mug. "*Aenti* has some issues with her memory."

Aenti nodded. "I tend to forget things and repeat a lot of questions."

Jonica fixed *Aenti's kaffi*, then took it over to the table. "Would either of you like a piece of pumpkin pie?"

"Sounds *gut* to me," he said.

Jonica placed the piece she'd been saving for Caleb on the plate, then removed a fork from the drawer.

"I heard you were selling your place, Edna." Ephraim glanced at Jonica as she took the chair next to her aunt. "That's the other reason I've *kumm*. I think I can help you figure out the paperwork, so it isn't delayed any longer."

Jonica forced a smile. "That's—"

"*Nett* needed," *Aenti* said. "We've decided *nett* to sell."

Ephraim shifted on his chair to face Jonica. "Then you're free to *kumm* back with me to Cedar Ridge?"

"Is your *kaffi* too strong?" Edna pushed up from the table. "Mine could use a splash of water."

"Let me help you with that." Jonica took *Aenti's* mug over to the sink. Her aunt liked strong coffee, but Jonica was grateful for the distraction.

"I don't see Stephen anywhere." *Aenti* craned her neck in front of the window.

"He was outside a few minutes ago," Ephraim said.

"I'd better call him inside." Jonica returned the coffeepot to the stove. "I don't want him to stay out too long and catch a *kalt*."

"It isn't going to hurt him to stay outside. *Kinner* should—"

Be seen and nett *heard.* She'd heard him say that about his own children. "I'll be right back." Jonica went to the door and called, but Stephen didn't reply. She was shoving her foot into her boot when Ephraim came out of the kitchen.

"He's *nett* answering?"

"*Nay*, I have to find him."

"*Buwe* explore. He'll *kumm* back when he's *hungahrich*."

"He's *nett* supposed to leave the yard." Her voice cracked. "He could be hurt." She fled the house, unwilling to waste another moment.

"Lord, where is *mei sohn*?"

Chapter 30

I messed up, God." Caleb signaled Nutmeg to turn onto the paved road. "I lost *mei* chance to tell her how I feel—tell her I love her. She's going to marry that man, isn't she?"

The still, small voice told him to turn around, but he couldn't. "I love her, God. But if it's Your will . . ." He ground the last part under his breath. "I'll let her *geh*." Then he silenced himself the remainder of the ride home.

He unhitched Nutmeg from the buggy and walked her into the barn. On most nights he brushed the mare as she ate, but tonight his leg was throbbing. He hadn't followed the doctor's instructions to stay off of it and he was paying the price now.

Caleb tossed a can full of oats in the feed trough. She had plenty of water. The barn door creaked open. "Caleb?" a small voice said. "I'm *kalt*."

"Stephen, what are you—? How did you get here?"

The boy hung his head. "I climbed into your buggy when you were talking to that man."

"Your mother is probably worried sick."

Stephen's lips trembled. "Are you going to marry *mei mamm*?"

"It's *nett* that easy."

"You said you love her. I heard you talking in the buggy."

Daed came down the wooden ladder from the hayloft. "I thought I heard voices." He eyed Stephen, then lifted his gaze to Caleb.

"This is Stephen." *Your grandson.*

"*Hiya.*" Stephen waved at *Daed.* "Is this your barn?"

"It is."

The boy's eyes widened as he looked around. "I've never seen a barn this big." He headed for Peter's roping horse's stall. "What's his name?"

"This one is Jet," *Daed* said. "He's a little high-strung sometimes. *Kumm* on, I'll show you the calves. They're a little more your size."

Stephen slipped his hand into his grandfather's, who startled at first, then chuckled quietly.

Caleb smiled. Stephen had a way of softening everyone's heart. Exactly what his father needed.

While the two of them inspected the calves, Caleb led Nutmeg out of the stall and outside. Jonica would be in full panic mode and rightfully so.

The barn door slammed. "Caleb," Stephen called as he ran toward him.

Caleb grabbed him before he got too close to Nutmeg, and picked him up. "You can't run up on a horse. Especially Nutmeg. She's skittish."

"What's skittish?"

"She gets frightened easily."

"Sorry," Stephen said. "I saw the *boppli* cows."

His father ambled toward them. "He's already naming them."

The screen door opened and *Mamm* stepped out on the porch, a dishrag in her hand. "It's time for sup—per."

"Hello again." Stephen waved.

Mamm shot up a quick wave, then squared her shoulders as if

303

correcting her moment of weakness. "Will you be having guests for supper?"

"Please, Caleb?" Stephen rubbed his tummy. "I'm *hungahrich*."

"Your *mamm* is going to be so upset." He carried Stephen to the house. "Can I get a small plate for him to eat in the buggy? I really need to get him back home."

His mother looked the boy over, then motioned them into the house. "Have you been sitting with the *boppli* all day?"

"I'm *nett* a *boppli*. I'm five." Stephen pulled off one of his mittens to show all five of his fingers.

"I stand corrected," she said. "You are certainly *nett* a *boppli*." She removed a small container from the bottom cabinet. "Darleen was here earlier." She added a spoonful of mashed potatoes on one side of the dish.

"Can we talk about that later?" This wasn't a conversation he wanted to have around Stephen.

"I just thought you might be interested." *Mamm* topped the potatoes with hamburger gravy. She peered down at Stephen. "Do you like green beans?"

He nodded. "Can I have a lot?"

His mother frowned. "Doesn't your *mamm* feed you?"

"*Mamm* says I'm a growing *bu*." Stephen attempted to stand taller by straightening his back, stretching his neck, and jutting his chin. The spitting image of Peter. Why hadn't he seen it earlier?

His mother smiled. "So I see."

Daed entered the house. "I finished hitching your buggy. They'll have a search party out if you don't get him home soon."

"*Jah,* you're right." Caleb gathered Stephen in his arms.

Mamm went to hand Caleb the container and sucked in a noticeable breath. Her gaze darted from Caleb to Stephen, to Caleb again, then back to Stephen. Was she seeing Peter in the boy's features?

"Is something wrong, Deborah?" *Daed* asked.

"*Nay*," she said, then composed herself. "Your *daed* is right. If you don't get him back, Jonica will have a search party out looking for the child."

"How did you know Stephen is Jonica's *sohn*?"

"She came to visit *mei mamm*," Stephen said.

"I invited her and Edna to the sewing frolic. Neither of them attended, so I'm *nett* sure why I bothered." She removed a spoon and fork from the drawer. "Please make sure *mei* silverware is returned."

"*Jah*, I will." Caleb went to the door.

"*Danki*, Caleb's *mamm*," Stephen said over his shoulder.

The boy was hungry. He'd eaten most of the meal by the time Caleb had him home.

Edna flagged Caleb down. "Stephen is— Young man, your *mamm* has been frantic looking for you."

Caleb climbed out of the buggy and lifted Stephen down. "He snuck a ride home with me."

"Stephen, where are you?" Jonica's distant voice came from the wheat field.

"I'll go tell her Stephen is *allrecht*." Caleb hobbled to the field, shards of pain shooting up his leg. He'd made it to the edge of the field when Ephraim ran past him, shouting, "Stephen's home!"

Caleb stopped. There was no reason going any farther. Jonica had clearly received the news, the two were hugging. Caleb turned. He hadn't made it too many steps before Jonica ran up to him. "You found him, Caleb?"

"*Nett* until I got home." He glanced over his shoulder at Ephraim hiking across the field, white puffy breaths escaping his mouth. "Is the old man out of breath?"

"Be nice, Caleb."

He snorted. "He's twice your age."

"And he wants to marry me."

"Are you in love with him?" Caleb stumbled on a rock and nearly fell.

Jonica came up beside him and placed her arm around his waist. "Lean on me."

"I'm *allrecht*."

She gripped him tighter. "Let me help you. You're limping."

"I've been limping for days. Don't do this *nau*." He forced himself to walk faster despite what felt like his muscles shredding. "I don't want to look weak in front of the old man."

"Caleb Schulmann, you're a stubborn goat," she yelled from a few paces behind him.

Ephraim caught up with them. "What's wrong with him?"

"Caleb hurt his leg."

Caleb kept walking. He had a decent stride and it wasn't too much farther to his buggy. He felt an arm too big to be Jonica's come up under his shoulder. His weight was lifted on his right side.

"What did you do to your leg?" Ephraim asked.

"I took on a bull in a fight and lost." If he was going to have help, he preferred Jonica's support. At least she was softer to lean into.

Jonica ran to Stephen and swept him into her arms. "Why did you leave without telling me?"

"I wanted to go with Caleb," he whimpered.

"*Danki* for your help, Ephraim. I have it from here." Caleb limped toward his buggy as Ephraim joined Jonica and Stephen.

She pointed to the house. "Stephen, go inside and go straight to bed. *Aenti*, would you mind taking him inside, please?"

Aenti and Stephen tottered toward the house, Stephen telling her about the calves he'd named.

"That's it?" Ephraim said. "You're just going to send him to bed?"

"I plan on talking with him later," Jonica said. "Once I cool down."

"The *bu* needs discipline. He needs a strong hand." He shook his open hand. "If one of *mei kinner* ran away . . ."

Caleb shook his head as he climbed onto the bench. God have mercy on Stephen—Jonica too. The man was domineering, reminding Caleb of his father.

"Caleb, can you wait a minute?" Jonica strode to the buggy. "*Danki* again." If she was disturbed by what Ephraim had said, she wasn't showing it.

"Don't do it, Jonica. Don't *geh* back to Cedar Ridge."

"I don't have a reason to stay, do I?"

"You're a strong woman. You've done a *gut* job with Stephen so far, and you've done it on your own. You don't *need* to marry anyone." *Please, don't do it.*

"I hope your leg gets better, Caleb." Jonica turned and walked away.

He waited a few seconds, hoping she would turn around and wishing he had the courage to stop her from leaving. But he had nothing to offer.

"Jonica. Wait." He climbed out of the buggy, his leg giving out under his weight.

"Caleb!" She fell at his side. "Is it your leg?"

Don't make a scene. He gritted his teeth and pushed up on his good leg. "I found this." He handed her Peter's notebook. "You chose faith over Peter."

"That's what I meant by us wanting different things. Peter wanted the world and I wanted to serve God. I couldn't choose him over leaving the Amish—over following God."

"I'm sorry for the way I treated you. I was wrong. You tried to talk about Peter, but I cut you off. If I talked about Peter, I would have admitted that his death was *mei* fault. I had said very harsh things . . . things that were hurtful."

"I'm sorry, Caleb. I struggled with telling you—and I know I should have told you. But pride got in *mei* way. I didn't want to be judged for past mistakes. I didn't want you to think less of me." She lifted the notepad. "*Danki* for giving me this. Good-bye, Caleb."

He closed his eyes so he didn't have to watch her turn away. He was letting the love of his life go and he couldn't muster enough courage to stop her.

He returned to his buggy, disengaged the brake, and clicked his tongue. He ran the mare home, then fed her extra oats and bedded her down with a blanket. Feeling the energy drain from his body, he could barely lift his bad leg. He didn't need to measure the size to know his leg was swelling. His pant leg was tight.

When he entered the kitchen, both of his parents were seated at the table, pensive expressions on their faces.

"Have a seat. Your *mamm* and I want to talk with you."

Caleb pulled out a chair opposite them and plopped down.

"You can't keep Darleen Yoder waiting," his *daed* said. "Your *mamm* and I believe she will make you a *gut fraa*."

Caleb shook his head. "I won't make her a *gut* husband—and I told Melvin that when I stopped by Yoder's Market to turn down his offer. I'm *nett* in love with Darleen. I'm in love with Jonica Muller."

His mother sniffled.

"She's a *gut* woman. A *gut mamm* to Stephen. And I want to marry her." If she doesn't go back to Cedar Ridge and marry Ephraim. Either way, he couldn't marry Darleen.

"You need to think about it more," *Mamm* said.

"*Nay*," Caleb said. "We all know life is short. I don't need to think about it. *Mei* mind is made up."

"The *bu*'s right," *Daed* said.

"But your future—"

Caleb held up his hand to stop his mother. "I've been thinking about that too. If I finish the *haus*, I can put it on the market. It should sell at a *gut* price, and you can use the money to pay medical bills."

Daed leaned forward. "You're going to start up your construction business again?"

"I'll cross that bridge after I finish the *haus*."

Mamm plucked a tissue from the dispenser and blotted her eyes. "What changed your mind?"

"I was at the *haus* today." He debated how much to say. "I met a man who was there when Peter fell. He didn't jump." As Caleb relayed the news, a supernatural sense of freedom overcame them. As though the strongholds had broken, they wept. The first thing they had done together as a family since Peter's death.

Chapter 31

It'd been two days since Jonica had turned down Ephraim's proposal, and she couldn't help but sense something was wrong. Not with her decision. Once she told him that she couldn't marry someone she didn't love, the burden had been lifted.

Ephraim seemed relieved and confessed afterward that he'd been praying about the proposal too. Although had she said yes, he would have kept his end of the deal, since she turned him down, he felt led to tell her about Eunice, the widow who had been helping him with his children.

It seemed both their prayers had been answered.

Only something was wrong. She felt the same impending doom as before her parents' accident and she couldn't shake the feeling, then or now. She kept a watchful eye on Stephen, not wanting to let him out of her sight.

Peter's letter gave her some peace. She opened the notebook and read it again.

Dear Jonica,

I was wrong when I tried to talk you into leaving the Amish. I'm writing to let you know that I've come back to the faith. I want to serve God. I know you were praying for me. *Danki.* I have to know—did I wait too long to get my life in order? Have you found someone else? I've been saving money to leave Posen. Maybe your *daed* has need of another worker in the sawmill?

The letter wasn't finished, but it said everything she needed to know. He had made amends with God before his death. God had answered her prayers.

But something was urging her to pray. Compelled to kneel on the kitchen floor, she bowed her head. "Lord, I don't know what I'm being called to pray about, but I ask that whatever is stirring in *mei* spirit, You will take care of it. Please place a hedge of protection around Stephen. Keep him safe. Watch over *Aenti* Edna. Lord, I pray for Caleb. He's hurting over Peter's death. Please, give him wisdom and strengthen his leg. He's in a lot of pain."

Jonica prayed for everyone who came to mind, including Ephraim, his children, and Eunice. Then she sat on the cold floor in silence, waiting for more prompting from the Holy Spirit of anyone she'd missed.

"*Mamm,*" Stephen called from the stairs.

"Amen." Jonica pushed off the floor. Stephen had only been down for his nap a few minutes. What was he doing up?

"*Mamm,* we need to pray," Stephen said. "Something's wrong with Caleb."

"We can do that." Jonica knelt back down and tapped the kitchen floor for him to join her.

Stephen got down on his knees, folded his hands, and closed his eyes. "God, I think something is wrong with Caleb. A voice woke me up and told me to pray." Muttering, Stephen continued to pray.

Watch over Caleb, Father. Keep him safe.

After a minute, Stephen looked up. "Okay." Then his eyes widened. "I forgot." He closed his eyes again. "And God, please, take care of Nutmeg." Stephen stood. "I'm done. Do I have to go back to bed?"

Jonica smiled. While she was still inwardly fretting about why God had called them to pray, Stephen was at total peace. Childlike faith. She cleared her throat. "If you promise to play quietly, you can stay up."

"Okay." He left the room.

Jonica sat on the floor a few moments longer. *Lord, please forgive me for worrying so much when You have everything under control. Give me that same childlike faith.*

Someone's knocking on the door brought Jonica off the floor. She opened the door and took a step back. "Deborah."

"May I *kumm* in? There's a few things I would like to talk with you about."

Jonica sucked in a sharp breath. "Is Caleb *allrecht*?"

She smiled. "He's *gut*."

Thank You, Lord.

"May I?" Caleb's mother motioned in the house.

Jonica wasn't looking forward to another talk after the last one didn't go so well, but she stepped aside. Maybe Deborah just needed reassurance that Jonica wouldn't interfere with Caleb and Darleen's plans.

It went against Jonica's grain not to offer Caleb's *mamm* a cup of coffee . . . But doing so would only encourage her to stay longer. Best to hear what the woman had to say, then encourage her to be on her way.

Deborah sat at the table. "I know this visit is . . . unexpected." She picked at her fingernails.

Was this display of brokenness another tactic to convince Jonica to leave town—leave her son alone?

"It seems you've been a major influence with *mei sohn* moving toward healing." Deborah linked her hands together on the table and lowered her head. When she glanced back to Jonica, tears pooled in her eyes. "Caleb has had periods of despondence since his *bruder*'s death. We all have been . . . overwhelmed with grief."

"I'm sorry. I know it's hard to lose—" She was repeating everything she'd told his mother the last time, and her words hadn't helped then. "I'm glad Caleb is moving forward." She cleared her throat. Best to set things straight once and for all. "I'm *nett* going to interfere with Caleb and Darleen's wedding plans, if that's why you're really here."

"*Nay*, that's not why I'm here. I came to apologize. *Mei sohn* is in love with you . . . and I don't want to lose *mei sohn* by interfering in his life. He isn't going to marry Darleen."

"He isn't?" Her lungs constricted, and she fought the urge to press her hand to her chest.

Deborah shook her head. "He said he wouldn't marry someone he wasn't in love with, and he also said the person he's in love with is you."

"He said that?"

She nodded. "I thought I owed you the truth."

"*Danki* for telling me." Jonica's insides fluttered with exhilaration.

Caleb loved her.

"Forgive me if I . . . appear out of sorts." The older woman's lips trembled, and she lifted her teary gaze upward.

Jonica reached out and placed her hand over Deborah's. "You won't lose Caleb." She shifted the conversation to a new topic. "How is his leg? I've been worried about him after he fell the other *nacht*."

Deborah sat up straighter. "He fell?"

313

"He's been favoring his right side. I think he's having more problems than what he's let on."

"Caleb and Abraham are working on the old house he's restoring." She stood. "I have their lunch in the buggy. I should go check on him. Would you like to ride along?"

"I don't like to leave Stephen and *Aenti* alone. Her memory isn't *gut* and she tends to sleep most of the day. Even *nau*, she's lying down in her room."

"I want to see Caleb." Stephen came up behind Jonica. "Please."

"I know Caleb would love to spend time with you both," Deborah said.

Jonica smiled. "I'd like to see him—and the project he's working on."

⁂

Caleb enjoyed working with his *daed* on the house. During the first few hours, the melancholy atmosphere was almost unbearable. Neither of them seemed to know where to begin and it wasn't from lack of knowledge. They both had an understanding of what had to be done before winter, such as windows, siding, and porch boards and railing that needed to be replaced, and what things could be done year-long, such as hanging interior doors, paint, and trim.

Without discussing the reason why, they both avoided the upstairs. But the dormer had to be addressed. The special-size window Caleb had gone into town to order the day of Peter's accident was still waiting to be installed.

Daed held the section of clapboard siding in place while Caleb hammered the nail. A fallen tree limb had hit the side of the house during a past lightning storm. "That tree is probably *nett* going to survive. It took a direct hit."

Caleb inspected the burned marks on the tree where the lightning had branded it. "It'd be a shame to take it down." He recalled the hot days he spent eating his lunch in the shade.

"It'll continue to be a hazard as it dies off and limbs fall."

Caleb nodded.

"Once it's down, we could haul it to the mill and have it lumbered." *Daed* studied the tree, probably figuring out how many eight-foot sections looked straight.

Caleb wasn't sure his leg was up to the task. It was one thing to do small odd jobs, but taking down an oak over a hundred feet tall was another thing. Swinging an ax took balance, and he wasn't that steady on his feet today. He'd caught himself twice from falling while hanging off the ladder, caulking windows.

"I agree. But I think that project is for another day." And more workers.

His father shifted his gaze from the tree over to the boarded-up dormer window opening. "I guess it's time to install that window."

Caleb wasn't sure he was ready to tackle such a huge project mentally or physically. His *daed* hadn't been upstairs, hadn't been in the room where Peter . . .

"I know being back at the *haus* you were working on with Peter is hard," his father said. "For me too. If I hadn't been working in the field, racing rain clouds, I would have been able to lend a hand." He nudged a fallen branch with the toe of his boot. "I knew Peter wasn't cut out to do construction. He didn't have your skill. Your math is better than all of us put together."

Caleb had waited all his life to hear his father say he approved of him.

"I always wanted Peter to be more like you. Instead, I think *mei* domineering way pushed him to jump the fence. Soured him toward God. That's why when *mei* prodigal *sohn* returned, I wanted him to do well."

315

"I shouldn't have been short-tempered with him," Caleb said. "I was upset at him for messing up the window opening when I should have been the one to do it. It was *mei* mistake too."

His father looked at the house, seemingly studying every piece of lumber. "I've been wanting to see you finish this *haus*."

"*Jah*, I know. You want me back in construction."

"*Nay, sohn*, I wanted you to work through Peter's death. I didn't want you stuck in the muck and mire that held me." *Daed* rubbed his beard. "If you're set on being a farmer, I'll support your decision."

Caleb twisted to face his father. "What?"

Daed held his gaze. "You deserve happiness, *sohn*."

"*Danki*, that means a lot." Understated, but with his *daed*, it was best to keep emotions at bay.

Daed patted Caleb's shoulder, his grasp strong and reassuring of what he said. "You mean a lot to me, *sohn*. I'm proud of you—always have been. Even when I was lost in my grief and anger, I was still so proud."

His father's words replayed in Caleb's mind before he said them out loud. "You're proud of me?"

"Always." *Daed* released Caleb's shoulder, his eyes flickering with tears as he redirected his attention to the house. "Well, are you ready to tackle that window?"

A buggy clattering down the road drew Caleb's attention. He recognized his mother's horse as it approached the driveway. "I think lunch just arrived."

"*Gut* timing. We can figure out a plan for the window while we eat." *Daed* headed toward the buggy.

Caleb hobbled behind him but stopped at the side porch to lean against the railing. His leg was getting stiffer, which was making it difficult to walk a long stretch. He set the hammer on the porch, and as he was removing his leather work gloves, he glimpsed a woman with her winter bonnet covering her face getting out of the passenger side of the buggy.

Darleen. Why did his mother have to be so relentless?

"Caleb!"

He heard Stephen call out his name before he spotted the boy running around the backside of the buggy. Stephen greeted him with a leg hug that nearly knocked Caleb over, but he didn't care.

"Hello, Caleb," Jonica said.

"I thought . . ."

She shook her head.

"Stephen," his mother said, "I'll need your help unloading the food."

"Coming." The boy scurried toward the buggy.

His parents chitchatting with Stephen about what foods he liked was a sweet sound to Caleb's ears. He would have never believed his mother would come around so quickly. And though he had prayed that Jonica wouldn't marry Ephraim, he knew she was the only one who could make that decision. Nothing he said or did would change her mind.

"I should probably help your *mamm* get lunch ready," Jonica said.

Caleb glanced at his father brushing snow off the picnic table and his mother directing Stephen where to take his corner of the large section of cloth. "Let's let them enjoy Stephen."

Jonica gazed at the threesome. "They have warmed up to him."

"Something tells me that Stephen can warm the coldest heart." Caleb motioned for her to follow him up the porch steps. "Do you want to see what I'm working on?"

"*Jah.*" She trailed him into the house, her gaze dancing around, taking in the open sitting room. "This is beautiful."

"I'm going to put a woodstove where the fireplace is." He took her hand and led her down the hall where they were free of being seen through a window.

"How's your leg?"

"Let's *nett* talk about that." He pulled her into his arms and kissed her. "I was worried you were going to marry Ephraim." He trailed kisses from her lips to her cheek to her neck.

"I don't want to talk about him." She brought her hands to his face and guided his lips back to hers.

Caleb's leg wobbled. He didn't want to ruin the moment, but feeling his leg ready to collapse any second he broke from the kiss. "Do you want to see the rest of the *haus*?"

"Um . . ."

"Neither do I." He pressed her against the wall, and feeling her warm, raspy breaths against his face, he kissed her again.

"*Mamm.*" Stephen's voice filtering through the open door broke their kiss.

"Time to eat," his mother added.

"We'd better go before they come looking for us," he said, struggling to even out his balance. Thankfully, Jonica was too busy fiddling with the few strands of hair that had come loose from her *kapp* to notice his stagger.

They joined his parents and Stephen at the picnic table.

Mamm passed Jonica a peanut butter sandwich. "How do you like the *haus*, Jonica?"

"I think it's beautiful." She looked at the house, smiling until her gaze stopped on the dormer.

"I have the window," Caleb said. "*Daed* and I were planning to install it when you all arrived."

Stephen lowered his sandwich. "Can I help?"

"*Nett* on the window. It's too dangerous. But there's plenty of other things for you to help with on another day."

"Like what?"

"We need to install baseboards in the sitting room, do some drywall work in the bedrooms, and the kitchen needs a coat of paint."

Stephen giggled. "I don't know what any of that is."

"I'll teach you," Caleb said.

Daed reached for another sandwich. "Me too."

The conversation shifted to horses with Stephen asking *Daed* what the difference was between plow and buggy horses. His mother and Jonica talked about needlework and recipes and nothing could take Caleb's moment of happiness away.

At the end of the meal, the women cleaned up the area while Caleb and his father unwrapped the packing material from around the window.

Caleb leaned the ladder against the side of the house and, with his tools tucked in his tool belt, started up the ladder. Now that Jonica hadn't left town, he was eager to finish the house. He took a step and paused, took another and paused. If only his leg would cooperate better.

"Stephen!" Jonica yelled. "You get down. Right this instant!"

Caleb looked down and found Stephen had started to climb up behind him.

"I can't. I'm scared."

Caleb came down to where Stephen was clinging to the ladder. "Just relax, Stephen. I'm going to help you get down." Caleb maneuvered around him, then wrapped one arm around his midsection. "Let go of the rung. I have you."

Stephen released his hold.

Caleb took the next few steps slow. The boy wasn't heavy but his added weight was on Caleb's wrong side. He'd made it a few feet from the ground when something snapped in his leg.

His foot went out from under him and they slid the remainder of the feet down the ladder. Twisting his body so Stephen would land on Caleb instead of the ground sent excruciating pain ripping through his body.

Jonica pulled Stephen off of him and checked him over.

"Is he okay? Tell me Stephen is *allrecht*!" Caleb cried.

"Lie still, Caleb," Jonica said. "You're bleeding."

Chapter 32

Jonica, Stephen, and Caleb's parents all stood at the same time when a woman in black scrubs entered the emergency room lobby and called for anyone from the Schulmann family.

"How is *mei sohn*?" Abraham asked.

"The doctor was able to stop the bleeding, but he does need surgery on his leg. Caleb has asked that you all be allowed to come back to the room so you're present when the surgeon is talking to him about his leg." The woman led them to a curtained-off area at the far end of the department.

Caleb smiled when the nurse pushed back the curtain.

His *mamm* and *daed* went to one side of the bed, Jonica and Stephen to the other.

"How are you, Stephen?" Caleb asked.

"*Mei* elbow has a bruise." He rotated his arm to show Caleb.

"I'm sorry I dropped you."

"It's okay. You didn't mean to." Stephen's attention skipped around the room. "What's that?" He pointed to a large machine next to the head of the bed.

"I don't know," Caleb replied.

Deborah grabbed her son's hand. "Are you in pain?"

He shook his head. "*Nay*, they gave me something that's made me feel like I'm part of the mattress."

The curtain opened and a man in a long doctor's coat came forward. "I'm your son's surgeon, Dr. Reynolds. Caleb has asked that you be here when I speak with him about his leg."

"Did he break his leg when he fell?" Deborah asked.

"I didn't see any fractures on the X-rays. I'll be repairing a ruptured tendon. Caleb said he's been receiving treatment from Dr. Mallory for an injury that happened a couple of weeks ago."

"Caleb," his mother sniffled. "I had no idea. Why didn't you say something? I had you doing all that work around the *haus* and I didn't know you were hurt."

"It's okay, *Mamm*."

"Were you injured when you fell off the horse? I don't remember much of that day," his father said, then lowered his head. "The bullwhip . . ."

"*Daed*, please. You didn't know how the livestock would respond and neither did I. What's done is done."

Jonica hurt for Caleb's parents, especially his *daed* who was looking pale.

Deborah stepped forward. "How dangerous is the surgery?"

"I'm not as concerned about repairing the tendon as I am with the bleeding around the tissues and damaged blood vessels. As I've already discussed with Caleb, von Willebrand disease is a critical factor. Any surgery is a risk. I've ordered more units of blood on standby in the OR and medicine to replace his clotting factors." He paused a moment, but everyone, including Jonica, was stunned by the news. "If you don't have any more questions"—Dr. Reynolds backed up to the curtain—"I'll see you in surgery, Caleb."

Caleb nodded. "*Danki*."

The moment the doctor disappeared behind the curtain, his mother gasped. "You have what?"

"Von Willebrand disease. It's a blood disorder that apparently I inherited from either you or *Daed*." Caleb shifted his attention to Jonica. "Stephen and I share the same condition."

"Me?" Stephen's face lit up.

Jonica's throat tightened and tears flowed freely down her face. Surgery was dangerous. Everything the blood doctor had told her about the disease meant Caleb's life was at risk.

Caleb held out his hand and Jonica snatched it and held on to it tight. "Don't cry," he said.

His mother stepped forward. "Why didn't I know about von—?"

"Willebrand disease," Caleb said. "I didn't want to worry you."

"I'm your *mamm*. It's *mei* job to worry."

"I'll be okay, *Mamm*." Caleb turned to Jonica. "Will you still love me if I lose *mei* leg?"

"Yes, you fool." She wiped her face with the back of her hand. "I will always love you, Caleb." Tears slipped down her cheeks. "You're *nett* going to lose your leg." She spoke with a boldness she wasn't even aware she had. "You can still live a normal life. At least that's what the *doktah* told me about Stephen."

"Are you . . . ?" Deborah lowered her voice. "Caleb, are you this *kind*'s *daed*?"

Jonica froze. She glanced down at Stephen. Thankfully, he seemed preoccupied showing Caleb's father his wooden animal. She took a cleansing breath, generating enough courage to face his mother. "Peter also had the disease."

Deborah's eyes widened. "And how would you know?"

Prepared to take the conversation out of the room, Jonica pulled her hand away from Caleb's.

"There's little ears in the room, *Mamm*. That isn't important right *nau*." Caleb reached for Jonica's hand and held it with a reassuring grip. "I want to be Stephen's *daed*. That is, if Jonica will have me." His gaze bore into hers. "Will you?"

"*Jah!*" Stephen shouted.

Jonica and Caleb laughed.

Deborah stood, holding her hand over her mouth. "What will everyone say?"

"Deborah," Abraham said. "Let's take Stephen and give these two a few minutes alone. I think they have some talking to do."

Stephen reached for Abraham's hand.

"I think it will be *gut* to have a grandchild around the *haus*," Abraham said. "Don't you, Deborah?"

"*Jah*, of course. But I would have liked to have known about . . . all of this sooner."

Jonica waited until they were out of earshot. "Your *mamm* may *nett* forgive me."

"She will. Give her time." Caleb took Jonica's hand. "I love you, and I want to spend the rest of *mei* life with you."

"I love you too, Caleb."

"I'd get out of this bed and propose properly, but that would be too embarrassing dressed in a hospital gown." He kissed the top of her hand. "Will you be *mei fraa*?"

"Yes, I will marry you, even dressed in a hospital gown." She leaned down and kissed him.

Epilogue

Five months later

Jonica and *Aenti* were busy making ham-and-cheese sandwiches for the picnic. She glanced out the kitchen window and smiled. Caleb and Stephen were loading the fishing poles and gear into the buggy.

"It's *gut* weather for a picnic," *Aenti* said.

"Finally. Stephen's been antsy for Caleb to take him fishing ever since the snow melted and the pond thawed."

Aenti added a quart-size jar of pears to the basket. "Are you sure you want me to *geh*? I don't mind staying home. I have *mei* knitting project to work on."

"Of course we want you to *geh*." Jonica placed her arm around her aunt's shoulder and gave her a sideways hug. "This is a family outing, and you're part of this family."

"I don't want to be in the way. Your new husband may want his *fraa* and *kind* to himself today."

Jonica chuckled. "Being alone will be difficult because Caleb's parents are meeting us at the pond. Besides, you know Stephen would be heartbroken if we all weren't there when he catches his first fish. He thinks he's going to get one the size of a yardstick the way he's been carrying on."

"Wonder what size worm it would take to lure a fish that size."

"I don't know, *Aenti*, but Stephen's been digging all morning. I'm sure his canister is stuffed with bait."

Aenti smiled. "I think it'll be a picnic for the fish as well today."

"Maybe so." Jonica chuckled.

The screen door creaked open, and Caleb poked his head into the kitchen. Jonica's heartbeat sped up. Even after three months of marriage, she couldn't help but tingle from head to toe when she saw her husband.

He scratched his bearded jaw. "Can you *kumm* outside for a minute? I want to show you something."

"I'll be right there." Jonica handed *Aenti* the pieces of sliced cheese she'd been dividing between the sandwiches, then grabbed a dishrag and wiped her hands. She hadn't picked up any urgency in Caleb's tone, but he'd already headed back out the door. She caught up to him in the driveway. "Caleb, what is it? Is everything *allrecht*?"

"You'll see." Using his cane for added support, he ambled toward the field at a quick pace. He reached for her with his free hand, holding her fingers tight in his warm grip. Perhaps he wanted to show her how well he was moving around.

Knowing he'd be cooped up indoors several weeks following surgery, Caleb had arranged for the bishop to marry them as soon as he was able to stand. Their wedding was perfect, and Stephen was thrilled sitting between his grandparents as Caleb and Jonica took their vows.

Jonica scanned the pasture. "Did one of the horses get out?"

"Patience, Jonica. Follow me." He continued walking, then stopped at the edge of the field and pointed down. "Look."

At first the ground seemed barren, then she noticed a light-green hue.

Caleb moved his free arm to encircle her waist and he pulled her close to his side. "The winter wheat is coming up. All of it."

She stared at the field, hardly believing her eyes. "*Ach*, it sure is!"

"I didn't think we'd get anything, but look at it all." Caleb's eyes sparkled as he held her gaze. "This is the thickest crop I've ever seen."

"*Daed, Mamm*." Stephen sprinted toward them carrying his can of worms. "Did you find more worms?"

"*Nay, sohn*. We're inspecting the wheat." Balancing on his good leg, Caleb leaned down to Stephen's level to show him the wheat. "Late summer, when the field is golden and the wheat is standing"—he held up his hand—"about yea tall, would you like to help me harvest it?"

"*Jah*." Stephen tugged on Jonica's sleeve. "Did you hear that? I'm going to be a farmer."

Aenti rushed across the yard, both arms swinging at her sides. "I saw you all gathered together. Is something wrong? What are you all gawking at?"

"Nothing's wrong—nothing at all. Look, *Aenti*, the winter wheat has *kumm* up," Jonica said.

"That's what all the fuss is about?" *Aenti*'s wrinkles across her forehead deepened. "I don't know why you two are so surprised. *Nau* that the snow has melted, it should be coming up."

"Caleb missed the planting season because of the early snow, and he didn't think anything would grow," Jonica explained.

"Actually, Mr. Jordan was the one who sowed the seed," Caleb added. "I had already counted it a loss, but *nau* we should do *allrecht*."

Jonica reached for his hand that held her waist. "We would have done fine no matter what." She sighed. "I wish Mr. Jordan were here to see the crop."

Caleb lifted his gaze to the sky. "Something tells me he knows."

"He does." Stephen smiled. "He's an *engel*."

Jonica cocked her head at her son. "Stephen, what did I tell you about—"

"The *bu* might be right," *Aenti* said. "'Be *nett* forgetful to entertain strangers: for thereby some have entertained angels unaware.'"

Jonica thought about the verse her aunt had quoted and smiled. "At first I thought Mr. Jordan was trying to swindle the farm out from under you."

Aenti chuckled. "He had you worried enough to stay, didn't he?"

Caleb squeezed Jonica. "I'm glad you decided to stick around."

Buggy wheels crunched on gravel behind them, and Jonica turned as Abraham and Deborah were getting out.

"I'll finish getting the picnic basket ready," *Aenti* said, walking away. She waved to Caleb's mother.

"Edna, we were passing by and noticed everyone standing in the yard. Is something wrong?"

"*Nett* that I'm aware of. Sure is a beautiful day for a picnic and fishing. Speaking of picnic, I better finish getting the basket ready." Edna continued to the house with a spring in her step.

"Nothing is wrong, *Mamm*." Caleb motioned to the field. "We were looking at the wheat, is all."

His *daed* stepped forward, squinting at first. But the longer he inspected the green growth, the wider his eyes grew. "Well, that's a first." He scratched his beard. "I've never seen anything like it."

Caleb nodded. "It's going to be a *gut* harvest too."

Abraham clapped Caleb on the back. "I'm happy for you, *sohn*."

Deborah leaned closer to Jonica. "Edna seems to be doing *gut*. I'm glad she's going to join us."

"Me too. The *doktah* said the best medicine for her is lots of interactions with others. I've seen some improvement after she gave up eating foods that the *doktah* said causes inflammation. Mostly bread. We're all trying to cut back."

"Oh, dear, that must be difficult."

"It's been worth it," Jonica said. Memories like today were something she always wanted to remember.

"*Daed*." Stephen nudged Caleb's arm. "Can we go fishing *nau*?"

"Do you have all your worms?"

"Yep." He held up the old coffee can with holes poked in the plastic lid. "Got them all."

Abraham turned. "Let's *nett* keep the fish waiting."

Stephen slipped his hand into Abraham's and peered up at him. "Are you going to fish, too, *Daadi*?"

"That depends. Do you have enough worms for me?"

Stephen nodded.

In the short time that she and Caleb had been married, Stephen had formed a tight bond with both of his grandparents. He needed them and they seemed to need him. Slowly, Jonica was learning to let go a little and not fret over everything Stephen attempted to do.

Deborah walked alongside Abraham and Stephen as they headed toward the buggies. "Would you like to ride with us, Stephen?"

He looked back at Jonica. "Can I?"

"*Jah*, I know you're eager to cast your fishing line. Get your pole out of the back of the buggy, and be careful. And listen to what *Daadi* and *Mammi* tell you. We'll be along as soon as we get *Aenti* and the picnic basket."

As Abraham pulled out of the drive, Jonica leaned closer to Caleb. "I think your parents are going to spoil Stephen."

Caleb nodded. "A grandchild is exactly what *mei* mother needed."

"It is?" Her stomach tingled with the secret she wanted to share.

He nodded. "*Jah*, God has been so good to me . . . to us. I can't think of anything else He could provide that would make me happier."

"God has been *gut* to us." She motioned to the house. "I have to run inside for the picnic basket and to get *Aenti*." She rose to her toes and gave Caleb a kiss on the cheek. "I'm so excited. This is our first family outing."

"Wait." Caleb stopped her from going ahead. "Have I told you how much I love you?" The gleam in his eyes told her everything. She needed no words, but they still took her breath away.

"This morning you did. But you can tell me all day long, and I still wouldn't grow tired of hearing it." There would be no better time than this to tell him her secret. "Caleb, is there really nothing else God could provide for you—for us?" She kissed his lips. "Nothing?"

He tilted his head and eyed her knowingly. "Nothing except— a *dochder*?" He gathered her in his arms and lifted her chin to meet his gaze.

"Or maybe another *sohn*?"

Caleb laughed, picked her up, and swung her around. "I love you, Mrs. Schulmann."

She smiled and laced her fingers behind his neck. "And I love you, Caleb. Forever."

Acknowledgments

As I was writing this book I found myself saying over and over, "To God be the glory. I will finish this book!"

And I did—finally. So I could easily sum up this acknowledgment by saying: "The glory is all Yours, God! Thank You for answering my prayer!" But my kind publisher gave me more space on the page, and God placed a lot of people in my life that came up beside me to help me through.

First, thank you, Becky Monds. You are a fantastic editor! I can't sing your praises enough for what you've done for me. Thank you to my publisher, Amanda Bostic, who is instrumental in publishing so many inspirational books. I'm proud to have you as my publisher. Jodi Hughes, you are so kind and helpful. I would also like to thank Julee Schwarzburg, my line editor. You are wonderful to work with and I look forward to doing more books with you in the future. Thank you to my agent, Natasha Kern. Natasha, you have great insight and I appreciate your candor. You've pushed when I've needed pushing, all the while guiding me through a difficult time in my life. Thank you for believing in me!

I would like to thank my family for their ongoing love and support. Dan, you are the best gift of all from God! I am blessed and highly favored because of you. Lexie, when this book hits the stands, you will be Mrs. Johnathan McKeen-Chaff, married to a wonderful, godly man. I'm proud to be your mother (and a new mother-in-law). You have both been a tremendous help with finishing this book. I hope you'll still let me hang out with you in coffee shops while I write. Danny, as you and MaKayla Clark start your lives together this fall, I pray your marriage will be centered around God because that is where you two will find strength and the endurance needed to grow in your walk with the Lord. I'm very proud of you both. To my last babe in the nest, Sarah, you are a unique and talented young woman. I'm so proud to be your mom! Thank you for all the help around the house. I thank God for blessing me with such a wonderful daughter. I love you!

I would like to say a special thank you to my parents, Ella Roberts and Paul and Kathy Droste. Without your love and continued prayers, I might not have found my calling as a writer. Thank you!

A writer's life would become lonely without other writers to share their journey. My critique partners are my sounding board, and without their honest feedback throughout the years, my manuscripts would still be in a slush pile on some editor's desk . . . or maybe used as shredded paper in some hamster cage. To all of you: Michele Morris, Jennifer Uhlarik, Sarah Hamaker, Ginny Hamlin, and Cindy Huff, thank you for your words of wisdom, and, most of all, your friendship. You ladies are the best!

Discussion Questions

1. Did you get a sense of how difficult it was for Jonica to return to her childhood district after having to leave the area shrouded in shame? How do you think the other members of the district treated her when she returned? Would you say her fears were realized?

2. Caleb often put the needs of his neighbor before his own. Do you see how the delay in planting his winter wheat opened the door for God to bless him? For Caleb, losing his crop meant confirming he was a failure in his father's eyes. Have you ever thought you lost an opportunity or something important only to discover God had a good and perfect gift waiting for you all along? The scripture that came to mind as I was writing Caleb's story was Jeremiah 29:11 "'For I know the plans I have for you,' declares the LORD, 'plans to prosper you and not to harm you, plans to give you hope and a future.'" Can you think of other scriptures in the Bible that offer God's love and encouragement?

3. Caleb's family is reeling after a recent tragedy. How did each family member deal with the grief in their own way? How did God work miraculously to bring them back together? What role do you think Stephen played?

4. What does Matthew 6:26 say about God's provision? Do you think the redheaded man taking care of an abandoned bird in the story portrayed God's plan for the characters in the book? Can you think of a time when God made provision for you?

5. Jonica often quoted the scripture 1 John 1:9: "If we confess our sins, he is faithful and just and will forgive us our sins and purify us from all unrighteousness" (NIV). Jonica didn't struggle with repenting to God. She struggled with forgiving herself for past mistakes. Do you think it helped Jonica to recite this scripture? If so, what did she gain from doing so? Do you have a favorite scripture that you recite in times of heartache or trouble?

6. Do you think Stephen's childlike faith gave him insight into who the redheaded stranger was? Hebrews 13:2 tells us, "Do not forget to show hospitality to strangers, for by so doing some have shown hospitality to angels without knowing it." Has there been a time or situation where you might have entertained an angel?

7. From the verse listed at the beginning of this book (1 Peter 5:10), can you describe how God restored, confirmed, strengthened, and established each of the characters in this book? Can you think of a time that while you were in the midst of your suffering the God of all grace did the same for you?

8. *Aenti* Edna was suffering from dementia throughout this story. Do you think the other members in the community did enough for her? Edna did what she could to help the redheaded stranger. She gave him food when he was hungry, water when he was thirsty, and she invited him inside the house and even knitted him a scarf to keep him warm. How did her acts of kindness exemplify

Matthew 25:35–40? Do you think the Amish community is better equipped to help their elderly members than the *Englischers*? Does someone in your community—maybe an elderly relative, neighbor, or shut-in—come to mind whom you might be able to help?

The beloved
Heaven on Earth series

"Ruth Reid is skillful in portraying the Amish way of life as well as weaving together miracles with the everyday."

—Beth Wiseman, bestselling author of the Daughters of the Promise series

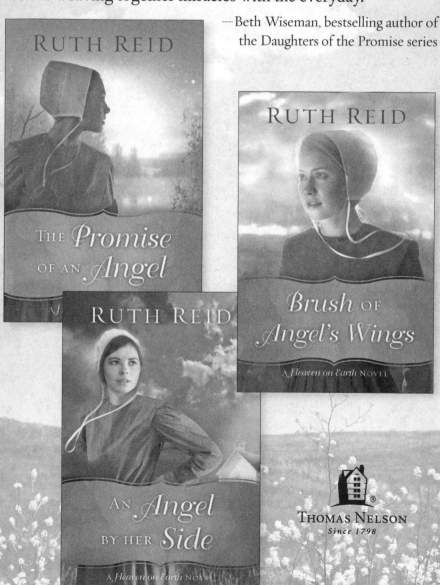

Enjoy Ruth Reid's Amish Wonders Series!

About the Author

R uth Reid is a full-time pharmacist who lives in Florida with her husband and three children. When attending the Ferris State University College of Pharmacy in Big Rapids, Michigan, she lived on the outskirts of an Amish community and had several occasions to visit the Amish farms. Her interest grew into love as she saw the beauty in living a simple life.

Visit Ruth online at RuthReid.com
Facebook: Author Ruth Reid
Twitter: @AuthorRuthReid